Witch Craft

Mythos Trilogy, Volume 1

Ruth Miranda

Published by Ruth Miranda, 2024.

NO AI TRAINING: Without in any way limiting the author's [and publisher's] exclusive rights under copyright, any use of this publication to "train" generative artificial intelligence (AI) technologies to generate text is expressly prohibited. The author reserves all rights to license uses of this work for generative AI training and development of machine learning language models.

Copyright © 2020 Ruth Miranda
All rights reserved.

This is a work of fiction, whatever similarity to actual people or events is a coincidence

This is a work of fiction. Similarities to real people, places, or events are entirely coincidental.

WITCH CRAFT

First edition. April 27, 2024.

Copyright © 2024 Ruth Miranda.

ISBN: 979-8227208408

Written by Ruth Miranda.

Prologue

Weaversmoor,
   Twenty Seven years ago

"Go into the woods, to the tree I showed you," she huffed, bending over her distended stomach, riding the wave of pain through shallow breaths and puffs. "Call his name out loud, Cress, as loud as you can." Another jolt of pain travelled through her lower body, this time bringing a wail in its wake.

The other girl shuddered, hand crushed by her friend's tight grasp. Eyes widened with shock and horror, she couldn't find words, nor could she move. Cressida Beckford was at a loss, and the most terrified she'd ever been in her entire life, aware of the urgency in her best friend's voice. Which meant she didn't really have time to be struck dumb like this.

"Cress, please," Erin Vaughn insisted, standing up to pace the room.

She pressed one forearm to her mouth and moaned against it with the next wave of pain, trying to keep the noise down. Both Cressida and she had worked on a blocking spell to keep all sound in the room from reaching the rest of the house - the last thing she wanted was to be eavesdropped. But her mother's powers far surpassed hers and Cress's tentative play at magic; soon the shields would drop and Corinna Vaughn come barging in, to do what she wanted with Erin's life. Unless Cressida left right now, to try to put a stop to it. Erin dragged herself to the bed, where her best friend sat in stunned silence, placed claw-like hands over her shoulders and gently rocked her.

"Cressida Beckford, listen to me," she insisted, and Cress's eyes focused on her, the glimmer of sentience returning to them. "This baby's about to come, and unless you go and warn his father, my mother will take our child away and ruin my life. Go to the woods, to the tree, call Fionn Sylvannar. He'll come. But go now, before mother severs my weave and locks him away forever, please."

Cressida's expression became stern, on a face that was losing pallor. She nodded, then stood up and marched to the window. Gliding through the open panes, she balanced herself on the narrow ledge; they'd been doing this for years, Erin and she. Coming in and out of the room through the window, and down the roof where it slanted closer to the ground. With a jump, she landed, running across the back garden on silent feet, towards the woods between Vaughn cottage and the Everley estate. Leaving behind a desperate girl about to give birth.

The night was dark, humid; clouds blanketing the sky, effacing the glow of the stars. Instinct led her steps across the jungle of mismatched trees, the hooting owls making her jump on her feet. How many times had she walked these paths with Erin, how many dark nights had they ventured into the deepest part of the woods, where magic ran stronger and filled their veins, swam across their skin? How many times had they come here to hone their talents, drink their fill of the strong, gutsy powers that seemed to hang around the leaf-strewn grounds? Why was she afraid, now? Why had she been so terrified of these woods, since Erin told her of the crossing by the weird oak?

The tree, that large mammoth, only discerned on certain days, specific circumstances, and not by all people. The tree with the strange, feather-like leaves, and the flocks of jewel-coloured birds perching along its branches. The tree where Erin had found a passage into another world, another realm, and Fionn's arms. Cressida had feared the woods from the moment her friend told her of him. The place where she'd once found peace and harmony had suddenly become menacing, dangerous, best left alone. And now she must come here, and be the light for Fionn to follow, guide the strange creature into her world, where none like him should roam? Yes, she must, for the sake of Erin and the baby. Corinna Vaughn would destroy her own daughter - she'd looked half-crazed ever since discovering Erin was pregnant, had locked her in the house as soon as the belly started to show, and only through gimmicks and tricks did Cressida manage to see her friend. So she must do this, before Corinna severed the threads Erin had left behind, to hold the breach in place and allow Fionn in.

Bracing herself, one deep breath filling her lungs with air and her body with peace, Cressida opened her arms, faced the looming tree.

"Fionn Sylvannar," she cried, "Fionn Sylvannar, your child is coming."

The air danced around her, lifting her hair and the fallen leaves. Birds chirped a tune that soon became a cackle; loud, threatening, as if they were about to attack. Cressida shuddered, but did not falter. She could feel the forces at war around her - Corinna's magic, Erin's weave - and knew she must lend energy to her friend's spells. Fishing for courage where she'd thought there'd be none, Cressida closed her eyes, curled her hands into fists, focused her will and sought for trace of Erin's particular brand of magic. Once she found the thread, followed it to its core and added as much of herself as she could to the pulsing beam. Her body rocked, balanced on the tips of her toes, hair on end over her head, as bursts of black lightening fled her fingers and joined the tree.

"Fionn Sylvannar, come forth," she shouted, the muscles on her face stretching and aching with the amount of energy she was forcing herself to emit.

The forest beamed with light - blue and white light that would have hurt her eyes, were they open - and the ground shuddered, rocking bushes and trees. She would have felt it, had her feet still been placed upon the forest floor, but Cressida now floated on air, like a broken rag doll upheld by strong winds. The birds cawed louder and louder, the surrounding atmosphere hissed with powers unknown. Thunder echoed far away, behind her, over the cottage she'd come running from. Rain and hail pelted her body, forcing cries of pain from her distended, distorted lips.

Then, the alien force that held her body aloft let go. She fell on pebbles, twigs, broken branches and leaves, and it all came to a sudden halt. It all came to a sudden halt and back to normal, as if those strong powers had never been; as if magic didn't really exist. Pushing herself on hands and knees, Cressida raised her head and opened her eyes, coming upon the strangest, most alluring creature she'd ever seen. Before her, a man stood almost as tall as the nearest tree, a thing of otherworldly strength and beauty, a being out of a nightmare and a dream. Wide shoulders over a torso that narrowed to a slim waist, strong legs made for running long distances, hands that could have snapped her neck, and a scowl on a face that was at the same time beautiful and terrifying. He trained light blue eyes on her, while twisting the long white mane of hair on his head in a hasty braid.

Fionn Sylvannar took a step from where he stood, still inside the safety of the shadow cast by the large, alien tree, reached a hand towards Cressida to help her up, scowling in a mix of pain and anger. His eyes swept his surroundings, taking everything in, searching for what wasn't there.

"You're the friend Erin speaks so dearly of," he said, a voice that sounded like thunder and hail.

Cressida nodded, tears brimming her eyes and starting to fall down her cheeks.

"And she has sent you here, to call for me?" Satisfied with Cressida's assent, Fionn Sylvannar gifted her with a smile that was like a bursting star, dazzling and terrifying, a thing of rare beauty and also pure evil. "I thank you. Here." Fishing a stone that very much resembled jet, he handed it to Cressida. "Take this. One day you'll have children and they'll want to wander these woods. This will protect them. This will protect your daughter, so make sure she has it. Consider it my gift to you."

With sweaty, shaky hands, Cressida fingered the stone, curled her knuckles around it, shoving her hand into the pocket of her coat.

"Where are they? Erin, the babe?"

She swerved her head towards the cottage, too far away to be seen. Fionn's eyes followed hers, as if understanding where he was meant to be.

A mesmerising shriek pierced the night, then another, forcing them both to attention. They exchanged a terrified look between them, Cressida startled by the sight of such a powerful creature looking scared and unhinged. Another shriek echoed loudly, followed by a fourth.

Then the wailing of a newborn babe silenced the woods around them, the very night going still.

Corinna Vaughn had threatened him once, not so long ago, and Fionn had laughed it off. She had then proceeded with a vain attempt at shredding Erin's weave, to assure the lovers couldn't meet. Again, Fionn had laughed it off, knowing Corinna was at the Crone stage, and her powers no match for those of her fifteen-year-old daughter. Erin had simply woven another pathway, brushing aside the broken threads of her former one. But something was different, now, and Fionn knew it. He couldn't quite place what it was, except for Erin's own powers having lost their formidable strength, perhaps due to the strain of childbearing.

He hurried across the lawn, aware that Cressida was falling behind, but Fionn couldn't care for the girl, now; he had no time. Corinna would do her best to abscond the babe, Erin even, if he didn't hurry and release them from her hands. She was a bigot, terrified of anything that was different, unusual, unknown, which, like her own daughter said, made her a hypocrite. For Corinna, like those of the blood, was herself different, unusual, unknown to everyone a stranger to the Craft. And she would have been as loathed and hunted in Ephemera as she despised Fionn in her own world. Maybe she was just scared for her daughter's safety, her grandchild's wellbeing, he pondered, long legs running across the dark meadow. It was a risk, taking Erin back to Ephemera permanently; a calculated one, but still a risk. Both for her and the child. But he had no other option, Corinna would never see eye to eye with him and allow his permanence in her daughter's life.

Jumping over the small, rough stone wall separating the pasture from the cottage's backyard, Fionn came to stand by the locked door. He'd never been inside; although many were the times he followed Erin's threads to come meet her at this spot. Taking a deep breath, he forced the anger away, filling his mind with only memories of the special moments he'd shared with a girl that was all but forbidden to him. He knew Corinna had a point, Erin had been just shy of fifteen when they'd met, and he... well, in human years, he'd have been far, far too old for the girl. But rules in Ephemera were not as those of Erin's and Corinna's world, and a girl on her menses was a woman, ripe and ready and prepared for a life of her own. When Erin weaved her first tentative pathway to his world, she'd proclaimed herself apt for womanhood and all it entailed. Fionn had been on the very end of that pathway, and as he rested eyes on her, he'd known himself lost. The attraction was immediate, the beast that was the Sylvannars' curse and birthright rising to the surface of his usually cold, blank face, and he'd laid claim to Erin on the spot.

It was the way of his world: whenever an Arbiter came across someone with magic, he was bound to leave his mark. And by the time Fionn and Erin crossed paths, he was so much more than just the local Arbiter; he was Lord Fionn Sylvannar, Governator of the East Baronies, Senator of Ephemera, Decurio of the Concilius at Chymera. Free to claim whoever he wanted, for to a Senator all was allowed, all was forgiven. The beast that had made him the highest standing man in the Sylvannar branch, that which had placed him as a Senator and raised him to the post of Decurio, this same beast demanded its fair share, and at the sight and sense of a Weaver, it had reared its ugly, ugly head. The downside of being an Arbiter. His capacity to sway and mesmerise had been put to good use, and if over the course of the first months he'd often questioned Erin's love, with time he'd come to know she was no longer under his spell, and all she felt was true. Erin loved him as much as he loved her.

When the baby took root in her womb, Fionn had been happy, ecstatic, despite being father to two sons, already. But Fioll and Rhysondel were grown men, with their own roles in the world, and he'd never been close to them, for he was not close to their mother. Theirs had been an arranged union, for procreation's sake alone. Children were rare amongst Everlastings, they'd been blessed with two, but as soon as the second son was born, Fionn considered he'd fulfilled his role, and found himself free to pursue other endeavours, other pleasures than that of being a family man. Until Erin, of course.

Long had they argued and studied and planned, together in the woods, since the girl had told him of the child in her womb. They'd discussed the odds and chances presented, the dangers, the possibilities, and come to the conclusion one of them must concede, forever leave their own world. It had been agreed Fionn would forsake Ephemera; he was of no need there, not when he had two sons ready and eager to take his place, his seat in the Senate, if not the role in the Decuria at Chymera. That was not a post heredity handed out, it was a nomination amongst the eldest living Everlastings. Fioll ached for it, but he was still too young. One day, he might ascend - that day was not when his father stepped down and left their world.

All had been arranged, until Corinna managed to gather around her four other Weavers, and lock the portals her daughter kept weaving. It had weakened Erin, the babe in her womb; it had worried Fionn. He was not to be made welcome here, after all; and on the wake of three weeks of Erin's absence and his own failure at crossing to her world, Fionn had taken to desperate measures and sent Venators to hunt those same Weavers. After all, they could be of use in Chymera, and their capture would ensure his continued high stance in the Decuria. For he'd known Erin must come to Ephemera with him, and not the other way around. He was vulnerable in Erin's world, a king in his own. The choice, if not to his liking, was the only possible one. When two of the Weavers fell to the Venators's traps, the strong wards they'd placed about came crumbling down, their counter-weaves shredded. Erin had woven her pathways once more, and Fionn had been there to hold her in his arms, feel the babe strong and ready to be born. Time had been short for all they had to say to each other, but a plan had been devised, so that Fionn could take Erin and the child to Ephemera once it was born.

That time had come.

With a flourish of his hand, Fionn burst the door open and crossed the threshold. His feet stomped across the pristine kitchen floors in rhythm to Erin's voice, calling for him. A man met him in a narrow, dark corridor, the stairs leading to where his woman, his child, were being held, obscured by his form. A boy, close to Erin in age, stood behind the man, a terrified look in his large, green eyes. Both trying to prevent Fionn from coming for what was his, doing Corinna's bidding against Erin's wishes. No, it wouldn't do, and he must see to it. The swipe of one hand sent the man flying from where he stood, the young boy's eyes widening even more. This must be Erin's brother, who she loved dearly; no harm should come to him. Fionn tried to recollect what she'd told him of the boy: he was weak, scared easily, a meek creature with no will and no power to oppose his own mother. Those had been Erin's words.

The spark of anger in his eyes belied what Fionn knew to be his sister's assumptions. The boy left his place by the stairs, running for the older man, who lay sprawled on the floor nursing an arm against his chest.

"Why?" the boy inquired, still frightened, but too furious to let Fionn pass by unquestioned.

"Erin doesn't wish to stay. And the child is mine."

"My father didn't deserve to be treated this way."

"Blame your mother, not I. It was her bidding you both were doing, against your sister's wishes. I came to claim what's mine, and no one will stand in my way. Erin and the babe's safety are all that matter to me."

"She's my daughter," Erin's father croaked, weakened and in obvious pain.

Fionn turned to face him, ice in his eyes. "She's my life."

He ran up the stairs, following the thread Erin weaved with her voice. Coming to a landing, dived down a corridor, stopped at the first door. Brushing it open, he gazed upon the scene.

Corinna Vaughn and another woman stood by the bed where Erin lay.

Sheets crumpled at her bare feet, bloodied and soiled, and her forehead was covered in sweat. A baby lay in her arms, mouth stuck to her breast, sucking peaceful and contentedly. Fionn smiled, walked in, ignoring the other two women, registering the one he didn't know must be a midwife. There was a scent about her which spoke of years delivering babes unto the world. Nearing the bed where Erin grinned back at him, Fionn fell on his knees, tears streaming down his pale, white cheeks. He gazed long upon Erin's eyes, the infinite, silent messages coursing through them laying bare all that they felt and thought and hoped for. He'd never love someone as much as this. Finally satisfied, Fionn reached one gentle hand to the top of the babe's head, caressed it's soft, downy hair.

"A boy," Erin said, voice hoarse from the childbirth's exertions.

Fionn received the small bundle in his arms, the baby's eyes locking with his, and his heart brimmed with love, with wonder at such a tiny, perfect little creature whose strong fist grasped his finger in a tight hold. His heart filled with pride for the child, and he smiled, delighted.

"I shall name you Noctifer Sylvannar, for you were born in the dead of night," he said, and sought Erin's eyes for trace of approval. "Here, hold him, let me carry you down."

The baby returned to his mother's arms, Fionn helped her up.

"Stop," Corinna whispered. "You mustn't take her away. She's my child."

"She's my heart. And has my son. Would you dare part me from what's mine?"

"Mother, I must go. This is my life."

The midwife retreated out the door, face hidden from view. Fionn curled his fingers; the woman stopped on her tracks, whimpering in sudden fear.

"Do not attempt to stop me, any of you. I'll guard Erin's life with my own, do you understand? At the first sign of danger, she'll return here, the child as well. This much I promise, but I hope to live a long, prosperous life with her by my side. I swear Erin will not be harmed, I'll die myself before I let that happen."

Corinna shook her head, Fionn mimicking her. Then seeing Erin was out of the bed, he grabbed her in his arms, the baby lying snug against her chest, and carried both down the stairs. The boy was still there, by the door where the man lay, his face caught in a scowl of pain.

"Spencer," Erin whispered, and Fionn stopped so she could say goodbye to her brother. "Look, this is your nephew."

He came closer, took a cursory peek. His lips curled in a small, fickle smile, and his eyes met his sister's. "Will you be all right?"

Erin nodded, Fionn did the same, as if wishing to reassure the boy.

"Stand up to her," Erin whispered. "Don't let her take away who you are, Spence, you're beautiful and strong, and brave. Don't let her destroy you. Be proud of yourself."

"You too, sister. What is the baby's name?"

"Noctifer Sylvannar," Fionn replied, voice booming with pride. "And he shall be known as Nox, for he'll be like the night, enchanting and alluring, a king of two worlds."

"King Nox," Erin said, and giggled.

"Nox of Ephemera and Weaversmoor," Spencer added.

Frowning, as if a less pleasant thought had crossed his mind, Fionn took a step towards the kitchen, wanting to leave the house as fast as possible. Nox of two worlds, Erin's brother had deemed the babe, never fully belonging to one, never entirely part of the other. The epithet sounded like a curse instead of a blessing, and for a split second Fionn feared for the future of his child, of his woman, his own. But as he caught sight of Erin's eyes, filled with hope, his heart rested at ease. Bearing both the girl he loved and their child in his arms, Fionn Sylvannar crossed the meadow to the woods in the dark of night, his silhouette lost amongst the shadows of the trees, as he marched his new family to his lands on Ephemera.

It would be quite sometime until any of them set foot at Weaversmoor again.

Part One

I

Present day
    Weaversmoor

Led Zeppelin's *The Immigrant's Song* blared through the car's speakers, its bass drumming a tattoo of punches straight through Nyx's chest. Painfully, she gulped, took a steadying breath; wincing at the guitar chords and the memories they woke. It shouldn't be this hard - after all, it was one of her father's favourite songs, she should be able to listen to it without agony. Her resolve lasted all of five seconds. With a twist of her wrist, she turned off the stereo, aware of her uncle's eyes studying her.

    He said nothing, though, and Nyx was grateful for it. Instead, his hand snaked across, took hers, pressed it reassuringly. She took another deep breath and studied the scenery. This was as hard for her as it was for him. Spencer had left Weaversmoor shortly after Nyx's parents, and hadn't returned since. Wondering what might be going through his head, she took in the looming trees on either side of the road - a never-ending forest that cocooned the small town in a blanket of safety. It felt secure; the place did. But her parents and uncle had still chosen to leave. Once again, Nyx wondered why. What could have happened to taint the place so much for them? They'd taken off and left friends and family behind. Well, on her mother's case it shouldn't be surprising; Erin

WITCH CRAFT

Vaughn had been doing the same pretty much all her life. Nyx hadn't yet turned five when her mother packed up and left the northern village they'd been living in, headed God knows where. Without one single explanation for her daughter to understand what could force a mother to leave her child behind.

Biting back tears, Nyx fought to keep those thoughts at bay. She hardly remembered Erin anymore, only a vague phantom with a cascade of dark hair and eyes as green as the grass on a sunny day. Better if she focused on the scenery, now that the thick clusters of trees gave way to a few houses. Large estates, hidden in the woods, barely seen from the road. Minted, her uncle had said, when describing certain locals. If these houses were anything to go by, Spence wasn't far off the mark. Her eye was caught by one peculiar construction atop a small, inclined driveway. Two circular turrets with steepled black roofs stood to each side of what looked like a thick, iron gate. The dark grey stone of the turrets was repeated along the enclosing walls, hiding the insides of the property from view, along with the house itself. She wondered who lived there.

"The Everley estate," Spencer said, and his voice was bitter, almost detached.

Almost, but not quite; so Nyx knew there was something here. Her head snapped in his direction, large eyes studying his gait. Spencer's lips were pursed in a slim line, green eyes focused on the road ahead, car speeding down it.

"Ok," Nyx responded, "care to tell me what's it about them?"

Spence shrugged, slowed their pace, the town's limits visible just ahead. "They're a bunch of entitled wankers. Don't bother yourself with them."

Shrugging, she went back to studying her surroundings, wondering how on earth she was going to fit in. She'd never been here, not even to visit her father's family, let alone her maternal grandmother. Neither Erin nor Spencer spoke of Corinna Vaughn, as if the woman was some sort of demon they only wanted to forget. Nyx's father had mentioned her once or twice, but never expanded on the subject - unless it was to say he disagreed with Erin and Spence, where it came to Nyx meeting her grandmother. But she'd never been allowed to; her father prisoner of whatever promise Erin forced out of him and Spencer made sure he lived up to. And now that Corinna was dead, it was too late to make up for it. She'd never meet her mother's mother.

As for her father's sister, Nyx had often spoken to her on the phone, and Sarah Wilson had come to visit a few times, dragging her brood along inside a packed van driven by her handsome, dark-skinned husband who drove Nyx to gales of laughter with his witty jokes. She'd been allowed a glimpse into what family life was supposed to be, whenever her aunt and cousins were around. Sarah was her idea of motherhood, fussing over her children and shouting at them when they refused to listen, but always present, always loving, always there. How good it must be, to have a mother around, someone she could talk to about things she'd never dare bring up to her father, or her uncle, for that matter. Even though Spencer was far more carefree than Nyx's father had ever been. Spencer was far more open too, what with being gay, growing up in a very small town.

She eyed him again, certain it was the fact he was gay that had driven him away from Weaversmoor all those years ago. Something must have happened, perhaps a star-crossed love affair, a broken heart, or just the locals being narrow-minded and horrid towards him. Whatever it was, Spence wasn't happy to be forced back into town. But Nyx's father had left nothing but debts and a house so vastly mortgaged they'd had to sell it. At least Corinna Vaughn had made sure to provide for her son and her granddaughter's welfare, by leaving her cottage both to Spencer and Nyx - even if under a permanence clause that forced them back to Weaversmoor. At least here they weren't alone, isolated, as they'd been in Havenleah; here they'd have family.

A smile crept up Nyx's lips as her uncle eased the car into the driveway of a large cottage on the edge of the small town. It looked almost fairytale-like, with the wilderness stretching behind it, and the front lawn looking like a savage jungle. A coherent, well cared for jungle, nonetheless, framing Sarah Wilson and her eldest son Jamal where they stood by the small, wooden gate.

Spencer drove the car towards the larger, double gates leading to the garage, sighing in what sounded like his personal failed attempt at braving himself for this unwanted return. He parked, closed his eyes for a heartbeat, and it was Nyx's turn to reach out a hand, fondle her uncle's arm over the lightweight jacket he wore. Then he opened his eyes and stared at her, and she saw the fear and the excitement deep inside, and knew for sure. He'd left his heart in Weaversmoor and had never got it back again.

"You ok?" she asked, Spencer nodded. "Then let's do this. Together?"

"Together."

Nyx opened her door and stepped out, being swept off her feet - even before these had touched ground - by her aunt. Sarah took her in arms, hugging the girl tightly, tears already streaming down her cheeks. It had been eight weeks since the family was notified of Tom Wilson's boat being lost at sea. It had been a little over a month since Nyx's father was declared dead, no body retrieved. The family held a small memorial service, while both Sarah and Spencer took care of everything legal and Nyx raged against a universe that robbed her of father and mother alike. And now she was here, the place her parents had run from.

"Hi, Sarah," she mumbled, patting her aunt's back.

"I'm so glad to have you here," Sarah wept into Nyx's curly hair. "We'll look after you, don't you fret, and you can talk to me at all times, about anything you want or need, and..."

"Come on, mum, giver her some space," Jamal said, breaching the distance from where he'd stood.

As Sarah let go of the girl and wiped tears and make-up from her cheeks, he approached Nyx and gave her an awkward, tentative hug.

"How was the drive?" he inquired non-committally.

"Long," was all Nyx said. She turned back to her uncle, who'd opened the trunk of the car and was fishing out suitcases and cardboard boxes.

"Spence, leave it," Sarah cried. "Tyronne will be here soon, he and Jamal can help carting all that in. Come check the house."

Spencer sighed again, caught Nyx's eye, and they both giggled - but still followed Sarah to the door, which Spencer hurried opening. Corinna had died less than a week after Tom's disappearance, which had been providential. What with the mess he'd left behind, the legal issues concerning Nyx had been enough to prevent Spence from attending his mother's funeral, or the reading of her will. He'd known what it would say, though, and had told Nyx. That they'd be provided for, both with extensive trust funds set in their name, and the cottage would be theirs too, as long as they moved in. Despite Spencer's misgivings, he'd known this was the only way they could make ends meet, and had been bluntly honest with Nyx.

She'd agreed to moving straight away, bracing herself for the change. Anything would be better than staying back at Havenleah, with all those memories. With all she'd lost in that sleepy little seaside town. Maybe a change of scenery would be for the best. And Nyx knew she'd never get the right kind of training at her previous school. She needed to be here, at Weaversmoor, if she were to learn how to control the strange things that kept happening to her. Things her father had known of, but couldn't quite understand, for he'd lacked the powers Nyx was born with. But Spence and Sarah knew, and they'd made her see it was in her best interest to join the elitist Weaversmoor Academy.

Following her uncle in, she lagged behind with Jamal, wanting to probe him on the subject. But Sarah was far too intent on seeing the insides of Vaughn cottage, a place she'd been banned from ever since Tom and Erin fled town. Corinna had blamed her son-in-law for Erin's departure, but Nyx knew it had been her mother's idea in the first place. Tom loved her so much he did all she wanted, including not trying to find her when she abandoned both husband and daughter six years into their marriage. Much like Corinna, this was something Nyx had a hard time forgiving, let alone understanding. If her father *did* love her mother, why wouldn't he at least try to discover why she'd ran away?

Because he already knew.

Because he knew he had to take care of Nyx, Erin never would have.

Because her mother had left *her*, not Tom. She'd been running away from her own daughter.

Pushing those thoughts aside, Nyx sought her uncle's eyes for reassurance, his dark pupils soothing her doubts and fears as he'd been doing ever since Erin had left.

"It looks so different," Spencer was saying, and Nyx found herself gazing around, taking in the cosy, modern décor of the place.

"Your mother did a lot of work on it this past year," Sarah elucidated. "It's like she knew..."

"She probably did. I'm glad she changed it all; it's like a whole new place. No more memories seeping through that chintz couch, or the horrible flowery wallpaper."

Nyx tried to picture the description, failed to envision what her uncle spoke of. The walls in the large living-room were painted a light, soothing grey, the sofas matching that hue. Everything looked bright and cheery, comfortable and homely, but not dated.

"She changed the rooms, too," Sarah added, gesturing them to the dark, polished oak staircase.

They joined her climbing up, Jamal rolling his eyes and forcing a snigger from Nyx. They lagged behind the grown-ups, as Nyx stopped by the large window on the landing and peered outside, greeted by a lush, fresh vision of greenery and the woods beyond.

"It's beautiful out here," she whispered. "Havenleah was all rocks and coarse sand beaches and the sea. This is... different. A fresh start."

"Are you excited?"

She eyed her cousin, a smile creeping up her lips. "Look, I won't lie. I had friends back there, I'm sorry to let go of them. But it was getting out of hand, and father had argued with Spence many times, that I should come here, to the Academy. I'm glad I'll be getting the help I need, despite everything."

"How has it manifested? Is it crazy? Mine was, but then again, I was much younger than you when it started happening."

"Yeah, it's not too wild, yet. But enough to make my friends look at me weird, know what I mean? I can do some stuff, like turn on the lights and close a door, or turn off the TV, the radio. But then it gets all out of hand, and if I'm upset... things tend to happen. It's either the wind, or the seas. It got me scared a few times, especially after dad..."

"Hey, you're all right, here. You'll do great, trust me. I'll introduce you to my crowd, Bryn will take you under her wing. She's always taking in strays, maladjusted kids. You'll like her, you'll see."

"Who's Bryn?"

"Bryn Everley." Sarah's voice reached them from the hallway. Her head peered from inside a door, ushering them to join her. "Jamal's girlfriend."

Nyx eyed her cousin with a grin, one that died as she saw the pained look in her uncle's eyes.

"Everley?" he said, trying to sound casual, but Nyx knew better.

So the mystery of his leaving involved this family. Weren't they the ones who owned that freakish estate they'd passed on the road?

"She's Max's and Cressida's eldest," Sarah explained, blushing a deep red. "I'm sorry."

Spencer shook his head, looked the other way, avoiding eye contact. A bit too late; Nyx had seen the brimming tears. So this was the reason her uncle had run away. Max and Cressida Everley. He must have nursed an unrequited love for the man, one she was sure he still nurtured. What a shame, Spence was such a great guy, he deserved someone who loved and made him happy. Maybe it wasn't such a good idea coming back to Weaversmoor, after all.

"Come here," he called, voice level as if he wasn't hurting. But the set of his shoulders told Nyx a different story, she knew him that well. "My mother had this room done for you, see if you like it."

She walked over. Eyes widening in wonder, Nyx studied every detail, from the white walls to the small, ancient-looking cast-iron stove. There was nothing inside she wouldn't have chosen herself, if left to her own devices. The swirls on the cast-iron bed seemed to match those of the vintage overhanging chandelier, the fuchsia pillows popping against the white bedspread. She took in the stacked old battered suitcases, the rustic chest at the feet of the bed, the French-looking wardrobe, it was all perfect.

"It's like she knew me," Nyx said. "Like she got into my head and knew exactly what to choose."

"Wouldn't put that past my mother," Spencer snapped, and turned away. "This was Erin's, when she was your age. It was her room. But it looked very different back then."

"Corinna asked me what Nyx liked," Sarah confessed, a slight blush covering her cheeks.

"I see. Well, as long as you're happy and comfortable, Nyx."

The girl marched to her uncle and hugged him, the bleakness in his voice matching her own. She wouldn't be happy for a long time, not when she missed her father this much, not when she felt so alone. But she had Spencer, and he had her – together, they'd overcome this. They'd learn to find happiness again.

"Let's see what she did with your room," she suggested, "so you can rant about your mother not knowing you at all."

Spencer hugged her back and smiled. "Problem is, my mother knew me quite well. She just couldn't accept me for who I am." They ambled down the hall towards a second door. "My teenage bedroom. Bet she hasn't changed it one bit, all dark greys and bright blues, that horrible single bed and the matching set of wardrobe and chest of drawers in that dreadful honey hue."

He opened the door, looked in and laughed. It was nothing like he'd described. Whistling under his breath, Spencer walked in, followed by Nyx.

"This looks lovely," the girl said.

"Well, guess I was wrong, mother did put in a bit of effort. Bet she was afraid I'd simply pack and leave if the room was still the same."

It was a far cry from what he'd expected, now a bedroom fit for an adult. Plaid and tartan in hues of red and dark blue fitted the fabrics, from the bed to the windows, the chairs to the rugs. The woods were all dark brown, and the walls gleamed in a light vanilla tone that infused the room with warmth and brightness. It was what he'd have done, had he the means to decorate a place of his own.

"What of that room?" Jamal pointed to the end of the corridor, where a dark door loomed forbiddingly.

"That's my mother's bedroom. A nightmare in yellow, it was. All chintz and flowers and that ghastly bright yellow. Used to give me headaches." Courageously marching to the door, Spencer opened it, gesturing Nyx to follow. "You need to see this, if only so we can gasp at my mother's less than impeccable taste."

The girl grinned, but as she looked into the room, the smile fled her lips. "I'll say one thing, she must have changed a lot over the years. From bright and cheery to dark and moody."

Spencer walked into the room, face mirroring his confusion. "My mother would never have slept in such a place."

The floorboards looked rough and untreated, the walls covered in dark wood panels all the way up to the ceiling. A folding stool made for a bedside table, and a few worn-looking chests filled up the empty space underneath the large windows, now covered with dark grey curtains instead of the old chintz ones. There was no wardrobe, nor a proper bed. A thick mattress stood on top of wooden palettes, the bedding all linen in grey and taupe hues, with a massive amount of pillows serving as headboard. Two clothes' horses were stacked against the farthest wall, separated by a dark-stain chest of drawers. The entire room looked unfinished, a work in progress, but at the same time, it felt complete and welcoming, for anyone who enjoyed that kind of stark, rustic décor.

"This must have been for dad," Nyx whispered. "Only he wouldn't have liked it much."

Wiping a stubborn tear from his eye, Spencer turned his back on the room. "Your father didn't really have an eye for interior design. As long as it had a bed, he couldn't care less what it looked like. This would have fitted him fine."

Even though it didn't feel like it was meant for Tom.

Another one of Corinna's mysteries, surely; she'd kept so much from him, from Erin. Until his sister had gone and discovered it all by herself. Shuddering, Spencer pulled Nyx out of the room and locked it, leaving the key. Better let the ghosts from the past sleep their eternal sleep, better not wake them, nor stir old memories. He was glad his mother had gone to the trouble of changing the house - it would help them settle. If everything had remained the same, Spencer would have had a very hard time returning to Weaversmoor.

As it was, he already regretted his decision to move back. But this was where Nyx must be, this was where Nyx belonged. People like her, like him; they couldn't afford to live on the outside world as if they were normal. Unless they spent a lifetime hiding their true nature, their very reality, that is. And he knew better than anyone else how taxing and life-depleting it was, to constantly pretend to be something he wasn't. He'd spent his entire life doing just that.

Nyx grabbed her uncle's hand and pressed it lightly, trying to catch his eyes. Spencer faced her, biting his lip to keep hold of tears. They both looked tired, and so sad.

"It's you and me, now," she whispered, but her aunt still heard her.

"No, it's not," Sarah said. "You have family, the two of you. We're here, too."

"Mum, maybe they kind of need to be alone? So they can settle in?" Jamal winked at Nyx, who smiled gratefully. "I can hear dad's car coming up the driveway, we should join him downstairs and help with the luggage, while Nyx and Spence take a break."

"It's fine," Spencer said, putting on a show, if only for Nyx's sake. "We're fine. And Sarah's right, we have family, we're not alone."

As mother and son walked to the stairs, Spencer held Nyx back, hugging her shoulders, resting his chin on top of her head.

"But it'll always be you and me, kid, it'll always be just us. For better and for worse."

Nyx nodded, her eyes on the play of light the rounded hallway window shed upon the wooden floor. Spence had been there since she was born, and he'd been a parent where she'd lacked one. He'd taken the place of his sister in Nyx's life, and was the nearest she had to her mother, the last remaining link. Along with her father, Spence had raised her; he'd nursed her through illnesses, suffered through scraped knees and tantrums. He'd driven her to and back from school, fed her, bathed her, played with her and the endless stream of dolls. Spence and her father were all she knew, and all she'd ever been able to count upon. Sarah was family, yes, so was Jamal, but they were almost like strangers and lacked the years of close living she shared with Spencer. So it would always be the two of them, even if others happened to come into their lives.

And she was fine with it.

Nyx grabbed the stick that had nearly tripped her and used it to beat a path out of the tall, yellowy dry grass. Staring over her shoulder, she studied the cottage, with its sturdy stone walls and the black roof. Not too different from the place she'd lived at in Havenleah, Vaughn cottage did lack the constant humidity, though. Despite its dark-coloured exterior, the house looked cheery and bright, with clumps of flowers growing around it and the way sunlight bathed it throughout the day. It felt like a home, but so had Havenleah. Only back there, it had been her father and her uncle who'd turned the damp, cramped little place into one. Their booming voices, their laughter, Spencer's loud music, the way he'd decorated, her father's cooking; it had all helped create a sense of homeliness to an otherwise cold space.

With Vaughn cottage the feeling was similar: it was a home, one she felt welcomed into, safe, loved, but Nyx couldn't afford it all to Spencer. It was as if the cottage had been put under a spell, one that made her belong, made her want to stay. From all she'd heard about her grandmother Corinna – be it from Sarah, her husband Tyronne, even her cousin Jamal and the occasional input Spencer threw in – she wouldn't put it past the old lady. An accomplished witch, she'd been, according to Sarah and Spencer. She must have done something to the house, to make sure they both wanted to stay. Especially Spencer.

She turned back to the path, now overgrown by years of abandonment that made it look as if it had never existed. But to Nyx's attentive eye. She could see where it had been once, a well-trodden route from the house to the woods, across the small, sunny meadow. A route she was sure both her mother and uncle must have followed in their youth, at least according to Sarah's hints, which Spencer had been quick to quieten.

As if he didn't want to speak of the past, *his* past at Weaversmoor. He was always on edge, since they'd arrived, ready to run at the first sign of... what? What was he so afraid of? Who was he so afraid of, more like it? They'd been to town a few times, and Spencer had avoided all the crowded places, the most popular spots, as if terrified of running into someone. Nyx had hinted at his odd behaviour while on a shopping spree with Sarah, trying to lure the story out of her, but her aunt had pretended not to hear, or understand what she was driving at. So Nyx was just as in the dark now, two weeks since they'd come to Weaversmoor, as she'd always been. But the sense that the house had been placed under spells that assured they both remained, wouldn't leave her mind. And she was certain Spence could feel it too.

WITCH CRAFT

The overgrown path ended at the edge of the woods. Tall, leafy green trees loomed ahead of her, sunshine playing hide and seek through wide boughs, the leaf-strewn ground speckled with pockets of light that seemed to sparkle and glint like gold. Nyx had always liked the woods, although she didn't have much of it back in Havenleah. They'd used to go hiking close by, on the weekends, just so she could infuse herself with nature and greenery. She wondered if she was like her grandmother, as strong a witch as she.

So far, none of her powers had manifested in a clear way. She could open and close doors without touching them, light a lamp or a candle, she knew what plants were poisonous and which were safe without having learnt it, and could even sense people's moods, what they felt, what they seemed to think, especially about herself. But it was all very flimsy, not like Spencer who played around with earth as if he owned it. Maybe she was like him, an Earthen, or a Waterling like Sarah and Jamal. Maybe she was a Feeric, did they have any in their lineage?

Her mother, what had she been? No one talked about it, but everyone hinted at her powers having been out of the ordinary, her magic very potent. Feerics were supposed to be the most dangerous, right? Because they could easily lose control of their emotions and of their magic, they could start a fire just by being slightly emotional. Adolescence must be hell for them. No, she wasn't one, what with her emotions all over the place as they'd been since her father's death, she would have started at least a hundred small fires. It was safe to say she wasn't burdened with being a fire Elemental. Smiling, she plodded on deeper into the woods, the thick canopies hiding the sun momentarily, bathing her surroundings in an eerie, greenish light. Water flowed to her right; Jamal had mentioned a creek, which he'd promised to show her as soon as he returned from his holiday.

Nyx realised she missed her cousins, missed her aunt, even uncle Tyronne. She missed them and was lonely for their absence, already sorry of not having accepted the invitation to join them on a week away at Mallorca. But then Spence would have stayed behind, and Nyx couldn't handle the guilt of knowing her uncle was stuck at Weaversmoor, a place he loathed, on his own. More than the guilt, it had been fear that prompted her to stay. Fear she'd come back to find Spence had simply packed up and left, run away as his sister had, all those years ago. She'd been too scared of losing yet another family member, and knew if she chose to stay, her uncle would feel bound to remain somewhere he'd been miserable, somewhere he *was* miserable. Why? What could have happened to him, to Nyx's mother, that they hated the town so much they wished never to return? Would anyone ever tell her? So far, Spencer refused to talk of his past, and Sarah pretended not to understand when Nyx prodded her.

She'd have to find a way to learn the truth, if only to keep her own mind from constantly wandering to thoughts of her father and his death. Maybe Corinna was a monster, one of those parents who constantly beat their kids. She knew her grandmother had never accepted Spencer's homosexuality; maybe she tried to beat it out of him? Maybe she'd lashed out at her daughter too, for defending her younger brother? Heart somersaulting at the thought, Nyx stopped suddenly, head swimming, sweat falling down her back. She gazed through the trees, turned around trying to see the way she'd come from, couldn't recognise any of it. Oh, she'd been so lost in her head she'd failed to mark her route, as her father had always taught her to do when out hiking in the woods. Now she was well and truly lost.

Well, maybe not.

Closing her eyes, Nyx cocked her head to one side, dark brown curls brushing against the nape of her neck and falling down one freckled shoulder. She listened to the sounds of the woods, the breeze through the trees, the birds singing, the din of the creek. To her left, then, the water; was that it? If she remembered well, Jamal had said the creek turned into a river and crossed the town on its flow towards the sea. She could hear it, but it sounded distant, as if she'd walked deeper into the woods than what seemed possible. After all, Nyx hadn't been walking for so long as to completely lose sight of town and its surroundings. She should still have been able to hear the water running along its bed.

What she could hear, though, were the birds, chirping happily.

But these didn't sound like the birds she was used to waking up to, the ones that flocked her garden and the woods close to the cottage. These sounded louder, clearer, more musical? Unlike any other bird she'd ever heard, these were. Peering up into the trees, Nyx tried to catch sight of them and was granted a peek of bright pink and green plumage jumping from branch to branch. Soon she was making out the entire flock, gaudy coloured birds that perched high up and broke the constancy of lush, dark green with their bright colours. Like fruit hanging from a tree. Only these trees were unlike the ones she was used to. These were nothing like those at the edge of the woods, amongst which she'd been taking strolls the past week.

Well, she was clear and truly lost, now. How was she to find her way back? Where was this supposed to lead to? She'd studied an old map of the area back home, one that hung in her bedroom and that Spence had suggested taking down. Nyx had wanted it to stay, and every night she found herself gazing at it, studying its lay, learning the land. The woods behind Vaughn cottage led to that eerie, strange place, what her uncle had called the Everley estate, a name that was replicated in flowery handwriting upon the map. So maybe she was close to that estate, and if she pushed forward, she might come to its walls. Not so lost, then, was she?

A noise brought her back to attention. A snap of twigs underfoot, a voice begging for silence, hushing its companions. Yes, a voice, now joined by another, giggling and chatting away, deeper into the woods. Straining her ears, she tried to make out the words, only to realise the pair weren't speaking anymore. Face red as a beetroot, Nyx realised it was a couple she was listening in on, a couple kissing and making out in the woods.

Suddenly upset beyond reason, shame taking over her thoughts, she turned and fled, hopefully to where she'd come from. Her legs, naked under the denim shorts, bore the marks of bristle bushes and weeds that scraped her skin. The white plimsolls were rapidly turning brown, with stains of green, and her white blouse clung to her back and chest, sweat marks under her arms, as she ran as far as she could from the couple meeting in the woods, hopefully back to the path she now knew, away from the deep of the forest.

Finally, Nyx's ears caught the sound of the creek. She stopped, took in her surroundings; these were familiar bushes, familiar trees. She was back on the route she knew, and the creek to her right assured her this was the correct trail back to the cottage. Taking a couple of deep breaths, hands leaning on her thighs, back bent as she recovered from running, Nyx giggled. Had she barely avoided walking in on a couple about to do it? It had sounded like it, hadn't it? Shaking her head, she composed herself, pulling unruly curls into a ponytail, brushing leaves and twigs from her clothes. Then she walked on towards the meadow, which she could now see in the distance, knowing beyond it lay home.

As she came to the cottage, her uncle's figure greeted her from the garden. He was by the low, rough stone wall, his back turned to the woods, eyeing the house as if taking it all in. Nyx cleared her throat, so he'd know she was here. The last thing she wanted was to scare Spencer; he already looked as if about to jump in fear at every breath. He turned to face her, smiled, but as he took in her stained shoes and scratched legs, his joy turned into a frown.

"And where have you been?"

Nyx blushed, but smiled even wider. "Took a hike in the woods, been doing it every day. But somehow I went deeper in, this morning. I think I was at walking distance of Everley estate, you know?"

Spencer's face darkened; he shifted his eyes. "You should stay away from the deep end of the woods, Nyx, it isn't safe."

"Oh no, it surely isn't," she said, and giggled.

Was that fear she saw in her uncle's face? Or worry?

"What did you see?"

"Well, I'm glad I didn't really *see*, but I heard enough. Spence, there was a couple making out in the woods, and I think they were about to... you know, *do it*. Almost walked in on them. I wouldn't be able to live with the shame if I did." Nyx laughed, Spencer joining her, but the mirth failed to reach his eyes. "What about you, where have you been? Woke up, and the house was empty."

"Maybe you shouldn't stay in bed so long."

Nyx jumped over the wall, joined her uncle in the garden. "I'm on holiday, cut me some slack. We should really do something about this, it looks like a jungle."

"I'm having someone look into it tomorrow. That's what I've been doing, young lady, taking care of things. You're now officially enrolled at Weaversmoor Academy. And school starts in less than two weeks, so no more slack, Nyx." He eyed her sternly, held her gaze until Nyx was forced to lower her eyes. "Tomorrow we go to Sunderleigh for your uniform and school supplies, I already have a list."

Shoulders slumping, Nyx faced her dirty plimsolls. Anxiety grabbed her stomach, the nagging bite of worry working away at her core. What if she didn't fit in? What if she made no friends?

She'd had no trouble amassing a group of them back in Havenleah, but what of Weaversmoor? The other children at the Academy would all have their powers manifest by now, she'd be the odd freak. Suddenly, the idea of starting school lost all the charm it had just hours before, when she'd crawled out of bed, bored out of her head for having nothing to do all day, again. She'd been pining for the start of the school term then, hadn't she? Well, not anymore.

"You'll do fine," Spence whispered, pulling her to him, one arm wrapped around Nyx's shoulders. "You're a clever girl, and talented too. Such an empath as you are, you're sure to do well at school."

"You hated it there, didn't you?"

Spencer eyed her, the look in his eyes impossible for Nyx to read. "I loved it. And so did your mother, your father, Sarah. We all loved school, because it's where we learnt and where we were free to be ourselves."

"Then why do you hate this place so much?"

He shook his head, emotion filling his eyes with misery. "I had my heart broken here. And it changed me, Nyx, I was never the same. I could never love anyone as much again. But let's not talk about that, it's all in the past." He pulled himself out of the sombre mood descending upon both; heading towards the back door. "How about driving off to Leavesford for lunch, huh? There's a nice little spot there Sarah told me about, and there's Houghton Castle not far, we could go visit. Bit of a sightseeing tour, what do you say?"

Nyx beamed, her silver-blue eyes gleaming with joy. "I think that's a massive good idea. Let me clean up first and you got yourself a date!"

WITCH CRAFT

II

Pulling on the dark grey blazer, Nyx studied her image in the mirror. Shoulders slumped, she eyed the hem of the skirt hitting just above the knee, demure and prim, as none of her previous uniforms had ever been. Her old school in Havenleah allowed shorter skirts on their pinafore dresses, and all the girls went for that hemline. Weaversmoor Academy seemed a bit old-fashioned in that regard, if she were to judge by the choice offered at the uniform store at Sunderleigh. Amongst all other schools catered by the place, the Academy was the one to sport the longest hems, and the only one demanding their students purchased two sets.

Either the black pleated skirt or the tartan one - which would have been cute, if only the length was shorter. Along white shirts, blazer, and a choice of cardigans that went from charcoal to dark red to tan. Plus, the brogues, meant to be worn all year round. They pinched her feet horribly, how was she ever going to get used to them? At least the boys were luckier, she'd spotted their uniforms on the store's front window, and they were allowed dark wash jeans. Yes, there was also a pair of charcoal trousers, the unobtrusive white shirt, the red tie, the horrible charcoal blazer, along with the black brogues. But they got to wear jeans, and that seemed unfair.

Just looking at herself in the mirror, Nyx knew she'd hate the school, and the other children there. They'd all be very arrogant and elitist; they'd all look down their noses on her. And the tartan skirt made her look fat. Sighing, well aware she had no choice but condescend, Nyx pulled one fallen sock up and reached for her cross-body leather bag - another one of the school's demands. It all looked so old-fashioned and dated it almost made her scream. Not that she was a fashion victim, but she did have her own personal style and preferences, and charcoal was far from being her colour. She liked deep pinks, and royal blue, and teal, and certain hues of gold and orange that looked like gems sparkling in the light. Not this... *darkness*. But this was what she'd been handed, and must to make do with it. Sighing yet again, Nyx took one last look in the mirror and braced herself.

The first day at school was always the worst.

Spencer waited for her at the sunny kitchen, breakfast spread out before him. Nyx tried to smile, but failed.

"I'm not hungry."

"You still have to eat."

Settling for a glass of milk and a toast with jam, Nyx forced herself. The toast was cold and dry, tasted like paper and rolled around her mouth, unwilling to go down. Her stomach cramped, and not even the cold milk seemed to appease the ache that had settled there. How she wished her father was here, if only to soothe and reassure her.

"I think I need to throw up." The kitchen lights blinked on and off; she was doing it again.

Her uncle put down the vial from which he'd been measuring careful drops onto a glass of water, grabbed her hand, pressed it gently. His dark green eyes came to rest on hers, appeasingly. Spence had always been able to calm her, far better than her father, but she still missed him madly.

"I know you're anxious, and scared. But it's going to be all right, Nyx. Trust me. Jamal will be there, and he'll look after you. Go brush your teeth, if you're finished, I'll pack you an apple so you can eat mid-morning. Hurry, you don't want to be late on the first day, do you?"

She wasn't late, in the end, and her anxiety levels lowered the moment she saw her cousin waiting for her at the Academy's front gates. Jumping off the car, Nyx joined Jamal.

"I'll take it from here," the boy said, head pushed through the passenger's seat window, winking at Nyx's uncle.

Spencer nodded, waved at the two teenagers and drove away.

"Right, let's brave the crowds, shall we?" Jamal ushered Nyx in, and as they marched off to the Academy's front door, he greeted other teens, introducing Nyx as his cousin.

She smiled and nodded at the new people, tired of keeping up the grin, jaws aching from the effort. But at least she wasn't alone.

"So, this building here is where we have most of the classes," Jamal explained, ushering her forward. "At the back we have the sports fields and the gym, and down that way, the refectory. To your left is off-limits for us, external students. Only boarders are allowed there."

"Didn't know this was a boarding school."

Jamal stopped her, eyes boring down on Nyx. "Look, this isn't your run-of-the-mill school, you know that. Every single student and teacher has magic, here. We're all the same and don't need to hide our powers inside this place. But the truth is, there aren't all that many people born with magical abilities in our world, are there?"

Nyx shook her head, in all of her sixteen years she'd met none aside from family.

"This is one of the very few schools for people like us across the country. It's only natural it doubles as boarding school, not every single witch in the world lives at Weaversmoor or close by. They come from all over, you know? The Academy's supposed to be one of the best, and everyone with magic wants to study here."

"Didn't know."

"It's silly they've kept this from you, really. You should have been attending this place for years, now, you'll be so far behind I bet you need special classes just to make up for all that lost time."

Nyx scowled, angry at Jamal's innuendos about her father, her uncle, who'd kept her away from Weaversmoor and the study of magic. "My father and Spence had their reasons. I may not know what those are, but I trust them, you know? They only wanted the best for me."

"Then they should have sent you here. Look, don't be cross, Nyx, but the truth is you're a witch. You have all these powers in you, some dormant, others not so much, and if you don't know how to handle and work with them, it can get very dangerous. The fact they kept you from studying ways of using your talents could have put you at risk. No matter how much Erin and Spencer hated their mother, or what they suffered at her hands, it was selfish of them to deny you access to learning. But now you're here, and it'll be all right."

Jamal patted Nyx's shoulder and smiled. She held back, eyes on the gravel under her feet, hurt by his words. Yes, he had a point, and it was true there'd been a certain amount of selfishness, of petty vengeance, at not letting her visit her grandmother or come to Weaversmoor, but there was also fear. For years, she'd seen the fear cross her father's eyes, her uncle's, whenever Sarah came to visit and they were forced to remember such a place as Weaversmoor even existed. Whatever had happened to them in this otherwise peaceful-looking town, it had made them live in constant terror of the past.

And now Spence was forced back home, and he'd been looking positively sick for it, but he still endured, and did it for her. He did it for her because he knew Nyx needed more than what he could give. Spence wasn't selfish, much on the contrary. He'd gone against his word of never accepting his mother's handouts, for the sake of giving Nyx a future and helping her learn how to handle what nature had given her. All she knew of her heritage, her magic, Spencer had taught willingly, but even he had limits to his knowledge. Jamal was mistaken claiming he was selfish, he was the exact opposite.

"You're wrong," she said, finally facing Jamal. "But I won't discuss my father's choices, my uncle's decisions with you."

"Nyx, I'm sorry if I've hurt your feelings, I only meant..."

Whatever he'd been about to say was left hanging in the air forever more, as what looked like some sort of clumsy giant jumped on his back. Jamal turned and laughed, squirming until he dislodged his assailant. They bear-hugged and patted each other's back, grunting in what was to Nyx a very unseeming fashion, while she simply stood there, being ignored and with no idea of what to do or where to go. Finally, the two boys let go of each other.

"How was your summer, Wilson?" the newcomer inquired, his smile large and open.

Nyx studied him discreetly, taking in the deep hazel eyes, the perfectly rounded nose, the near symmetrical lips. She lingered over those lips for longer than needed, and blushed at the thoughts flaring through her mind.

"Not as swanky as yours, your lordship," Jamal joked, hugging his friend again. Then, as an afterthought, he turned to Nyx. "This is my cousin," he introduced, "Nyx Vaughn."

The newcomer finally deemed to notice her existence, the hazel eyes coming to meet hers with a look that was all too telling. "Oh, so this is the famous elusive cousin, is she?" He reached out one hand, which Nyx reluctantly took. "I'm Trystan Everley, the black sheep."

"Make nothing of him," Jamal said, and guffawed. "This is my best friend, Nyx, he's actually an all right bloke, once you get to know him." He punched an elbow into Trystan's midriff, who woofed and doubled over himself. "Even though sometimes he can be a total oaf."

"Would a total oaf tell you you're about to be sent to the doghouse if you don't hurry finding my sister? She's been looking for you all over school."

Jamal's face lost all signs of mirth, eyes widening and tongue swiping over suddenly dry lips. He actually looked scared, which made Nyx giggle.

"But I have to get Nyx to Mrs Taylor's office, so she has her schedule cleared with the Principal. Bryn's going to kill me, isn't she?"

Trystan grinned openly, nodding in compliance. "Go, I'll walk your cousin to the Principal's." His attention returned to Nyx, eyebrows raised in a failed attempt at playful seduction. "It'll give us a chance to get acquainted."

Jamal smirked. "Are you ok with this, Nyx?"

"Go, it's fine. The young esquire here can escort me to wherever I need to be."

"Ooh, pretty and with a sense of humour, see, you've been hiding all this from me, Wilson. I shan't forgive you the deceit! Shall we go then, milady?" He offered an arm to Nyx, who blushed and forced her eyes to the ground.

Trystan leading the way, she had no choice but follow and try to keep up with his impossibly long strides. In a matter of seconds, Nyx found herself as good as running by his side.

"So," he said, slowing his pace as if realising the girl was struggling to keep up. "How long have you been in town?"

"We got here early August."

"How do you like it so far?"

Nyx shrugged. "Can't say much about it, it's been less than a month. I figure it's ok?"

"I need to show you around, then. Bummer you got here when everyone's away, know what I mean? We've been out of town since July, to my sister's chagrin. She and Jamal only started dating last year, and she's already freaking out. Because he's a ten and she's only an eight, she says."

"A ten? Jamal? I guess he's all right."

Trystan cackled, amused. "Don't let him hear you say that, boy's very proud of his looks. Most girls at the Academy swoon for your cousin, you'll soon have more friends than you signed up for, you'll see. Ah, here we are. This is the Principal's office. Just make sure you don't get on my sister's bad side, she'll make your life hell. See you around, Nyx Vaughn."

With a wave and a smile, he took off running down the corridor they'd come from, leaving Nyx facing an imposing locked door. She took one deep breath, and braced herself, but before she could knock, the door opened from the inside, and a short, plump woman stood facing her with a stern look in her eyes.

"Yes?" she asked, rather forbiddingly. "Shouldn't you be headed for Assembly? What do you want here?"

"I was told to see the Principal first thing this morning," she explained, face blushing so hard heat spread all over her head. "I'm Nyx Vaughn."

The woman's eyes widened, but she soon regained her composure, shoving the door wider for the girl to pass. "Well, why didn't you say? I'm Elspeth Buckford, Mrs Taylor's personal assistant. Have a seat, I'll announce you straight away."

Closing the door behind her, the small woman disappeared into another room, leaving Nyx alone in what looked like an antechamber. She gazed around; spotted an uncomfortable-looking armchair, but before she could take a seat, the lumpy secretary was back, holding the door for her.

"Go right in, Miss Vaughn, the Principal will see you now."

Staring at the timetable the Principal had handed her, Nyx repeated the name between her teeth. Jacintha Tate, what kind of name was that? It sounded Australian, or Kiwi at best, didn't it? Maybe in her head. Miss Tate was sure to be a lovely old spinster who taught magic to those so far behind on their use of it they needed a tutor just to keep up.

A *tutor*. The word alone sent cramps down her stomach, a sense of inner shame shattering her already shaky self-confidence. A tutor, three times a week, filling up her afternoons so she barely had any free time. *Just until you get a grip of your talents*, the Principal had said, but how long would it take for her to actually know what her talents were? Well, there was no point wallowing in self-pity now, she'd have to endure. At least it kept her busy and masked the sense of loneliness.

Glancing at the timetable, Nyx realised she was far too late for Assembly, there'd be no point joining now. Best to search for Classroom 8, where her History lesson would take place in about twenty minutes. That would give her enough time to find her bearings through the maze of corridors, stairwells and rooms that constituted the insides of the Academy. Searching the numbers above the doors scattered throughout the corridor, Nyx realised she must be in the wrong wing. These were all Labs and Workshops, for the practice of chemistry and potion-making, surely. History class would be located elsewhere, wouldn't it? Searching through the array of leaflets, booklets and forms the Principal had handed her, she was distracted by a whimpering coming from one of the rooms. Like someone crying, or in pain.

Nyx straightened up, strained her ears.

Yes, from two doors down the hallway. Someone was in pain, maybe hurt. Perhaps she should help? She tried to make sense of what the person was saying, her feet moving towards the Lab door of their own accord.

It was a boy's voice. He was complaining of something; no, he was begging. Begging for someone to stop. Was he being hurt? Lurid, horrifying stories of bullying she'd read online came to mind, filling the empty spaces of her imagination with vivid images she'd rather discard. Bracing herself, Nyx walked to the half-open door, took a peek inside.

"It won't stop, just help me make it stop, I can't take it," the boy whimpered.

He was of medium height, and slim. Eyes that were very blue and brimming with tears shed a pained look upon the girl seated by his side, holding one of his hands and caressing it in a comforting manner. The boy had loosened the tie and opened the first few buttons on his shirt, exposing a glimpse of tattooed skin. His fingers were covered in symbols, as were the back of his hands and one wrist. He held a cigarette butt between his fingers and took long drags from it. His black hair was pushed back on his skull, exposing a face that was at the same time handsome and terrifying. He looked the proverbial bad boy, the kid who kept getting himself in trouble, the never-do-well, who was sure to end up tragically short of his potential. And at the same time, he looked far more mature than any kid his age should be. As if he'd seen far more than what was good for him, suffered through a lifetime of pain and despondency. He looked scared, vulnerable and lost.

He looked scary

"I'll draw you a sigil as soon as I can, but I need to know where it's coming from, Pip," the girl seating with him whispered, and tried to pull the boy into her arms, but he fled her reach.

"It's here, it's so loud, so overbearing. All this pain, all this rage, all this hatred. All this fear. There's so much fear."

The boy stood up, made as if to leave the room, but the sight of Nyx stopped him. Their eyes met; he cocked an eyebrow in silent interrogation, as if curious about who and what she was, but then his face changed. He let out a growl of pain and doubled over, hands grabbing the sides of his head.

"Make her go," he murmured, and his companion turned a confused face to the door.

And saw Nyx.

Her eyes had flecks of green that glowered with anger, eyebrows knitted in a scowl. She stood up from where she sat, tall and lean in her uniform, which she somehow managed to look stylish in. Maybe it was the rolled-up cardigan and shirt sleeves, the myriad of leather bracelets on her wrist, the ear pierced through the entirety of its lobe. She marched confidently towards the door, which she held, closing it an inch and hiding the boy from view.

"What do you want?" the girl asked, aggressive in manner, chin jutting out. "Do you take a perverted pleasure from seeing people in pain? Or are you just an eavesdropper in search of the next school rumour, so you can bring attention to yourself by telling tales?"

"I... I was just..." Nyx stuttered, face burning.

"Get out of here! You stupid little girl, don't let me see your face around us again."

Lights flickered overhead. Turning on her heels, Nyx sped down the hallway, biting back tears of shame. As she crossed a set of swinging doors, heart beating wild, breath raspy and laboured, she collided with a running figure and landed on her butt. Satchel and forms went flying around her, in a display resemblant of a flurry of autumn leaves fallen off a tree. The girl she'd ran into fell on her knees, releasing a screech either of pain or disconcert. Could this day get any worse?

"Are you all right?" Nyx inquired, grabbing around for her belongings, blushing once more.

The other girl handed her a ream of paper, the forms Spencer still had to fill for her admittance in the Academy to be complete.

"I'm fine, sorry I bumped into you. Are you hurt?"

"You bumped into me? Thought I'd been the one throwing you on your knees."

The girls giggled.

"I'm Penny." The girl extended a dainty, chocolate-brown hand covered in fashionable rings. "Penelope Lattimer, but everyone calls me Penny."

"I'm Nyx. Vaughn." Helping her up, Nyx pulled the satchel over one shoulder, stuffed the forms inside.

Penny's eyes widened at the sound of her name. "*The* Nyx Vaughn? Corinna Vaughn's granddaughter? You're Jamal's cousin, then. How lucky."

Trystan's words echoed in Nyx's head, claiming she'd soon have an entourage of girls wanting to be her friends because of Jamal. She shook her head; this wasn't what she'd signed up for.

"My cousin's in a relationship," she said, voice frosty and clipped.

Penny's eyes opened a tad more. "I know that, Bryn Everley won't let anyone forget. But he's still the cutest boy at school, you know. A girl can only dream."

"I guess."

"Why were you running? If any of the Monitors catch you speeding through the corridors, you'll get in trouble."

"I was trying to find Classroom 8, for my History lesson. This school is a maze, I can't seem to get my bearings around here."

Penny slid an arm through Nyx's, directing her to a side corridor. "You'll soon know this place like the palm of your hand. Come on, I'm going to Classroom 8 myself, looks like we're classmates! Can I sit next to you? I'll put you up to speed with everything Academy, and you can tell me what it's like to attend a non-magical school. Weren't kids freaked out by you?"

"Why would they be?" Nyx stepped into pace with Penny, frantically watching their surroundings so she could memorise the route taken.

"Well, I don't know, maybe because they don't have magic? Got to be weird, seeing someone do the kind of things we do."

"I didn't show my magic around them. Not that I have all that many powers."

"You've been dormant all this time?"

"Not quite. I can do small stuff, but dad and uncle Spencer always said I had to keep it to myself, mustn't allow others to witness. So I simply didn't use it at all."

"You've lived your entire life like one of them!" Penny sounded excited, as if Nyx was to be admired for attending a non-magical school.

Sensing the students' eyes on her, now that Assembly was over and the corridors full, she felt far from being commended; only regarded with suspicion and even a little mockery, for the exact reason that held Penny in awe. Girls pointed and giggled behind their hands when they walked by, boys sniggered and shook their heads in detriment. As if she was a weird sort of animal they wished they didn't have to lay eyes on, let alone endure. Shame drenched her, and she wished herself back at Havenleah, where her friends liked and accepted her, and no one saw her as the new, shiny freak. But then Trystan Everley walked down the hall in their direction, smile beaming, hazel eyes warm and mischievous, his wink reassuring and calming. Jamal marched on his side, and he dished around cold looks to all those who seemed to be poking fun at Nyx.

"Hey there, Nyx," Trystan greeted, his voice warm but loud enough for everyone around to hear.

She blushed deeper, but nodded in silent greeting, unwittingly holding on to Penny's arm with increased pressure. The girl flinched, said nothing though, enduring the tight grip and Nyx's nails that dived into her skin through the flimsy fabric of her white shirt. Both girls stood aside to let the boys pass, Jamal and Trystan walking into the room, which Nyx gladly noticed was Classroom 8. So they'd be taking lessons together. All of a sudden, her stay at the Academy had become a lot less daunting. As the rest of the students filed inside, Penny pulled her back a couple of steps, her face serious.

"Be careful with the Everleys," she warned. "They're not very good people and think they can throw their weight around. They fancy themselves lords of town, know what I mean? A step better than the rest. It's Cressida Beckford's fault, of course, she's such an arrogant..."

"What? An arrogant what, Penny?"

"Never mind, let's get to class."

"You said you'd dish everything, if I let you sit with me."

The girls slid through the door, took a desk by the window. Nyx looked around discreetly, registered Trystan and Jamal sitting side by side on the back row, Trystan's eyes still on her. He smiled, she smiled back, warm flutters like wings brushing through her stomach, over her skin.

"Cressida Beckford's Trystan and Bryn's mother. She comes from one of the oldest resident families, much like yours. The Vaughns, I mean. Fancies herself a cut above the rest, and taught her children to regard themselves much the same way. They're royalty and we're their minions. You mark my words, Jamal Wilson will come out of this with a broken heart. No way Cressida Beckford's going to allow her princess of a daughter to seriously date a Wilson, one that's black at that. She's such a racist. Only thing holding her back is Jamal's dad and where he stands inside the school Council. See, he's the Academic Overseer, and responds to the Magisterium alone, so he kind of holds the future of the Academy's students in his hands. Cressida would never openly antagonise him, she wouldn't dare."

"Trystan seems nice."

"Yeah... nope. He's a wanker, Nyx. Most boys around here are, but that's to be expected, right? Teenagers, hormonal, all they can think about is... well, you know. But Trystan uses people, so be careful around him."

Their conversation was cut short by the teacher's arrival, shortly followed by a latecomer student. Nyx's eyes widened as she watched the boy she'd witnessed whimpering and wailing just minutes before stroll into the classroom, as if nothing of the sort had happened. He swaggered inside, a cigarette tucked behind his ear, blazer held nonchalantly in one hand, hems of his dark wash jeans rolled up farther than school policy allowed. He looked like a modern day James Dean, a true rebel without a cause, except Nyx knew better. She wondered what the story was, what was wrong with him.

"Don't stare at Pip," Penny whispered, "or the Everleys will make your life hell."

Nyx turned her face towards the teacher who droned on about school rules, the academic year ahead, his particular class. She zoomed out of the man's dull voice, eyes fleeting towards the outside, through the window. It was a lovely, sunny day, one she'd rather have used to hike through the woods instead of being locked in a stuffy classroom. She wished Penny would tell her more about Pip, the Everleys. Nyx had recognised the name Cressida Beckford as associated with her own mother. Spencer had mentioned her once or twice, regarding Erin Vaughn's group of friends. Along with Sarah Wilson, Cressida Beckford had been her mum's best friend, and Nyx wondered what the woman might tell her about Erin, secrets she might share, everything her father and uncle always refused to let her know.

"Pip?" she asked after a few minutes, to divert her mind from the woman who'd birthed and later abandoned her.

"Pip Thomson, Philip John Thomson the third. Now, *he's* royalty, unlike the Everleys. Not *royalty*, you know what I mean. He does descend from the Tudors, though, or is it the Plantagenets? I was never very good at history."

"What's his story?"

"He's the family rebel, as you can see. His entire family is squeaky clean, Pip's a mess, just look at him. *Don't*," Penny hissed, as Nyx turned in her chair to watch the boy in question. "Has all these tattoos, and is always acting up, being silly and aggressive. Gets violent, sometimes, and only Jamal and the Everleys can get a hold on him. They protect him, you know. Bet his family has some sort of agreement with the Everleys, they came into a huge amount of money not long before Pip enrolled at the Academy. See, he's from up north, but was thrown out of a couple other schools for his hectic behaviour. So his father sent him down here. He's a boarder, but stays over at the Everleys more often than not."

"Why does he have all those tattoos?"

Penny shrugged. "Rumour has it he's just trying to shock his family. I think they're sigils. You know, magical ones, to ground and protect him? I've seen Bryn draw a couple of them, and he later showed up with these new tats that were far too identical to Bryn's designs."

"I get it you and Bryn used to be friends?"

"Sort of. Trystan took me on a couple of dates, but his mother soon put an end to it."

"Oh." Could Penny be in love with Trystan? Was that why she acted as if she couldn't stand the boy? "You still like him."

The other girl giggled. "That's all in the past, trust me. Wouldn't be caught with Trystan Everley if he was the last man on earth."

"But that's what ended your friendship with his sister?"

"No, she took my side, actually. It was once she started dating Jamal that she changed. Pushed every one away. Well, most girls. She's so insecure where he's concerned, always terrified he falls for someone else. It's silly, I mean, Bryn's... well, *Bryn*." Penny said it as if it was something obvious, so Nyx merely nodded.

"And Bryn's been drawing sigils for that Pip bloke, is that it? Why?"

Penny shrugged. "They're a tight-knit bunch, those four, always together, with their secrets and their mysteries. You'd do well to steer clear of them, even though Jamal's your cousin."

Nyx stole a glance at the back of the classroom, where her cousin sat with Trystan, Pip Thomson occupying the table behind them. She didn't want to steer clear of them, much on the contrary. As she eyed Trystan Everley's jawline and plump lips, Nyx realised she very much wanted to get to know that group a lot better.

WITCH CRAFT

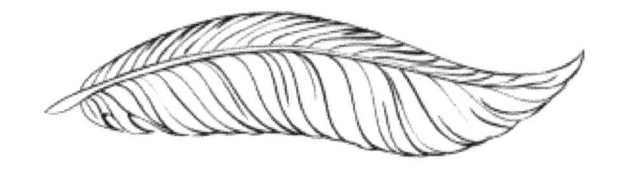

III

The first school day dragged on for what felt like ages, Nyx running around the corridors in complete disorientation, trying to find the correct classrooms for the subjects she was taking in sixth form. After the success on her GCSE's, she realised the Academy expected her to take her courses seriously and strive for academic excellence, alongside the extra-curricular classes she was demanded to attend and that comprised the learning of those capacities particular to the students of this school. Seeing she was so far behind on subjects as History of Magic or the rather dull Potion and Apothecary Studies, alongside more specific lessons such as Moon Magic, Herbology, or Rune Casting, Nyx was rather eager to meet up with Miss Tate, if only to start catching up on that.

When she finally got to her tutor's office, sweating with the exertion of running up and down endless stairways in search of it, Nyx no longer cared for the extra work, the extra classes, or any sort of academic prowess she might have dreamt of achieving. All she wanted was to go home, curl up in bed and have herself a good cry. The first day at school, although it had thrown her into a couple of classes alongside Trystan Everley and his mischievous hazel eyes, had been tiresome and stressful, making Nyx wish she was back at Havenleah with her friends.

But her former life was over; and this was what fate had dealt her, she must make the best of it. Her father would be very disappointed if his daughter were to let herself be disheartened just because she was finding it hard to keep up with schoolwork. After all, this was only the first day. Yes, she was a bit overwhelmed, a bit emotional, but several classmates had offered to help her. She'd already been invited to a couple of study groups, so it wasn't as desperate as Nyx seemed to be making it. There was no need for tears. But constantly missing her father set a dull, lingering ache in her chest, making it hard for her to breathe, burdening Nyx with misery.

Bracing herself, she knocked on Miss Tate's door, a crisp, clear voice inviting her in. Nyx turned the knob and was greeted by a spacious, light office where a couple of armchairs and a couch huddled around a cosy fireplace. A desk stood in front of the window, littered with papers; and a round table surrounded by chairs nestled by two ceiling-high bookcases, filled with books of all sorts. Seated at that table was a woman so far from what Nyx expected she did a double take, only to make sure this was the right room.

"Nyx Vaughn?" the woman inquired. "Come on in." Standing up, Miss Tate smiled a wide, welcoming grin and gestured Nyx to the table.

She wasn't very tall, nor was she short. Eyes of the brightest, most vivid blue Nyx had ever seen, they seemed to sparkle with pure joy at being alive, if that was even a thing. Glossy brown hair fell down her back and framed a face that was slightly pinched, with delicate features and healthy colours, covered in freckles just like Nyx. The coincidence made her smile. Having expected an old spinster dressed in tweeds and sensible shoes, Nyx was taken aback by the stylish, well-polished woman in front of her.

"Hi, did you find me all right?"

Nyx shrugged, unsure of understanding the question. Miss Tate smiled.

WITCH CRAFT

"I'm Jacintha," she went on. "Come, sit, I thought we might get acquainted before we start any sort of work." She gestured at the comfy-looking armchairs, and Nyx took one. "So, Nyx, what's your special brand of magic?"

"I'm not sure I know what you mean." What special brand? Her magic was all over the place, she didn't know how to use or control it, didn't even know when it was about to come to life and do something that might just embarrass her in front of others.

It had been easier, back in Havenleah, when the really weird stuff only took place at her home, never at school or out in the streets. But since coming to Weaversmoor, she seemed to be flying sparks off her fingers at every step. It was just a matter of thinking *something*, and it came to life in the freakiest way possible. Like at Herbology, when the teacher had been lecturing them with an outline of what the classes would be like, and the classroom was just too hot and stuffy. So Nyx caught herself thinking how much she'd enjoy a breeze, and all of a sudden, the door and a window opened of their own accord and a draft filled the room. The teacher had immediately known it was Nyx's fault, as had the rest of the class, but no one said a word, despite the few sniggers hidden behind carefully placed hands over smiling lips. Only Pip Thomson had given her a reassuring nod and eyed her as if she weren't a complete freak.

"You don't know what I'm talking about?" Miss Tate insisted. "Well, you're far more behind than I thought."

I've never had a dormant before, what am I supposed to do with the girl?

The words echoed inside Nyx's head, and she blushed. So now she was listening in on other people's thoughts? This may prove to be an even bigger problem. She averted Miss Tate's eyes, instead trained hers on the fireplace, where a couple of logs sat unattended, waiting for a drop in the temperature for someone to build a cosy fire that warmed the room. As soon as she thought it, a flame erupted on one of the logs, but it lacked force of permanence, and dwindled to nothing in mere seconds.

"Oh dear," Miss Tate said, having paled considerably. "Are you a Feeric? This could be a bit dangerous, if you can't control your flames. I remember we had a similar problem a couple of years ago, with this Year Two student, he could hardly keep himself from lighting flames at each breath he took, poor boy. Incinerated a sapling out there in the gardens, was so distraught by it he came down with a fever. But all's well, he got his training, and is one of the best in his class now. We just have to find you a proper tutor, then, a fire Elemental that can guide you."

I'm useless with Feerics as it is, wonder why the Principal would send the girl to me.

There. Again. She was hearing Miss Tate's thoughts, surely? What if the woman happened to think about something personal, something... intimate? Blushing deeper, Nyx fanned herself with one hand. Why was this room so warm, why had Miss Tate not opened a window on such a hot day? She couldn't breathe, and her head was swimming, what if she fainted and made a spectacle of herself? Why was this so hard? If only she'd stayed back at Havenleah, where she wouldn't need to deal with this. If only dad hadn't been lost at sea. If only she wasn't as alone as this.

The sound of a window latch opening broke the silence in the room, both Nyx and Jacintha jumping in their seats. The window pane swayed on its hinges, the white lace curtains floating with the breeze. It was turning chillier, and there was a scent of humidity in the air that promised rain. Miss Tate stood up and shut the window, turning the catch so it didn't open again, but her face translated the thoughts Nyx fought not to hear. The woman knew it wasn't a draft that opened the window; it had been Nyx. The girl hung her head in shame, but raised it back up when Miss Tate presented her with a glass of water.

"Go on, have a drink. Don't be nervous, Nyx, there's no reason for it."

Taking a seat again, Jacintha studied her pupil, the thoughts in her mind too fast and convoluted for Nyx to make sense of them. She gulped down the water, one small sip at a time, in fear of choking. Everything was getting out of hand, and out of her control, what if the water started attacking her? The thought brought a smile to her lips, and a giggle found its way out.

"Feeling better?" Miss Tate asked, and Nyx nodded. "Do you mind if we try a little experiment? I just want to make sure I know what I'm dealing with here."

"What if it goes wrong, whatever it is?"

"You don't need to worry. Can you try and turn that water to ice? Or heat it up some? Maybe make a small scale tsunami inside that glass?"

Nyx laughed, what did she mean, make a tsunami in a glass? But Miss Tate's expression left no doubt to the seriousness of her words, so she gulped down her mirth and focused on the water instead. Soon, it was spinning like mad inside the clear glass, forcing a vortex to the deeper end, like a whirlpool. Scared, Nyx put a stop to it.

"Good," Jacintha whispered, her eyes intent on the girl's face. "Was it hard to do? Now, see that plant over by the window, the one on my desk? It's looking a little sad, isn't it? I keep forgetting to water it. Do you mind trying to perk it up a bit?"

"I can't do that."

"Humour me."

Nyx closed her eyes, snapped them open again, staring straight at the plant. She stood up and marched herself to the desk, where her fingers alighted over the droopy, lacklustre leaves. For what felt like long seconds, nothing seemed to happen, but a subtle change was indeed taking place. Where the tips of its leaves already looked browned, now they were turning a deep, lush green, and the plant seemed to revive and thrive under Nyx's gentle touch. She turned around with wide eyes, mouth set in an *'O'* of awe and confusion.

A Weaver. When was the last time I came across a Weaver?

Something else floated through Miss Tate's mind, a fog, a shadow Nyx couldn't quite make out or read. What had the woman called her? A weaver? At Weaversmoor? What were the odds? And what on earth was a *weaver*?

"A Weaver is a witch that isn't bound to any particular element," Jacintha clarified, once again gesturing the girl to take a seat. She seemed to have read the questions crossing Nyx's head. "Most witches are elementals, as you know. Feerics, Waterlings, Aerials, Earthens. Then they have their own personal abilities, which means they can be Spellcasters, Hexers, Omen-Clairvoyants, Haruspexes, Draught-Makers, Sigilists. Did you not know any of this?"

"My uncle filled me up on these. He's an Earthen Draught-Maker."

"Weavers, like me and you, we don't fall under any of these categories. We don't have an element, rather we can summon them all. And we can do a little bit of everything. We don't excel at a particular subject or discipline, but can play with them all to a certain degree of effectiveness. Of course when compared to a Sigilist's our sigils will be lacking, but they work. And the same for every other speciality. We can do them all, we can use it all, but we don't excel at anything in particular. Are you getting this?"

"I think so. What you're saying is that I'm capable of using all sorts of magic, and that's why weird things keep happening to me?"

"Yes. Because you don't know how to channel energies, you don't know how to control your abilities. I'll teach you, of course. First of all, I'm going to show you a trick to lock other people's thoughts out of your head. This is very good when you're around Haruspexes, because it also prevents them from entering your mind and controlling you. Then I'm going to show you how to draw a sigil that will lock this neat little trick in place, but you need to have it tattooed somewhere in your body. We'll go for a small design, something you can tuck away where only you can see it, all right? Of course you need to ask your uncle's permission, first, but him being of the blood, I'm sure he won't oppose."

"Of the blood?"

"Witches' blood, Nyx. It's what we call ourselves around here; we're of the blood, contrary to those who aren't. Granted, there aren't many in this town, but you can find some. Those of the blood tend to flock to places like this, unlike folks who aren't like us. It's like a calling."

"Why's that? Because there's a lot of magical people in one place?"

Miss Tate's expression took on a dreamy quality, a faraway look spreading across her eyes, as if she was lost in thought. "I really don't know... I was drawn here, after the fall. And many of the Academy's teachers were also called into this town, by some sort of force."

"The fall?"

Jacintha's eyes cleared. She smiled at Nyx, suddenly back to the insides of her office. "Yes, I used to do a lot of rock climbing a few years ago. One day, I took a nasty fall and shattered my hip, and that was the end of my career. Woke up in hospital riddled with pain and fogged with drugs, and the worst case of amnesia I can think of. Luckily, one of the doctors attending me was of the blood, she recognised me for what I am and helped me quite a lot. I still can't remember much of my life prior to the fall, but sometimes I get these flashes... anyway, as soon as I was well enough, I started getting this itch to move from the city I was living in and find a place that was less crowded, less daunting. When my doctor mentioned Weaversmoor, I knew I had to come here. And the rest is history, as they say."

"How long have you been here? How long have you been tutoring students at the Academy? Were you always a teacher?"

Jacintha shook her head. "Like I said, I don't remember much. I think I worked as a pharmacist or something like that, because I distinctly remember mixing medicine. Maybe I was a potion-maker, but we couldn't find trace of me, nor did I match any of the missing people's reports. I've been here for two-and-a-half years, now, and before I became a tutor, I did a lot of baby-sitting and a lot of nanny service. I realised I like working with children, so when the Principal offered me this job, along with my new identity, I accepted."

"New identity?"

"Those of the blood take care of their own, Nyx."

"So you can't even remember your real name? Don't you want to?"

Jacintha cocked her head to the side, smiled. "I can't remember my real name but know it was similar to Jacintha, so when I was told to choose one, this was the first that came to mind. Some days I want to remember, most I don't even think about it. If I matched none of the missing persons' reports filed at the moment of my accident, then that means no one missed me, I had no one. Right now, I have friends and a career, an entire community of people who care, respect and value me. If I were to disappear, I'd be missed, and there'd be a report matching my description. So no, I don't really care. I feel complete, here. Maybe this sounds odd to you, callous?"

"No, that's not what I mean. I just think I'd want to know, but then again, it's like you said, if no one missed you, you're better off not knowing what that other life was like." She faced the window, frowning.

It made sense. Nyx herself hardly ever thought about her mother, didn't care to meet her. If the woman had chosen to abandon her, then why would Nyx want to know and remember her? She didn't, most days. And wouldn't, if it wasn't for the memory of those hushed conversations she'd happened to overhear, between her father and uncle, late at night when they thought her asleep. If it wasn't for Spencer's silence regarding his life at Weaversmoor, his childhood here, his youth. If it wasn't for the muddy, messy tendrils of thought she'd grasped from his mind, that hinted at hidden secrets, a secret history as to her mother's past, one that might explain why Erin Vaughn had left her own daughter behind and made her estranged husband promise to never take the child back to Weaversmoor. Nyx wouldn't care one bit, if it wasn't for all this.

"I couldn't agree more," Miss Tate replied. "Well, look at the time. I think we should call it a day. Meet me here tomorrow and we can start work on that sigil. In the meantime, please give your uncle this form so he can sign his permission for certain procedures. I'm sure you have quite a few more documents for him to sign."

Nyx grabbed the piece of paper from her tutor's hands and shoved it in the satchel next to the others. She hadn't even noticed time pass, but it was nearing five, and she still had homework to do. Grabbing her blazer, she followed Miss Tate to the door, saying her goodbyes with a sense of ease she hadn't yet experienced; not since leaving Havenleah after the weekend spent there celebrating her sixteenth birthday with her old friends. That had been mid-August, it was now early September, had she really walked around all this time with the weight of the world on her shoulders? Because it did feel like it, what with the sudden lightness to her step and the sudden ease in her head, that assured her she was doing fine and wasn't a freak. She was one of them, and at the right place.

After all, she was of the blood.

Trystan sat at the kitchen counter munching on a bacon sarnie and going through the list of mandatory readings for the first term alone. He was already knackered with the load of school work he was expected to put through. Dripping fat on one of the forms he'd brought home for his father to sign, Trystan winced, aware it would be cause for argument. He grabbed a paper towel and wiped it, but not before his father walked into the room and caught him at it.

"It's nearly lunchtime, what are you doing eating a sandwich?"

"I was hungry," he replied, keeping his voice down and neutral, while fire bubbled up inside him.

"You'll ruin your appetite for lunch. Look at those forms! How'm I supposed to sign them now, Trystan? Why can't you be careful? Why are you such a slob?"

"It was an accident, all right?"

"Everything's an accident, with you. When are you going to grow up, son? I won't always be around, nor your mother, to pick up after your mess."

Trystan clenched his fists, tried to take a couple of deep breaths to steady himself, in vain. His head already ached, the pounding of his heart nearly out of control, the familiar throbbing at his temples riding down his veins to the tip of his fingers, where flames demanded to be let out.

"Well, you can go whenever you wish, good riddance. It's not like you're here because you want to," he mumbled between his teeth.

His father's hand slapped him across the face, left side. The sarnie he'd been about to bite flew from a suddenly strengthless hand, food spat from between his lips, tears brimming his eyes. As unexpected as the slap was, it was painful, leaving his cheek tingling and red. But Trystan pulled himself together; he'd not give his father the satisfaction of knowing how much his actions still affected him. He sat up on the stool, back straight, eyes shadowed by anger he forced under control. There was no point throwing fire at his father, the man was quite capable of staving off any sort of magical attack.

"You watch your mouth when you speak to me, Trystan. I'm still your father, you owe me respect."

Cackling, Trystan pushed the forms at his father, stood up from his seat, wiping greasy hands down the length of his jeans. "Maybe you should have thought of that when you decided it was fine to make out with a man in your family home, with your children inside."

Before his father could say anything, Trystan ran out the kitchen door, crossed the backyard towards the woods on his family's property. Knowing he'd certainly hear it once he was back – after all, it was Saturday and father demanded they had lunch together, like the proper, happy family they were not – he still fled the house, intent on staying away as long as he could, just so he avoided his father's presence. It had always been like this, nothing his son did was ever good enough for Max Everley, always finding fault in everything. Not that the man was any different with Bryn, but she was his favourite and had their father wrapped around her finger. He was proud of his daughter, if only for the way she stood up to their mother, who was always trying to pick a fight with Max, always throwing some sort of shade at him.

All that in the seclusion and privacy of their home, of course. Outside these walls, they were the perfect family. Privileged, beautiful, rich, cultured and talented, they were the closest thing to aristocracy within Weaversmoor, and played the part. Or at least their parents did. Trystan couldn't care less, in fact he didn't much care about anything. He went through life looking for fun, and anything that meant too much hassle, too much stress, he gave up. He didn't care about school or his education, didn't care about his future; in fact, he could hardly see a future for himself. Unlike his sister, who was so driven, despite looking the exact opposite. Where Trystan was the poster boy for preppy young men, Bryn was all rebel, with her leather jacket and biker boots, the torn jeans, the tattoos and the pierced ear. But she was studious and bright, she had a life plan; she had intent. Trystan lacked everything. All he had about him were his friends. And his lack of interest for all the rest.

Ever since catching his father kissing a man one night, downstairs by the front door, Trystan had lost all respect for him. The vision - unexpected as it had been - of his father holding his PA in his arms in a way he'd never held his own wife, had seared itself into Trystan's brain, and shed light upon so many of his family's idiosyncrasies. Not that he shunned his father for being gay, or bisexual, or whatever. Trystan's best friend fancied both boys and girls, he was fine with it. What he wasn't fine with was the cheating, the betrayal. His father hadn't just betrayed his wife; he'd cheated on all his family. After having witnessed that kiss, a lot of his mother's erratic behaviour made sense, her drinking, her blaming, her constant jabs at Max as a faulty father and husband, it all made sudden sense. Why didn't he just divorce her, why put them through all the constant misery that was living with parents who loathed each other?

Because of his reputation, of course. Max Everley was royalty in the eyes of most of the town's residents, and that was a statute he didn't intend to lose. So he kept on with a fake, poisonous marriage, forcing his children to live in a toxic environment, constantly exposed to the vicious, violently verbal attacks Max and Cressida threw at each other. No wonder Trystan just didn't care. No wonder he shut everything out and locked himself away in his head. No wonder he ran from every responsibility. He simply couldn't allow himself to care. But that wasn't quite accurate, was it? Trystan cared about Bryn, about Jamal and Pip, too. And he now found himself caring for that new girl, the one with the freckles, Jamal's cousin.

The Vaughn witch.

Shaking his head, he strolled leisurely through the clump of trees that his family called a backyard, headed straight to the small gate at the end of the Everley property. He had zero to no intention of staying home on a day such as this, early September with a persistence of warmth and sunshine blazing across a cloudless blue sky. Such days were rare, and meant to be enjoyed. He'd go off to the woods and follow down to the creek; he could laze about for an hour or two before even thinking of meeting up with his friends. He could sit by the water and daydream, he mused, as the image of a pair of silver-blue eyes filled his mind. Blushing, he grinned; life seemed full of promise lately, ever since Nyx Vaughn moved to Weaversmoor and started attending the Academy. Bryn had already alienated the girl, what with her silly jealousy and the way she suspected everyone but those closest to her. Which was also an outcome of their parents' relationship, of the lies and deceit they fed each other. They tainted everything they touched, his parents did, and he and Bryn were the usual victims.

He left the property through the gate, remembering to lock it behind him. The act was so ingrained, from years and years of his father droning it in his ears, it was automatic, by now. The thought of his father sparked up a new surge of anger. How could a man so flawed, so lacking in morals, come and demand his son be perfect? How could his father have the gall to criticise everything Trystan did? When he himself had so much to be ashamed of?

Allowing rage to take hold of him, the boy grabbed clumps of dry, tall grass in his fingers and ripped them from the soil, leaving a trail of destruction behind. He kicked at bushes and pebbles on the ground, at clusters of weeds, all the while letting loose irate roars that scared birds off their perches. Finally, and as Trystan came to a clearing amidst a thick grouping of trees, exertion overtook him, and he let himself fall on the dusty ground, soiling the seat of his jeans.

Only one thing would work for him. He had to vent his rage, had to let it loose, push it out of him. If Trystan allowed it to remain inside, it would fester and hurt him more. So he stretched himself on the dirt floor of the forest and spread his arms wide, eyes closed, legs apart, as he breathed deep of the tangy, moist scent of the woods. Then he called forth his fires, allowed his flames to run the course of his body, dancing over the palms of his hands, his arms, neck, across his torso and legs. Mother would have a fit, what with the singed clothes, but he couldn't care less. He'd go around wearing ruined garments if he had to, fully aware it would be a cold day in hell before Cressida Everley allowed one of her children to go out sporting clothes that weren't in mint condition. Right now, he needed this. Right now, he needed to let the blazing heat steam out of him, so he could get back to being cool-headed and disinterested, the boy who thought of nothing but having fun, the golden child of his father's loins and his mother's womb, who was nothing more than a privileged kid with a loaded bank account and a pretty face.

If that was what Weaversmoor demanded him to be, then that was who he'd be. Anything was better than being open to emotions and pain, or the hassle of trying to prove everyone wrong. If people saw him as something, why would he try to fight it? He must be what was made of him, why else would everyone assume he was like this? This empty, shallow thing, the bag of strong, well-structured bones that was him and yet, not him? This wasn't all there was to Trystan Everley, couldn't be, but why bother searching his inner self for a trace of who he might have been? Why bother trying to be whoever the world didn't want him to be?

A sudden noise forced his eyes open, a gasp, a loud intake of breath. Trystan turned his head right, towards the direction the sound had come from, and met a pair of silver-blue eyes set on a face full of freckles.

Because of her.

He must search inside himself all he was able to be, because of her.

The Vaughn witch.

IV

The first roar took her by surprise.

Heart catapulting against her ribs, Nyx jumped on her feet and frantically searched around for the source of such upheaval.

The second roar had pretty much the same effect.

She still jumped, her heart still raced – even though it had seemed impossible for such a small muscle to beat faster than it already did – and cold sweat ran down in rivulets over her chest and back.

The third roar did nothing, Nyx had been expecting it.

No longer thinking she was on the verge of crossing paths with a lunatic murderer turned beast, she knew what to expect. Some kid, about her age. Venting fury and frustration alone in the woods, as she'd done, as well. On her first day at school, after coming home to find it empty and Spencer gone. The moment she'd most needed him to shed comfort on what was otherwise a hard, bleak day. She'd run into the woods and screamed her fury and fear, her sadness and anger at the trees, the bushes, the sky. She'd screamed herself hoarse, and felt much better for it, while picturing the scornful gazes that had followed her around school throughout the day - the sniggers, the comments, the girl in the lab shouting at her to leave. The girl Nyx now knew to be Bryn Everley, Jamal's jealous girlfriend, and sister to Trystan Everley.

Closing her eyes, she allowed the image of Trystan's lips to flood her mind, for a fraction of a second only. The boy was way out of her league, as Bryn's scornful looks had hammered into Nyx. Best to keep him out of her head, right? Then why didn't she do it? Why did she go to bed every night reliving each and every second of the few scattered moments she'd seen Trystan around the Academy, analysing his every word and the way he looked at her? Why did she daydream of him, if she knew it wasn't to be? If she wasn't even sure she *wanted* it to be? Ah, who was she kidding? Trystan Everley was dreamy, and she was on her way to develop a full-fledged crush on him.

A fourth roar brought her out of the reverie, attention focused back on the conundrum at hand. Should she go and see if the person needed help? Should she offer comfort? Nyx would have liked to have someone approach her, that day, when she found herself on her knees, crying in the woods under pouring rain. What if it was Pip Thomson? The boy always looked as if burdened with the world's entire stock of pain. Or he looked as if he just couldn't care and was the coolest cat in school. A smile graced her lips, she liked Pip. Not that they'd spoken often, but he always smiled at her and said good morning, and he'd held the door for her a couple of times. He was always nice and polite, unless in one of his moods, where he ran out to the schoolyard and smoked cigarette after cigarette, pushing away everyone, including his best friends. So if it was Pip losing it out there, wouldn't he just lash at Nyx?

Wouldn't he wish to have someone look out for him, though?

Mind made up, Nyx crossed the few yards that separated her from the source of the furious yells. Careful not to be too noisy - she didn't want to scare him - the girl came to a clearing, in the midst of which a boy lay down on the leaf-strewn forest ground, eyes closed, mouth wide open in a grimace of anger, from which roars of rage still erupted, echoing through the still, late morning air. But it wasn't Pip Thomson having a fit.

It was Trystan Everley, and his body was covered in leaping flames that danced across his clothes, his very skin. Even his hair was on fire.

Nyx gasped, unsure of what to do. Call for help, perhaps? Diving a hand into the pocket of her jacket, she brought out her phone, frantic fingers already searching for her uncle's number, so she could at least call him. Spence would be home, getting lunch ready, he'd be able to get here in minutes. But before she put the call through, Trystan silenced his screams, turned his face towards her, meeting Nyx's eyes. A smile crossed his lips, and the flames died. He sat up.

Nyx turned and ran.

Deeper into the woods, far from the cottage, with Trystan's voice calling for her and his steps right behind. Why was she running? What was she afraid of? What was she *ashamed* of? There was no reason for this. Nyx stopped, waited for the boy to catch up, her face red and sweaty from the exertion. Trystan tumbled into view and came to a halt mere steps from her, grinning and pushing a fringe of light brown hair back on his head. His hazel eyes gleamed with the specks of light breaking through the thick canopy of trees.

"Did I scare you?" he asked, one hand reaching for Nyx's. She surrendered hers without a second thought, marvelling at the warmth and softness of his skin, delighting in his touch.

"Sort of. I thought it was Pip."

"And you went to help him?" He sounded doubtful, as if he couldn't bring himself to believe someone would willingly approach Pip out of worry.

"I know what it's like to cry alone in the woods, all right?"

"You don't need to be offended. Why would you cry alone in the woods?"

Nyx shrugged, pulled back her hand and shoved it in her jeans' pocket, as if hiding it from sight would keep it safe from Trystan's reach.

"I'm sorry, that was callous of me. This must be hard for you, what with your father and the move, and all the changes. How are you even holding up?"

"I'm not that weak."

Trystan's eyes darkened, his smile transformed into something bitter, as if her words had stung him. "Can't seem to say anything right, today," he whispered, and stared at the trees.

Nyx could have slapped herself for her callousness. He'd been out here alone, venting whatever pain was hurting him, but instead of focusing on his own problems, here he was, asking after her wellbeing, and Nyx antagonised him? What kind of fool did that? Well, apparently a fool like her, who couldn't seem to hold it together in the presence of a boy like him.

"I didn't mean to be rude," she said, "sorry. What's up with you? Want to talk about it? Sometimes it helps. Had no idea you were a Feeric, didn't that hurt, all those flames?"

He kicked a twig ou of his way, scratched his head, cheeks blushing. But kept his eyes trained on Nyx, a warm, soothing look inside them. And something more she could almost see; there was something more in the way Trystan looked at her, wasn't there? Or was it all wishful thinking, an illusion from her eyes, a fantasy?

"Had a row with my father. The man drives me mad. He's too demanding, and expects perfection from me. Well, it's just our luck, innit? I'm far from perfect."

She would have disagreed with him on such subject, were she courageous enough to share her thoughts. Of course she didn't know him at all, but from where Nyx stood, Trystan Everley was just about as perfect as can be.

"Parents just want the best for their children, don't they? Sometimes they just don't know how to show them that, know what I mean? Maybe you should cut him some slack?"

Trystan snorted, one hand reaching for the bough of a tree. He pulled himself up, hanging from his arms, muscled biceps visible through the cotton fabric of his jersey. The jersey that rode up his torso and shed a glimpse of his stomach, the promise of a six-pack underneath. Nyx flushed, warmth rushing up her body, and she turned away from him.

"I wish he'd cut me some slack, honestly," Trystan said from behind her.

Nyx nodded, her attention diverted to the woods ahead. Again, those odd, strange looking trees. And the colourful, loud, beautiful birds. She took a step closer, one of the birds swooping down a bough, talons grabbing the wood firmly, as he perched so close Nyx could have reached a hand and petted it. Its black, beady eyes met hers, and the bird cocked its head to the side. It spread its wings, wide and bright under the sun, feathers that went from dark grey to rich, deep blues, with specks of purple along the tips. Above its bough, another bird came to perch, this one bearing feathers of intense crimson mixed with darker hues of red and grey. They were beautiful, and like nothing Nyx had ever seen. As the first bird flopped his wings and closed them, one solitary feather came loose and dwindled to the forest ground. Keeping an eye on the trees, Nyx bent down and grabbed it, admiring the colours and its silky feel, before pushing it into the pocket of her jacket.

"Can you see these trees?" she asked, turning round to look at Trystan, who'd joined her.

"Yeah, what about them?"

"Don't they look weird? And what's with these birds? I've never seen anything like them before."

Trystan studied the clump of trees, searching among the leaves for signs of the birds, which seemed to have flown away silently. "These look pretty common to me, they're just oaks. Lots of birds in these woods, it can be a right racket in spring."

"There you are."

A girl's voice reached them from the right. Both swirled to face her, Nyx's smile dropping at the sight of Bryn Everley. The newcomer cocked one eyebrow, trained hard eyes on Nyx.

"What's *she* doing here?" she asked, and Trystan bristled.

"You need to stop that, Bryn," he replied, one arm instinctively reaching across Nyx's shoulders, pulling her to him. "She's your boyfriend's cousin, why do you keep antagonising her?"

"She knows."

Nyx blushed, she didn't. Well, she could guess what Bryn meant, but the girl was mistaken, Nyx hadn't been doing anything wrong.

"I wasn't eavesdropping on you and Pip," she barked, squaring her shoulders in a lame attempt at standing up to Bryn.

"Sure you weren't, it was all a massive coincidence, an accident."

"Actually it was, I was trying to find my classroom and got lost."

Bryn snorted, crossing arms laden with bracelets over her chest.

"She's new at the Academy, of course she got lost, Bryn," Trystan insisted. "Look, if you came here to further ruin my day, I suggest you take yourself elsewhere and go fight with Jamal or something."

"I was forced to come here, after you storming out of the house like that. Mum made me. Says you have to come home for dinner, we're having guests." The girl rolled her eyes, as if that was just about the most boring thing she could be submitted to. "Fancy going to Haver's for a bite, now you ruined lunch?"

Trystan smirked. "I could eat. Want to join us, Nyx?"

The girl blushed deeper, knowing Spencer had been fussing around the kitchen all morning to prepare her a nice meal. He'd let her go, if she asked, but would be disappointed, after all his hard work. And Nyx didn't want to do that to her uncle.

"Spencer's counting on me for lunch," she said. "Rain check?"

"I'll hold you to that. Catch you later?"

She nodded, and Trystan swooped down to plant a chaste, hasty kiss on her cheek, forcing her to blush even deeper. Bryn sniggered behind her hand, eyes amused and mocking.

"Oh Nyx," she called, as the girl marched off down the path back to Vaughn cottage. "Tell your uncle my father said hi. He's asked me to give you the message before, but it keeps slipping my mind."

Nyx turned to face her, studying the girl's expression. There was still some sort of mockery in it, but her eyes spoke of something deeper, a sorrow that was hard to define.

"I will."

"That's Max Everley," Bryn insisted, and now she sounded serious, and a little frantic, too. "Tell your uncle Max Everley says hi and would love to catch up."

"I know your dad's name. I'll pass the message, don't worry."

"Tell him to call Max."

"Are you for real?" Trystan bellowed. "It's got to be some sort of joke, right?" He stomped back towards the Everley estate, face red and tarred by an angry expression, eyes set on the path, ignoring both girls.

"Is he all right?" Nyx couldn't help asking.

"He's throwing a tantrum, ignore him. Will you give your uncle the message?"

"I already said I would."

"Ok. Goodbye, Nyx."

Taking off at a run, Bryn followed her brother through the path, both soon lost to sight from Nyx. She shrugged, wondering what was up with those two, they managed to be weirder even than her or Pip. Hurrying back home, Bryn's insistence she delivered her father's message kept running through her head. Spencer must have known Max, if Cressida was Erin's best friend. It stood to reason her boyfriend would know Erin's brother, right? And they'd all frequented the Academy at about the same time, didn't they?

Spencer was what, two years younger than Nyx's mother? Not even that, they'd all have been at school together. And Nyx had the distinct impression Max Everley was behind her uncle's flight from Weaversmoor. But what could the man want with Spencer? Maybe Max Everley had news of Erin Vaughn? Maybe Cressida did? Perhaps they just wanted to catch up, understand what had happened to Erin that had driven her to leave behind an infant daughter? Whatever it was, she needed to know, if it concerned her family.

Marching through the kitchen door, she found Spencer busy around a salad, and the scent of homemade cannelloni filled her nostrils. He'd remembered. She'd been throwing him shady hints about cooking her something Italian, and now he had. Folding her arms around him, Nyx hugged her uncle.

"I love you, you know that? Can't wait to dive into this."

"Wash your hands, first. Had a nice walk out there?"

Nyx opened the tap and hastily wet her hands, wiping them on a fresh towel by the sink. She was that hungry.

"Met up with the Everleys. Trystan and Bryn, I mean. Asked me out for lunch at a place called Haver's?"

Spencer placed a tray of cannelloni on the table and served Nyx. "Local eatery," he clarified. "Can't believe it still exists. Youngsters tend to favour it, it's nice and cheap. You didn't want to join them?"

Nyx shook her head. "I knew you'd been cooking." Her voice came out muffled through a mouthful of steaming hot food, but she still closed her eyes and moaned in delight. "Would I willingly miss this? No way." She loaded salad into her fork and ate, taking her time munching while Spencer poured water into their glasses. "By the way," she finally said, eyes intent on her uncle, ready to take in every reaction, so she could analyse it later. "Max Everley says hi. Asked that you give him a call."

Spencer dropped his knife on the plate, kept his eyes down, but Nyx knew him too well. His breathing became shallow, and sweat beaded his forehead, while a pallor crept up his neck and face. Whatever Max Everley wanted, her uncle didn't wish to hear; he didn't want to meet the man. There was actual fear in Spence's eyes, in the curling of his lips, and the trembling of his hands. Had Max bullied him when they were kids, because of Spencer's sexuality? Was he the person Spencer had been trying to avoid since coming back to Weaversmoor?

"When did you meet Max Everley?"

What was that in his voice? A catch? A tremble? A show of emotion that didn't quite sound like fear.

"I didn't, it was Bryn gave me the message."

I can't see him, I won't see him.

Oh, this was bad. She couldn't allow herself to eavesdrop on her uncle like this. Pulling down barriers like Miss Tate had taught her, Nyx closed her senses to Spencer, the voice of his mind lost in static. Why wouldn't he see Max? What was he afraid of? What was he trying to avoid?

What if Max Everley knew Erin's whereabouts?

"Do you think it's about my mother?"

Spencer trained wide, wild eyes on her. "Huh?" He sounded like he didn't even know what she was talking about.

"That Max Everley wants to talk to you about. My mother? Maybe he knows where she is?"

Standing up, Spencer paced around the kitchen, running hands through his hair and taking deep, paused breaths. As if he needed to calm himself. Why? What for?

"What's wrong? Did I do something?"

He came back to the table, caressed Nyx's face gently. "No, darling, you didn't do anything. I just... don't really want to meet up with certain people from my past."

"Look, you don't have to. Even if this is about mum, you don't need to speak to him, I'll do it if you want me to, if you think he'll tell me..."

"It's not about your mother, Nyx. Just keep away from Max and Cressida, all right?"

"You'd rather I not be friends with their kids, then?" Her voice was filled with gloom, and it helped push a smile onto Spencer's lips.

"I don't know their children, but if you think they're all right, I trust your instincts. And you do need to make new friends. Now eat, don't you have an appointment this afternoon, at the tattoo parlour? For the sigil? I'm so sorry I didn't know enough about being a Weaver to teach you better, Nyx. You never said you were getting hints of people's thoughts, or that it scared you."

"It's not your fault. You're not a Weaver, how would you know?"

"Because your mother was one. But she was always so secretive about it, I hardly knew all she could do with her magic. I'm not sorry I had to come back here, not if it's helping you. But do get that tattoo, if only to protect yourself."

And other people's privacy, Spencer thought, the message echoing loud and clear in Nyx's head. She cut the inflow again; it was easy to do when it was only the one person. Being in a crowd was what made it hard; she could only focus on a single individual and block that one out, but every other thought would come at her with no barriers. She needed the sigil to keep them off all the time and only allow thoughts from the person she might want to read. Which according to Miss Tate was a safety trigger she'd hexed onto the sigil, for Nyx's protection. It didn't mean it was okay to read people's thoughts, she should only use it in extreme necessity. They'd worked on the design during the week, settling on a bird, wings spread in flight. Come to think of it, the drawing resembled the bird she'd seen out in the woods earlier, the one that came to stare at her, opening its wings to showcase the beauty of its coloured feathers.

Feathers.

She had one of the feathers still in her jacket. It would look lovely on her arm, the bird on her shoulder. Would the tattoo artist mind that she added the feather to the design? Well, he didn't know it wasn't part of the original drawing, did he? She could add it to the bird quite easily. In fact, it hit her this was of the utmost importance - she must have that feather tattooed into her upper left arm, the bird flying out of it. Nothing else would do, nothing else would protect her magic; nothing else would guarantee her powers were hers and hers alone to use.

Nothing else would keep her safe.

But from what?

Wincing in pain, Nyx clamped her mouth shut, tired of her own whimpering. If anyone had told her how painful it was to get a tattoo, she'd have settled only for the bird, as small as she could get it. But no, she'd had to have the feather as well. The tattoo artist, a girl in her mid-twenties, sporting a healthy array of ink over her body, had turned the bird feather Nyx showed her into an intricate, elaborate, delicate design that marvelled her eyes. It was like fine lace, she could think of no other comparison. Beautiful and exquisite, it matched the bird to perfection. But instead of looking like the feather had fallen from the bird, it was as if the bird was breaking loose from the feather. As if the feather symbolised the entirety of Nyx's powers, and the bird was only one small part of it. As if the feather marked her as a Weaver.

The front door opened, the little bell over it ringing cheerfully and drawing eyes towards the entrance. Nyx was no different, her attention latched to the door and the person walking through. For some absurd reason, her heart cartwheeled to the thought it might be Trystan.

It wasn't him.

But it was the next best thing.

Pip Thomson strolled in, cigarette tucked behind his ear, leather jacket opened to display a white tee-shirt underneath, the hem of his jeans rolled up showcasing black Creeper shoes and matching socks. Nyx smiled openly and was relieved to see him smile back at her. The girl at reception stopped him from further venturing in, though, as she checked his appointment. Once that was cleared, she gestured him in, and Pip walked over to Nyx.

"Hey," he greeted, peered at the tattoo that was just about finished. "Getting inked?" He seemed to study the design a while longer, and once finished, lay curious eyes on her. "You're in a world of pain, aren't you?"

They laughed, and another tattoo artist came to speak to Pip, leading him to the next chair. He handed the man a square of paper with a small cross drawn on it, and proceeded to take off both his jacket and the tee shirt, pointing to his already inked chest, right over the sternum.

"Here," he said, "ink it right here." Then he turned to Nyx, still smiling, but looking tired, his eyes glazed. "Looks good." He pointed his head towards the tattoo she'd just got, and she stood up to check it in the large mirror covering one of the walls.

"Doesn't it?"

"Are you in a hurry?"

Nyx searched his eyes, wondering what this was all about. "Not really, why?"

"Wanna grab a coffee with me, after I'm done? Should be quick."

"All right," she said, doubt crossing her mind. Was he coming on to her? "Why a cross?"

Pip shrugged. "Why not? It's a symbol as good as any other, right? Why the feather?"

Nyx smiled, seeing what he was getting at. "Right, why not. So, you didn't go home this weekend?"

"I hardly ever go home, there's no one there." Seeing her blush, he grinned. "My parents both work, like, *a lot*. My siblings go to other boarding schools and we mostly meet up for the holidays, you know. Otherwise, we're stuck each at their school."

"How many of you are there?"

"We're four. Three boys, one girl. Poor mite, she's the eldest, puts up with a world of crap. You're an only child, right?"

"Yep. Though I would have liked to have brothers and sisters, it can get real lonely when there's just you."

"What's the deal with your folks? That bloke who drives you to school, he's not your dad, is he?"

Nyx frowned, how did he not know? It was all over school, surely; everyone at Weaversmoor must know of her family's awkward past.

"He's my uncle, Spencer Vaughn. You're a bit in the dark, aren't you? Here I was, thinking I was that obviously notorious new girl, and there's at least one bloke who knows nothing of my history?"

"I don't usually pry. Rumours tend to skip by me, couldn't care less for school gossip, what with being constant victim to it."

"I can only imagine. Good thing I came along, to give you a respite."

Pip pulled on his tee-shirt and jacket, the tattoo being finished. "So, what's the deal, living with your uncle?"

"What if I don't want to talk about it?"

He held up his hands, smiling. "Fair enough. But can we still go for coffee? I really wanna talk to you, somewhere private."

Could it be about Trystan? Why would Pip want to talk to her alone, it wasn't as if they were on friendly terms; more like acquaintances. Just kids who greeted each other whenever they met down the halls, but who'd never hang out together at recess. Or maybe they would, maybe Pip wanted them to? She followed him across the street, down a narrow alley, into a secluded, dark and moody coffee shop.

"My father was a fisherman, where we lived. Havenleah," she clarified. "His boat was lost at sea, with all his fishing crew, five men lost. The bodies were never retrieved, but the ship was located, it had sunk during a freak storm at high seas. My uncle's all the family I have now, seeing grandmother died soon after dad. Well, I have Aunt Sarah too, of course, and her children, but Spencer's my guardian, and he's been like another father to me."

Pip ordered coffees and directed Nyx to a table by the window. "I see. What about your mother, why isn't she here? She's a Vaughn too, right? You're supposed to be the cat's whiskers around here."

"Wouldn't know about that. My mother left when I was five. Never came back, so she's as good as dead to me." Nyx tried to keep all trace of emotion from her voice.

"I'm sorry I asked." The boy snaked a hand over hers, pressing it gently. Nyx's first instinct was to pull away, but she allowed it to linger. Somehow, it felt different from when Trystan held her hand, it carried a different intention and a different meaning. "But it doesn't matter, does it? It's not what I wanted to chat to you about."

Cold washed over her, as a million thoughts crossed her mind. The sigil was working, Nyx knew these were all hers; she was getting nothing from Pip, nor did she intend to plunder into his mind. But what could he want to talk to her for? It sounded ominous, and scary.

"Go on, then." This time, she did pull back her hand, and hid both under the table, clasped together over her legs.

"This is awkward." Pip lowered his eyes, a lopsided smile on his lips and a blush covering his face to the teardrop inked just below his eye. "Ok, so, the tattoo I got done today? That was a sigil meant to keep your thoughts out of my brain. Well, not your thoughts, or not just. But..." he stopped, noticing her wide-eyed stare. "Do you not know this?"

"Know what?"

"Ah, man. Should have listened to what people were saying, that you were never trained in the Craft. You're of the blood and don't even know what that means, right? Thought you were being tutored."

"I am, but it's only been one week. What's with my thoughts?"

"Right. How'm I gonna explain this without you finding me a creep?"

"You can read my thoughts."

It was Pip's turn to be perplexed. "Well, yeah, kind of. So you *do* know? That I'm a Haruspex?"

"Had no idea you were one until now. That cross was to keep me out?"

"It's not so simple. One single sigil is usually enough to keep a Haruspex safe from being bombarded with all sorts of thoughts and voices, know what I mean? But I'm an Aerial and an Empath, and you... well, you're a bloody Weaver, aren't you? And boy, do you emit."

"Emit?"

"So you're aware you're a Weaver? Was that what you were doing at the tattoo parlour?"

Nyx grinned. "Yeah, I was getting a sigil to keep the voices out, too. But not one single, specific voice, you know, all of them."

"The feather?"

"The bird."

Pip frowned. "What's the feather for, then?"

Nyx fished inside her jacket's pockets, brought out the feather she'd picked in the woods, handed it to Pip. Who released a low whistle.

"What? You know what kind of bird this is from? Because I never saw birds like these."

He played around with the feather, turning it one side then the other, studying its silky threads and the gem-like blue. "Never seen anything like it. What was the bird like?"

"Big. But not huge. It looked a bit like a kestrel, but the colours were all wrong. Mainly because there were all sorts of them."

"What do you mean all sorts of them?"

Nyx shook her head. How had the conversation turned from Pip telling her she emitted to her dishing about stuff she saw out in the woods and that she'd kept secret? "What do you mean I emit?"

Pip laughed, finished his coffee. "Fair enough. I mean you send out your emotions. Most people can keep a tight hold of their feelings, you get perhaps a whiff of them, the sense there's something wrong with that person, just a hint, a feeling, know what I mean? Not with you. The first day at school, you were *very* loud. The moment you walked in the building, I knew. It was like someone screaming in my ears. Your anger, your fear, your revolt. *Your pain.* It was all out there, and any Empath would get waves of it, which they could effectively block as soon as it started. But I'm not like other Empaths, nor other Aerials or Haruspexes. I need to ground my shields and blocks *on* my skin. I need sigils. Does this make sense?"

Nyx nodded. "You spell your blocks into the drawings, and once they're inked, you're safe from that person's energies, is that it?"

"Sort of. With people like you and Trystan, things get a bit rougher. Whenever he's upset I still get a beating, despite the massive sigil I got done to lock his energies out. But he's Feeric, so... and you're a Weaver, which can make it better if you and I work together. You need more ink."

She laughed. "I do, do I?"

"Only to reinforce my block. You need to get a safety catch, so that you don't emit as much. Or you try and get a hold of your emotions, of course."

"I'm working on it. So that big skull in your arm, that's for Trystan? Why? What's he got to be upset about? It's like he leads a charmed life, innit?"

"Don't assume what you don't know. Trystan's my best friend, so is Bryn. And Jamal, of course," he said, as an afterthought. "But only because he lives in a big house, has all that money and dresses like every mother's dream boy, doesn't mean he's that squeaky clean, well-adjusted young man he seems."

"So Trystan's the rebel, and you're the nice bloke?"

Pip grinned again. "I *am* a nice bloke, and if it weren't for the bloody Empath thing, I'd be a lot less inked and a lot less troubled, I think."

"Are all Empaths like that?"

"No. Some are like me, but it's kind of rare, according to what I've been told. Like Weavers, they're rare too."

"Maybe we should get matching tattoos," Nyx joked.

"I was thinking about that, actually. I know being a Weaver you're prone to be an Empath too, it can't be easy."

"The bird seems to be doing its job, haven't been hit by thoughts that aren't my own since I left the parlour. I could dig into people's heads, if I wanted to, but won't, of course. So my sigil seems to be enough."

"What about the feather?"

She shrugged. "I don't know. I just had to have it inked. As if it's part of me. I think it's supposed to claim me as a Weaver, does this make sense?"

"Actually, it does. You know the spiderweb on my elbow? I had to have it done. It's not a sigil, it carries no spells, no hexes, nothing. But I had to have it done because it claims me as a Haruspex. It links me to my particular type of powers. Does your feather do that, too?"

"Yes, that's exactly it! The feather links me to my powers."

"Where did you see those birds?"

"In the woods. Somewhere between my house and the Everley estate."

"The thickest part, right?" He nodded as if in agreement to his own words. "Been down that path a few times. Actually, we all have, me, Trystan, Bryn, Jamal. It feels different, there, do you also get it? Because they don't."

"What do you mean? They don't?"

"I get a different feel out there. Can't explain, but it's not the same as the rest of the woods. There's one specific patch, near a clearing..."

"That's where I saw the birds and the weird trees. Where I got the feather, too, Trystan was burning on the ground and..."

"Trystan was *burning*?"

"Well, not burning, he had these flames dancing across his body."

"Ah, so that was what I was getting earlier today. He must have had an argument with his dad, it gets him so upset he goes into the woods to let out steam."

"Let out fire, you mean."

They locked eyes and laughed.

"Weird trees?"

"You didn't notice? Maybe it's because I'm not from around here. There's a small clump of trees that look different from the rest. And the birds were perched there. Blue, and green and red and bright pink, their feathers looked like jewels. I never saw anything like it."

"Never saw the birds myself, but I do feel differently there. As if there's a magical vortex in that area, as if the Craft is much stronger there, more powerful. For some reason, Trystan always heads there when he's in one of his moods. The same reason Bryn is always working her spells there. It's strong mojo, that clearing."

"Do you think it's dangerous?"

"No. I don't know. But I think I need more ink done. Want to tag along?"

Nyx shook her head. "Got tons of homework, and my uncle's waiting for me. But it was really nice talking to you."

"Oh wow, that sounded *so* not good," Pip joked, standing up and ushering Nyx towards the door. "I actually enjoyed myself, you're one cool cat, Nyx Vaughn. I hope we can do this again?"

"I'd love to. I mean, I'd like to, if you want. Oh, bother, I don't even know what I mean. I didn't mean it like this."

"I know what you mean." Pip held the door for her and winked. "I've seen how you look at him."

V

Three years before,
   Daylesford

Eli Sylvain's eyes snapped open, and his mouth released a loud gasp.

Turning a sore neck over to one side and then the other, he took in his surroundings, bathed in dim, milky light made mellower by the taupe curtains pulled shut. He still recognised his own bedroom, though. What he did not recognise - or understand - was the hospital-like bed he lay on and the array of tubes and wires coming off him.

And he had no memory of how he'd got here.

He had no memory of the past couple of days. The last he remembered was packing up to go camping with his father, during spring half-term. One week living rough and in the wild, just the kind of thing Eli enjoyed. How he ended up strapped to a bed was beyond him.

Sitting up, he tried to dislodge the needle stuck through the thick vein on the back of his hand. A sway came over him, and Eli had to lie back down.

That hand.

He didn't quite recognise that hand.

It looked little like his, a fifteen-year-old schoolboy's hand. It was bigger than what he remembered, and the skin looked thicker, older.

Just how long had he been lying in this bed?

Taking a long, studious look at his own arm, he found his heart rate catapulting, lungs oppressed by whatever fist got hold of them, his breathing shallow with either shock or fear. His forearm was covered in a fuzz of blond hair he didn't remember being that profuse, or long. Sure, he'd had a few scattered short and soft hairs on his arms, like any teenage boy, but this wasn't a boy's arm any longer. This arm and hand belonged to a grown man. Tears brimmed his eyes - tears of confusion and dread at the possibilities presented by the changes to his body. Carefully, he pushed away the bed-covers, to see long legs inside sweat pants. Pulling at the waist of those same pants, Eli took one single peek inside the dark blue briefs he was wearing, and let out a moan.

He wasn't fifteen anymore, that was for sure. His anatomy was no longer that of a fifteen-year-old, this was the body of a grown man.

Before he could break down, the bedroom door swung open, and a woman walked in, face flushed, eyes widened in shock. As she ran to the bed - arms already wide so they wrapped around his frame, smile pulling at the corners of her mouth - Eli recognised the hard, loving face of his mother. And he registered the years gathered on that face, with wrinkles that grabbed the corners of her eyes, and streaks of white that peppered her hair.

How long had he been in this bed?

"Oh, Eli, you're back," she wailed, and hugged him to her bony chest, weeping softly into the shoulder of his grey tee-shirt.

"Mum," he whispered back, inhaled the fresh, clean scent of her neck, the aroma bringing back a surge of memories from his youth. "Where's dad? What happened?"

"Serge," the woman called, Eli wincing as her voice echoed in his head. "Serge, he's awake."

A tall, large man shadowed the doorframe, pushed himself into the room. His father came trampling to his other side, legs as wide as tree trunks, arms strong as a lumberjack's. Which he looked very much like, come to think of it, with his faded jeans, the outdoorsy boots, the chequered shirt on his back. He remembered they'd been wearing pretty much the same, the day they headed to the woods for a holiday. The thought his father hadn't changed out of those clothes all the years Eli had been strapped to this bed made him giggle.

"Son, how are you?" The man caressed a mane of long hair Eli had failed to notice.

He squinted at it now, hair that came down to his shoulders, blond and wavy where it had been short, cropped against his skull. He'd never liked long hair on himself. How many years had it been growing, unattended to? How long since that day out in the woods?

"I... I don't know," he replied.

"Are you hungry? I can get you something to eat. Broth, perhaps, to build up your strength," his mother said.

"How long?" Eli croaked, throat raspy and dry, unused as it was to working; as if he'd been years without speaking. "How long has it been?"

The couple exchanged one long, silent look, pregnant with meaning Eli failed understand. It was ominous, though, and placed a heavy, blazing stone down his stomach.

"What do you remember, son?" His father took a seat by his side, wrapped one large, strong hand around his.

"I was getting ready to go camping. *We* were, you and I."

"Yes, that's right."

"I was what, fifteen? Wait, I'd just turned fifteen, hadn't I? This was April, wasn't it? I'd had my birthday in November, but this was part of the birthday gift you two had for me. A camping trip."

"You remember that. What else?"

"Dad, how long? Please," he begged, eyes moist with fear. "I'm not fifteen anymore, am I?"

"We went camping, the two of us. Do you remember setting up tent? Do you remember the can of baked beans and the cheese?"

"I... yes, I remember you told me to set up the tent, while you went round clearing up a space for the fire. I remember sitting down on a log to eat. I remember the fireflies and the cold, cold night. Then we went to sleep."

"We went to sleep, and I forgot to clean up because I was tired, and a fox came round and started rummaging through our trash. That woke me up; it was nearly dawn. I came out of the tent to scare it away, and the entire thing collapsed. The aluminium beam hit your head, and you lost your senses. When I finally managed to drag you out of the fallen tent, you were in a faint, and I couldn't wake you. There was a gash on your forehead, blood oozing, I tried to clean it and stop it as best I could. Then I..."

"Then your father took you to the hospital, and the doctors couldn't make head or tails of what was wrong with you," his mother interrupted. "Everything was fine, your vital signs were fine, you just didn't wake up. We ended up bringing you home, seeing hospitals and doctors couldn't help. And you've been here ever since."

"Ever since when, Mum? How long ago was that?" Not that he wanted to know; he dreaded hearing those words. But he had to, hadn't he? He had to understand how much time he'd lost, and why he'd lost it. He had to know what was going on.

"Seven years, Eli," his father said. "It's been a little over seven years since that night in the woods."

He closed his eyes. Pulse lowered and then sped up again. Air refused to enter him, nose clogged and throat clamped. His hands oozed cold, pasty, sticky sweat. Seven years? He'd lost seven years of his life in some sort of weird coma? What else had he lost along with that? The capacity to use his legs, his arms, his hands? Actually, his body didn't look atrophied as it should have been, after years of immobility. His back must be covered in scabs, but it didn't hurt. He felt nothing besides a tingling on his feet, as if he'd been sitting on them for too long and they'd gone numb and asleep. Wriggling his toes, Eli realised he had perfect control of his limbs, so he shoved one hand down the blankets, grabbed hold of his thigh, kneading it. The muscles were taut, well-defined, as if he'd gone about his normal life - a young man's normal life. Walking, running, working out those muscles, bringing them to definition. He touched his abdomen; it was the same.

How could he have spent seven years in a coma and still his body had grown and changed as if he'd been awake?

"What's going on?" His voice shook. He coughed to clear his throat and get rid of the tears streaming down his face. "What the hell is going on with me? How can this be happening?"

His mother caressed knotted streaks of his hair, kissed his head gently. "Don't you worry about that now, there'll be time to work things out, Eli. First you need to eat, get your strength back, then we can talk it through. Maybe you'll remember it all, after you get some rest."

Pushing the woman away, Eli sat up straighter in bed, a scowl filling his handsome face, lips trembling in ill-hidden fury. "Remember what? Just what on earth are you talking about? I was seven years in a coma, what is there for me to remember?"

His head hurt and swayed, a cloud of confusion settling over it, a fog that numbed his entire brain. A surge of images ran across his mind's eye, in rapid succession, like shots being fired by a machine gun, a stream that ran too fast in its bed down to the sea.

And then he remembered.

At least, the horrid hospital bed was gone. The room already looked lighter and larger without it, a simple pinewood, single bed having taken its place. Eli eyed it longingly, despite knowing sleep had evaded him. And it wasn't as if he needed it, after seven years immersed in a kind of slumber that was akin to hibernation. Living an altogether different life, being an altogether different person, in an altogether different world. Was coma like that, every time? Did every coma patient experience what he did, to the point of being so vivid Eli still caught glimpses of it when he closed his eyes?

He'd not gone back there, not even in his dreams. One week from his return to the world of the living – if he could even call *this* living – and he still longed for that other place, still hoped to reach it every time he lay down in bed. Or the sofa, where he spent countless hours dozing to the sound of really bad TV. Unless he was jogging, that is. He'd taken to spending long hours in his joggers and trainers, running around the neighbourhood, if only to avoid his mother's constant fussing. If only so he could recall his other life, try to piece the details back together, remember everything about it. There were still holes, entire blanks the size of years. He'd been fifteen the last time he was a part of this world – a healthy, happy, feisty fifteen-year-old, well-adjusted and clever, if somewhat snarky in his remarks. Now, he was a twenty-two-year-old man who hardly recognised his parents' house and the world he lived in; a man with no memories but those he could hardly consider being true. He'd grown up elsewhere, inside his head, and was having a very hard time coming out of it.

WITCH CRAFT

Eli walked to the window, pushed aside the curtains and stared out. Cars were parked up and down the street in front of square, small houses that looked the same, with their carefully manicured but minuscule gardens and their pristine front doors. The world he remembered had houses built in the middle of the woods, some attached to large, beautiful trees. The world he remembered had no cars, nor any such objects. It had animals roaming free, a creek where he used to fish; it had game in the forest which he was allowed to hunt. He'd traded the meat for fresh rolls of fragrant, sweet bread baked in the nearest village, in that particular barony.

There were no baronies here. There were no villages in the woods, and no cliffs nearby where he could go and sit, and gaze at the sea. There were no large estates where the Governator overlooked the progress of his people and his lands, he who ruled over the East Baronies of Ephemera, where Eli had lived. Where Eli hadn't been Eli, but Nox to his closest friends and family. Which was something he didn't have, out there in the East Baronies. He'd been alone, in his dream, no mother nor father to guide and raise him. He'd been on his own, a young boy on the cusp of adulthood, able to provide for himself, which he gladly did. Noctifer, he was, out there in the East Baronies, named for having been born in the dead of night – and how did he know this, if there'd been no parents to inform him of such intricacies?

He'd not been alone, though.

Well, at least not completely.

There'd been *her*, to keep him company. Stella of the blond hair, queen of the owls, enchanter of birds, which swarmed down the trees to be with her. Stella of the blue eyes and the sweet, sweet lips, and how he had ravished those lips, how he'd kissed her every time they were together, how he'd crushed her in his arms and promised never to leave.

A plume of fire rose up his stomach, invaded his chest, took hold of his throat and spit out a moan. Eli could see her clearly, the large eyes, the delicate lips, the hair like fine spun silver, so blond it was nearly white. The curve of her shin when Stella took off her boots so she could dive dainty, small feet in the creek; the round of her knee as she flashed it at Eli, taunting, playfully; the soft warmth of her skin; her hand, as it trailed caresses down his face, his neck, his arm. How could he see her so clearly, how could he almost feel her touch, if it had all been a dream, a product of a troubled mind caught in an unnatural sleep?

He'd made that world up, and Stella too; there was no such place or being.

But the feel of her hand upon his naked arm still lingered, resting on the invisible feather inked there that marked him for his magic and what he was, what he must grow up to be.

The feather.

Inked on his upper left arm, and the flock of birds that flew from it up to his shoulder. Dark, black ink, just a flock of birds in flight, as if breaking free of their prison in that feather.

Letting go of the curtains, lips trembling in doubt and eyes widening in hope, Eli marched to the en suite bathroom. The overhead light flared into his eyes like fire branding his cornea, blinding him momentarily. He blinked, faced the sudden glare, stared at himself in the mirror. How could he remember the face of a woman who didn't exist so clearly, and not recognise his own features in this mirror? He still expected to see himself as the fifteen-year-old that graced the numerous pictures spread across his parents' house, but it wasn't him he now saw. The face staring back at Eli looked far older than his years, as if he'd lived a lifetime and not known it, as if he'd aged far more than the seven years passed since he'd last seen himself in a mirror.

WITCH CRAFT

His hair had darkened. Now a golden hue, where it had once been like bright straw in the sun, it was finally cut short again, after his father had driven him to the closest barbershop. He'd kept the short beard, lighter than the hair on his head. His face was gaunter, slimmer, lines already etched into his forehead, cheeks sunken where they'd been plump and full. But the chin, the lips, the blue of the eyes, all these were as he remembered. Only older, much older than Eli expected to see.

Shaking his head, he ran a hand through his face, his hair, grabbed the hem of the long-sleeved t-shirt he wore around the house. He pulled it up, studied the muscled abdomen, the pectorals, the fine line of hair travelling from his navel down to the waist of pyjama pants. Then he pulled it off, dropped it on the floor, turned to his left so he could see that arm reflected in the mirror.

It hadn't been a dream.

It couldn't have been a dream.

Eli hadn't noticed it yet because he hadn't been looking for it, nor thinking of it, until memories of Stella filled his mind. Memories of Stella and how she used to touch that spot in his arm, fingernails lightly scraping his skin over a tattoo Eli didn't have when he'd set off on a camping trip with his father at the age of fifteen. A tattoo he must have brought back from Ephemera and the East Baronies, for he doubted his parents would have him inked while he lay unconscious, barely able to breathe.

So, if the tattoo existed, and he hadn't had it done here in this world, then it meant that other world was real, and somehow, *someway*, Eli had spent his adolescence there, amongst those cliffs, those trees, with Stella for company. No wonder he felt so uneasy here, it was a place he hardly had any memory of. Sure, he remembered his childhood, parts of it, at least. Going to school, making friends, playing around in the small garden outside, or at the park with the other children. He remembered that. But not as clearly, not as vividly as he remembered riding a horse through the tree-shadowed road that led from the village of Viridans, on whose outskirts he'd lived, to the larger town of Fulvus, just so he could have the crystals he'd been collecting in the woods cast into a tiara to grace Stella's brow. Not as vividly as he remembered chopping wood that he'd store away for winter, so he could warm his lonesome cabin in the woods. The cabin near that little house built in a tree, from where he could watch the world below, as far as the Governator's manor and its surrounding estate. As far as the pretty white house where Stella lived, with the profusion of flowers gracing its gardens in spring, flowers tended to by her mother and her blind younger sister.

There.

How could he remember this amount of detail, if it was all a dream, an illusion of his fevered brain? It could not be. Stella had a sister, yes, a blind girl one or two years younger than her. Eli couldn't quite remember her features or her name, but nor could he remember the faces of the villagers in Viridans, Stella's own parents, the Governator's Sectarius who had him cast out for...

For what? Why had he been sent away? Was that the reason he'd woken up from his coma? Was there a way to go back? There must be, and he needed to find it.

Sleep, of the deepest kind; *that* would help. He must go back to sleep. Pulling the t-shirt back on, Eli walked on cold, naked feet to the bedroom, slithered into bed. Turning on one side, he forced his eyes shut, slowing his breathing and the rate of his heart. Maybe thoughts of Stella would help. Picturing her as he best remembered the girl - standing still and silent in a clearing, surrounded by tall, looming trees, an owl perched on one shoulder, a falcon on one arm, a raven alighting at her feet - Eli traced back his memories, to the moment he'd come across her for the first time, and the first kiss he'd dared shed upon her lips.

WITCH CRAFT

And still sleep refused coming to him.

VI

After two weeks of sleepless nights and declining health, his moods swinging from euphoric to desperate, Eli slithered slowly into a dark hole he found hard to climb out from. No more did he hold any pleasure in being alive, in fact, it was a burden he could no longer conceive. This world, with its noises, its smells, its disrespect for the sanctity of nature, held no wonders for him. He felt the same in his parents; they didn't belong here. A notion had formed in his mind, that they, as well as he, had come from elsewhere, that magical elsewhere he longed to go back to - Ephemera, land of trees and blue skies and the crags above a roaring, grey sea.

But probe as he could, the couple never said a word about it. They seemed to misunderstand his veiled hints. Worry for his mental state grew with each passing night Eli failed to fall asleep, pacing around his room like a caged tiger, despair seeping from him, invading and pervading through the entire house, filling cracks and nooks and poisoning everything. They finally caved in, not in the way Eli had wished, but with his father running off to the nearest pharmacy and buying him a pack of sleeping pills. Oh, how Eli had gazed at them longingly, wishing night would hurry so he could go to sleep. And night did come, and he did take one pill as it said on the packet, and he did lie down in bed, the buzz of cicadas that didn't exist on his parents' street humming at his ears, the sweet scents of a summer breeze through the night woods gently lulling him to sleep, while Stella's eyes beckoned him forth, deeper into the woods, back to Ephemera, back to the East Baronies.

He slept, deeply. Profoundly. The entire night, Eli snored and slept, not tossing and turning as usual, but soundly. He woke up mid-morning, rested, refreshed, his head somewhat cleared, but dreamless. Or at least, unable to remember whatever dreams there might have been. He was still in this noisy, smelly world, though. He wasn't back amidst the trees; he was still here, the place he'd come to loathe with every fibre of his being. But it had just been one night; he mustn't give up yet. Facing the day with far more hope than he'd lately managed to, Eli put on a show, if only for his parents' sake, and gobbled his breakfast, not really hungry for food. He then went out for a jog, two hours of his day running around the neighbourhood, clearing his mind of the nagging doubts clinging to him - that he'd never go back, he'd never return, he'd never be free.

He went about the day as if normal, and come night, instead of one, Eli took two pills. And fell fast asleep.

Only to wake up again in this bed, which he didn't want, in a room where he didn't belong, minus the woman he loved and wanted back in his arms as he needed air to breathe. Despair clung to him. Darkness filled his mind momentarily and Eli couldn't think. All he could do was cry bitter, hot tears, sobs muffled by the pillow stuck to his face or the running water from the showerhead that drenched his entire skin. He couldn't give up, *mustn't* give up, not yet. It may take some time, but he'd find his way back. He'd find his way back to Stella.

So two months went by, and the more time passed, the further Eli got from his memories of that place - Ephemera no longer so bright and vivid in his mind's eye, Stella's blond hair no longer as shiny under the imagined sun, her lips no longer as tantalising, no longer as begging. He was losing her, losing himself to this ugly new world; and the longer he waited, the harder it would be to find his way back. For he'd eventually forget everything, and Ephemera would become a word he'd once heard but couldn't remember where. And Eli couldn't allow that to happen. After all, his place was there, not here. Some intuition, some certainty, prodded him like needles, assuring him he had a role to play in the destinies of Ephemera. He belonged there; it was his birthright; he was of Ephemera as much as the entire land was of him; he was a lord amongst the East Baronies.

So why didn't it work? Why didn't sleep take him there, if it had, during his coma?

Because he was doing it all wrong.

Coma wasn't as akin to sleep as it was to death. It was that in-between place, that limbo, where life and death met and stared each other in the eye, but none made a move. It was the wrinkle in time no one saw coming, the fold in the fabric of life, the magical space where worlds met, collided, merged and ran free. It was the spinning wheel from which possibility rose, and although it wasn't death, it wasn't life either, nor was it sleep. It was the space in between.

And that was what he needed. To place himself back in that moment, before death took him, but when life, *this life*, no longer quite held him. It was risky, of course; he might dive straight from one state to the other, skipping the black hole in the middle, the one hole he must fall down so he could find himself where he longed to be. But he had to try. What had Eli left to lose? He couldn't even claim to love his parents, he barely remembered them. Oh, he was grateful to the couple, and loathed the thought of hurting them, but he didn't feel as a son should, not for them, at least. He had a heart, but it wasn't set on them, or this place. He must go where his heart told him, and that wasn't here. If he stayed, if Eli allowed himself to linger here for much longer, he'd end up losing himself; and then, what would there be? A long stretch of nothingness, an empty life, a desperate, lumbering state of existence he couldn't bear the thought of.

He must try this.

Whatever the consequences, he must try this.

It was one cold, dark, winter night - days before his first Christmas since he'd woken from the coma - that Eli Sylvain took a sharp blade in his hand and cut a line along his wrist.

Blood, thick and red, oozed to the bathroom floor where he sat, back propped against the shower cabin, a smile on his lips as his mind numbed and he flitted into sleep. Cold hit him first, and exhaustion, every muscle in his body sore and heavy and unresponsive. His heart slowed, and his breathing took on a shallow rasp, one that dimmed with every blink, until his eyelids no longer opened, and Eli was no longer here.

Nor was he there.

He was exactly where he'd hoped to be - *in between.*

And it was in that state of altered consciousness that the truth came for him, and slapped him in the face, ripped his stomach open, pulled his guts outside and feasted on his heart.

It was in that state that every inch of him was shredded to pieces, and the pain from knowing how he'd come to leave Ephemera, why he'd been made to leave Ephemera, was more than he could admit. The treachery, the treason, was impossible to believe. But it was there, and he could see it all plainly. He remembered everything, every little detail of a life he'd longed to return to, a life that was now running from his veins onto the cold ceramic floor of this bathroom - a world away from where his mind watched, perplexed, the story of his heartbreak unfold before his weeping eyes and his broken heart.

Before death lay claim to him, though, his mother came and saved his life.

"You must never do such thing again, son," his father whispered, handing him a glass filled with an amber liquid. He gestured him to drink, and Eli did, gulped it all in one go, wincing at the taste and the burning fire it lit down his throat. "Next time, we may be forced to call for help, and you don't want that."

Eli lowered his eyes, focused on the bandage wrapped around his wrist. It hadn't even worked, he hadn't returned to Ephemera, only to the part of his memories he'd refused to acknowledge, the reason why he was no longer there, where he belonged.

"Why did you do it?" His mother's voice was harsh, her face set in a cold glare, as if all the love she'd been showing him was just another lie, and this was how the woman really felt.

It broke his heart, sapped light from his spirits, draped fear through his brain. He'd counted on this woman, he'd needed her, after all. Even if Eli had wished to go back, he'd felt for her what a son feels for a mother, in the end.

"You wouldn't believe me if I told you. But it was the only way."

"A suicide attempt is the only way, Eli? For what? For you to be taken to a mental facility, locked away and pumped full of drugs for lord knows how long? Is that what you want, son?"

His mother wrapped a gentle hand around his father's wrist, the soothing touch calming him. Eli's eyes sparkled with unshed tears; how could he tell them, what could he tell them, that they wouldn't think him crazy and send him off to one of those facilities his father had just mentioned?

"Child, where have you been? All those years asleep, where have you been?"

"Ora," his father whispered, fear draining the colour from his face.

"Serge, we must speak of this. It is time."

Eli sat up in bed, locked eyes with his mother. "What do you know?"

"What do you remember? From before the accident, that is. From your childhood."

He closed his eyes, resting back against the pillows Ora had plumped up for him. Thinking, forcing his brain to bring forth all it had hidden, so it made space for memories of Stella and the East Baronies. But then it was there, like a thread of silk he could cling to and follow, all the way to the memories that seemed to elude him.

Memories of Ephemera and life at the East Baronies. But not those of the past seven years, no. These were far older, from a time long gone, when Eli had been a babe, a toddler, an infant child running wild and growing in those woods, with Ora and Serge, yes, but others too.

His *real* parents.

Clinging to Ora's hand, he tightened a claw-like grip on it, eyes wide and terrified. "Who are you? Who am I?"

The woman who was not his mother caressed the bandaged wrist, her face a portrait of pain and misery as she took in the self-inflicted wound. "You're Noctifer Sylvannar, third son of Lord Fionn Sylvannar, Governor of the East Baronies, Senator of Ephemera, Decurio of the Concilius at Chymera. Your mother was Erin, a Weaver and dweller of this world."

Eli sighed, took a tentative deep breath, found his lungs caught in a noose that didn't allow for air to seep in. "You're not my parents."

Serge shook his head. "We aren't. But we're as good as, and love you as a son."

"You said *Ephemera*. I remember that place. The East Baronies. I remember the house in the woods, where I lived with you. And there was this woman, and occasionally a man. I remember him, he used to throw me up in the air, and his hair was bright and light like the full moon. I remember him well."

"That'll be your father, Lord Fionn. We were Silvares in your father's lands, our loyalty was to Fionn alone."

"Silvares? I don't understand."

Ora sighed. "We're Ephemerals, Nox. This is your real name, son: Noctifer, Nox, not *Eli*. But Eli is who you are here, Eli Sylvain. Ephemera, part of the Mythos, is divided into Baronies, each ruled by a Governator and his or her family. Your father ruled over the East Baronies, but he was also a Senator of Ephemera, which meant he must spend a given amount of time at the capital, Chymera. Because he was wise and learned, with the experience of years behind him, he was made a counsellor for the ruling Concilius, a Decurio. He would have ascended to the Regia in time, I'm sure. An Everlasting of so many years..."

"Everlasting? What's that?"

"You don't remember these terms? Are they unfamiliar? I thought you might have spent those seven years living in Ephemera, from the changes I noticed to your body," Ora said. "It did not weaken, but grew strong, and aged, so it must mean you, as a Weaver, were living your life there. Was it not so, son?"

Eli covered his face with shaky hands. "This is giving me a headache. What's a Weaver?"

"Think, Nox, you should know all this."

"*Everlasting*. They're immortals, right? Every few years a selected group of young people who carry magic in their blood are chosen for the Eligens. If they pass the tests, they ascend and become Everlasting."

"Everlastings aren't immortals," Ora explained. "They live long and prosperous lives, yes, sustained by magic. But they decline, of course, and new ones must be brought in. Some are tainted, and those are put to death after a few years, and another one takes their place. Children are very rare, amongst the Everlasting, and entire branches have disappeared for lack of offspring. Their lands and privileges are given to others then, newly risen ones. Your father, he's from good ilk. His father before him bore two infants, a boy and a girl. Fionna Sylvannar ascended to Everlasting on her sixteenth birthday and ruled in the Concilius for many a year. She had one daughter, who now rules over the Seaside Barony of Terabina. Fionna has joined her daughter so she can end her days peacefully. Not many step down from the Concilius of their own accord, but the Sylvannars are different. As for your father, he took as wife a newly risen Everlasting when he came into his third decade after his change, and she bore him two sons, Fioll and Rhysondel. We made no acquaintance with the youngest, Rhys, but your father spoke highly of him."

"He spoke highly of Fioll as well, and look where it got him," Serge spat. Ora shushed him with a gesture.

"Does any of this ring a bell, Nox?"

"Yes. I remember the Governators, and Chymera. I remember the titles and their meaning, I remember the Eligens only too well. And I remember Rhysondel."

The woman's eyes widened in surprise.

"It was he who had me cast out from Ephemera. He cast his own brother out."

"Wait, Rhys never knew of you. Hear me out, child, learn the history of your father and your mother and how their love for one another brought you here."

Leaning back on his bed, Eli nodded, ready to allow Ora her say. Maybe if he were to learn of his real origins, maybe if he were to know of his parents and his legacy, he could find a way back to his homeland, the place he belonged to. And where apparently his birthright made him something other than what he'd thought, during the seven years spent there. For if he was the child of a Governator, a Senator, a Decurio, he was sure to have a say in his own defence. His word should be given more power than that of a village dweller, a girl of no standing, a woman who was yet to pass her tests and be granted the privilege to ascend.

His words should bear more weight that Stella's lies, and she should be the one cast out of Ephemera, sentenced to a life of woe and misery, away from the world that had seen her grow.

And if there was a way for Eli to return and claim his just place, he'd make sure Stella Dellacqua paid for her treason, repented her mistakes.

"I don't know the details," Ora said, as she settled on a chair by the bed, Serge sprawled on the armchair by the window. "All I know is Lord Fionn was very particular to a certain part of the woods, and he came often to hunt there. One day, and this I heard from your mother herself, Fionn found his surroundings changed from what he knew. He stood at the very same spot, beneath the very same trees, yet not two paces ahead, the woods were different. The trees were of an unknown type to him, as was the quality of light and the surrounding vegetation. At hands' reach, a girl unlike any he'd ever seen. She was young, and fresh, and free. According to your mother, she wasn't yet fifteen when she first weaved a path from this world to Ephemera and ended up at the East Baronies. Fionn was immediately taken by her, and she by him. They spent that first day talking, Erin on her side of the chasm, Fionn on his, and that's how he found out your mother was a Weaver. Because only Weavers can thread paths to Ephemera."

"Does this mean I'm a Weaver, too?" Eli asked, right hand instinctively reaching for his left arm, alighting over the feather tattoo inked there.

"I realised you must be one when that feather became visible," Ora replied, nodding towards his arm. "Weavers are marked. Actually, anyone who carries magic also carries a mark. In this world, they tattoo sigils to their skins that mark them as of the blood, workers of the Craft. In Ephemera, these marks show up when children come of age, at fifteen, sixteen. When their magic starts to unravel and awake. That's why they must be at least sixteen to enter the Eligens. You remember the Eligens?"

How could he not? It was for it Stella had betrayed him.

"You're a Weaver, and I'm sure that's what saved your life. When you went into a coma, your magic took you back to your rightful world, and you lived there, while your body here slept through it all but also changed. There were days when you were so dim, I was certain you'd die. If you died here, that meant you were alive there, and I hoped and prayed you would. I also hoped and prayed you wouldn't, for your life would be in danger out there, without us to help."

"I don't understand."

"Let me tell you of your parents, then. Fionn and Erin fell in love, as expected. Her mark happened in Ephemera, not in this world; she needn't have it inked, for it came to life there, after her first crossing. Fionn knew she was precious, Weavers are so rare, and crossings even more so. He knew it was his duty to take her to Chymera so she could be of service, but your father was in love, and he dreaded the thought of losing her, of ruining such a precious being as Erin."

"*Ruining* her?"

"It's Weaver magic that's used in the making of the Everlasting, child. Weavers are milked of their powers, to provide for the energy that allows turning normal life spans into nearly eternal ones."

Eli's eyes widened in shock. He didn't remember this. Being a Weaver himself, he'd be at risk in Ephemera. Unless no one knew. He'd make sure of that.

"So they met in secrecy, and she fell with child. Barely fifteen, and she carried your father's seed in her. You. She was very distressed, afraid your father would shun her, but he loved her so much, and the life growing in her womb, too. Serge and I had recently been wed, and we'd petitioned the Governator for a living as Silvares in his woods. He granted us, as long as we provided a safe place for him to meet with your mother, which we promptly did. No one who knew them could be indifferent to the sentiment they had for each other. And it was a joy to see her grow with the promise of new life. Now, Lord Fionn wasn't free, he could never have taken your mother as spouse. Not in Ephemera, at least, and I know there were plenty of talks between the two, for him to cross over and live with her in her world."

"Why didn't he?"

"Your grandmother. Your mother's hometown is one of the few vortexes in this world. A place where the fabric between worlds is thinner, easy to shred. Weavers can always cross, of course, but it takes difficult, taxing magic. They can step across worlds in these borders, because there's already a rip and they're the ones who can see it. Your grandmother soon realised her daughter had been crossing over, and found out Erin was with child. She put an end to their meetings, locked her out of Ephemera, but as soon as the baby was born, Fionn managed to part the fabric and cross to this world. He wasn't a Weaver, at all, only an Aerial, but somehow, he knew the babe was born, he told us so. Ran out of our cottage with a mad look in his eyes, not knowing why Erin had failed to cross so many days in a row, terrified something had happened to her and the child.

"And he came upon your grandmother's cottage, where Erin and the baby howled inside. He dashed through the door, and was your grandmother shocked at the sight of him! She had an idea who he might be, the father of her grandchild, and all thought of stopping him ended at the sight of his despair, his half-crazed countenance. The moment Fionn entered the room where Erin had given birth to his child, the wails subsided, and both mother and baby were appeased. He took them away to Ephemera, Erin came to live with Serge and me in the woods, along with you. I've been watching you grow since you were a babe, Noctifer Sylvannar, and I love you as if you were mine. But you were Erin's, and she was a good, loving mother, as long as she had Fionn by her side.

"His responsibilities and ties didn't always allow him to stay there with us, but still he spent an unusual amount of time in those woods. Watching you grow, spending time by your mother's side, happy as only they knew how to be when they were together, lost in each other. Five years went by before Fioll became suspicious of his father's constant travels to the East Baronies.

"See, Fioll was to be made a Senator after his father, if only the man stepped down. But if Fionn had offered his seat to his eldest son, he'd no longer be Governator, and he'd be forced to reside in Chymera. Fioll was always ambitious, unwilling to wait, so he followed his father on one of his travels and came across Erin. He dubbed her for his father's mistress, and was angered, but not as shocked as you might expect. The nobility, living such long spans, have a tendency to take lovers, forced as they are into marriages that last as long as their lifetimes.

"Only when he realised his father intended to give everything up for Erin's sake, so he could take her as a spouse, did Fioll start to worry. If he shunned his wife, Fionn would be made to give up all his titles and power, he'd be cast to shame and ruin, and his children along him. Despite already being Everlasting, as fitted them from birth, they'd be cast out of their seats of power and made to work the lower ranks of their caste. I believe Rhysondel would have been fine with it, but not Fioll. No, not Fioll. He argued with his father that he was condemning his own children to squalor, shame, poverty. Fionn wouldn't listen, he didn't care.

"But Fioll saw the feather inked on Erin and knew. She was a Weaver, and his father had committed the ultimate treason, he'd absconded the most powerful magic from the Concilius, he'd be sentenced to exile or death for that. So he made a bargain with Fionn. That he'd keep Erin's secret and her safety, if his father renounced her. He'd step down from his Decuria, Fioll would step in after him, Rhysondel would become Governator, and Erin would be free from a lifetime imprisonment in Chymera. How could Fionn refuse? He had to let her go. What Fioll didn't know was that you were his brother, he assumed you were mine and Serge's son. So when he decided to show Erin the scope of his powers and force her to leave Ephemera for good, he used us for the lesson he intended to provide."

"He cast you out," Eli whispered.

"He cast me and Serge out. If what you say is true, that Rhysondel cast *you* out, then you know how much it hurts, physically, to be extricated from what ties us to Ephemera. Maybe it's not the same for you, as you were born in this world, but for Serge and I, it was excruciating. We were standing in the clearing one moment, inside our woods, that part of our world we knew so well, and then we were two steps to the right and couldn't move back there. We shook all over, fell to our knees, the contents of our stomach spewing before us. Erin was terrified by what she saw, aware she might suffer the same torment and be forever locked out of Ephemera. Locked out of Fionn's life, and yours.

"Fioll thought you were our son. He didn't cast you away, just to make it a little more cruel. To show Erin all he could do, to show his father too. Fionn understood, and knew he must keep you away from your brother, lest he found out who you were. He took one final stand as the Governator, as a Senator and a Decurio, he gave us his child. Pushed you away from Ephemera and into this world."

"I remember this." Eli's voice shook, palms of his hands sweating with the pain of the memory. "I remember Fionn telling me not to cry, to go over to where you were waiting for me. That one day he'd come find me and take me back home. He didn't speak, but I heard him clearly in my head."

"Your father was an Aerial, a Telepath. He must have said something very similar to Erin, for she took your hand and crossed you over to us. Then Fioll had her thrown out of Ephemera too. The breach closed, and they all disappeared, the woods, the clearing, Ephemera, the Sylvannars and the Weaver Fioll had brought along to force us away from the land we knew and that was ours too. But at least you were safe, and so was your mother."

"What happened to her?"

Serge shook his head. "Erin was heartbroken. And terrified. She feared Fioll would change his mind and come after her, to take her to Chymera and force her to a life of subservience, handing her powers to the Everlasting. She feared he found out about you and that this, too, came to be your destiny. So she sent us away, with the help of her mother. They provided for us. Found us a home, jobs, new names and papers so we could take up a living here, in this world. We were to be your parents, Nox, so that you were safe."

"What of my mother?"

Ora shrugged. "She couldn't be with you. But she couldn't stay in her hometown either. She tried, for a few years, she tried to go back to her old life, prior to meeting Fionn and moving to Ephemera. I know for a fact she tried to cross over many times, until she realised her mother had placed a hex that prevented her from ever weaving a path back to Ephemera. She was terrified, you see. Of the Everlastings realising they could cross over themselves, with the help of the Nigrum they had in Chymera, and round up more of the blood they could use for their personal sakes. She locked the crossing in those woods, and your mother was heartbroken for it. She'd met a nice young man, though, who longed to protect and make her happy. They were wed at her mother's insistence, and when Erin got pregnant with this man's child, she was terrified the baby might also come to be a Weaver, so she moved away. They went north, not far from here, in fact. Havenleah, you may remember going there when you were younger?"

He nodded.

"We often took you on day trips so Erin could see you, so you could see her other child. A beautiful baby, all freckles and blue eyes. When you went into a coma, I warned her straight away. She came as soon as she could, took one look at you and knew. I had my doubts, I did, but Erin just knew."

"Knew what?"

"That you were a Weaver who could weave paths to Ephemera with only your mind. That your body was here, but your mind wasn't. That somewhere in the East Baronies, a body much like the one you'd left behind had been replicated, and you were living your life there, in the place that saw you as a baby, in the lands that were your birthright. And she feared for Fionn's life."

"She feared for my father's life?"

"As well as yours, of course. She knew she had to go back, find you, find Fionn. I don't know what she expected to do, if she thought she could bring the two of you back... I don't know, but she took off, and we never heard from her again. She left your comatose body here, fighting for life, left a little girl back at Havenleah, and took off to Ephemera, leaving everything else behind."

"Do you think she went back to her hometown?"

"No. Her mother's wards would have still been in place, Erin couldn't cross over from there. She must have gone elsewhere, looking for a rip she could use."

"So she may be in danger herself. What if Fioll found her, what if he sent her to Chymera to help breed more Everlastings?"

"We cannot help, son."

"We don't belong in this world, mother. We should be back there, doing something about this, about my mother, my father, my birthright. I was cast out for a lie, and I must avenge that. I *need* to go back."

"Was that what you were trying to do?" Serge inquired. "When you cut your wrist? It wasn't a suicide attempt, was it? You wanted to get to the in-between state, so you travelled back to Ephemera, right?"

He nodded, lowering his eyes in shame.

"I doubt it works that way."

"Then how? How does it work, what can I do?"

"Son, you'd need another Weaver to cross you over."

Eli lifted his eyes, taking in his father first, then his mother. "Isn't my grandmother a Weaver too? She owes me this much."

"She'll never help."

"I'll make sure she does. Where's my mother from, what's the name of her hometown?"

"Weaversmoor," Serge said.

"But you can't go there like that, unprepared. You need a plan. Corinna's a strong witch, and has an entire town of those of the blood at her beck and call. Study your Craft, learn your arts, and prepare. Then, you can go and try to reason with your grandmother, although I very much doubt you'll get her to help."

"Didn't you say I have a sister? What if she's a Weaver, as my mother feared her to be? Is she still at Havenleah? What's her name?"

"She's still at Havenleah, yes, lives with her father and her maternal uncle, Erin's brother. Her name's Nyx Vaughn, and she's as much of a Weaver as you are."

VII

Present day
    Weaversmoor

WITCH CRAFT

"Miss Lattimer, Miss Vaughn, are you quite done?"

The girls blushed, faced Mr Carter, who eyed them with an annoyed glare. They nodded, aware the teacher had every reason to be cross - after all, they'd been disturbing class since its start, with their hushed conversation and the giggles.

"Good. For tomorrow, you'll bring me five pages on the various uses of Alchemy in modern day witchcraft. Each."

Both girls gasped, eyes widening in shock at such a harsh punishment for what was really not so bad, just a bit of innocent girl-talk. A snigger reached their ears from the back of the classroom, Nyx turning round to shed a murderous frown upon Pip Thomson, belied by the amused smile she couldn't erase from her lips. Pip grinned back and winked.

"Seeing you find this so amusing, Mr Thomson, you'll bring me a list of the most common alchemical ingredients and their various uses throughout times. And the next one disturbing my class will have a surprise test tomorrow."

From that moment, Mr Carter found himself teaching an attentive and silent class, until the ringing of the bell turned his well-behaved students into hormonal teenagers, high on life and youthful spirits.

As the class filed out, Nyx stood next to Pip, who elbowed her lightly. "Want to meet up at the library so we can work on Mr Carter's assignment?" he asked.

"My uncle's expecting me for lunch. I was thinking I could do it at home."

Pip shrugged. "It was just a thought."

"But yeah, sure, I'll have to be back at school anyway, for my tutoring with Miss Tate. Meet you half-past two, at the library?"

"It's a date."

He strolled off with his usual swagger, leaving Nyx blushing at his choice of words. Penny joined her, ushering her friend to the wide front doors.

"Pip Thomson, huh?" she joked. "That'll keep Trystan Everley away. Or not," she added, seeing the subject of her speech approach from the left.

"Hey, Nyx, Penny," he greeted, a shy look on his face that belied all Penny had told Nyx about him.

"Hi, Trystan," she replied.

"Talk to you later, Nyx," Penny said, and sauntered off, head held high as if she hadn't even seen Trystan.

"Well, I guess she hasn't forgiven my past trespasses, then," he mumbled apologetically.

"You *did* ditch her in a rather callous manner, what do you expect?"

"I was fourteen, what does one know at that age? And it's not as if her parents approved, either. They were the ones calling my mum, all worried about us dating."

"I didn't know that."

"Nor does Penny, so please keep it to yourself. Are you headed home?"

"Yes."

"Mind if I walk with you?"

"Sure, why not?" Blushing, Nyx stepped out.

Greeted by a drizzle, she fished the umbrella from inside her school bag, holding it as high as she could for Trystan to fit under the canopy. He laughed, grabbed the handle from her hands.

"I think it'll work better if I carry it, what do you say?"

They walked out of the gates and took a side street that led away from the town centre. Nyx's house was two roads from it, and Trystan's could be reached through her back garden and the woods that bordered both properties.

WITCH CRAFT

"So, how are you holding up?"

She squinted, momentarily lost in thought. She'd been at the Academy for nearly two months, now, and at Weaversmoor for almost four. To say she'd fitted right in would be a massive exaggeration, but things weren't as hard as Nyx had expected them at start. Kids no longer eyed her as if she was the curious alien who'd been dropped at school; no one made snarky or funny remarks about her lack of knowledge, and she was catching up with magical subjects. Regular subjects were easy, she'd always been a straight-A student and keeping her grades wasn't hard at all, it was just the magic she found herself struggling with. Theoretic subjects, like Mr Carter's class, or Herbology, she found herself catching up with ease, but anything demanding the practice and use of magical powers, Nyx still struggled with, and sometimes her spells came out the opposite of what she'd meant. But as Miss Tate said, it was early days, she was supposed to be tutored for a few more months.

"I'll get there," Nyx said, and eyed Trystan with a grin.

The boy threw a careless arm around her shoulders, pulling her closer. "This umbrella's too small, you'll get soaked."

The warmth in his voice and face hinted at much more than his words. Nyx found herself blushing, a rush of heat swimming across her.

"So," Trystan said. "Do you have any plans for this weekend?"

She shrugged.

"Because Bryn and Jamal have extra tickets for the cinema, and I thought we might join them? Then we could grab a bite to eat."

"I don't think your sister will enjoy my company."

"Ok. Then we don't go with them. Come on, Nyx, I'm trying to ask you out on a date, here." He blushed, bringing a giggle out of Nyx's lips. "You drive a hard bargain, don't you? What do you want to do, tell me? For a first date, I mean."

"A *first* date? So you plan to have more, do you?"

Trystan smirked, his hazel eyes twinkling in mischief. Nyx's stomach did a wild turn, and her heart pummelled her chest. Why did he have to be so cute, with that sweet smile of his?

"I plan to have much more with you. If you're willing, that is. I'm asking you out on a date, what do you say?"

She lowered her eyes, shrugged, not knowing how to respond. The image of Pip Thomson's blue eyes and awkward grin assaulted her mind, conflicting emotions taking hold of her. Pip had called it a date, meeting up at the library, hadn't he? But he must have been joking; he hadn't meant it like that, not like Trystan, surely. Who was being open and straightforward about it, he *did* want to take her out, he *did* ask her for a date. Pip had been horsing around.

"All right. We can go see a film, if you want to. Just don't choose anything stupid."

They reached the gate of Vaughn cottage, Trystan bending forward to open it. They kept it on its latch, but being such a small gate, as was the surrounding wall, anyone could simply jump over. The rain had stopped, but the sky was still covered in dark, moody clouds that prevented light from filtering through. Everything looked grey and foggy, even the lush greens of the bushes around the front garden, which Spencer had had landscaped into something less jungle-like than what his mother had allowed it to become. They walked across the drenched gravel to the back of the house, where another gate led straight into the woods and the Everley estate further on.

"I won't, we can see a comedy," Trystan suggested.

"I hate comedies."

"Drama, then."

My life has enough drama already, Nyx thought, but bit the inside of her cheek to keep from speaking out. Did it really matter the genre of film they'd end up watching? All she wanted was to spend time with Trystan and get to know him better. She'd been daydreaming of him since the first time their paths crossed. But recently, she'd been daydreaming of Pip Thomson too, wondering what it would be like to be held in his arms, as well as Trystan's; pondering on how their kisses would feel like. Not that she'd been kissed often, only a few times, back in her old school, by the boy she'd secretly run out of the house to meet. That hadn't lasted long, soon interest dwindling on her part, as he was incapable of holding a proper conversation and all he seemed to want to do was kissing and groping, taking her to his bedroom so they could get intimate.

Putting the past away, she looked up at Trystan, who jumped over the wall on her grandmother's property. They smiled at each other, and Nyx's insides seemed to melt at the sight of those hazel eyes, those lips. Made for kissing, they were, for nibbling with her teeth. Another blush covered her throat and cheeks, a giggle softly erupting from her pursed mouth.

"So, this Saturday?" Trystan asked.

It was Thursday, anything might happen.

"Sure."

"Five o'clock session, then a bite to eat?"

"All right."

"Will your uncle be ok with this?"

"I guess."

"Are you going to be this monotone the whole time, Nyx?"

She covered her face with moist hands and laughed. "No. I'm sorry. Yes, Trystan, my uncle will be fine with this, and yes, I'd love to go on a date with you. There, happy?"

He bent over the low wall, pulled Nyx into his arms and hugged her tight, face drowning in the cascade of curls on her head. Lips placing a soft kiss over her temple, Trystan's mouth travelled down to her cheek, and Nyx's muscles locked in place, a surge of cold sweeping over her, drenching her in eager anxiety. Was he going to kiss her? Arms wrapping around his torso, Nyx closed her eyes, parted her lips, apprehensive but excited, longing for him to dive in and take her mouth.

Trystan delivered another soft peck, this one on her lower cheek, close enough to her lips to act as a promise of what was to come the next time they stood this close together. Legs weak, stomach fluttering with butterflies that felt as if they carried flames in their wings, Nyx offered Trystan her silliest smile, eyes dimmed with want and the hope for that elusive kiss.

"I'll see you tomorrow, Nyx."

"I'll see you tomorrow, Trystan Everley."

She stood at the gate watching him run across the meadow straight into the woods, where the boy turned to wave goodbye. Nyx stretched her arm high, returning the wave, and as soon as he was lost amidst the trees, ran into the house, where Spencer awaited her, lunch ready and set on the table, while he stood against the counter, arms crossed over his narrow chest, a smile she couldn't translate set on his lips. He must have watched the entire thing, and the mere thought turned her face red, smouldering with shame.

She crossed the kitchen carting a dripping umbrella behind her, placed it on the stand at the hall by the front door, discarded her school bag on the floor and hung her coat. Then, walked back, ready to face her uncle and whatever he might have to say about what he couldn't have failed to witness.

"What was that all about?" Spencer joined her at the table, where he served both a healthy dose of roast fish and vegetables.

"Trystan was asking me out."

"Like a date?"

"Do you have a problem with that?"

"Do you?"

Nyx faced her uncle, registered the worry in his eyes. "I like him, Spence. I mean, I really, *really* like him."

"As much as that bloke in Havenleah you used to sneak out to meet?"

Another surge of heat rose up her head, and she lowered her eyes to the plate, biting mouthful after mouthful of food. So he knew. Who did she think she was kidding, Spencer had known her better than anyone, than her own father even, and he was *always* home. Like a good mother, he'd been around the entire time; of course he'd have seen her leave to meet the boy.

"No, nothing like that. Paul was a bore, Trystan isn't. Spencer, he's so dreamy, and I think he likes me. Look, it's just a date, cinema and a bite to eat this Saturday. I already said yes, you have to let me go. I'm sixteen, after all."

"You can go, as long as you have your homework done and all your chores finished. But be careful, Nyx. The Everleys... they think they're a cut above the rest, better than anyone else, always did."

"According to general opinion, so did the Vaughns. Mum, grandmother, grandad even. It's only you who have such low self-esteem," she murmured, squinting at Spencer to take in his reaction.

The pained look in his eyes dropped her stomach. What a callous thing to say; Spencer didn't deserve this. He'd been everything to her, given everything up for her. When did Spence ever have a life of his own? He'd become a stay-at-home-parent for her sake, so that her dad could work; he'd done nothing but care for Nyx, his life revolving around hers. Maybe this was what was wrong with him. Spencer should have lived his life, found himself a job, made friends, maybe fall in love. What horrible thing could have happened in his past that he'd locked himself away from everyone but Tom and Nyx? What had he been running from, leaving Weaversmoor? Bryn Everley's words floated to mind, Trystan's elder sister insisting Nyx told her uncle Bryn's father said hi and asked him to call. Spencer had reacted badly to that.

He'd tried to disguise, of course, pretend it hadn't shaken him, but it did. He'd been unable to drop the gloomy mood he'd been under for the rest of the day. And now he belittled the Everleys, advised her to be careful dating Trystan, why was that? Because he feared she might suffer the same fate Spencer did at Trystan's father's hands? There was a story here, all right, she'd suspected it before, and was more and more certain, now. Spencer must have carried one hell of a torch for Max Everley, and had his heart broken by him. But if Max wanted to catch up, might he have had feelings for Spencer, after all? Oh, what a blasted mystery this was; why did her uncle refuse to shed some light upon his past? Didn't he think it was important for her to know? Not only what had driven him away from Weaversmoor, but what had made her parents leave. Why had Erin and Tom been so intent on staying away from this town, and keeping Nyx from the rest of her family? Why had Erin left her own child at age five, if she'd been so worried about her safety? What had her mother been running from?

"Spence, you have to tell me," she said, pushing the empty plate away from her.

He sat up straighter, a genuine look of confusion in his eyes. "Tell you what?"

Glancing at the large clock mounted on the kitchen wall, Nyx realised she had no time for this. In about fifteen minutes, Pip would be waiting for her at the library. The idea of meeting him and spending time alone with the troubled boy inflamed her. How could she nurture feelings for both boys? What game was she playing at, what was she trying to do? Pip and Trystan were best friends; she had no right to come between them. A choice must be made, and Nyx stick to it, she'd already agreed to go on a date with Trystan. Pip must be regarded as a friend, a study mate, no more than this.

"Tell me who broke you heart that made you leave Weaversmoor."

"Another time, maybe. Are you done? Can you put the dishes in the dishwasher, please?"

"I have to get back to the Academy. Have a tutoring session at half-past three and promised to meet a mate at the library. We have homework that requires research; I need to do it there."

"Helping Trystan with his studies, are you?"

She blushed, averted Spencer's eyes, started piling dishes on the sink. "No, it's Penny."

Why was she lying? Why not tell her uncle she was going to meet Pip? Because she knew her intentions were all the wrong ones, her reasons for meeting him the worst possible ones? She mustn't play with him, not Pip. He already had so much on his plate; she couldn't do this to him. What if he hadn't meant anything? What if what Pip wanted was really just someone to do the research with? What if she was seeing something that didn't exist, and his interest in her was nothing like the feelings she kept experiencing for him? Now *that* would be fun, surely. That would be a great way of making a fool of herself and losing both him and Trystan, as friends and possible love interests, too. She must stop this. Pip was a mate, and that was all he was going to be.

"Fine, go on, then. But you need to sort yourself out, Nyx, and start helping more around the house. Please."

Running to her uncle, she wrapped her arms around him and gave it a gentle squeeze. "I promise I will. I love you, Spence, be back at about five, all right? See you later."

Grabbing hold of her school bag again, Nyx reached for the waterproof parka and the umbrella, and ran out, already late to meet up with Pip.

Spencer halted abruptly, halfway into the small café, forcing Nyx to swerve in order to avoid walking into him. She still bumped against her uncle's back, forehead colliding with his shoulder, as Spencer turned on his heels.

"I don't think I need that coffee, after all," he said, and she studied the insides of the café, searching for the reason behind her uncle's sudden odd behaviour.

He reached for the door handle, fumbling with it, fingers sliding as sweat ran down his hands. Nyx placed one of hers, cool and soothing, over his, opened the door.

"Spencer," a man called, before they had time to leave.

Nyx watched her uncle straighten, back stiff, eyes wide, lips pursed and forehead brimmed with tiny beads of sweat. She turned to see the man who'd spoken. A tall, well-built bloke about Spencer's age, with eyes between blue and green that reminded her of someone she couldn't quite place, a chiselled face, and a boyish grin all too familiar to her.

Like a slow motion film, Spencer spun on his heels and faced the man. He'd somehow managed to collect himself, and looked calm enough, although Nyx could see through his ruse and spot the turmoil going on inside. Why was he so nervous in face of this man? Could this be the one Spencer had been running from, the lover who'd jilted and broken his heart?

"Hello, Max."

Max? Was this...? Before Nyx could react and think further, the man walked over, one shaky hand groping a coffee cup, the other extended towards her.

"This must be Nyx," he said, a little too eagerly, a tad too loud. As if he, too, was under immense stress. "Hi, I'm Max Everley, Trystan's father. My son speaks highly of you."

Nyx shook the hand he presented her with, large and strong, but clammy. He seemed to be in the same world of pain as her uncle. What was this?

"Hello, Mr Everley, nice meeting you."

At a loss for what to say, she balanced on one foot, then the other, while the two men stared each other down. A contest Max Everley lost, as he was first to avert his eyes. He cleared his throat, took a sip of his coffee.

"So, how are you holding out, back at Weaversmoor?"

"I'm doing fine, Max. We have to go."

The man reached out and took hold of Spencer's wrist, who looked down as if he'd been bitten by a poisonous snake. But Nyx noticed he didn't pull free; in fact, his shoulders seemed to relax somewhat.

"I... I'm really glad to see you. I've missed you."

Spencer sniggered.

"Somehow I doubt you've had time to miss old friends, Max. What with two kids and that high-maintenance wife of yours." Spencer turned a grinning face to his niece, but the smile failed to reach his eyes, which held a painful, harsh glint inside. "Max's wife was your mother's best friend, they were very much alike. Both very self-centred, they always had to come first. Especially Cressida, she always had to have her way, didn't she?"

Max Everley studied his shoes attentively, in an attempt at avoiding facing Spencer. "Cress was always difficult, but so was your mother. She had to have her own way too, didn't she?"

"And some of us were too weak to oppose her, I guess."

"Spence, please, let's not do this here."

Nyx studied the two men, watching the drama unfold before her eyes, one she believed she was starting to understand.

"No, you're right. Let's just not do this. Nyx and I have to go, her classes are about to start."

"Give me a call."

Spencer looked up at Max, his entire composure gone. A blush had risen up his cheeks and fire sparkled in his eyes, an anger beyond anything Nyx had ever seen. Only similar to his reaction when Erin had fled Havenleah, leaving behind a heartbroken husband, a scared little girl, and her brother to pick up the pieces.

"Seriously? You have the gall to..."

"This is business, Spence. About your mother. My firm handled her affairs, but apparently, she'd been consulting with a few other lawyers in London. I've had a letter from them, all very official. There seems to be another, more recent will. You need to give us a call and come into office so we can discuss this."

Spencer finally pulled back his wrist, freeing himself from Max's grip. "Have someone else handle it for you, then. I don't want to see you again."

Grabbing hold of Nyx's shoulder, Spencer opened the door and led her out, dragging the confused-looking girl to where he'd parked the car. Why had he lied? She wasn't due at school for another forty-five minutes; he could have spoken to Max Everley, whatever the subject might be. What had the lawyer meant, there was another will? Had Corinna Vaughn not left them the house, or the trust funds, after all? Were they destitute, made to live out in the streets? Would they have to leave Weaversmoor, would she need to drop out of the Academy? But where would she learn about magic, then? Could they even afford to pay the school fees?

Sliding inside the car, Nyx sat back and stared blankly out the window, while Spencer took the driver's seat. His hands rolled into fists, and he slammed them into the steering wheel, punch after punch, releasing low grunts of either pain or anger. Nyx sat up straight, heart hammering; she'd never seen him like this. It was scary, and upsetting. What was she supposed to do? Folding one hand over his, she pressed it, forcing her uncle to stop and stare at her, realising he must have frightened her.

"I'm sorry," Spencer said, eyes brimming with tears. "He drives me out of my head."

"What happened between you?"

Hiding behind shaky fingers, Spencer allowed himself the luxury of silent tears, but only for a few seconds. Pulling himself together, he wiped one arm across his face, took a deep breath, steadied himself. Nyx deserved to know, after all she'd seen.

"Remember when I said I had my heart broken here? It was him."

"I'd figured as much. So, you were in love with him and he didn't feel the same, huh? Did he bully you, did he...?"

"Nyx, Max and I were together for five years."

What? This was far from anything she'd expected. Max and Spencer were actually a thing? Trystan's father was gay? Then why had he married a woman, had children with her?

"I don't understand."

"Max and I fell in love in our senior year. We'd known each other for ages, of course, but didn't hang out with the same group of people. It was only that year that we had a few classes together and began to get to know each other better. We fell, madly. I had no idea he was gay until that time, he hadn't come out. Nor did he do it that year, too scared of his parents' reaction, of my mother. But we stayed together, and went off to college, where we shared house and lived like a couple. We were so happy." A dreamy stare filled his eyes, reminiscing about the past. "We were happy, and free, and Max wanted us to stay together, so he decided he'd come clean to his parents and tell them he was in love with me."

"I gather it didn't go well, huh?"

Spencer shook his head, one fat teardrop running down his cheek. "No. His father wouldn't hear of it. I don't know what he told him, but that was the beginning of the end for us. And when my mother decided to step in, Max and I were through. He didn't have the guts to stand up to her, to all of them. Broke up with me and immediately started going around with Cressida, who'd always had her eye on him. By that time, your mother had already left Weaversmoor with Tom, and she suggested I joined them at Havenleah. I was so desperate and heartbroken I didn't even ponder, just packed my bags and left. Never came back. Nor did he come after me."

Nyx caressed her uncle's hand, gave it a gentle squeeze. "You're still in love with him."

Hanging his head, Spencer snorted. "That's the kind of fool I am. Man's married, has two kids, and here I am, still longing for him. I've been dreading running into him for months, afraid of how I might feel, well, now I guess I know. Yeah, I still love that wanker, still want him, my heart still misses all the beats when I see him. But I can't allow that man back into my life, Nyx, he'll never assume who and what he is. Cressida won't let him, either."

"Spence, this is 2018, come on. Things have changed; you two can even get married, now. Maybe you should give him a chance to come clean? I'm not saying you should forgive and forget, get back with him, but if the man needs to make amends and apologise..."

"Max Everley does not apologise, Nyx."

"Well, he did say it was business, right? Grandmother's will."

Spencer started the car, eased off the parking slot, joining the little traffic usual to the town's centre this time of day.

"Yeah, that's something I don't get. Mother wanted me back here, she wanted you to grow up here, attend the Academy, what's with this new will? I'll need to speak to the lawyers, eventually; I just don't want Max to be part of that team."

"Do you think we're going to lose the house? The trust funds? What are we going to do?"

Eyeing his niece, Spencer smiled briefly. "You don't need to worry about that. Part of the cottage will always be mine, and Erin's, provided she still lives. When our father passed away, we were his natural heirs, along with mother, so twenty-five per cent of the property is mine. Even if we don't get to live there, for whatever reason, I'd still get some money from the sale. As for the trust funds, I don't think anything can happen, there. We've been granted access to the accounts, so it's all legal, even if there's a new will. Those were set long ago. If mother didn't want us to have them, she'd have locked the accounts and cleaned them when she made the new will. Actually, I think she must have put an end to Erin's trust fund, no one mentioned it, and seeing she's been gone for so many years, declared dead at Mother's request, if the fund still existed it would have passed to you, as her daughter and sole heir. Nyx, don't worry."

She snorted, held tight to her school bag.

"No matter what happens, we'll stay here, all right? At Weaversmoor. And you'll still attend the Academy. Worst-case scenario I can get a job, I worked my way through university at a coffee shop, still have my old barista tricks. We'll be fine. Now go to class, and try to clear your head of this. I promise I'll look after you, let me do the worrying. I'm the grown-up here."

He stopped the car in front of the large Academy's front gates, leaned across his seat to place a kiss on Nyx's cheeks.

"I don't want you to take it all upon your shoulders, Spence, it's not fair. You gave up everything for me, I can't have you give up more."

"Then we'll work it out together, when the time comes. As of now, we have no idea what this is about, so let's not worry in advance. I'll call the offices and schedule an appointment, listen to what they have to say. Then we take it from there. But now, please, get to school. Want me to pick you up after? Think it's gonna rain."

"Yes, please, if you don't mind?"

"I don't. Half past four, then?"

Nyx nodded, curls swaying over her shoulders.

"Now go on, school. I love you."

She stepped out of the car, sneaked her head back in, before shutting the door. "I love you too. Drive safely, see you later."

As she ran off towards the Academy, Spencer lingered at the gates, watching her, his mind far from the sight of his niece. All he could think of was what sort of Machiavellian plan had his mother conceived, that she'd needed a new will arranged by a firm in London, away from Weaversmoor, so that no one in town knew what that was all about. What had Corinna been hiding that she meant to keep secret from the whole of Weaversmoor? As doubt crossed his mind, Spencer waved his arm absent-mindedly to a grinning Nyx, wondering how this would affect her in the end.

VIII

Pip came out of the Everley estate, hands in the pockets of his leather jacket, shoulders scrunched up to his ears to keep away the biting cold. A bitter wind had started blowing from the North, picking up fallen leaves and carrying them in a dance of red, amber and gold that never failed to mesmerise him. He stopped at the short lane leading to the road, closed his eyes, inhaled deeply of the midafternoon. The scent of rain filled the air, but it was still too far away - he gave it until early evening for it to start falling. Sodden, decaying leaves also infused the aether with their pungent stench, one he was particular to; and in its wake, the woody, warm, brittle aroma of log fires from every home. And that was his favourite smell in the whole world.

The sense of being watched forced Pip out of his reverie, eyes snapping open to take in his surroundings, a sheepish, lopsided grin gracing his lips as he saw Nyx Vaughn standing across the road from him, an amused smirk on her face. He lowered his head, but kept his eyes on her, studying her features and the soft, slow blush that ran up her cheeks. By all the elements, this girl was like none he'd met before. This girl was pure lightning to him, riveting the air with an unbridled, unshaken, unspoiled energy. Just like Trystan; and he didn't find it at all surprising that his sentiments for her were akin to what he'd been feeling for Trys over the years. Shallower, for Pip had only just met her, but similar.

"Hey, there," he greeted, and watched as she crossed the road and came to join him. "Headed home?"

"Yep, tutoring session lasted forever, today, and I still have a ton of homework."

"Cut through the woods, then," he suggested, "it'll save you at least fifteen minutes' walking up that road."

Nyx smiled, shook her head. "Never done it, I'll just get lost. Better stick to what I know."

Pip threw a careless arm around her shoulders. "You need to be more adventurous, young lady. Listen to the voice of experience, let yourself go."

"Yeah, and get lost in the woods as it darkens and starts to rain; no thanks." Nyx giggled, freed herself from Pip's hold.

"I'll walk you home, come on." He headed for the woods, and the girl followed, frowning in apprehension. "Can I carry that for you?" Pip gestured at her school bag.

"I'm fine, thank you. Blimey, it's got cold, hasn't it?"

"Wait until late December, January. Whole place turns into Winter Wonderland. Makes for a pretty sight, but folks keep forgetting how freezing it gets."

"We hardly ever had snow at Havenleah."

"Do you miss it?"

Nyx cocked her head to the right, which Pip had come to notice she often did when pondering things. "Sort of. I miss my friends. But I've made new ones here, and I feel more at ease at the Academy than I did at my old school."

"Are you enjoying yourself at the Academy? Do you like the subjects, all the new stuff you get to learn?"

"Yeah, I do, I love it. Feels like...I don't know, like I belong?"

"It does, doesn't it? But all work and no play isn't good for you."

"Says the boy who's all play."

Pip laughed. "Not fair, I work hard and study a lot. I'm just not very clever."

"Yes, you are. You just like to act as if you don't care, as if you're a bad boy, a rebel. You and Bryn. It's a wonder how she and Jamal are together."

"True. He's very focused, responsible, hard-working. Bit like you. She's wild and rambunctious, by I think that's exactly why they work, he tones her down, she gets him to be more adventurous. I think that does him a world of good, or else he'd be stuck at home all day, studying, or going on bland, placid dates with the likes of Penny Lattimer, Deanna Morris, or, God forbid," Pip lowered his voice, "Angeline Huntley. I swear there's never a hair out of place on that girl's head. She never gets unravelled, does she? She doesn't even live. Don't become like them, please."

Nyx smirked, lowered her eyes to the leaf-ridden forest floor, stepping carefully over a fallen branch. "And how do I avoid becoming one of them?"

"Let yourself go. Loosen up. Get your socks stained with mud, your shoes ruined, your shirt untucked. Dance naked in the rain on a dark night, brave the woods without learning the lay of the land, kiss the earth and thank it for all the blessings you have, fall madly in love. Lose your head over that love," he said, voice louder and excited, eyes glistening with emotion, arms thrown wide into the skies.

Nyx laughed, twirled around, hair caught in branches that she pulled free with a wince of pain, sides of her shoes clogged with thick, reddish mud. Pip stood watching, entranced by her innocence, her surrender, her faith. She was untainted by her magic and the powers it granted her; she was unafraid; free like no other kid at their school would ever be. Only because she'd grown away from a system that cast them immediately into roles supposed to last them a lifetime. She was like him, didn't fit one particular shoe - she could be and do anything.

"Come here," he whispered, and Nyx stopped her wild twirling.

"Why?"

"Let me show you a trick."

The smile on her lips changed momentarily, from one of amusement and joy to a snare of ill-hidden seduction, something crude and experimental, for she had no experience with it, nor did she realise what she was doing. The fact it was unplanned and unthought of served to allure Pip even more, ready to fall into Nyx's net as he'd fallen into Trystan's two years ago. The girl came to stand by his side, and he grabbed her hand, curling his fingers with hers, arm outstretched towards the sky.

"Now, focus. Close your eyes and focus, follow my lead. Think about how much you want the wind to stop. Think how much you want the day to warm up."

Nyx giggled and he pressed her hand.

"Shh, take it seriously. You'll be surprised."

Silence surrounded them, broken only by the banshee-like wails of the wind, until this, too, dwindled into nothing. Nyx opened her eyes, mouth agape, a giggle escaping her lips as she clapped hands in pure delight.

"Did we just do this?"

"Of course we did. You're a Weaver, the final element. You're Spirit."

"What?"

"Miss Tate hasn't taught you this?"

"We spoke of the elements, of course, but there are only four."

"No, there are five. Five elements, one to each tip of a pentagram. Fire, water, earth, air and spirit. You're spirit, and so can work with other witches' magic, enhancing their powers and your own. I'm sure she'll get into this soon, maybe she doesn't want to overwhelm you. Come to think of it, I kind of screwed up showing you this, didn't I?"

"No, no way," Nyx assured him, hands instinctively going for Pip's face, cupping it, thumbs dishing gentle strokes upon his cheeks.

A hot blush climbed up his neck, and his heart took on a wild tirade of frantic beats. Pulling on every reserve, Pip used all his strenght to not bend forward and kiss Nyx. Somehow, he sensed she wasn't yet ready. But she would be. He was certain she would be.

"Listen, what are you doing this Saturday?"

"I'm going to the cinema," Nyx said, and the moment was gone, her eyes avoiding his, her hands no longer pressed against his cheeks.

"Okay. You make sure you take time off to do stuff you like, or it can get hectic and stressful. Take it from me."

They resumed their walking, Vaughn cottage just visible beyond the next line of trees. Pip sighed; it had taken less time than he wished, and he didn't want this moment to end. He longed to stay by Nyx all hours of the day, as he had when he'd first fallen for Trystan. Did this mean he was falling in love with this weirdly beautiful girl? He mustn't let it hang out unspoken, then, not like he'd done with Trystan, who'd always left it clear he wasn't into boys. He must take a stand where it came to Nyx, if he wanted to be with her. But he'd never asked a girl out, nor a boy, for that matter, and the very brief flings he'd had were resumed to groping sessions and passionate kisses when the mood hit him. Nothing serious, or lasting. But that wasn't how he felt about Nyx. With her, he wanted more. More quality time together, more commitment, more surrender.

"Hey, what about the Everley Halloween? They throw this huge party every year, want to come with me? We can dress up as, oh, I don't know, Henry the Eight and Anne Boleyn?"

"I'm not going to dress up as some beheaded old queen," Nyx said, giggling. "I think we should go as Natalie Wood and James Dean, in 'Rebel Without a Cause', what do you say?"

"Is that a yes?"

"Huh?"

"You're coming to the party with me, is that what you're saying?"

For an instant, her eyes seemed to shadow, and Nyx hesitated. Pip's heart caught in his chest, his breath locked inside his lungs, refusing to be let out. Fear washed over him.

"I think so, yeah. We'll go together, why not?"

His breathing eased, heart returning to its normal rhythm. When had he last felt like this? He still remembered; he'd been fourteen and only just realised how in love with Trystan he was. Those first months of finding himself in love with the boy who'd become his best friend were still fresh in his mind, despite Trystan's reserves, his denials, his incapacity to admit what he really felt. The boy who claimed he had no interest in Pip other than as a friend, a brother. The same boy who'd kissed him once, not that long ago, on a night they'd both had far too much to drink. A kiss that had prevented Pip from allowing himself to fall in love with anyone else, hopeful that Trystan would come round.

But this was a change, a turning point. For two years, Pip had felt no interest in others, neither boys nor girls had sparked up a flame in his heart, until Nyx came. And this time, he wasn't being shunned; she'd just agreed to go out on a date. His face erupted into a smile, and his eyes sparkled with joy. They came out of the woods into the clearing, and Pip didn't feel so crushed they'd have to part, now. Because he knew he stood a chance, he knew deep in her heart, Nyx must have a place for him.

"Well, here you are, young lady, safely delivered to your door," he said, twirling his hand and bowing before her in an exaggerated curtsey.

"My, aren't you in a chirpy mood! What's got into you?"

Pip eyed her mischievously, his grin exposing well cared for, bright teeth. "I suddenly realised how much in love with life I am, know what I mean? How much of a blessing just being alive really is, able to experience this wonderful, beautiful world with what we have, what we are. With the people I'm lucky to have in my life. And you're one of them. Thank you, Nyx, for wanting to be part of my life."

He took her in his arms briefly, her body stiff under his hands, only to melt and relax as Pip tightened the embrace.

"I'm so glad you're in my life too, Pip Thomson, you're one of the most special people I've ever met." Disentangling herself from his arms, Nyx fidgeted with her coat, her skirt. "I'll see you tomorrow at school, hmm?"

"You certainly will."

"Thank you for walking me home, Pip."

"It was my absolute pleasure, Nyx."

Unable to move, he stood in the middle of the clearing as Nyx ran off, waving goodbye, curls bouncing, eyes sparkling, hem of her skirt riding up her thighs.

When the rain finally came, Pip broke from the spell he'd been under and ran to the road, knowing it was still a bit of a jog to the Academy and the dry warmth of his dorm room.

There was something about these woods; Jacintha couldn't deny it. She'd felt its strange allure before, in the two years she'd lived here. In fact, it was what made her so certain her place was at Weaversmoor, the very day of her arrival. Once she'd settled at the small flat provided for her, she'd taken a stroll around town. Had never quite made it to the centre or the high street, her feet following the river's course upstream and directing her to a shady glade, where Jacintha had sat down on a log and breathed in the warm June air. That exact moment was still vivid in her head – the peace she'd felt with her eyes closed and the hum of bees around her, a soft breeze blowing through the canopy above her, the deep, strong scent of the forest reaching for her. Begging her to enter, take a walk, meander along those tree-lined streets that weren't really streets but pathways leading... where? A forest had no streets. Trails perhaps, but never streets. Still, she'd sensed the calling and responded to it willingly.

Further in, Jacintha had gone; further into the copses and the thickets, the bushes that spread their magic all around, and oh, the bounty she'd met with, along her way. From hawthorn to wild roses, she'd found an immense array of natural ingredients that would make any Draught-Maker the happiest of witches. They'd made her one very joyful witch, and she'd picked a few leaves, a couple of roots, twigs and berries and seeds she could later use. And delved even further in.

It was somewhere beyond a wild bramble she found herself ill-at-ease. Jacintha couldn't have named it then - nor could she now - the unease taking over her, the sense of dread, of doom. As if something unspeakable lurked in the deepest folds of those woods, something unreadable, posing such dangers as to have her arms break out in goosebumps. And still Jacintha had walked towards the source of that unease. A copse of trees, beautiful and lush, where an orchestra of unknown birds erupted into unexpected melodies. Birds whose feathers were the rich colour of jewels, birds whose beady black eyes seemed to train upon her, birds whose claws and beaks promised a world of pain and injury, should she cross them. But for whatever reason, Jacintha didn't fear them; she actually longed to touch them. And knew they'd allow her to gently caress their colourful, smooth, silky feathers, if only...

If only she could reach them.

Jacintha had walked towards the trees, but before even alighting upon the first, the day turned dark. As if the canopy of leaves above closed down on her, preventing light and air from spilling into the woods, darkening the world around until she could no longer see. One moment all was bright and coloured and vivid, next second Jacintha was blind and couldn't see.

Blind.

Her eyes hadn't worked, and she'd panicked. Hands reaching out, she'd tried to find guidance amongst her surroundings, fingers alighting over leaves, branches, thorns, the corrugated trunks of trees. She'd ran out of the woods, or at least, she'd hoped to be running out of the woods, using her other senses, her inner eye, to lead her to safety. Shrieks had come out of her lips, evidence of her fear. Finally, tripping over a large root, Jacintha fell face down, scraping her bare knees and hurting her wrist. But her eyes were working again, and now she could see. She'd come out of the woods upon a clearing, a meadow filled with tall grass and the remnants of last spring's profusion of wild flowers. A cottage stood just ahead, dark grey rough stone and black rooftop, its green door and window frames inviting and safe.

A woman had leaned by the small gate opening onto a jungle of a backyard, where everything seemed to grow profusely, with neither head nor tails about it. A woman had leaned there; face stern and harsh, grey hair pinned on a loose bun at the top of her head, a black and red fringed shawl around her shoulders, and a fist closed so tightly her knuckles had turned white.

Jacintha had stood up, taking a look at her bleeding knees, nursing the injured wrist to her chest. Every single muscle and nerve hurt, and she dragged the twisted foot, trailing behind her a path through the grass and the dry clumps of earthy soil.

"Hi," she'd greeted. "Seems like I've taken a bit of a nasty fall, might I bother you for a bit of..."

"Get out of my property," the woman had hissed, such venom in her voice as Jacintha had never seen. "The likes of you better stay away from here."

"Excuse me?" She'd been shocked, hurt, but mostly angered. Who did that woman think she was to treat Jacintha like this? To treat *anyone* like this?

"Stay away from those woods," the woman had insisted. "The patch between Everley estate and this cottage is off limits to you, young lady. Stay out of it, if you know what's good for you."

Jacintha had picked herself up and hobbled back home, tired, scared, in pain and furious. She'd mentioned the woman to the school's principal on their first meeting, and had been duly informed this was Corinna Vaughn, who, like the Everleys, belonged to one of the most ancient witch families in town. A Weaver like Jacintha, one that weaved her powerful spells on the surrounding area in order to keep them safe, secluded, free. She was advised to do as the woman suggested, and keep herself to hiking other parts of the large forest that didn't lead to that particular patch of land. For two years, Jacintha had obeyed - unwillingly. Whenever she drove down that road, the woods beckoned, called her in. She ignored the summons every time, but it was physically depleting, and painful to do so. Well, not painful, not really. It was more a question of pride, that of being locked out of what was actually free. But she'd obeyed, and kept away from the woods.

Until one stormy day at the end of March; the sky falling out in gales of wind and rain, like the world was coming to a drowning, blowing end. Jacintha had been home, minding her business, working on a few worksheets for the students she tutored, when her entire body spasmed, and flickers of energy crossed through her. A harsh, coarse energy that demanded spending, immediately. She pulled on her running shoes, a waterproof wind-breaker, mobile and set of keys and left the comforting cosiness of her home to go for a speedy jog around town. She must run this course of energy to the ground, or become a stalked, caged, wild beast waiting for the weather to improve. Jacintha had never feared a little wind, a bit of rain.

She'd ran on and on across the small town, to find herself delving amidst trees, convinced she was way on the other end, giving the Everley estate a wide berth. Only she hadn't, and soon her feet came to pound the same route, and she found herself upon the same hallowed grounds, the same weird, strange trees locking in on her. But there were no birds, not today, not with the rain.

The same sudden darkness fell over her, and her eyes no longer could see. This time though, Jacintha had expected it, and been better prepared. She'd stayed calm, breathing in and out with pause, then turned on her heels and marched away from the clump or trees. To happen upon the same clearing, now sporting the first signs of spring, with Vaughn cottage just ahead. Where hell or something of the same mount seemed to have broken lose.

She'd taken to the road, skirting the back of the house, coming up the front as if she'd ran from Porsley Street on her mid-morning jog across town. And there, at the door of Vaughn cottage, a police car, an ambulance, Max Everley and an array of important people gathered under drenched umbrellas, speaking in hushed tones. Jacintha had approached the narrow wall, gestured the Academy's principal, who came to join her.

"What's the matter?" she'd asked, feigning concern, unable to hide her curiosity.

"Corinna Vaughn passed away. She's not been seen around town the paste couple of days, and when the boy who delivers her groceries came to call this morning, she wouldn't open the door. Worried, he peered through the living-room window, saw her lying on the couch, thought she was asleep. Only when she still didn't wake up with him fisting the glass and shouting her name, did the young man consider she might be dead. Hence the spectacle."

"Why the police? Do they think it was...?" Jacintha had let it hung unspoken, the principal smiling at her.

"No, Corinna was an old woman, with a heart condition. Her time was come. Well, her death poses a few problems; I only hope they don't make everything more difficult than it already is."

"*They?*"

"Corinna's children."

And thus she'd been put up to speed with the Vaughn's drama, and why Corinna had no family in town. A daughter who'd been a constant runaway from age fifteen, a son who'd been caught up in some sort of scandal the principal had implied at but not clarified, a mother who'd pushed her own offspring away, only to end up alone in that house, with both of her children swearing never to return to Weaversmoor. Thus the town's ingrained fear Corinna's heirs turned out to be difficult, in the wake of their mother's death.

It hadn't happened like that, after all, Jacintha mused, as she came upon the gates of Everley estate. Turning on her right, she entered the woods close to the tall, forbidding walls surrounding the place, wandered through the trees, lost in thought. The Vaughns hadn't made things difficult, much on the contrary. Corinna seemed to have kept an eye on her offspring, and she'd known her daughter was missing, having left a small child at the care of her father and maternal uncle. The poor girl. Nyx Vaughn had lost both parents and a grandmother she'd failed to meet, and been forced to a place she didn't know, away from her friends and all that was familiar. Corinna Vaughn had seen to it. She'd made it imperative her son and granddaughter came to live at Vaughn cottage, and against local belief, Spencer Vaughn hadn't opposed his mother's last wishes. He'd left everything behind and moved back to a town that had run him out, only for the sake of his niece.

A strange girl, she was. Powerful but untalented, she still struggled with the basics of her magic and the control of her art. But she was studious and applied herself to work with what was a hopeful heart, unlike many of the students Jacintha tutored, who were downright lazy. Nyx wasn't, and even though she struggled with the lack of magical knowledge provided by ten years of living in the dark about whom and what she was, the girl worked hard. But there was something odd about her, something Jacintha couldn't quite pin. Something that came at her in waves and had her sway on her feet, searching for an answer to that mystery. What exactly was wrong with Nyx Everley? Why did Jacintha feel such a connection to the girl, such a sense of recognition? Could they have met before? The years prior to her climbing accident were still a blur - worse than a blur, they were non-existent. Doctors kept reassuring her it was normal, she may never remember her past again, she may be struck by a sudden surge of memories unexpectedly. Maybe she'd come across Nyx somewhere in her foggy past.

The sound of voices chanting brought her to a halt. Swerving left, Jacintha slithered through a thicker clump of trees, hid behind a tall, large bush, took a peek. Her lips broke into a smile as she watched the four figures out there, forming a circle under round-canopied trees. So, she wasn't the only person sensing the allure of these woods. Something here was replenishing, fulfilling. As if magical creatures found nourishment and an added source of energy, just by standing amidst these trees. Even though the place didn't call to every single witch around town, it whispered to these. The Everley siblings and their two usual sidekicks.

    They'd gathered round a bonfire, each placed upon a cardinal point, according to the element ruling over their magic. Jacintha wondered what kind of spell they were working, and watched them more attentively. Jamal Wilson took the North, wore a moonstone hanging from a raw leather cord around his neck. The stone seemed to pulse with their canticles. To the South, Trystan Everley held his arms towards the fire, and flames danced in his direction, as if trying to reach for him. Jacintha couldn't see, but was sure the leather cord on his neck held an amber amulet cast in silver. She'd glimpsed it before. On the West side, Trystan's sister Bryn was the only one with her eyes open, and she watched the flames attentively, hands stretched by her side, palms down. The jet stone on her cord vibrated to the inflexions in her voice. Finally, to the East, disturbed and overall bad boy Pip Thomson stood bare chested on what was a cold, late afternoon, arms held high towards the sky, torso achingly thin, a sapphire nestled against the base of his throat, and every single tattoo on his body pulsating with a life of their own.

    Jacintha reeled; this was powerful magic these kids performed out here in the woods. She wondered what they were about, worried they might take it a little too far, until the words the group was chanting became clear to her ears. This was a protection and shielding spell, directed at Pip Thomson, the Aerial, the boy constantly haunted by the side effects of his particular powers. Life mustn't be easy for the likes of him, being an Empath and a Haruspex at the same time; no wonder the kid was always troubled and tended to act out. An odd sense of pride glided through her, watching how this odd group of children had banded together and managed to work out their individual powers in order to create such strong magic, only for the sake of their friend.

WITCH CRAFT

But this was a private moment, and she had no place here - this belonged to them alone.

Silently standing from behind the bush, Jacintha veered to her right, turned deeper into the woods, away from the borders of Everley estate, following the lure singing out to her. Knowing what was bound to happen, if she chose to dwell there. The siren song from the trees was stronger than her fear, though, so it was with a hopeful yet heavy heart she found herself once more near the odd clump of trees. Where those weird birds sat perched on now nearly bare boughs, not singing their joyful songs but training black, intrusive eyes on her, as if they could read her mind.

The darkness fell again, blinded Jacintha, who eased herself down to her knees. She wouldn't run, not this time, she meant to brave it. The birds, the trees, they had a message for her, something to impart, perhaps a clue into her forgotten past, a helpful reminder of who she'd been. Burrowing her hands into the soft, moist soil, she became one with the earth, and it was through nature's eyes she now seemed to see.

A long, stretching forest ahead of her, with narrow alleys winding amidst the trees.

A log cabin built up one of those trees, a child's tree-house, perhaps?

A silence that was shattered by the odd cackle of a bird, the swaying of leaves chiming to the breeze. A horse's hooves, far in the distance. Water running far, far away from where she stood. Waves crashing against rock walls so high she couldn't see down to the bottom, unless lying on her stomach and inching herself to the edge of the cliff.

A man, just a shadow, whistling as he walked along the trees.

A man, tall and well-built, with a face she couldn't see, but one she knew closely, intimately.

A man whose voice she was so familiar with as to know its every cadence, the rise and fall of his breathing, the soft threading of his feet, the sound of his every step and the laughter he often shared so openly.

Then the turmoil and the shrieks, loud accusations she couldn't properly hear, the running of many, many feet in pursuit of their prey, the crying, the baying, the darkness descending around her as if to clothe her in a shroud ready to take her away.

Dread prompted her feet to run, flee this place, arms pumping by her side, eyes blind. She darted across the woods, through trees, bushes and brambles, hair snagging in low branches, skin scratched by hanging twigs. She didn't know where she was going, and didn't really care, as long as it was away from this place, where she was sure something very bad had happened one day. The past tended to linger and infuse the present with its memories, if these were of blood shed into the land, of pain inflicted so harshly as to leave a deadly print behind. And that was what she'd sensed, back in that clearing, deep in those woods. Pain so strong it hung about the very fabric of time.

Jacintha ran, and only came to a halt when she fell down and scraped her knees, the sound of brakes screeching in her ears, wet tarmac beneath her hands, the acrid smell of exhaust pipes filling her nostrils. She stopped, and stayed down, her sight returning to normal, the light of the sun slowly filtering through closed eyelids, while she inhaled deeply.

Heart stampeding, breath laboured and raspy, Jacintha found herself shedding fat, scalding tears, shoulders hitching with sobs she couldn't place a reason for. She cried earnestly, as if her heart had been shattered, her life ended. She cried in shame, in pain, in fear. And when a pair of strong, soft hands came to lay over her shoulders and pulled her up, she didn't as much cry as she shrieked, feet sliding in the tarmac as whoever had taken hold of her dragged her away from the open road.

As her eyes snapped open and she took in the man who imprisoned her in his arms, Jacintha's heart subsided, her tears dried, her sobs halted.

And she found herself lost within the blue eyes staring back at her from a face that graced the loveliest smile she'd ever seen.

Part Two

I

Eli braked, motorbike screeching in protest at the sudden halt. He barely managed to hold it up, swerving to the side of the road, arms shaking with the effort of preventing the bike from cartwheeling. It had been so unexpected.

She'd come running from the woods, like a mad dryad on a high, thrown herself into the open road, careless of what might hit her. The woman had seemed drugged, really. He'd barely had time to swerve and brake, another inch and he'd have hit her full on. Heart hammering, Eli killed the engine and ran to the woman, who'd fallen on her knees, crying like her heart was breaking. Had she been attacked, in those woods? She was obviously out for a jog, evidenced by the choice of attire, but her clothes were dishevelled, her hair breaking loose from the high ponytail, she had scratches and bruises all over arms and face. The wind-breaker she wore was ripped, one sleeve hanging limp over a skinny arm.

He approached her, grabbed her by the armpits, and pulled her up. Lord, she was heavy, or made herself so by helping him as little as she could. As if she wanted to stay down until a car ran over her. What on earth could have happened in those woods? Pulling on his strength, Eli managed to drag her to where he'd parked his bike, the woman growing calmer and more relaxed in his arms. She opened her eyes and trained them on his, gifting Eli with the sight of the bluest pair he'd ever come across. Finding he couldn't help smiling, his grin widened at the sight of her. Something about this woman felt oddly familiar.

"Are you all right?" he asked, voice seeped with concern, studying her demeanour for clues of deeper injuries. Apparently, there were only scratches, but that was just the physical side. Whatever had driven her out of the woods in such panic was sure to leave mental scars. "What happened out there?"

The woman followed his gaze to the edge of the woods, her cheeks blushing crimson as if she'd only just realised what this looked like.

"I... I think I freaked myself out."

"Freaked yourself out? You weren't attacked, then? No one harmed you?"

"No, nothing like that. I went for a jog and got lost amidst the trees, they're kind of all the same, you know? Then there's all these noises in the forest, and it's dark and eerie in there, I started imagining all these wild things and got scared. Pretty silly, huh?"

She tried a smile, it looked more like a grimace than a grin, and Eli wasn't fooled by her words. There was more to it than what she said, but if the woman insisted she wasn't attacked, there wasn't much he could do about it.

"I nearly ran over you," he whispered, this time eyeing his bike with something of concern. As if he was more worried about the injuries it could have suffered than what might have happened to the woman had he slammed into her.

"I'm sorry. I'll be more careful, from now on."

"Maybe you should just stay out of those woods."

She trained her attention back on the border of trees, the light in her eyes dimming for one split second, her face drenched with something that wasn't quite fear. "Maybe I should. Anyway, I'm sorry for the inconvenience. Thanks for the help."

"Don't mention it. I'm Eli." He offered her a gloved hand.

"Jacintha." Taking it in hers, she squeezed, shook, smiling openly.

Stomach burning as if hot stones had been dropped in it, Eli blushed. This woman had something about her he'd not encountered before, she did something to him he'd not yet experienced. Since waking up from the seven-year coma he'd been under, Eli hadn't come across many women, and of those, few were the ones who'd grabbed his attention for more than five minutes. He'd spent the previous three years hard at work, making up for lost time. He'd studied, taken his driver's licence, worked a few odd jobs, and overall accustomed himself to this world, where he must now dwell. That had meant meeting new people, making friends, going on dates. He'd asked a couple of girls out, but the interest they'd sparked wasn't long-lasting. None had given him this feeling, like worms trailing inside his stomach, a noose around his heart that forced it either to completely stop or rush on in a speedy beat. This woman had a different effect on him, and Eli wasn't sure he didn't quite like it.

"What a lovely name, very unusual."

"Bit old fashioned, but I rather like it too. Well, I should get going. Thank you once more."

"I'll see you around," Eli offered, watching her take off down the road.

Jacintha turned around, grinning, and waved at him. Goosebumps trailed across his forearms, and the burning coals inside his stomach seemed to melt to something mellow and sweet. Laughing under his breath, Eli got back on his bike. According to the GPS, he wasn't far from his destination; in fact, the place he sought must be just up the road, around the bend he spotted a few miles ahead. Revving the engine, he sped towards it, keeping an eye on the gloomy skies above.

WITCH CRAFT

Who decided to travel across the country on a motorbike in such a wet October? His parents had offered him use of their car, but he'd stubbornly declined, his mood embittered by worry at the possibilities hinted in the letter he'd recently received. A letter that had prompted a phone call to some London-based law firm, where all he was told was he should be at Weaversmoor on November 2nd, at a certain address, for the reading of his grandmother's will.

He was a few days early, all right.

The thought of showing up somewhere like a piece of bad news, a nasty surprise, had prompted Eli to pack up and finally do what he'd proposed himself to, three years ago. He'd wanted to meet his sister, his uncle, start building a relationship with both, especially Nyx. She was the one who could help him, after all. But playing catch up with those lost seven years had taken up most of his time, and frankly, he'd feared his family's reaction. They didn't know him, probably didn't even know he existed, what was he going to say? *Hi, I'm Eli, Erin's long-lost bastard son*? Would they even believe him?

His plan had then changed; he'd give Nyx a wide berth for the time being, and focus on Corinna. When he came down to Weaversmoor, it would be to meet his grandmother, the one person he was certain would believe him, for she'd known of him. So Eli had taken his time to improve, and learn how to navigate this world with his particular talents – he'd have to live in it longer than he might wish to – before confronting Corinna Vaughn. The truth was, he'd feared her. He'd been terrified of her reaction. She'd shunned him before, what if she did so again? How ready was Eli to face rejection, how prepared was he to deal with a biological family that might not even wish to acknowledge him?

Close to three years had passed, and he'd not made up his mind about what to do, the memories he still had of Ephemera dimming further and further as time flew by. Even the wrongs he'd been done seemed to matter less and less, as if this world had a stronger pull on him than the one held by the place he'd known far better, and loved more.

Then the news had come.

That Corinna had passed away - news his adoptive mother received by way of a phone call from the very same law firm who later contacted Eli. They'd been instructed to contact either Ora or Serge Sylvain in the event of Corinna Vaughn's death, why, they had no idea. Nor did they care - it was a job, nothing more. But the news had disrupted Eli. There was no one left now, who knew for sure he was Erin's son. There was no one left who could attest to him being Eli Vaughn, and the plans to make friends with his sister came to a sudden halt, forced by the loss of the one person who could have vouched for him.

Spring dwindled into summer, followed by autumn, Eli no longer caring for the whereabouts of his sister. Serge had looked into it, though, and insisted he reach out to her, saying the girl had lost her father recently. She was as much an orphan as Eli, and could do with family around. But she had her uncle, *their* uncle, didn't need a brother she'd never met and probably didn't even know existed. So he'd chosen to stay away, keep out, thoughts of Ephemera already so sporadic he spent entire weeks without even remembering such place existed and he'd belonged to it. The letter from those fancy London lawyers had changed it all, though.

If there was a will, Nyx and Spencer Vaughn were sure to be at the reading, right? And Eli didn't want to show up without some sort of previous meeting, without having at least reached out to them, made himself known. The decision to leave for Weaversmoor before the required date had been an easy one. What was not so easy was dealing with the anxiety provided by constant wondering how they were going to receive him. The odd, unexpected encounter with Jacintha had served as a distraction, but now that he could see the muddy road leading to the cottage's front lawn, Eli's innards jumped and coiled, performing a dance meant to leave him heaving and gasping before he could utter a single word.

    He stopped the bike in front of the low wall surrounding what he knew was his grandmother's house. Not anymore, he corrected, this was no one's house, now, seeing the will was still to be read. But Spencer and Nyx had been living here for a while. Bit presumptuous of them, perhaps? Or maybe clear evidence they were in the dark about Eli's existence? Well, they'd soon learn of it. He only hoped Grandma Vaughn had left some sort of letter explaining how he'd come about. Fancy having to tell a sixteen-year-old girl about the existence of another, parallel world. What of Spencer? He'd have Eli committed for lunacy the moment he started raving about the Sylvannars and what not. Best to keep those details out of the way, say he had no idea who his real father was.

    Bracing himself, Eli unlatched the miniature gate and stepped in, following the narrow flagstone path to the front door. Taking a steadying breath - lungs aching with the effort - he knocked. He waited, then knocked again. Spotting a bell, Eli smirked. Of course they wouldn't hear him knock, what if they had music on, or were at the back of the house? Pressing the button, he let it ring, its chimes sending a trail of fire down his throat to the pit of his stomach. And still no one opened, no one came. They were clearly not at home. Which he would have realised, had his brain been working properly. There was no car parked on the empty driveway, surely Spencer would have his own car? Well, they'd have to return any given time, he might as well wait. Worried that the impending rain chose this moment to fall, he eyed his motorbike, wondering if he should lug it in, park it by the garage, where a jutting awning would provide ample coverage from the deluge. Before he could even move, the sound of a car reached his ears, coming into view mere seconds after.

The vehicle halted by the wider gates leading to the spacious driveway, and a teenage girl jumped from the passenger's seat. Her round, blue eyes met Eli's - suspicious, thoughtful, measuring him. He watched her too, noticing the freckles covering her face, which brought a smile to his lips. So this was his sister. A surge of emotion travelled across his frame, and he stood up, eager to reach out and scope the girl in his arms. She was family, and he'd had so little of it he was starving for connections. Those of the blood, that lasted through misery and pain, those who were always there because they belonged, they were the same. An annoying thought crossed his mind, along with the image of a pale, lovely face. Stella Dellacqua still haunted his mind, but less and less every day.

The girl opened the double gate, and the car drove through. Her eyes were still on Eli, they shared the same colour - the same clear blue - if not the shape, his sister's being slanted. Hands sweating, he wiped them on the legs of his jeans, stood up from where he'd sat waiting, as the man he assumed was his uncle emerged from the car. They walked over quickly; the man pushing the girl slightly behind him.

"Yes, can I help you?" he asked, and Eli studied him eagerly.

Dark of hair, and eyes that were of a deep olive green, large and soulful, this man stood nearly as tall as the girl, and nearly as slim. His hair shared the same curls as his nephew and niece, only he wore them close cropped like Eli.

"I'm Eli," he replied, voice shaking as much as his legs. "Erin's son."

Nyx turned an alarmed face towards Spencer, both having spotted the bike parked outside their front gate, and the man sitting on their front steps.

"Who's that? Doesn't look like one of the lawyers, does he? Have you met with Max Everley yet?"

Spencer shook his head, eased the car up to the double gates. "Open those for me, will you?"

His eyes were still on the young man. Something about him looked familiar. The curve of his jaw, the drawing of his lip, the curls on his head, the blue of the eye. His heart halted, painful inside an already tense chest. Driving through the open gates, he waited for Nyx to close them before pulling out of the driver's seat. Nyx's scolding tone had not gone unnoticed. He should have contacted Max's firm, if only to understand what they wanted with him. He'd have to do it now, today, before the end of office hours, or risk having to call Max personally. Not that he had his phone number, but Spencer was sure Nyx could get it for him, in case of dire need.

Nyx waited for him to join her, and allowed her uncle to push her slightly back, as she, too, took stock of the young man on their porch. The girl was also riddled by the familiarity she discerned in him, as if she knew those traces. Then realised he looked a lot like Spencer, albeit her uncle's eyes being wide and large and this man's smaller. And their colours were also different. Spencer was warmer, his hair darker, he was also much smaller and leaner. But they could have been related, chin, nose, lips being so similar.

"Yes, can I help you?" Spencer inquired, sounding haughty and distant.

Nyx knew him well, though, and she alone could see through the ruse - he was anxious, he was nervous, scared, even. Of what, he didn't even know.

"I'm Eli," the young man said, and Spencer's hand reached out for Nyx's, grabbed it with a tightening grip. "Erin's son."

The girl's eyes darted from the man to her uncle - huge, moist, terrified. What was the meaning of this? What had he just said? Nyx tried to free her hand.

"What?" She wheezed, face paling, lips colourless as if she was about to faint, which Spencer feared she might.

He, too, was on the verge of losing it. But hadn't he known? Or at least suspected? Hadn't he looked at this young man and wondered? There was a resemblance to his sister in him, yes, if one pushed hard to find it.

"Spencer, what does he mean?" Nyx broke free, took a couple of tentative steps towards the man. "What do you mean? Who are you, to come here spreading lies about my mother?"

"Nyx," Spencer called, she ignored him.

The air crackled around them, and the earth seemed to rumble. Spencer wondered who was losing control of their powers - it had to be Nyx. Did the man even have powers of his own? If he was Erin's child, he would have, what with a father like his. Shaking his head, he grabbed Nyx's shoulders, trying to impart a sense of calm upon her.

"Are you just going to let him lie?"

"You must be my sister," the man said, reaching a hand out to her, which the girl chose to ignore. He then presented it to Spencer, unfazed. "And you're my uncle, Erin's brother?"

"I'm Spencer Vaughn, yes." He *did* take the hand, and shook it. Whoever this man was, he'd soon clear up his origins. "Nyx, we should have told you before, but your parents didn't want to. I respected their wishes. Didn't agree, but had to respect their wishes."

"What are you talking about?" she hissed, turning her attention to him. A gust of wind blew leaves around the front lawn, rocked them on their feet.

"Calm down. Maybe we'd better get in."

"You're not going to ask this person into our house, we don't even know who he is. Well, I know who he *isn't*, and that's my brother, because I don't have one," Nyx spat, facing Eli once more.

"What is your father's name?" Spencer asked.

"Which of them?"

Nyx cackled, but her uncle gave her shoulder a tight squeeze, forcing her to wince and shut up. Could he really have any doubts of the veracity of this man's words? Hadn't he known all along he'd come here one day? Despite everything Erin had done to keep him away from Weaversmoor, ignorant of his origins, Spencer had always known it wouldn't work like that. Corinna would see to it, if the boy himself didn't. What child wouldn't wish to know the truth about his parents?

"Both," Spencer insisted.

Eli sighed, lowered his head, eyes on the toecap of his biker boots. "The man who raised me and who is a father to me is called Serge Sylvain. But my biological father is Fionn Sylvannar."

Spencer let out the breath he'd been holding. Would anyone other than Eli Vaughn even know these names? A couple of people, perhaps, but they'd never tell. *He* hadn't, and doubted either Max or Cressida ever would. As for Corinna and Tom, they were no longer alive to speak of the past.

"Come, let's get in. It's about to rain."

Nyx stared at her uncle, shocked. He was going to invite that liar into their house? Was he mad? Searching in her core, she touched the source of her powers, readying it for use, should she need it. This was insane, but seeing Spence had clearly lost his mind, it came down to her to make sure they were safe.

"My bike." Eli pointed at it. "It's gonna get drenched. I'll just go and cover it, if you don't mind, I have something for that in the saddles."

"Bring it in," Spencer said, "leave it under the awning, it'll be dry."

At a run, Eli left the garden, sat astride his bike and drove it through the double gate, parking in front of the garage's door, wondering why Spencer didn't use it.

"My mother's car is still in there," Spence clarified, reading Eli's expression.

They huddled through the front door, Nyx stomping off straight to the stairs, so she could hide in her room. Spencer grabbed her by the arm, shook his head, nodded towards the capacious living-room. Then he ushered Eli and followed them in.

"Sit down." The invitation sounded more like an order, one Nyx didn't dare disobey. For whatever reason, neither did Eli, and they sat on opposite chairs, eyes on Spencer. "Right. Look, Eli, I'm of a mind to take you on your word. The names you just said, I doubt you'd know them if you hadn't been raised by Serge. How long have you known?"

"Only just recently."

"What are you doing? Spence, why are you even talking to him?"

"Nyx, pull yourself together. Your mother had a child ten years before you were born, all right? Our mother made her give up the babe, handed it to a couple by the names of Serge and Ora Sylvain. So there's a good chance this man here is your brother, my nephew, Erin's son. Now shut up and let me think."

Pacing the room, Spencer studied his options. He'd have to call the law firm. "How recently? Why did they tell you after all these years?"

From inside his leather jacket Eli fished an envelope, handed it to Spencer, who raised his eyebrows in question.

"Just read it."

Spencer opened the envelope and fished out an official-looking letter, which he studied in silence for what felt like an inordinate amount of time.

"I see," he finally said, and handed the envelope back to Eli.

The young man handed it to Nyx, the girl sitting back in her chair as if afraid it might contaminate her.

"Please, just read it," Eli begged, and she caved in. "I was told everything, after this came. Even that my adoptive mother used to drive us to Havenleah, after Nyx was born, so I could spend time with Erin and my sister. I don't remember much of it, though. Think I must have been about ten, eleven? Then we stopped going because Erin wanted us to stay away. That's what I was told."

"Spence," Nyx whined. "How can any of this be true?"

"Honey, I'm sorry. My sister did have a child when she was younger than you, a child she had to forsake. I'm sorry, Eli, but I need to be sure you are who you claim to be."

The young man stood up, wiped his hands down the leg of his jeans. "I understand. Is there a B&B I can stay at, for the time being? The reading of the will is not until next Thursday, I don't fancy going back up to my parents only to have to drive down here again in a few days."

"Yes, there's the Pointer House, I'm sure I can..."

"Why did you come?" Nyx cut in. "I mean, why did you come here so many days in advance?"

Eli blushed, and Spencer felt sorry for him. What must he be going through, finding out after what, twenty-five years? That he was adopted, had a sister, a grandmother who'd left a will he must attend the reading of, and everyone who was supposed to be his family only doubted his word, his identity? How must that feel like?

"I wanted to meet you first. The two of you. Had no idea if you knew I existed, but I wasn't going to let this hit you in the face the day of the reading. Had to make sure you knew."

"Well, looks like I'm the only one who didn't, right?"

"He hasn't known for years, either, Nyx, don't be a victim. Like I said, I was only respecting your parents' wishes."

"My mother abandoned me when I was five, my father passed away before I turned sixteen, don't you think that between then and now you could have told me something about this? After all, they're no longer in the picture, are they? You've always known, and you never went looking for him?"

"I had no idea where he was. Come on, Nyx, my sister gave him up for adoption, what was I to do? Our mother saw to it that..."

"That what, Spence? This is unjustifiable, you know? Have you never asked yourself if he was safe, well-cared for, loved? Your own nephew."

"My adoptive parents did all they could for me. I've been very much loved and well-cared for," Eli whispered, placing worried eyes on Spencer.

"That's not the point. He should have searched for you, I should have been told. I had the right to know I have a brother. There were times in my life when I could have used someone who understood."

"Understood what?" Spencer asked, sounding tired, defeated.

"What it's like to have a mother who doesn't care for us, doesn't love us." Storming out, Nyx stomped up the stairs and shut herself in her room with a loud bang of the door, which echoed through the entire house.

Spencer made as if to leave and follow her, but Eli grabbed hold of his arm.

"Let her, it'll be for the best." Letting go of his uncle, as he noticed the dissatisfied look in his eyes, Eli held up his hands. "Look, it's none of my business, I just thought... never mind, I'd better go. It's been nice meeting you, uncle. And my sister, too. Pointer House, you said?"

Spencer shook his head, ran uncertain fingers through his hair. "I'll take you there. I need to go into town, need to talk to the law firm that's been handling our family's affairs. Just follow me with your bike, will you?" Stepping towards the landing, Spencer eyed the upper floor, hoping Nyx would come out of her room and join him. He didn't fancy meeting Max Everley on his own. "Nyx, I'm going out," he shouted at her. "Going to talk this through with the lawyers. Eli's coming with me, I'm taking him to Pointer House. Nyx?"

"Drive carefully," she bellowed from her room, but didn't bother coming out.

Spencer shrugged, directed Eli to the door. "Let's go, I'll sort her out later."

II

Nyx paced the room for a few seconds, then found herself running out to the landing, headed for the small round window. Balancing on her toes, she took a peek, hands on the window-ledge, spying the two men. Spencer sat in his car, engine revving, gates open so he could drive out, waiting for Eli to stride his bike.

Eli.

How could he be her brother? Studying him, Nyx took in his features, seeing Spence in them, but something else, too, equally familiar. She'd come across a couple of pictures of Corinna Vaughn and their own mother - Eli did bear a resemblance to both women. His colours were Corinna's: the honey-hued hair, the blue of the eyes. His smile, though, that was Erin Vaughn to a dot. Nyx had a photo of her parents in her bedroom, when Erin had been in her late twenties, and the smile on her mother's lips was just like Eli's. Crooked, shy, elusive, but so appealing. Making it easy to believe he could indeed be her elder brother. A child Erin had also abandoned, a child she'd hidden from her own daughter, as much as she hid Nyx from Eli, preventing them from getting to know each other, and growing up together.

What sort of mother did that?

What sort of mother abandoned her children?

A sense of relief washed over her. It wasn't Nyx's fault, after all, it never had been. There was nothing wrong with her, she hadn't pushed her mother away. It was all Erin. Erin was intrinsically flawed, broken, defective. It was she who'd run from her own children, left them to the care of others, and for what? Because she couldn't be bothered, couldn't be burdened? Because she lacked a mother's capacity to love and care, to support, to be present? Maybe she'd feared being like Corinna, who according to Spencer was only capable of demanding and ordering, who'd never tried to understand or support her children, never stood by them.

Or could there be something else? Hadn't Eli said something about going to Havenleah so Erin could see him? If she'd wanted distance, why would she have Eli's adoptive mother drive him there? Something wasn't right, what was Eli hiding? What had Erin been doing, why had she left? What if Eli himself was as much in the dark as Nyx about their mother's reasons for leaving them both? What if Eli was really her brother?

She couldn't afford to not let him in, *didn't want to*. There was no one else but her and Spence, no more family. Well, that wasn't really correct, was it? There was Sarah, and all her kids. But they weren't as close to Nyx as Spence, who'd been a surrogate parent all her life. And if Eli was her brother, it made him even closer. They shared the same mother, the same blood.

Watching him ease the bike out of the yard, Nyx sighed. If only there was a way to be sure. Hopefully, Spence's conversation with Max Everley would shed some light on the subject. A small, amused smile drew itself on her lips. Spence and Max, forced alone and into intimate, painful subjects. Well, maybe it would bring about the closure her uncle sorely needed. Or rekindle the flame that once was there? It wasn't fair, now; Max was married and with two children, what would something like this do to his family? How would Trystan react?

Her mobile pinged, and Nyx ran back to the bedroom. A new message from Trystan, as if on cue - hadn't she been thinking of him? She slid a finger across the screen, read it eagerly, already composing a reply in her mind. She wanted to talk to someone about this, about Eli, but couldn't. No one had asked her to keep her would-be brother a secret, but before it was official, Nyx knew it was better to drop it. Settling for a bland reply, she texted him back, stating she wasn't doing much except homework. A lie, but a white one, and Trystan wouldn't know. Before she could drop the phone back on her bed, it rang in her hand. A phone call, this time from Pip. He'd be harder to elude. For a brief moment, Nyx considered not answering, but courage failed her. She needed a friendly voice to distract her uneasy mind.

"Hi," she greeted.

"Hey, are you ok?"

He was an Empath, this shouldn't surprise her. Maybe Pip was right, and she did need more ink, if only to maintain her privacy and his sanity.

"What do you mean?"

"Nyx, come on, we've been over this. I can feel your moods. There was a change a while ago, it hit me like a stone, and at first I couldn't make sense where it came from. Thought it was Trystan having another row with his dad. But then I knew it was you. What's wrong? How can I help?"

She sighed. Why did he have to be so nice, so obliging? Why did he have to make it all so much harder? "It's a family thing, there's nothing you can do, no one can. It'll sort itself soon, I hope."

"Fine. Do you want some company? I can sense your distress."

That's it, she was having another bird inked next morning. One that harnessed her emotions and kept them private at all times. Why was she settling for birds? After the feather, Nyx had already returned to the tattoo parlour and had a couple more birds inked on her arm and shoulder. Birds she'd drawn, and that looked a lot like the ones she'd spotted in the woods, those uncanny birds that resembled kestrels, but weren't kestrels, not with those coloured feathers of theirs. She'd inked them in black, though, as the feather, but couldn't deny inspiration for her motifs had come from that flock.

"I'm fine, just waiting for Spencer to come back home. But thanks for your concern, I mean it."

"Sure. Listen, if you need to talk, I'm here, Nyx. I'm a pretty good listener. You can call me anytime, all right? Night and day."

"Thank you, I will. Have to go now, Pip. Talk to you soon."

"Bye, then. Take care."

She cut the call and scrolled through the screen to read the texts that had come in while she was on the phone with Pip. All from Trystan, jocose and playful, a distraction from the thoughts cramming her mind. She replied in the same vein, laughing out loud at each new message, until Trystan had to go. Then Nyx found herself alone, with only her thoughts to keep her company, and she didn't much care for them. She didn't much care for the confusion in her mind, jumping from a state of elation and joy at the thought she might have an elder brother, to the opposite state of fury and panic, that she might have a brother she'd been kept away from. It scared her, not knowing what was behind all this. It terrified her not knowing if Eli was honest and could be trusted, it horrified her not knowing what the future might bring, after all this. Because it had to be connected with what Max Everley had told them, that there was another will.

The thought hit her like cold water. The bedroom. The *third* bedroom.

Jumping from her seat, Nyx ran towards what had been Corinna's room. The room both she and Spencer had assumed was meant for Tom, were he still alive. How wrong they'd been.

Folding one hand over the round doorknob, she turned it and eased the door open.

This was never meant to be Tom's room.

This was Eli's.

Corinna had known about him all along, and kept an eye on him, knew him well enough. For Nyx could see the young man who'd turned up at their doorstep feeling very at home inside this room. It matched him to a dot, the clothes he'd been wearing, the bike, the personality. This room was meant for Eli, and Corinna had arranged for them all to meet. But why now, after all these years? Because she felt guilty of all she'd done? Because she wanted to force her family back to Weaversmoor? Because she knew they'd be safer here? Their place was amongst the magical community, with people like them, that was a given. Maybe this was the only way Corinna knew to make them come back home, where they belonged.

Maybe this wasn't a bad thing, after all.

"How can I help you?" the stern, professional-looking girl at the reception desk inquired.

Spencer ran a hand through his hair; he hated dealing with this kind of people. He didn't much like to deal with people, and that was that.

"I need to see someone on the team who handled my mother's affairs, I told you already. Corinna Vaughn."

"Sir, if you don't have an appointment, then..."

"Is Max Everley in?" he finally asked, stripped of patience. "Tell him Spencer Vaughn is here, I guarantee he'll see me."

The girl paled, pressed her lips together into a thin, forbidding line. "If you'll take a seat, please?"

Spencer headed back to the chairs she'd gestured, perched on one, leg shaking, heart drumming like a machine gun. He couldn't hear what the girl said, but soon after putting down the phone she'd been talking on, Max Everley's figure loomed over him. Spence stood up, sweating, face reddening as his eyes met Max's. Lord, he'd aged well, hadn't he? Still looked as handsome as ever, if not better. The same bright eyes, the same lips, the high forehead - he was a vision. Still looked fit, too; Max had always been much more of a jock than Spencer, who'd used to sit watching him work out his firm body inside their dorm room.

"Spencer, I'm glad you came. Come on in, please."

He followed Max across the corridor, into a spacious, light office room. Max had done well for himself, in the career he'd dreamt of throughout their school years. A career he'd have been forced to forsake if he'd stayed with Spencer. Well, not quite; Max would still have been a lawyer, just not on his father's firm, and not with his father's money. Would he have ended up resenting Spencer, if they'd stayed together, back then? Pushing those thoughts away, he declined Max's offer of something to drink and took a seat on a chair facing the impressive desk dominating the entire room. Instead of taking his place behind it, Max opted to sit across from Spencer, their knees so close together they almost touched.

"So," the man said, and actually looked lost for words, as if he hadn't expected Spence to be here. "About Corinna's affairs. We thought it was all taken care of, but then we got this." He fished an official-looking letter from a folder and handed it to Spencer, who read it eagerly.

"Your *constituents*?"

"You and Nyx. We are your legal representatives, after all."

"Do you have any idea about the contents of this new will? Nyx is terrified we have to leave Weaversmoor."

Max reached out a hand, placed it over Spencer's with a gentle squeeze. Pulled it back the moment he saw the forbidding look in his eyes. "Not quite, but... look, I might as well say it, you'll know soon enough. Your mother seems to have located..."

"Erin's first child, I know. Well, it was mother who saw to the adoption, after all, I'm sure she must have kept an eye on him all along."

"How do you know?"

Spencer ran a shaky hand through his hair once more. "He just showed up at the cottage, and I swear to you, Max, his resemblance to my own mother is uncanny. I'm pretty sure he's who he claims to be, Erin's eldest son, Eli Vaughn."

"Did he present any evidence of his identity?"

Spencer sighed, closed his eyes, sitting back in the chair. "How much has mother told you? Cressida?"

"Your mother never said a word to *me*. She did confide somewhat in my father. Cressida told me the whole thing. I confess I've had a hard time believing her, especially because she did so when massively drunk. Which seems to be every other day."

Spencer eyed him, and his stomach cartwheeled at the thought there might be trouble in paradise for good old Max. It was oddly vindicating to learn he didn't have a happy marriage, but then again, Spence never expected him to. Max wasn't bisexual, he was gay, and being in a heterosexual relationship was sure to drive him up the wall. But it was the choice he'd made.

"What of your father? He never said a thing?"

"Oh yes, he had a lot to say in the weeks prior to his death. Corinna must have given him the green light, he'd never spoken of the subject before."

"What did he say? Why is Erin's son being brought back to Weaversmoor? Actually, why are both my sister's children being forced here?"

It was Max who sighed, now. "Are you sure I can't get you a drink? Fine. Cressida told me about Erin's powers as a Weaver. That they can weave a way into another world? They can open portals between our world and this other realm, where your sister met the father of her eldest child."

"Yes, that's true. Fionn was not from our world."

"Did you ever meet him?"

Spencer nodded. "The day Erin gave birth, he crossed over by himself. Demanded the child, and took him and my sister away. Remember mother saying she'd run away? It was to this other world she did. They were forced out of it five years later, along with a couple who helped them. See, from the little I was allowed to understand, Fionn was someone of importance in that realm, and his attachment to my sister was forbidden. Somehow I think Weavers are forbidden there. So she tried to keep her children out of this place, because they're Weavers too. That's about all I know."

"Where's your sister?"

"I have no idea. Took off ten years ago, never said a word again. I thought something had happened to Eli, or to Fionn, but the boy seems to be well and thriving, if indeed the bloke who showed up at my door is Erin's son."

"Corinna arranged for extensive DNA testing, according to this London law firm. There's no doubt the boy she was monitoring is Erin's son. Here, they sent us a small file on him."

Max retrieved the folder, gave it to Spencer, who opened it to the sight of the same man he'd just accompanied to the reception desk at Pointer House.

"It's him, the bloke who came to the cottage."

"So he's Erin's child, Spence. Corinna was monitoring him all along, I think. At least for the past couple of years, look at all these reports."

"But why would she arrange for him to come here? I mean, she was the first to insist Erin gave him to that couple and stayed away from him. She prompted my sister into marrying Tom and forget about the boy. She herself wanted nothing to do with him, so why this, why now?"

Clearing his throat, Max stood up, paced around the room, clearly shaken. "According to my father, the Weavers have a preponderant role. There seem to be spots where crossing to this other realm is... easier? Where those who belong in that other world can easily step into ours, at least. Weaversmoor is one of those places. It takes the combined powers of a few Weavers to keep this pathway locked. My father was one, and when he died, Corinna was left alone. She probably knew the moment she passed away these locks would be open?" He returned to his seat, balanced himself at the edge of the chair.

Spencer nodded, he'd hinted as much from his mother's several loud arguments with Erin. Maybe Corinna had wanted Erin away from Weaversmoor. His sister had been so intent on opening a route back to that other realm, if only to be with Fionn, whom she'd never stopped loving, even after marrying Tom Wilson.

"They didn't want that to happen. For some reason I wasn't told, it's adamant creatures from that other world don't step into ours. They're supposed to be dangerous?" Max went on. "So I think your mother wanted to make sure there were two Weavers here who could keep those gateways closed. She orchestrated your return to Weaversmoor, along with Nyx and Eli. I'm sure this new testament will present Eli as heir to the house along with you and Nyx. And there'll be some sort of trust fund in his name, too. But we'll know more when the meeting takes place. So, how are you?"

Their eyes met, lingered over each other, as if taking in the changes time had ravished upon them. Spencer wet his lips. How could this man still hold so much power over him, how could Max still have such an effect on him, after all he'd done and the way he'd crushed Spencer's hopes and dreams, along with his heart?

"Max, I don't want to do this."

The other man slid from the chair he sat upon, came to kneel in front of Spencer, grabbing hold of his hands.

"You have no idea what it's been like," he whispered, and Spencer's resolve faltered at the ache he heard in Max's voice. "Cressida and I, it was a mistake, and I always knew it. I was terrified of my father, your mother, I was weak." Max tightened the grip on Spencer's fingers, sensing him pull away. "But I never stopped loving you, Spence. I never managed to get you out of my heart. I pleaded with her, that she told me where you were, I was ready to give it all up. This was some twelve years ago, I'd just realised how toxic an environment Cressida and I were providing for the children. I asked her for the divorce, so many times. Begged Corinna to tell me where you were living, so I could go to you. She said you were in a relationship, very happy with your partner, that I shouldn't intrude."

Spencer pulled his hands free. "She lied. But it doesn't matter, Max, we're not doing this." He stood up, eyes searching for the door, judging the distance. All he wanted was to get away from Max, lest he crumpled and fell under his spell again. "You're a married man, you have children, and I won't be the side dish. Ever."

Max took hold of his shoulders, turning Spencer round so they faced each other. He was stronger, taller, and a lot more intent on his purposes than Spence. "I love you, don't you get it? Always have. Never stopped loving you. I've been miserable all my life since I let you go. I've hated myself for letting you go. I've hated you for finding someone else, even though I had no right, even though I knew I should be happy for you. But I just couldn't, I love you and want to be with you. I tried to find you, but your mother and sister did a pretty good job of keeping your whereabouts secret."

Spencer shook himself free, walked towards the door of the room, shaking his head. The bruised look in his eyes turned to a cold, soulless stare, when he managed to face Max again.

"You mustn't have tried very hard. You used to know me better than anyone else in the world, Max. You were my best friend, my lover, my everything. So you surely remember how I held grudges, back then, right? You must remember how it was always impossible for me to forgive others, when they hurt and betrayed me knowingly. My mother stands as the perfect example, I never once spoke to her again, after all she did to tear us apart. So what on earth makes you think you can waltz your way back into my life?"

Max opened his mouth to speak, but Spencer held up one hand, preventing him. "You broke my heart, you as good as destroyed me. I was never able to trust again. So we're not doing this. You're married, with children, and your son is sort of dating my niece. There's not going to be an *'us'* again, ever. All our dealings will be purely business."

"I'm going to divorce Cressida. Have already started the procedure," Max went on, despite Spencer's head shaking. "I'm not doing this for you, stop being so self-centred, that was always your biggest fault, Spence. I'm doing this for me, for my sanity, my mental health. I need to be who I am, not this puppet my father demanded I became. It's a shame I took this long to take a stand, but Cress never made it easy, and I was wrongly mistaken it would be better for the kids that we stuck together. It isn't, it's toxic, and I'm going to put an end to it. It'll get messy, but I *will* be free. And I will spend the rest of my life trying to make it up to you, if I have to."

Spencer held the doorknob, his back to Max, dreading the moment he'd have to face him. Heart bursting against his ribs, he tried to tone down the meaning of the other man's words. Max had played him before, he'd never have the guts to come out, he'd never be man enough to face Cressida, even with his own father gone. But goosebumps still erupted all over his arms, at the thought of what he'd just been told, and the possibilities Max's promises seemed to hold. Promises Spencer wanted so much to believe, to give in to, just so he could hold Max in his arms again. Just so he could love him once more.

"I have to go."

"Spencer, please don't hate me."

That sweet voice of his, how could he fight it? How could he fight the emotions it woke, the memories it brought, the extreme happiness he'd once known with this very same man, who'd later ripped apart his heart? How could he allow Max to do the same again? Without another word, Spencer opened the door and walked out. If Max did divorce Cressida, then maybe he'd give him the benefit of doubt. Maybe he'd try to trust him again. But until then, all Spencer wanted was to keep a safe distance between the two of them.

Because he wasn't sure he was strong enough to resist, if Max came for him.

III

Trystan waited for Nyx to strap the helmet under her chin and hop back on the bike behind him. A chilly wind gusted around them, lifting clumps of sodden leaves off the ground in pockets that fell back a few inches from where they'd originated. The night was cold but clear, not one cloud in the sky. The weather had been holding after the intense rainfall on Friday, Saturday offering Weaversmoor a beautiful autumn day - golden in colour and brisk in temperature. And it had held for the entire evening, to the point he already regretted having spent it cooped up in a musty cinema instead of taking Nyx for a bike ride and a walk, followed by a nice meal. Well, the meal had been nice, if a bit silent. He suspected Nyx would still have preferred going to the cinema, something was off with her. She'd been morose and in a bit of a mood the entire time. Maybe he'd read the signs wrong, and she wasn't much into him, after all.

Once he felt her safely seated behind him, one hand coiled around his waist for balance, Trystan ventured reaching for the other one, tucking it under his shearling-lined biker's jacket. Nyx didn't pull back; in fact she burrowed her hand further into the coat, caressing his stomach, muscles crisp under her touch. Good thing Bryn had let him borrow the bike. He revved up the engine and took off, the night stretching before them with the road, a starlit sky lighting their way. It felt good to have Nyx here, warm against him. Even the silence had become somewhat comfortable, as if both were too entranced by each other's company to manage much of a conversation. But the ride from the town centre to Vaughn cottage was a short one, and she did have a curfew Trystan intended on keeping, loathe as he was of having her uncle oppose their dating.

Slowing at the curve, he eased the bike up the driveway, eyes trained on the chopper parked under the garage awning. Here was a sight he hadn't expected; whose bike was this? Trystan parked by the front gate, waited for Nyx to hop off before doing the same. She freed her head of curls from the helmet and tossed them around, hair bouncing up and down her neck. He wanted to touch those curls, run fingers through them, pull her towards him so they kissed, but shied from the action. What if she didn't want to be kissed? Ridding himself of his own helmet, he received Nyx's, placed them both on the seat. Then inched closer, hands grasping the lapels of her coat.

"Everything all right?" he asked. "You've been oddly quiet the entire evening."

Nyx blushed. "I'm sorry, not much of a company tonight, am I?"

"Wanna talk about it?"

She shrugged. Sensing her discomfort, Trystan settled for a change of subject, turning his head to the right so he caught sight of the chopper again.

"Didn't know your uncle had a motorbike. Bryn's going to freak when she sees it, that's the one she wanted, but mother put her foot down."

Nyx's eyes darkened with a shadow of irritation, as she, too, focused on the bike.

"It's not Spencer's. Apparently, I have an elder brother no one bothered telling me about, and now he's here. He's *always* here."

Trystan was taken aback; this was the last thing he expected. "What?"

"Yeah, shows up last Thursday at our doorstep claiming to be my mother's eldest child. Like, mother had a baby when she was younger than me. And no one told me this. Spencer kept this from me."

"Wow, that's just... wow. Are you sure?"

Nyx shrugged, eyes brimming with tears. Trystan pulled her into his arms, no longer caring how she might perceive his actions. The girl was obviously disturbed by the news, and in need of some comfort. The little he knew of her assured him she relied on her uncle as if he was a parent, and this must have felt like the ultimate betrayal. Something Trystan could understand and relate to.

"According to your father, there's been DNA testing, and yes, he's..."

Pushing her slightly away so he could look into her eyes, Trystan kept his arms around Nyx. "Wait, my father knew of this? And he didn't tell your uncle?"

"He told Spencer there was another law firm with a new will. Told him to meet him so they could talk about it. We were in a coffee shop, I'm sure your dad didn't want to blab about it in front of all those people. In front of me, probably. So Spence went to see him, but Eli had already shown up at our door and introduced himself as my brother. There were photos, though, on the file, and according to Spence, it's the same man. Grandmother had him followed or something."

Head reeling, Trystan took a deep breath. "I'm sorry, you're not making much sense. A law firm? Another will? What's your grandmother got to do with this? And where did this brother come from?"

Nyx sighed, annoyance resounding through her entire frame. "Apparently mother had a fling with an older bloke when she was fifteen. It ended badly, she got pregnant, and he bailed, as expected."

Trystan winced at what her voice hinted. He'd have a lot to make up for, just for being male. "Ok, what else?"

"Mother had the baby and grandmother forced her to give him up for adoption, but kept an eye on him. Well, so did mum, according to Eli. He used to come see us at Havenleah when I was just a baby. But then mum stopped taking me, and years passed, and he never saw her again. I think he had some sort of problem, he says the oddest things sometimes, and doesn't know like, basic stuff? Like, he didn't even know how to use social media, or WhatsApp. I mean, it's not as if he's old, not like Spencer, and Spence knows how to use all the apps, know what I mean? But he doesn't talk much. Or I don't listen, I guess."

"What about the will? And my dad?"

Sighing again, Nyx leaned against Trystan's chest, inhaling deeply of his woody scent, the soft wool of his cashmere jersey against her face relaxing her shoulders and her countenance.

"Grandmother had another will done in London. She kept Eli's existence from everyone. Well, not everyone, obviously, because certain people must have known Mum was pregnant. Like Aunt Sarah, she must have known. And your mother, they were best friends. Your Dad found out when this other firm contacted him, because his firm handles Spencer's affairs, and mine too, I guess. Anyway, the new will is being read next week, on the second. They're coming in from London, so as to not be too disruptive."

"But what of this brother? He always knew and never tried to contact you, your Mum?"

Nyx shook her head. "He only knew for sure when he got a letter from the lawyers. That's when his adoptive parents told him the whole thing. He wanted to come here before the reading of the will, because apparently," her words were infused with sarcasm and disbelief, "he didn't want me to find out from someone outside the family. He didn't know if Spencer was aware of his existence, either. Should have been mad the truth was kept from him all these years, but no, he's all chummy with Spence, as if they've known each other all their lives."

"Maybe they're trying to make up for lost time. Maybe they hit it off straight away. Maybe you should give him a chance?"

Nyx pulled away from Trystan, his arms falling to the side of his body, hands hanging for lack of what to do with them. He wanted to hold her again, but the darkening of her eyes told him he'd better hold back.

"You're taking his side?"

"I'm taking *your* side. I can tell you're conflicted. I can see you want to let him in; after all, he's family, your brother. But you're scared, and suspicious, I get it, it's only natural. Look, what I'm saying is I'm here for you." Trystan held out his hand; Nyx took it.

"Maybe I should go in, then, see what they're about."

"You do that." He smiled and ventured pulling her closer.

Thumb softly caressing her cheek, Trystan took in her freckles, the blue of her eyes, the moist, plump lips. Those charming, bewitching, spellbinding lips he longed to kiss. What the hell, he was gonna try for it and deal with the consequences.

Lowering his head, guts coiling like snakes around his belly, Trystan closed his eyes, parted his mouth. A soft breeze caressed him; he realised it was Nyx's breath, the scent of bubblegum forcing him to smile.

But then he no longer wanted to grin. Well, in fact he did, he wanted to whoop for joy and his face wanted to burst apart in the largest, widest smile the world had ever seen, because he was kissing her. Their lips were locked together, tongues tentatively reaching for each other to start learning their own particular dance - and his spine tingled with excitement and joy, and his chest burst in happiness, and his heart stampeded like a wild horse on an empty meadow, his entire body flaring in a fire the likes of which he'd never experienced.

The kiss was brief, and sweet, and Nyx didn't push him away. They parted lips with soft, teasing pecks, eyes opening to greet one another, smiles drawn across their mouths. Joining his forehead to hers, Trystan sighed. This was what he'd hoped for ever since Jamal had introduced them. This was what he wanted, and the fact she wanted it too was beyond his belief.

"I'll call you tomorrow," he whispered, gifting her another kiss. "Listen, we're having a Halloween party on the 31st, it's also Bryn's birthday, will you come? I'll get you an invitation; you can bring your uncle and your brother, if you want."

Nyx eyed him, a blush gracing her cheeks. "I already agreed to go with Pip."

Trystan's eyes widened, he hadn't expected this. Pip hadn't mentioned it either, which usually meant it was no big deal. Whenever Pip was actively into someone, Trystan and Bryn were the first to know, he just couldn't keep such things to himself. But Trystan hadn't even realised the two had become friends.

"Is that a problem for you?"

Kissing Nyx again, he grinned. "Nah, as long as you're there. You're my girl now, aren't you?"

"Am I?" she teased, and softly bit his lower lip. "When was I consulted about this?"

"Just now, when I kissed you. Ah, don't be mean, Nyx, say you're my girl." His voice came down a couple of notches, throaty and shaking with emotion. "I don't believe you don't feel the way I feel."

She nodded against his head. "I do. I want to be your girl, Trystan. But now I really have to go. Text me when you get home, will you?"

Trystan kissed her, deep and long. "Promise. Now go."

He watched Nyx run off towards the house, and only when she shut the door behind her did he get on the bike and leave, a stupid grin on his lips.

Making sure he parked at Bryn's preferred spot and hung the helmets on their pegs, Trystan fished his phone from inside his jacket and texted Nyx he was safely home, laughing at her reply. Was this really happening? He still found it hard to believe. What about Pip?

Wondering why his friend had asked Nyx out without mentioning it to him, Trystan searched his number and pressed dial. It was best to have it out as soon as possible, on the off chance they were both going for the same girl. It wasn't as if Trystan had said anything about his date with Nyx either, but he'd wanted to keep quiet until he knew it was a sure thing and he could officially call her his girlfriend. After a couple of rings, Pip answered.

"What's up, Everley?"

"Where are you?"

"Dorm. You?"

"Backyard. Just came home from a date with Nyx Vaughn." The silence on the other end of the line was uncomfortable and lasted longer than Trystan had expected.

"You and Nyx, huh?" Pip finally said. "Had no idea you were into her. How did it go?"

"We kissed."

"So, it's not a one-off."

"Nope. We're officially a thing."

WITCH CRAFT

The silence stretched a bit longer, Trystan sweating uncomfortably. It had never crossed his mind they might one day fall for the same girl. He knew Pip almost as well as he knew himself, knew about his friend's feelings for him. Trystan had made sure Pip understood there was no chance Trys would come to fancy him, but he'd also made sure his friend knew how much he loved him, like a brother, a mate, his best friend. They'd talked about the uncomfortable subject of Pip's infatuation for Trystan only once, and that had been it. Pip had gone on to snog other people, boys and girls alike, Trystan had acted as if nothing had changed, nor been said between them. But it had never crossed his mind this could come to happen, and now he had no idea what to say, what to think.

"Okay. So, I should tell you I asked her to the Halloween party. Hope you're all right with this? I can always take back the invitation, now the two of you are an item."

That would make him look petty, wouldn't it? And it wasn't as if Nyx was going to spend the entire party with Pip, not when the two of them were dating, she'd want to be with Trystan. Deciding not to make a big deal of it, he shook his head. "No, it's fine. It's not as if she won't be with me, right?"

Another odd silence, and Trystan's misgivings grew. Pip *did* have feelings for her that went beyond mere friendship. He just hoped they hadn't taken a more serious turn; not this early, surely?

"Right. So, talk to you tomorrow?"

"Yeah, sure."

"Have a good sleep, Everley."

"Behave yourself, Thomson. Bye."

He cut the call just as he opened the front door and stepped in. To be greeted by the loud voices of both his parents on one of their shouting matches. Wincing, he made as if to run up the stairs and avoid them all together; he was in too good a mood to allow it to be ruined by this. But the sight of his drunken mother staggering out of the library, tears streaming down her face, made it impossible for him to ignore what was going on. Searching around, Trystan wondered where Bryn was, she'd been minus her bike, where had she gone off to? Jamal's perhaps, to be driven back later by one of his parents? Hadn't she mentioned Sarah Wilson asking them to baby-sit for Jamal's twin sisters and his kid brother this evening, so his parents could go on a date? Just his luck to be home alone for this.

His mother tottered towards the stairs, ignoring him. She ran up to her room, the loud sound of her sobs reaching down to him, until she closed the door behind her with a bang. Should he go after her? Knowing Mum as he did, she'd want to be alone for a while. Then she'd come find one of her kids so she could complain about their father and how horrid he was to her. Which Trystan knew only too well to be true. Max Everley had been cheating on his wife practically since they'd first said their vows in the local chapel, and Trystan had seen with his own eyes the evidence of his father's misbehaviour. Angered by yet another treason, and the horrible effects his father's affairs had on his family, Trystan sped into the library, hands clenched, face red and fuming.

"What the hell did you do this time?" he barked, his father turning to stare wide-eyed at him. "What did you do that got her like this? Aren't you sick of hurting her constantly? You hurt us all, can't you see?"

Max gulped down the rest of his drink, shaking his head at his son. "You don't know what you're saying. I'm sorry if the constant arguments hurt you and your sister, but I'm not the only one at fault, here."

"Why don't you simply divorce her? For appearances' sake you put us all through this hell when you could just set her free, set yourself free to go around with whoever you want. Just because you're ashamed you're gay?"

His father's hand slapped across Trystan's face. He placed a cooling palm against it, fighting the tears that threatened to spill. Max ran trembling hands through his thick, dark hair, shuddering.

"I'm sorry I hit you, that was uncalled for," he whispered, seating himself on the corner of a square table, laden with trinkets and frames filled with photos that depicted the lie they all lived in: a perfect, happy family. "I'm not ashamed I'm gay. I was, though, for many a year, my father saw to it. How many times do you think I've asked your mother for a divorce? She's the one who won't let go, Trystan, not me."

"Liar," he whispered, eyes blazing with an anger Trystan knew could become dangerous. If he lost control, his powers would come blazing, literally, and starting a fire inside a library was a sure recipe for disaster. "I've seen you go behind her back, you and your lovers. But then you come home all sweet talk and red roses, and you cover her in jewels and lavish holidays, and think it makes up for everything, every single treason, every humiliation? You're disgusting; the world's biggest hypocrite."

His father stared numbly at him. His eyes, which at first seemed blank, sparkled with hidden emotions, an ache so acute it shook his son's beliefs. He realised he must have hurt him like never before. Good, Max Everley deserved to be told a couple of truths; he deserved to be as hurt as he kept hurting his family.

"You have no idea what you're talking about, son."

His anger grew. Was his father going to deny his blame much longer? Was he just going to keep skirting responsibility? Fire flared inside his brain, threatening to burst forth. A pair of hands alighted over Trystan's shoulders, his eyes frantic in search of who it could be. Bryn stood behind him, shaking her head. He reined in his emotions.

"He just drives me mad, Bryn," he whispered, turning away from his father.

Max got up from the table, walked off to the door. "I'm sorry you don't believe me, but it's no surprise. Your mother's a master manipulator, after all. She's been feeding you lies all along. I'm not innocent, nor do I pretend to be, but it's Cressida who constantly refuses to set me free." He stomped out of the room, shoulders drooping as if defeated.

"Dad, where are you going?" Bryn shouted after him.

"Out. Don't wait up for me."

"Can you believe the nerve? Out, after he brought her to tears. Out, to be with one of his lovers. I hate him."

"Trystan, you don't know shit," Bryn said, letting go of her brother. "It's mother who refuses to let go, she won't give him the divorce."

"That's not true, he just wants to keep up appearances."

Bryn shook her head. "He's filed for a divorce, though it won't be uncontested. Things may get messy, if Mother insists on making it so, but Dad's intent on really doing it this time, he's intent on being free to live his own life. Don't you think it'll be better for every one, if they do get divorced?"

Trystan shook his head, eyes liquid with unshed tears. "You're always taking his side, no one sees to Mum, the two of you gang up on her and..."

"And what? Good heavens, you're such a fool! You can't force someone to love you. Dad doesn't love her, never did. Ok, he made a huge mistake marrying her, but look, he's been trying to do the right thing for years, now, ever since Granddad passed away. She refuses, all the time, she hinders him, threatens him, that she'll kill herself, that she'll hurt one of us, take us away from him. Mother's been manipulating you and dad all these years, don't you see?"

"No, Bryn, I don't. What I do see is you being played by dad, just like he does everyone. He's telling you what he wants, and you buy into every lie he feeds you. Man's a scoundrel, and you're so into the role of daddy's little girl you couldn't see the truth if it hit you in the face."

Trystan stormed out of the room, Bryn trying to get hold of his arm. Shaking himself free, he ran up the stairs, leaving his sister behind. As he walked past their mother's bedroom, he stopped, glued one ear to the door. Silenced greeted him from within; then the soft, low purr of his mother's snore. She was asleep, which was a relief. He'd just had what he thought was the best night of his life, only to see it ruined by his parents' constant fighting; at least he got to recover some of the peace and joy he'd been experiencing. Running off to this own room, Trystan locked himself in, intent on getting into bed and croon himself to sleep with memories of kissing Nyx.

Leaning back on the door, Nyx shut it silently, eyes half-closed and a soft smile on her lips. She traced them with a thumb, stomach dropping like heavy stones as her body remembered the kisses she'd traded with Trystan. A sigh escaped her. She was being silly, but couldn't help the rush of joy brought by the memory of what had just taken place between them.

Then the voice of her estranged brother called her back to reality, and her entire demeanour changed. Bracing herself, Nyx walked into the living room, where Spencer and Eli sat drinking whisky. Spence rarely indulged, and when he did, it was for social reasons alone, the spirits sitting at the bottom of a glass while he nursed his barely touched drink an entire evening. Unless it was wine, and even that he drank moderately. Her mother had liked to drink, hadn't she? The memory caught her unaware, an image of her mother's round face smiling down on her while she sipped her drink, bottle in the other hand, ready for a refill. Yes, Erin had liked to drink. Maybe Eli did, too.

"Hey," Spencer greeted, patting the spot to his left on the velvety sofa, suggesting she sat with them. "How was your date?"

Nyx shrugged. She longed to tell her uncle everything, every little detail of what had happened between her and Trystan, but not with Eli here. She didn't care there were DNA tests to prove he was her brother; didn't care he, too, had been abandoned by their mother, Eli was a stranger and she didn't want him here, breaching her privacy and the close, familiar relationship she shared with Spencer. Eli was meddling, and he had no place.

'Maybe you should give him a chance.'

Trystan's voice echoed in her head, like a shot of guilt straight to the vein, running across her body to the centre of her heart. Which sped in its already hasty drumming, at the thought of Trystan's voice, his eyes, his lips. His kiss. Oh, why couldn't Eli just pick up and leave?

"What's he doing here?" she asked, gracing her brother with her coldest, harshest look.

He blushed, averted his eyes, downed his drink.

"Enough of this, Nyx," Spencer said, his voice loud, unusual on a man who was generally mild and easygoing.

She could count by her fingers the number of times Nyx remembered him shouting. So this was one more thing that was down to Eli. Why didn't he leave?

"Maybe I should go," he finally said, and Nyx exhaled in relief.

"Absolutely not." Spencer stood up and poured Eli another drink, topping his own, which he gulped, as if in need of some respite.

This also had to be hard on him, Nyx realised. Eli was his sister's child, the one he'd been robbed of. Eli was his nephew, one

Spencer wasn't allowed to know and care for; of course he'd want to make up for it, now he had him back. Had Eli told him anything more of what his life had been? She could sense something else lurking beneath his composed demeanour. There was always an undercurrent to Eli, as if he hid something, as if he was reining himself in, baulking from showing his true face, who he was in reality. He put on a mask for them, but Nyx could almost see him underneath.

"My date was fine," she finally said, capitulating to her uncle's will. Crossing the room, Nyx took the armchair across from Eli and sat. "The film was good, the meal could have been better."

"That place is meant to be nice, but cheap. That's why students flock there. You didn't expect Trystan to take you to a five-star restaurant, did you?" Spencer joked, and they both laughed, Eli left out of their personal, private joke. The thought alone comforted Nyx. "Are you seeing him again?"

Nyx blushed, and a mischievous grin crossed her lips. "Yes, next Monday at school. We have classes together."

It was Eli who laughed now, and his entire face smoothed and softened, the blue of his eyes mellowing with the mirth. "Girl's got sass," he said. "Is he your boyfriend, this what's his name?"

"Trystan Everley." Nyx's voice turned colder, as if offended that her own brother didn't know her boyfriend's name. "Yes, he is, why? Do you have a problem with that?"

"Oh, so it's official, then?" Spencer ignored her rudeness, tried to veer the conversation to a milder tone. "Well, he better treat you right, or I'll have a few words with him."

"My thoughts exactly," Eli added. "He better be good to my sister, or I'll sort him out."

Nyx eyed him. Her chest had warmed at the sound of his words, her face too. It hadn't been awkward, much on the contrary. She found herself taken by a sense of belonging, of gratitude, relief even, that Eli was so keen on being her elder brother. The emotion was something unknown, unusual. Akin to feelings she experienced only relating to Spencer; or her father, every time she thought of him after his disappearance at sea.

Love - could that be it? An innate, unconditional love, that wasn't learnt, nor grown, it was simply there, part of her. For Eli was part of her as much as Spencer, Tom, Erin. It appeased, but also scared Nyx. He was a stranger, after all, and she'd had enough loss to last her a lifetime. The last thing she needed was for a brother to show up as a lifeline which she found herself clinging to, family that stood in place for those she'd been robbed of, only to have him leave as soon as the will was read and he had what he'd come for. She realised she was holding back in fear of being hurt.

"Leave Trystan alone, the two of you." Crossing her legs, Nyx turned her attention to Eli. "What about you, do you have a girlfriend?"

"Nope."

"I find that hard to believe, you're the kind of bloke girls throw themselves at, aren't you?"

Eli blushed, smiled his shy little grin, one Nyx was becoming familiar with. "What does that mean?"

"Well, you're good-looking, aren't you? Fit, and handsome, with those blue eyes and that rough shadow of a beard, I can see girls going for that. The biker boy, slightly dangerous, a misfit. Yes, you're the type women like. Unless you're gay, that is," Nyx added, blushing for having been callous to the point she never even considered the option.

"Gay?"

There it was, what she'd mentioned to Trystan. As if he didn't know certain things. How could a twenty-six-year-old not be familiar with terms like that?

"Like Spence; you don't like women, you're into blokes."

Eli looked puzzled, turned to Spencer, studying him. Then his eyes widened in understanding and he grinned. "Ah, no, I'm not gay, I like women."

"What did you say your adoptive parents' names were?" Nyx asked, a sudden thought forming in her head. Maybe he didn't know enough English? She fanned herself with one hand, the room suddenly cloying and far too warm. Had Spence messed up the heating again?

"Ora and Serge Sylvain."

"Sounds French to me."

"It does, doesn't it?"

"So they *are* French? Is that why you seem not to understand certain expressions, not recognise certain things? Because you were raised elsewhere?"

A flicker lit his eyes, it was momentary, but it had been there, Nyx had seen the flare sparkle in the deep blue, knew she was on the right track. Eli had been raised in France, probably. No wonder he struggled with certain expressions. Another flare of heat flooded the room, followed by a distinct jolt of energy. Nyx checked herself, she couldn't afford to lose grip on her powers, not in front of Eli, at least. Not until they were sure he could be trusted.

"I was in a coma for seven years. Only woke up three years ago."

The shock took her by surprise. Nyx had expected pretty much anything: a foreign upbringing, his first language not being English, a secluded infancy, whatever. But not this, surely not this. Her eyes sought her uncle's, saw the stunned look on his face, realised he hadn't known, either. Spencer reached across the coffee table and placed a hand over Eli's, squeezing it. Every nerve in her demanded she did the same, but her legs didn't move, and Nyx sat rooted to her chair, mouth slack and eyes wide.

"Hey, it's no biggie," Eli tried to tone it down. "I'm here now, aren't I? With absolutely no physical sequels."

"What...? How...?" Nyx clamped her mouth shut, finding herself lost for words and any capacity of verbalising her inner turmoil.

"Freak accident," her brother explained. "I was fifteen, went on a camping trip, was hit by the rod sustaining the tent. For some reason, my brain shut down and I went into a coma. Means I had a lot to catch up in the past few years, and certain expressions still elude me."

Nyx shook her head, it all made sense now. He'd been living the past years as a child, re-learning everything. He'd lost his entire adolescence, his early twenties. How awful he must feel, not having finished high school or gone to university, but being old enough to have to provide for himself, find a job, live as an adult when he'd never even been a teenager.

"I'm so sorry," she whispered.

"How on earth have you coped?" Spencer inquired, and Eli looked from Nyx to him.

"It was... awkward? I finished my studies, just didn't apply to university, what's the point? I'm nearly twenty-six but have the emotional range of a kid younger than Nyx. Sometimes I don't know how to react to things, what to say or do, how to respond to people. Because they expect an adult behaviour from me, and I don't always give it them." He grinned, but took another sip from his whisky.

"But there were no sequels? You're fine?"

Eli nodded, took another drink. The subject was obviously making him uncomfortable, Nyx could almost sense his unease. A shadow brimmed her brother's eyes, and she found herself pitying him, he'd lost so much, far more than she had. Mother and father had both given him up, and then this? Seven years in a coma, unaware of the world around him, seven years of his life lost to... what? A black hole of nothingness. Where nothing happened, nothing existed. It wasn't as if he'd been living it up in some alternate reality, was it? Eli had spent seven years sleeping his life away. No friends, no school, no dates. No girlfriends. She was suddenly very self-conscious at the callousness of her question, had he ever had a girlfriend? He must have, these recent years, but how awkward would it have been? He'd become lost to the world at fifteen, and missed all those milestones, only to wake up at twenty-two, having nothing to show for all that lost time. Unless he'd had girlfriends before, dating would have been really awkward for him after waking up from the coma, wouldn't it?

"Maybe we should get you an appointment with a specialist, just to be on the safe side." Spencer insisted, and Eli's face denoted a certain impatience, which Nyx was quick to register.

"Spence, I'm sure his parents took care of everything," she said.

He eyed her with mild irritation, but seemed to ponder and understand her meaning. "Of course, I'm just overreacting; Nyx will tell you I tend to do this. I'm sorry, Eli, didn't mean to hint your parents weren't thorough enough with your health."

Eli nodded. "It's fine. I'm glad to see you care. I was actually very unsure as to how you'd react to my existence, my presence here. I was terrified you wouldn't accept me. It's a relief to see you do."

"I knew of your existence, I'm just sorry I didn't do enough to find you. You have no idea how guilty I feel that I let my mother and Erin give you away."

"Erin was too young to care for a baby, she was a child herself. It was for the best they gave me to the Sylvains, really, I love them and they've been amazing parents."

"Erin was flawed, there was something wrong with her," Nyx cut in. "She left you, left me, obviously she didn't love her own children."

"Don't talk of your mother like this."

Nyx jumped from her seat as if bitten. "It's the truth, you know? Mum couldn't be bothered with us, she wanted more from life than just being a mother. Well, good riddance to her. You were my parent, along with dad. And I'm glad Eli got to experience a really good family, one that loved and cared for him like a real son. Because our mother didn't."

Lights flickered, and a sudden gust of wind pushed the French window doors open, displacing a small table that stood in their way. The vase and the frame placed upon it tumbled to the floor, cracking and breaking with a loud clang. Spencer latched his eyes on Nyx's, a silent message crossing through them - that she was to get a hold of herself, rein in her powers, lest she wished to give herself away. They had no idea if Eli was aware of the odd blood running in their family, coursing through their veins; best not bring that subject out in the open just yet. She took a deep, steadying breath, crossed the room in fast strides, and locked the window. Then she picked up the broken vase, the shattered frame, placed them over the table.

"Is that our mother?" Eli asked, and his eyes held a strange, curious light. Nyx handed him the photo. "I remember her, but not quite like this."

"She was fifteen here, already pregnant, you can see by the roundness of her face."

"How beautiful she was. You look a lot like her, Nyx."

"You don't."

"I must take after my father. Did you ever meet him, Spencer?"

The buzz of his mobile had Spencer reach for it, shaking his head as he frowned, confused with the unknown number across the screen. "Saw him only once. He was much older than Erin. Their relationship was very frowned upon. I'm sorry, I need to take this."

He stood up and left the room in a hurry, Nyx watching after him, wondering what that late call was about. Who'd be phoning him at this hour? Spencer hadn't made any new friends, and it wasn't as if he was getting all chummy with his former ones. In fact, Nyx doubted her uncle had ever had many friends, he was very much a loner. Except for family, that is.

"Is he all right?" Eli inquired. "He looked troubled, wonder who that is."

Nyx squinted, what was it to him? He'd just met Spencer, why would he care who called him this late on a Saturday night? Then it dawned on her, it must be, it *had* to be.

Max Everley.

It had to be him, no one else would have had such an effect on Spencer. What could he want this late? Had he come across something about Eli, some information that he wasn't who he pretended to be? But what about the DNA tests?

Could Max be calling Spencer to rekindle their flame? What had her uncle said? He'd apologised for his actions, and told Spencer he'd never stopped loving him, hadn't he? Oh, boy, that was one big mess, it was. Max was married, father to her own boyfriend, how much would this affect her and Trystan's relationship? But Spence had a right to be happy, and loved. Max had been the only one for him, and if Spencer wanted to get back together with the man, she'd support him entirely. Trystan would understand, he was sensible, sensitive. It wouldn't be a problem for him, surely.

"It's probably a friend."

"I'd say it's a very special kind of friend, by the look in his eyes and the redness on his cheek," Eli joked, and Nyx giggled.

"Maybe. He's never gotten over his first love, actually. I can't remember when Spence last went on a date, you know?"

"Well, let's hope it's a mind-blowing romance that's about to happen for him."

"What about you? You missed all this, the first dates, the first kisses, the... had you had any girlfriends before?"

"Before the coma, you mean? No, I was just fifteen. Oh, I'd kissed a couple of girls at school, yeah, but never had a proper relationship."

"So, did you date when you woke up?"

"A couple of times. Nothing serious."

"So you've never..." Nyx blushed, and shut up, lowering her eyes to the rug beneath her feet, which suddenly looked quite entrancing.

"Why, have you?" Eli leaned forward in his chair, blushing. "How was it?"

"You're not really asking me this! Spencer doesn't know, and I'd rather he didn't." She waited for Eli to nod his agreement. "It was... okay? Fine, the first time was horrid, it hurt like hell. But the other times, it was really good. We broke up because it was all he ever wanted to do, and as much as I enjoyed it, I wanted more from the relationship, you know? And he couldn't give it to me. So you're still...?" Taking a quick peek at him, Nyx studied her brother.

The colour on his cheek was a tell her assumptions were right. Eli was far more inexperienced than her where it came to the opposite sex. The thought amused her, and she swallowed back a giggle.

Eli nodded, his entire face covered by a red blush. "Fancy talking about this with my kid sister, who happens to be a lot more experienced than me in this area. If you'd have told me two years ago I'd be doing this, wouldn't have believed it. But I'm really glad I've met you, Nyx. Although I adore my parents, you and Spence are the only blood relatives I have."

He reached for her hands, which Nyx submitted to his grip. He wasn't so bad, after all. Maybe she could do this, welcome him in, accept him, even enjoy having an elder brother she could talk to about certain things. And he'd had it hard, hadn't he? All that time lost, no mementos of his youth, no memories. A thought flashed through her mind, she knew someone else who'd also lost their memories. Only this was different. Miss Tate hadn't been in a coma, she had long-term amnesia. Eli had been robbed of the chance to carve his own memories; Jacintha Tate simply couldn't remember her past.

That would be a good pair for Eli, wouldn't it? They were roughly the same age, and Miss Tate was so caring, such a nice person, really. And she was real pretty. With that lovely, upturned nose covered in freckles and those eyes of hers, Eli would surely go for her, wouldn't he? Now, here was a project, bringing those two together. Nyx grinned mischievously, as a plan formed in her head, not even realising she'd just opened herself up to Eli, handing him his rightful place as her brother.

"I'm sorry if I've been a bit of a bitch," she said, "but it hasn't been easy for me. Look, I want you in my life, of course I do, if you're really my brother. I want to get to know you and all that, but cut me some slack, Eli. I'm sixteen, hormonal, used to being an only child and the centre of attention within my own family. It's bound to set me off, having to share the spotlight with an unknown brother. Even if he's less experienced than me."

Eli laughed out loud, stood up from his seat. "Can I give you a hug? Or is this too soon?"

Nyx jumped into his arms, squeezed him against her narrow frame. "I'm really sorry if I was mean. But I'll make it up to you, promise. First thing I'll do is find you a girlfriend."

Eli pushed her away, slightly alarmed. "You're joking, right?"

Nyx's phone pinged, and she fished it from the back pocket of her jeans, eyeing it distractedly. A new text from Trystan. "Maybe," she replied, loosening herself from her brother's grip. "Maybe not. Excuse me while I read this."

She texted Trystan back, still eyeing Eli's uncomfortable stance, and laughter bubbled up inside her. Oh, this was going to be fun, much more than what she'd anticipated. Eli was so awkward, so shy, women would be falling at his feet. That bad boy style he had, betrayed by all this bashfulness, was sure to get him into more trouble than he was prepared for. Her elder brother may have failed all the milestones, but he wasn't going to remain a virgin for long, now. It was actually endearing that he might need his little sister's help navigating the wonderful world of passion and lust, the magical experience of falling in love for the first time.

Magic.

Again, she wondered if he had it, and if they should talk about it with him. If Eli was like them, some sort of power would run through him. He'd need help working it, surely. He'd need someone to guide him in the use of his talents, so he didn't risk something dangerous. Maybe his adoptive parents were also of the blood, and had already put him up to speed with this. Maybe all he needed her help for was to meet a nice girl he could take on a date. And that, Nyx was already on top of.

Brought back from her musings by Spencer's sudden entrance, she eyed her uncle with curiosity. Something wasn't right, but it didn't look as if it was all that wrong. Spence's eyes were moist, as if he'd been about to cry, but there was a trace of a smile threatening to implode on his lips at any given moment, if only he let himself go. He kept checking himself, though, so whatever he'd just been told wasn't yet a *fait accompli*, but something in the realm of possibility. He wouldn't speak of it until it was certain, and Nyx knew him enough to leave him alone. Something Eli obviously didn't.

"What happened?" her brother asked. "You look like the cat that got to the cream."

Spencer put on a stern look, trying to disguise his sudden bliss. "Look at the time," he said, eyeing the large clock on the mantle. "And you've been drinking, same as me. Nyx, I don't care about tantrums, your brother's staying here, tonight."

"I was about to suggest he did. After all, there's that bedroom I'm pretty sure grandmother meant to be for him."

"What are you talking about?"

"My mother did some work on this place, she had it fixed and decorated to our personal tastes. Only there's a bedroom, which used to be hers, that doesn't fit either Nyx or me. We thought it was meant for her father, my mother died a few months after him, but the moment you introduced yourself, I knew it was for you."

"It does fit him like a glove," Nyx said. "Come on up, let me show it to you."

She grabbed Eli by the hand and pulled him up the stairs, excitedly, Spencer following them.

"Actually, Eli, I think you should close your tab at the B&B and stay here with us until the will is read and you decide what you want to do. What do you say?"

"If you don't mind?" he asked, eyes focused on Nyx.

She nodded, and Eli's face lit up with a grin.

Trystan had been right, she just needed to give him a chance.

IV

Eli watched Nyx saunter off with her date, skipping from one foot to the other and twirling around the boy, whose face showcased the most massive grin he remembered seeing. His sister was a bit of a conundrum, one he couldn't solve. One moment, she was all warm and loving and asking for his opinion and advice, and the next, Nyx would get into one of her moods – as he was now calling it – and become sulky, childish, throwing temper tantrums. Maybe it was only natural, and all teenagers were like that, but he didn't quite remember himself being this moody, not like Nyx.

Those formative years, he'd spent them elsewhere, in a world that was as different from this as the sun was to the moon. He'd woken up in a different house one morning, knowing exactly where he was, for he'd lived out in those woods until he was five, and knowing this time round he was on his own and must take care of himself. Unlike Nyx, Eli's adolescence was one of self-sufficiency. He'd known how to hunt, fish, mend his clothes, cook his own meals and tend to his house. Unlike Nyx, he had no idea what social media was, or what song was popular, or even how to behave like regular kids did. His had been a different life altogether, and if he failed to understand his sister, he couldn't really blame her, could he?

Leaning back on the car-seat, he watched the young couple climb the massive stone staircase leading to the door of the Everley mansion. When Nyx's date had shown up at their doorstep, Eli had expected to meet the much-spoken-of boyfriend, Trystan Everley. Instead, he'd been introduced to Pip Thomson, a boy with a chip up his shoulder, far too many tattoos, and a sullen attitude Eli didn't much care for. Nyx had clarified they were friends, and that the party – which she'd insisted Eli joined them for – was to be held at Trystan's house, hence her going with Pip. It still sat wrong with him. If Trystan was her boyfriend, why would Nyx go out with another boy? He'd told her so in clear terms, and apparently, it had been his biggest faux pas, the one that put him in the doghouse through the car ride from Vaughn cottage to Everley estate. A car ride Spencer had practically begged him to drive, claiming to be late for whatever secret appointment had had him as good as drenching himself in cologne. Hot date, probably.

So that was Nyx out with her boyfriend, their uncle slipping away for his secret rendezvous, and Eli playing chauffeur to his adorable yet maddening sister. And no date for him. Not that he longed for one, he thought, but an image sprang to mind unbidden. A pair of light eyes, brown hair, a dainty, upturned nose. Jacintha. As much as he distrusted women, most women, this particular one had clung to his mind, ushering a rush of unexpected, unwanted sensations through him. He'd not seen her again, and propriety had kept him from grilling Nyx or Spencer about her. But Eli caught himself wondering about the woman more often than not, knowing he wouldn't mind seeing her again, maybe even taking *her* out on a date. To what purpose, he didn't know.

For three years, he'd constantly reminded himself he didn't belong here, in this world. But memories of that other place grew dimmer and dimmer in his mind, faces completely gone from his head, names he could no longer recall, and even the places and forest roads Eli had thought to know so well, became figments of a dream he once had, the more time he spent in this world. And now he'd crossed paths with a woman that seemed to push everything else further and further away, including his wish to return to where he felt at home.

Shaking his head, he grinned, started the car, pulled back for a U-turn as soon as he spotted Nyx and her date enter the large front doors of the massive house. And ran into something that hadn't been there. Braking the car, Eli jumped out, face paling at the thought of having hit someone, possibly injured one of the kids. He'd gathered from Spencer the party attendance would be mostly kids Nyx's age, a few years older, perhaps, with no adults around. That had made up his mind, and he'd declined his sister's invitation to tag along with her and Pip, an invitation she'd made prior to his apparently offensive remark that she shouldn't go out with another boy if she had a boyfriend. What was it with him running over people, lately? The day he got to Weaversmoor he'd almost crushed Jacintha under his bike. The fact he was thinking about her again didn't fail to register.

Eli walked to the back of the vehicle, heart hammering in fear of what he'd find, the extent of injury he might have caused, the damage to Spencer's car. What he came upon was a YZ125 Yamaha lying on its side and a girl kneeling beside it as if it was a wounded pet. He tried hard not to laugh, and searched for damages to the bike. It looked fine, but he'd have to check closer to be sure.

Before Eli could utter a word, though, the girl jumped up and faced him, cheeks red with anger, eyes blazing and a scowl so deep he took a step back, hands held up in silent apology.

"You stupid animal," she shouted, voice shrill. "No one taught you to look in the rearview mirror before reversing? You could have killed me!"

"I... I'm sorry, I *did* look, you weren't there."

"Well, the bike was. You crashed into it."

Crash was a massive exaggeration, but Eli kept his opinion to himself. "It's dark, the bike had its lights off, I didn't hear you come up behind me. It sure wasn't there when I first got here, all right? Let me check," he offered, bending down to help pull the bike back up.

The girl slapped his hand away, fingers brimming with rings, nails covered in chipping black nail polish, rows and rows of bracelets over her thin wrist.

"Hey, what's your problem? Let me see if there's any damage, I know bikes." It was pretty much the only thing he knew, the one thing that had caught his interest and attention not long after he woke up from his coma.

"That's not your car," the girl said, chin pointing to Spencer's black Toyota. "It's Mr Vaughn's, why are you driving it?"

Frowning, Eli took the girl in. She must be about Nyx's age, perhaps a little older. Wearing a pair of black jeans ripped at the knees and a leather biker jacket, much like his own. Boots on her feet, a helmet hanging from one arm, dark hair loose on her back, and bright green eyes. The proverbial rebellious girl, trying to look edgy and cool, when fear and inadequacy still shone bright inside her eyes. He sighed, not knowing how to handle her.

A current of energy lashed out of her, in constant streams, as if she was putting up some sort of barrier that kept Eli out of her head. He hadn't even realised he was trying to glide into her thoughts; it was something that came naturally to him. Aside from Nyx's date, Pip Thomson, whose brain seemed surrounded by a fortress, Eli had only once failed to read someone else's mind. Jacintha's thoughts had been unreadable, but Eli had put it down to the circumstances in which they'd met. She'd come running out of the woods terrified, and fear clouded her brain. He'd been kept out of it by the sheer block wall of panic he'd sensed. But now this girl came along, and he had no idea what to make of her. Behind the green sparkle of her eye, all he could sense was an unbreachable dark block of... nothingness.

"I don't see what you have to do with who Spence lends his car to," Eli replied, grunting with the effort of pulling the bike back up. His eyes did a thorough search of it, saw no damage, not even a scratch, but then again, it was night time and the outside barely illuminated.

"Spence, huh? Pretty intimate."

Eli's head snapped up, locking eyes with the girl; his cold and forbidding, hers widening in sudden surprise and a little alarm. "What's this? Don't you think he's a bit too old for you?" he snapped. "And I seriously doubt you're his type."

The girl's face twisted into a mask of disgust. "Eww," she whispered, "you're not really suggesting I'm into him, are you? That's just sick. Are you his boyfriend?"

Eli shook his head, quickly tiring of the girl's line of questioning. He stepped back to the car, grabbed the door handle, ready to slide inside and drive away.

"Look, Spence let me borrow the car so I could drive my sister and her date to this chick's birthday bash, not that I owe you an explanation on what my uncle does or doesn't do. I don't see how this is any of your business, really, so why don't you get back to the party and let me go back home, little girl?"

The girl frowned, offended, and Eli couldn't help being amused. But then her countenance cleared, and her eyes softened as she seemed to connect whatever dots her brain had been working out. "You're Erin Vaughn's son!"

Sweat, cold and profuse, broke down his back, under his arms. Who was this girl, that she knew this? Of course it would be all over the small town in two days' time, but until then, only Spencer and Nyx knew of it, her date Pip and probably the boyfriend too, as must his father. He was Spencer's lawyer, after all. Fear hit him like a fallen tree trunk on his skull, dizzying him on his feet, head swimming. Eli placed one unsure hand against the cool glass of the car's window, shut his eyes, took a deep breath.

"How do you know my mother?" he inquired. "She left this place before you were born, didn't she?"

His ears caught sound of soft footsteps over the gravel, walking towards him. A hesitant hand came down over his shoulder, pressed it gently. Eli opened his eyes, turned to meet the girl's.

"Are you all right? You *are* Erin's son, aren't you? Nyx's brother."

Eli nodded. "How can you know of me?" But it suddenly made sense. She must be the birthday girl, Trystan's sister. "I see. Happy birthday, Bryn Everley."

Her lips widened in a satisfied grin. "Why, thank you." She held out one hand, which he took, smiling a defeated grin. There was a hint of amusement in his eyes, though; the girl was nothing like he'd expected her to be. "It's a pleasure to meet you…"

"Eli Vaughn."

"Eli. Mother used to talk about you, ages ago. She'd say the oddest things. Mind, she was usually drunk."

"Your mother? How does she know me?"

Bryn laughed. "She knew *of* you. Erin was her best friend. She'll go mental once she knows you're here. Actually, how come you're here? I remember her saying you were adopted."

"Ask your father, I'm sure he can clarify that for you. Shouldn't you be at your own party, Bryn Everley?"

She shrugged. "Bunch of kids, gets pretty boring. You're much more interesting."

Sensing an odd current pass through them, Eli studied her. The look in Bryn's eyes, the smile on her lips, the way she used the tip of her tongue to wet those very same lips, it all sent a message not even his inexperience kept him from understanding. What was the girl trying to do? Hadn't Nyx said something about her cousin Jamal dating the Everley girl? Why was she coming on to him, then? Or was he reading more into it than what she meant? He opened the car door, slipped inside.

"Well, it was nice meeting you, Bryn. I need to go now, enjoy your party."

"Wait," she said, one hand on the door holding it back so he couldn't close it. "Why don't you come in, have a drink?"

"Like you said, bunch of kids, gets pretty boring. I've places to be, people to see." Eli pulled the door, managed to dislodge it from her hand and shut it. "Listen, about your bike? Do you know the auto-repair shop downtown?"

She nodded. "My friend's family owns it. What about it?"

"Meet me there on the second, will you? Let's get that bike checked, I don't want to risk having caused it any harm. It looks fine, but better safe than sorry. What time do they open?"

"Around eight."

"Well, then, that settles it. November second, eight o'clock outside the shop, is that okay?"

"I have to be at school by half past, though." She sounded unsure, but an odd, unreadable light shone in her eyes.

"I'll drive you to school, don't worry, you'll be there on time. It's a date, then?" Bryn nodded once more, lowering her head as if trying to hide a smile. "Have a nice evening."

"Thank you. See you soon." The grin she offered him was nothing short of disconcerting. Starting the car, Eli drove down the wide lane, out the large front gates, taking the road into the town centre, instead of back to the cottage. Spencer had asked if he minded dining out, as he was having someone over. It didn't take a genius to understand Spence had some sort of date going on, and he wondered if it was with the same man who'd broken his heart before, Trystan and Bryn's father, Max Everley. Nyx had put him up to speed with what she knew of the story, and although Eli considered Spencer a fool if he allowed Max back into his life, it served his personal purposes to a dot, that his uncle was invested in a new relationship, his attention diverted to someone other than Nyx. It would give Eli a chance to bond with the girl, infiltrate her heart, her life, become that one single person she relied on the most. It was of the utmost importance to his plan that she did.

Driving down the high street, Eli wondered what he was to do with his time, until he had to pick Nyx. Maybe he should have accepted Bryn's invite; it might have given him a chance of meeting the girl's mother, who could have told him about Erin and his own father. Ora and Serge had related all they knew, but whenever they spoke of Fionn Sylvannar, they did so with awe and reverence, not with deep, intimate knowledge. His father had been a man of high stance in their world, Ora and Serge mere serfs where it came to him, and it was with the kind of respect owed one's lord they talked of Fionn. Maybe this woman would speak differently; maybe she did know more about him. She'd know Erin intimately, and that served him well, too.

What could have happened to his mother, that she'd disappeared so effectively, abandoning both her children? Nyx seemed to believe she was just flawed, the worst mother in the world, but Nyx didn't know everything. There'd come a time when Eli must tell her, there'd come a time when he must take his sister into the woods and see if she could help. Because if Nyx was a Weaver but unable to open the pathway for him, he'd have no need for her and was just wasting his time. Time he felt he didn't really have much of.

A familiar figure strolled ahead of his car, along the sidewalk. As he drove by, Eli took a peek in his rearview mirror. It was her, the woman he'd nearly run over four days ago. Jacintha. Speeding towards the first vacant spot he could find, Eli parked the car and got out, heart hammering in a contracted chest, lungs constricted and unable to take a breath. What was this effect she had on him? He found it impossible to hold back the grin rising to his lips, as well as the overall feeling of joy at running into her, *finally* running into her. Did he really have time for this? Hadn't he set on a plan, a life course? How could he allow himself to be distracted from it, now? But here she was, walking like she had a purpose, eyes on the pavement, lost in thought, and he found himself wishing those were thoughts of him. Then she raised her head and looked straight at Eli. His smile widened, his cheeks reddened, hands sliding into the pockets of his tight-fitting jeans. Jacintha smiled back and hurried towards him.

"Hi," Eli greeted, suddenly lost for words.

"Hey, it's you. Eli, right?"

He nodded.

"Fancy running into you here." Her eyes fell on the car by his side. She studied it with a frown, as if the vehicle was familiar but she couldn't quite place it.

"I was looking for a place to dine," he said. "Know any good spots around?"

"Sure, there's a couple nice places."

"Have you had dinner?" His mouth seemed to run ahead of him. What was he doing?

Jacintha blushed, averted her eyes, seemed to ponder for a few seconds, then turned her face back to him. "No, I haven't, I was going to get something to eat. Why don't you join me?"

"I'd really like that."

"What do you fancy? Chinese? Indian? Oh, there's this nice little French bistro round the corner, but it must be packed. Actually no, tonight's Halloween and half the town will be partying up at the Everleys. We may just be in luck, come on."

Eli followed her down the street, until they came to an awning and a sign indicating a small, cosy restaurant. The place wasn't packed, but it wasn't quite empty either, it wouldn't be hard to get a table. Opening the door for Jacintha, Eli ushered her in, wondering if this was really happening, and how he'd been so lucky as to run into her inadvertently for the second time. They needed to stop meeting like this. Bracing himself, he swore he'd get her phone number before dinner was through, and smiled all the way to the table a pristine waitress led them to.

Spencer sat in the car, eyes on the falling rain, Nyx and Eli still bickering about whatever had them at each other's throats since breakfast. He'd come down to them already at odds with each other, busy cooking breakfast and arguing at the same time. It was tiresome, and although he'd been slowly guilt-tripping himself about spending the weekend away, so soon on the wake of Eli's arrival and official introduction to the family, Spencer couldn't wait to leave. If only for a couple of hours. If only to willingly place his heart, his hopes and dreams into the hands of the very same man who'd shattered them before.

Had he completely lost his head? What was he doing? How had he given in so easily, after all the years nursing the broken heart Max left him with? What kind of weak, brainless man was Spencer to welcome back the same person who'd been too scared of others' opinions to admit to his feelings? This time was different, he just knew it. Not because Max had assured him – which he had – but because Spencer had already seen it. Max had left home two days before the massive birthday party the Everleys threw their eldest daughter every year. He'd left a marriage that was all but a lie, moved into a small flat of his own, started the divorce proceedings. He hadn't lied about it. And he hadn't tried to sway Spencer, allowing him the time he'd asked for, when Max called him the very night he decided he wasn't going back home. The same night

Spencer had thought Nyx was starting to accept her brother's existence, and his permanence in her life.

But if Max had kept his word and lived up to Spencer's expectations, Nyx had failed. Or rather, Nyx and Eli had failed; he couldn't place all the blame on the girl. Not when his nephew insisted on acting as if he was living in the middle ages. It had started with the Halloween bash and escalated from then on. Eli had frowned at Nyx going to the party with a date other than Trystan. Even before setting eyes on Pip Thomson, Eli had made a couple of unnecessary remarks about Nyx showing up with someone other than her boyfriend.

The girl had stormed out of the room with her dinner unfinished, hissing about her brother being a sexist pig. Not that Spencer thought Eli was that bad, he didn't much care for his niece going out with two different boys at the same time, but he knew Nyx, knew she'd accepted Pip's invitation before things with Trystan had progressed into a more serious relationship. Eli apparently didn't, or refused to acknowledge it. And then he'd met Pip, and taken an immediate dislike to the boy, for whatever reason. Although Eli insisted it had nothing to do with Pip's tattoos, his leather jacket, his bad-boy looks and attitude, Spencer had his doubts. And so did Nyx.

She'd called her brother a hypocrite a couple of times, whenever Pip was mentioned and Eli snorted. Said he dressed the same as Pip, had the same attitude, acted the very same way. Spencer had forced a hand over his lips to hide his smile, she had a point but he intended to stay out of that particular argument. But Eli had also disliked Trystan, saying the boy looked cagey, hinting Nyx shouldn't even be seeing him. That had been the final drop, and Spencer had found himself needing to butt in. Eli had ended up apologising, assuring he trusted Nyx's judgement and wasn't trying to order her around, and things had gone back to normal, with the three of them tagging along to Sarah Wilson's for lunch on the first of November, where Eli was formally introduced as Erin's firstborn. It had gone well enough, without arguments or bickering, just Eli being his usual endearing, shy, charming self and Sarah asking too many uncomfortable questions.

Next day, Corinna Vaughn's new will had been read, claiming exactly what Spencer expected: that Eli Sylvain was Erin Vaughn's eldest child and should henceforth change his name to Eli Vaughn, so he could share ownership of Vaughn cottage along with his sister Nyx and their uncle Spencer, as well as use of the trust fund set in his name.

Eli had looked somewhat shaken at the thought of having to change his name, but a phone call to his adoptive parents had put his mind at ease and assured him he was doing the right thing. Max Everley had offered his assistance in the legal procedures, for which Spencer was grateful, and Eli even more. The young man always looked as if he had no idea how to go about in the world, and the only moments he appeared remotely comfortable were when sat astride his bike, riding away down an empty road.

The arguing and bickering had taken a break that day, too, with Nyx delighted at Eli being now officially her brother; and the entire family had gone out for dinner to celebrate. Eli had been in high spirits, so had Nyx, but the moment Trystan called her, interrupting the meal, a dark shadow fell across Eli's face, and the drive back home had brought back the sullen, passive-aggressive stabs between the two siblings.

He wondered if that was simply the way of things. Spencer remembered well enough what it had been like with his own sister, their age gap considerably smaller than the one between Eli and Nyx. They'd fought like cat and dog, arguing for hours, shouting at each other and generally driving their parents mad, so it shouldn't be surprising that Eli and Nyx acted in a similar way. They were siblings; it was normal. It was constant, yes, tiresome - but normal. At the end of the day, the two always made up, and could go from the loudest row to the most intimate of conversations in the space of mere seconds. He'd just have to get used to it, and keep in mind that if Nyx was only sixteen, her brother - despite physically being twenty-five - wasn't much older emotionally. Spencer couldn't expect mature, adult behaviour from someone who'd slept through his entire adolescence. For good or for worse, Eli was still going through his teenage years, at least mentally.

There was still the problem of his entire genetic inheritance. Not that Spencer had seen any signs Eli had magic running through him, but he was Erin's child, a strong Weaver, and his father... well, his father was something else altogether. Eli must be dormant, but soon his powers would awake, wouldn't they? And if he was a Weaver like his mother, like his grandmother and sister, it fell down to Spencer to talk to him extensively on the subject, and tell him what Max had shared about the need to keep the pathway across worlds locked and secured, so none from that other place could enter Weaversmoor. That other place, which was as much Eli's home as this world. How was he supposed to handle all this?

A respite would be welcome. He'd had a couple of days' quiet, when Eli had gone north to visit his adoptive parents earlier this week, but it had been short-lived. All there seemed to be around him was constant, nagging bickering. Three weeks since Eli had arrived, three weeks with those two either laughing or shouting at each other, and Spencer was drained, tired, in need of some time for himself. In need of being so far from Weaversmoor he needn't worry who saw him nor where, or most importantly, with whom. Funny how things changed. In the past, it had been the other way around: Max worrying they'd be caught together, always terrified of who knew about them, always hiding their relationship whenever they were at Weaversmoor. Now, Max had done everything by the book, giving Spencer the time he'd asked for, only coming round or calling if business so demanded, never trying to steer their awkward conversations into the personal, intimate scope.

It had been Spencer who'd brought up the subject, when Max had unexpectedly visited the cottage to drop a few legal papers Eli must sign. As they sat in awkward silence, waiting for the new member of the Vaughn family to arrive, Spencer had thrown caution to the wind, and asked Max how the divorce proceedings were coming along. It had led to a long, boring, full of legal jargon explanation that Spencer had found himself interrupting by glueing his lips to Max's.

And that had been it. They'd gotten back together on the spot, as if they'd never really been apart. Max was all Spencer knew, the only person he'd ever loved, and although there had been others, lovers who never stood the test of time, it was Max he still knew best. The taste of his lips, the shape of his waist, the curve of his knee, the way his mind worked and the meaning of every single gesture and look he dished, it was all still so familiar as to feel like they'd never parted.

Max had been ecstatic, full of promises of ever-lasting love, and how happy he'd make Spencer, how he was going to make up for all he'd put Spencer through, how he was going to redeem himself from the errors of his ways and the harm he'd done. Spencer had been more careful, taking every promise with a pinch of salt, but basking in the joy of being reunited with the man he loved. He'd had one demand, though, and Max had been loathe to comply, but comply he did.

Knowing the divorce procedures were due to take a while, Spencer had insisted they kept their relationship to themselves, at least for the time being. He hadn't said anything to Nyx, or Eli, and hoped Max had also shied from sharing the news with anyone. But who would Max share it with? The partners at his law firm? His estranged wife? His children? Actually, given the close relationship he had with his eldest daughter, Max might just have told Bryn everything. The girl would keep it to herself, though. According to Max, she'd always taken her father's side in detriment of her mother, and had vied for the two to get a divorce and Max finally come out, assume he was gay and live a life of far more freedom than what he'd done so far.

Spencer wanted to take it slow. The fact Max was still a married man weighed on his decision to keep their affair from common knowledge, at least until he was sure it was meant to last; it wasn't just a one-off thing. But the lure of a weekend away, somewhere no one knew them - with enough time to spend together, without having to hurry because there were responsibilities, people depending on them - had made a dent in Spencer's resolve. He'd agreed on going, allowed Max to book them the hotel and a bunch of fun activities, but hadn't yet mentioned his trip to Eli or Nyx.

Seeing he was supposed to take off after lunch, maybe he should say something before dropping Nyx off at school and Eli in town, where he'd had his bike being serviced. Where he'd been spending an unusual amount of his free time. Either his nephew had an unhealthy dependence on that bike of his, or he'd met someone, which he'd also been keeping a secret. The thought put a smirk up his lips.

Taking a deep, steadying breath, Spencer braced himself, unsure of how much to impart. No matter how he looked at it, it was something that would end up affecting Nyx; after all, she was dating Max's son.

"You two need to stop that," he said, tired of the ongoing argument between them, this time related to Eli's refusal to come pick Nyx up from school after her tutoring session.

The inside of the car fell into an unexpected, unusual silence, and Spence risked a look at the rear-view mirror, where he caught

Nyx's eyes. The girl blushed, but the rebellious spark was still inside. Given some leeway, she'd be back at the argument, insisting her brother come get her.

"I'm sorry, Spence." Eli averted his uncle's eyes, instead placing them on the large driveway in front of Weaversmoor Academy. "I know I don't have much to do with my spare time, but I was actually thinking of finding myself a job. The local auto-repair shop is looking for..."

"Tell him he doesn't *need* a job," Nyx cried. "He has enough money, why does he want a job? You can come and get me at four, why is it so hard for you to do what I ask at least once? What kind of brother are you, that..."

Eli broke out in laughter; not an amused one, though. "Are you for real? That is so shallow, Nyx! I'm not Spencer, and you're not going to turn me into your private chauffeur or maid. I don't need a job but I *want* one, okay? I want to feel useful, with a purpose. Why is this so hard for you to understand? What kind of man do you want me to be, huh?"

Spencer smirked, the boy had a good head about him, did him proud. "Your brother's right, Nyx. And it's a great idea, Eli, that you get a job. I've been thinking about it myself. Maybe investing the money Mother left me in a business of my own, a bookstore, perhaps. Weaversmoor seems to have an uncommonly short amount of bookstores."

"You mean there's none." Nyx's expression had sobered, and darkened even more.

Spencer knew she'd be uncomfortable with the idea of him working, instead of being constantly at home for her, which was her notion of a good parent. But he was her uncle, not her father, nor her mother, and he was a human being who had the right to a life of his own. An independent, private life away from his family, something that belonged to him and him alone. Taking another peek at the rear-view mirror, he watched Nyx unfasten the seatbelt and grab her school bag, ready to join the yawning mass of students headed for class. He couldn't let her leave just yet, though. She was already annoyed with him, so what better time to inform her he'd be taking the weekend off?

"But that's not what I wanted to talk to you about," he added. "I'm going away for the weekend. I leave today after lunch and only return Sunday night. Late."

The silence grew tendrils, like a live organism that clung to him, wrapping around Spencer's chest, obstructing the way in for air. He found he could hardly breathe, waiting for their reaction.

"Have a great time," Eli said. "Are you driving? Drive carefully then, give us a call when you get to... where?"

"Spreigh," Spencer said, "up by the coast."

"Are you going alone?" The glint in Nyx's eyes, filled with mischief, assured him she knew he wouldn't be. Throwing her arms around his shoulders and the car seat, Nyx hugged him. "I love you, Spence. All I want is for you to be happy, you know? I'll support your decisions, whatever they are. All of them. So go and have fun."

The look they exchanged was ripe with meaning, a message passing through them. So she knew, she must, that Spence and Max were back together. Contrary to what he'd expected, Nyx seemed to approve. It was a weight lifted off his shoulders.

"I won't, if the two of you keep arguing and fighting like you do."

"I'm sorry. Promise you I won't. But Eli never does what I ask him."

"Nyx, that's not true. You can walk home with Trystan. There's no need for Eli to come get you. By the way, I'm leaving the car, you can use it anytime," he added, turning to Eli. "Nyx is allowed out with friends and Trystan but has a curfew, and that's half-past eleven for Friday and Saturday. I want you home by ten thirty on Sunday, young lady. I'll try to be here by that time, but..."

"Don't worry, I'll sort her." Eli cackled, locking eyes with Nyx. "She can stay home and play board games with me. You can have Trystan over, if you want, or that friend of yours, Penny."

"Eli, I don't want you controlling your sister's outings, her friends, or her dates. You're old enough to know better, please."

"I was just joking. Look, I'm not Trystan Everley's biggest fan, nor Pip Thomson's, but if she is, then it's not my place to butt in. Unless they do something to her."

Nyx punched Eli's upper arm. "Don't talk of me as if I'm not here. Spence, I promise we'll behave, all right? Go enjoy yourself, you deserve it. Have a safe drive, call me when you get there, promise?"

Spencer kissed her cheek, her forehead, and nodded. Nyx slid out of the car and ran towards the slippery stone steps, where Penny Lattimer awaited her. The girls entwined their arms, Nyx waving back with her free hand, and marched through the double doors. Only when he could no longer see her did Spence start the car and drive out of the courtyard, Eli chatting about the job opening at the auto-repair shop he wanted to apply to, Spencer barely registering what he was saying. The fact Nyx didn't oppose his relationship had taken a massive burden off his shoulders, maybe now he could relax and actually enjoy himself on his weekend away with Max.

V

Sparks rushed through her body as their hands brushed. They'd both reached for the bottle of wine, the touch of Eli's skin shooting flares of heat across her arm, unleashing swarms of butterflies inside her. Their velvet-tipped wings beat a wild tattoo against the wall of her stomach, begging for release. Jacintha pulled back her hand, smiled awkwardly, melting at the sight of the shy, lopsided smile on Eli's lips.

Why did he have this effect on her? He was just a man.

And this was all shades of wrong, after all. Maybe the fact these regular dates were morally and ethically inappropriate was what made them so exciting, and the reason behind her emotionally charged moods, regarding him. She should have put a stop to it after that first dinner, the only justifiable encounter, for it had been unplanned and accidental. But during the course of that innocent first meal together, Jacintha found herself saving his phone number, him doing the same. She found herself diving into the clear pools of his eyes and drowning in the husky melody of his voice. Lost in the way he smiled at her, long-fingered hands gesturing along with his words. She found herself hungry to see him again, so when he'd called her suggesting lunch, Jacintha had been unable to refuse. She hadn't wanted to refuse. Just like she hadn't wanted to refuse the other dates, some of them of her own initiative. Like tonight's dinner.

Her intentions had been the best, when she texted Eli suggesting they meet up. She'd meant to put a stop to their dates, of which nothing had come about, frankly, so why was she worried? Not once - not one single time - had Eli attempted anything physical. He hadn't once tried to kiss her, or hold her hand, hug her, come up to her flat when he dropped her home. The most intimate he'd been was placing one smooth, warm hand over hers as they rode his bike. One smooth, warm hand she'd often found herself wishing he'd place over other parts of her body.

What was it with this man, after all? Why did he feel so familiar, why did it feel so right, so fitting, being with him? Why did it feel so lacking, at the same time, that their relationship – whatever it was – hadn't progressed from the long conversations, the comfortable silences, the veiled looks, the heavy, heavy weight of the physical attraction between them? An attraction that was nearly palpable, one she was sure he could feel. Why hadn't he tried for more? Maybe it was for the best. Eli's sister was one of her students, after all; if the Academy got wind of this, they might not like it. Searching around the small bistro she and Eli seemed to favour, Jacintha spotted a few familiar faces, some belonging to parents of students at the Academy, others to employees. Surely the sight of Jacintha Tate and the long-lost member of the Vaughn family sauntering about town together had already been noticed. Surely her employers knew they were at least on friendly terms. But did Eli know that she tutored his sister? Did Eli know the truth about the town?

Stealing a glance, Jacintha watched him sip the wine, take a bite from his dinner, apparently lost in thought. Did he even have magic? There *was* something, a hint at special talents lying just below the surface, but flimsy, as if hidden by static. Sometimes, she nudged his thoughts, tried to break in just slightly, but it was like trying to cross a thick, foam mattress. No matter how hard

Jacintha pried and pushed, she kept bouncing back. He must have something, being a Vaughn, but perhaps his dormant magic had kept his uncle, his sister, from talking about the town's secrets, waiting to see how Eli's blood manifested. For he must be of the blood, even if he had no idea how to work his craft.

"Listen, I should tell you something," Jacintha said.

Eli's face depicted a sudden flare of panic, eyes widening, tongue wetting lips in a nervous tell she'd already come to recognise. The sight of that tongue, tip over the soft-looking skin of his lips, sent a chill down her back, a blaze of fire erupting at the pit of her stomach. How she longed to have her mouth glued to those lips. How silly of her, such a strong infatuation for a man, as if she was a teenager again. But Eli was unlike any other man she'd dated, there was an innocence, an authenticity to him most people lacked. There was also a veil of mystery, like a thick, dark drape folded around him, encasing him in its safety. What did he hide? What secrets lurked within? Why hadn't he made a move yet, but kept asking her out? Any other man would have already kissed her, tried to sleep with her. What was wrong with Eli Vaughn?

"Have I done something?" he inquired, visibly uncomfortable.

Jacintha sniggered. "No, of course not." *'You're pretty much perfect, and that's what's terrifying about you.'* Grasping the stem of her glass, she took a long drink of the wine. "You do know I tutor your sister, right?"

Eli frowned, mouth slack as he tried to comprehend the meaning of her words. "Nyx is struggling at school? I had no idea, Spence and her make it sound as if she's top of the class."

Oh, this wasn't going well. How could she justify the need for tutoring without giving away secrets that weren't hers to tell?

"She is, she's a straight-A student."

"Then why...?"

"Nyx studied at state-funded schools most of her life. Weaversmoor Academy is independent, therefore, has its own curricula. She's just a bit behind on certain subjects, and I'm helping her with it."

"Oh, I see. So she's doing well, is she?"

"Yeah, don't worry."

"There's just so much I don't know about her, about them. I had no idea you were her teacher." His face darkened, a shadow falling across the usual smile Eli always had for Jacintha.

It must be hard, living your entire life thinking you're someone and then suddenly having this whole other identity thrown your way, like he had. A family he didn't know, a mother who'd given him up, a father who didn't care, an uncle, a sister. It was a lot to take in, but he was handling things pretty well, wasn't he? Warmth seeped through Jacintha's veins at the thought he was an exceptional man. So why didn't he make a move?

"But this seems to worry you," Eli said, and she blushed.

"Well, I wanted you to know, see, people might frown upon it, upon us." Now he had a weird smirk on his lips, she wasn't handling this well. "I mean, they see us together and make assumptions, right? With me being Nyx's tutor, I don't know, the Academy might not be too pleased with us..." Oh, she was making it all worse. "I mean, there's nothing wrong, right? We're friends hanging out together, aren't we? I just thought I'd make sure you knew. That I'm her tutor, I mean." Could she make it any more awkward? Blushing, Jacintha trained her eyes on the food, shoving a spoonful of dessert in her mouth.

Eli finished his meal, downed the rest of his wine, gazing around as if in search of people observing them. His face had sprouted a scowl, Jacintha already sorry she'd brought up the subject; it had ruined the evening.

"Are you done with that?" he asked, still managing to force a smile to his lips.

Jacintha pushed her plate away, nodded. "Yes, I believe I am."

They stared at each other, as if measuring the real meaning behind their words. Eli shook his head, a minute, nearly imperceptible gesture, but one she couldn't fail to glean. Now, she'd done it, ruined it all, he'd never make a move after what she'd said. Jacintha watched him gesture the waitress, ask for the tab, a sudden ache taking root in her chest, driving prickles to the corners of her eyes. She blinked, drank a sip of wine, the silence between them no longer companionable but awkward, empty, uncomfortable.

"Come on, I'll walk you home," Eli offered, after paying the bill, and Jacintha stood up, nauseated and cold.

She wrapped the thick wool scarf around her neck and put on her coat, fingers numb from the sudden shift in their usual light banter into this barren, cold exchange. Outside, the night hung ripe with the scent of impending rain, unseen clouds shielding stars and moon from sight. The wind picked up, frosty as Eli's current demeanour, and Jacintha huddled further into her coat, hands diving into the large pockets where she fished for her gloves. Falling behind, she stopped to pull them on, shivering from the drop in temperature. The bistro had been warm and inviting, now all she wanted was to get home, where central heating would place some warmth back on her frozen nose and toes. Her attention diverted back to Eli, who had ploughed on ahead, as if he'd forgotten about her, or simply didn't care. Had she offended him? Why was he acting this way, so childishly, throwing a tantrum for reasons not even Jacintha could discern? Perhaps not even he knew.

She marched slowly after him, keeping a few paces' distance between them. Suddenly, Eli stopped, turned back, brow darkened by whatever impish mood had bitten him, and turned him from the polite, charming young man into this spoilt, self-gratified brat.

Jacintha stopped, wondering what he was about, lacking the time to even puzzle at the expression on his face. He reached her in three large strides, eyes moist with an emotion she couldn't quite read.

"What if I don't want to be *just* friends?" Eli whispered, cold, cold hands cupping her cheeks, mouth claiming hers in a blazing, unexpected kiss.

She let go.

Wrapping suddenly tingling arms around him, Jacintha let herself go and gave in to the kiss. It was all she'd wanted. It was all she fantasised of, whenever thinking of him. Their lips glued together, tongues dancing to the same song, bodies pressed against each other, and his strong, soft, gentle hands on her face, just like this. His strong, gentle hands holding her in place, like couldn't get enough of this kiss.

A moan rose up his throat, left his lips to alight upon hers, ripe with meaning. The kiss intensified, becoming urgent, as if they were about to burn or explode, the world about to end, or some devilish catastrophe might come to pull them apart - forever apart. Jacintha held tighter, gloved hands caressing the short-cropped hair on the back of his head, almost lost for air, as the kiss became more and more inflamed. Then, out of nowhere, he pulled back. Letting go of her face, one hand over his mouth, the other running through his hair, Eli took a step back, cheeks flushed with either shame or lust.

"I'm sorry," he said.

"Why are you apologising?"

He sniggered, watched the cracks on the pavement instead of her face. "I shouldn't have done this. You mentioned your worry at the impropriety of our relationship, and I disrespected that. I'm really sorry, Jacintha. I just never know how to behave around you."

Her jaw slackened, he'd gotten it all wrong. One shaky hand reached for his arm, grabbed the thick leather of his jacket, pulled him closer. Eli came willingly, another moan - this one barely audible - leaving his lips.

"What do you mean, *behave*? I think I've given you the wrong idea." Tugging at his arm, Jacintha tried to bring him nearer, while the wind around them picked up strength. "I wanted you to kiss me. You behaved perfectly well."

"You wanted me to...? Why did you say those things about us being just friends, then?"

She shrugged. "I was only trying to warn you, in case my professional relationship with your sister left you uncomfortable. Because it doesn't leave *me* uncomfortable, Eli, at all."

"Come here, let me hold you," he begged, voice thick and husky in her ears.

She went willingly to his arms, and Eli ventured kissing her again. "I've been dying to do this, ever since I first met you. The day I almost ran you down, remember?"

Jacintha smiled, nodded. "What took you so long, then?"

Eli shook his head, wrapped an arm around her shoulders, directing their steps to where Jacintha had her flat. "There's a lot of catching up I still need to do. I'm never quite sure how to act in this kind of situation."

Staring into his eyes, Jacintha tried to read his expression. It wasn't the first time she noticed something off, odd, about Eli and the way he dealt with normal, daily issues. As if he was learning how to live, how to act, who to be. It reminded her of her own condition after the fall she'd taken when rock climbing, she'd had to learn everything again, because of her amnesia.

"Listen, it's still early." Her head pointed towards the closest pub. "Want to go get a nightcap? We can talk about this, if you want to. There's so much you still don't know about me, and so much I don't know of you."

Eli checked his watch, nodded. "Nyx is out with Trystan, I still have some time before I need to head back. Come, let's get inside where it's warm and we can have a good chat."

Reaching down to steal another kiss, Eli directed them towards the pub, and hand in hand, they crossed its doors, to the warmth of a crowded interior.

"So what's the deal with your brother?" Bryn Everley let herself drop to the couch in a dramatic gesture, Jamal sitting by her side and pulling her into the crook of his arm.

Nyx eyed her, unsure of how to react to such a question. Trystan held her hand, tugging so she joined him in the armchair, but she ignored him. Her eyes went to Pip's, who sat across the room from them, returning the stare. Whatever it was Eli didn't care for about the boy, Pip felt the same, Nyx could sense it. It was glaring and loud, as if the two of them mistrusted each other despite being so similar. Maybe because they were so similar.

"What of him?" she asked, and relented, sitting over Trystan's legs, folding herself against him.

"Dunno, you tell me."

"Why are you so interested in Eli?" Jamal asked, and the silence that followed was awkward, with Bryn's entire face darkening in displeasure.

"I'm not interested in him, but what if I was? His mother and mine were best friends, and from what I gathered, it was pretty messy, when he was born and Erin ran away. It was pretty messy for my mum, for your grandmother, your uncle too, Nyx. And when she came back, there was no son with her any longer, was there? Why would she give him away?"

Nyx frowned; there was something Bryn wasn't telling her. Something else being kept from her, perhaps from Eli too? What more could Spencer be hiding? What if he was also in the dark, and only Cressida Everley had been made privy to it, what with being Erin Vaughn's best friend? Did Aunt Sarah know of it as well, whatever it may be?

"This is none of your business," she said, "but seeing you're so eager to know, my mother had issues. She must have; after all, Eli wasn't the only child she abandoned. At least he was given to a good, loving family."

"It must have been hard, finding out you have a brother no one told you of," Bryn insisted.

"That's enough," Jamal warned her. His face mirrored his displeasure, which only made Bryn smirk.

"Oh, come on, you're all a bunch of sissies. This is why things fester and people get mad at each other, because no one properly speaks of stuff, no one dares say what's really on their mind, how they really feel. I know I would have felt betrayed, if I were in Nyx's shoes."

"But you're not."

"So you're *that* accepting, are you? You've welcomed in a bloke claiming to be your long-lost brother with no doubts to the veracity of his words?"

"There were DNA tests, Bryn, Corinna Vaughn made sure he was her grandson. Eli is who he claims to be, there's no issue with that, go ahead and ask Father."

Bryn eyed her brother momentarily, before focusing back on Nyx. "Well, I can't, can I? Not when he's gone away for the weekend." Her voice was infused with innuendos only Nyx seemed to understand.

Both girls grinned at each other, as if reaching an agreement. So it was *Max* Spencer had gone off with. Good for him. At least he might get some closure, if nothing else. Nyx stole a quick glance of Trystan, trying to figure if he knew about it, but Bryn's sudden, brisk shake of her head assured her he was in the dark. It wasn't her place to tell him; that should be his father.

"What have you got for us to drink?" Bryn asked. "Let's have some music, too."

Nyx made to stand, but before she could move, the speakers blared with music, way too loud. The volume lowered straight away, though, as if someone had turned it down. She gazed about, saw the smirk on Pip's face, and knew.

"How'd you do that?"

He shrugged, blushing. "Get us a drink, will you?"

"My mum's picking us up, do you really think it's a good idea to get plastered before she gets here?"

Bryn caressed Jamal's cheek, planted a kiss over his lips. "We won't get plastered, babe, we'll be careful. You'll be here to put a plug on our fun, after all."

"What's with you, tonight, why are you being so mean?" he asked, the others averting their eyes as if to avoid the awkwardness of being witnesses to their bickering.

Bryn twisted her wrist in the air, the bar cart wheeling forward of its own accord, with Nyx laughing excitedly at the sight.

"I need to learn how to do this," she said, and stood up to pour drinks for everyone. "Spencer will kill me if he finds out we've been drinking. What do you want? There's whisky, gin, rum, and vodka in the fridge. That's Eli's."

"Gin for me," Bryn said. "Trystan and Pip prefer the vodka, though."

"Eli won't like it if we drink his booze."

"Your brother won't mind," Bryn insisted. "Your uncle, on the other hand... but Jamal will see to it, won't you, love?" Once again, the girl stroked his cheek, and they kissed.

Nyx poured gin into a tumbler, watching the level of the bottle lower considerably. When she placed it back on the cart, the liquid seemed to rise, returning to its former amount. Eyes widening, she searched around for the culprit, spotted her cousin's reddening cheeks.

"Get out, you did that? How?"

"I'm a Waterling, it's easy for me to bend liquids to my will. Get me a vodka too, will you?"

Nyx nodded and ran off to the kitchen, Bryn following her, and grabbing the vodka from her hands.

"Here, let me pour," she offered, placing three tumblers on the counter. "Do you want some?"

"No, I don't drink."

"You're so uptight, here, live a little." The girl handed Nyx a half-full tumbler, holding one in her hand, which she proceeded to down. "Go on," she urged.

Nyx frowned, but mimicked Bryn, the vodka burning a trail of flames down her throat and into her stomach. Pulling a face, she coughed and gasped, the other girl giggling at her discomfort.

"Ugh, this is horrible. I thought you were having gin."

Bryn shrugged. "I like mixing my booze. So," she lowered her voice, filling the tumblers with more vodka, "you know they're together?"

"Are they?" She didn't bother confirming who Bryn was talking about; sure enough it must be Spencer and Max. "My uncle didn't come out and tell me straight up, but I assumed it was your dad he took off with. You're all right with this?"

Bryn faced her, looking sobered and serious for the first time. Not argumentative, rebellious or mocking, as she usually did. "Of course I am. Dad's been miserable all his life, and it stemmed from letting your uncle go. He's always repented it."

"Then why did he?"

Bryn's hand clawed at Nyx's wrist. "Those were different times, you know? My grandfather was a bully, he terrified his children into doing whatever he wanted. Corinna Vaughn didn't help either, being such a bigot she couldn't stand having a gay son. Dad was weak, terrified of losing his father's support, caved in and married Mum. Your uncle was braver, and that got him a broken heart, but look here, dad loves him, he never got over Spencer, and he won't ever hurt him again."

"It's none of my business."

"But you're fine with them being together? Because Trystan won't. Mum's got him wrapped up her little finger and he *will* make their lives hell, Nyx. For her sake."

She shook her head, picked one of the tumblers, leaving Bryn to carry the other two. "I won't let him."

Bryn laughed as they stepped back to the living room. "You're no match for him. My little brother's a player, and as soon as he tires of you..."

"Oi, that's out of order," Trystan said, taking the drink Nyx offered him. She placed the bottle on the floor by her side, taking back her seat. "Don't you listen to a word she says," he whispered, placing a kiss over Nyx's lips.

"Am I lying, though? You're only out for fun, that's all that matters to you. Once things get real, once it becomes serious, you're out the door, Trys. Why would it be different with Nyx?"

Trystan lowered his eyes, not in shame but to hide the anger Nyx caught sight of. Her stomach coiled, Bryn's words far too reminiscent of Penny's, who'd also warned her Trystan was never in for the long run - he was a player and once he'd had his amusement, he'd skip and leave Nyx to nurse a broken heart. She'd refused to believe, hanging on to the way Trystan treated her, and how good they were together, but there were times, in the dark of night, where she'd find herself questioning the veracity of his feelings, and hers too.

There were times, in the dark of night, when sleep evaded her and her mind would fill with images not of the boy she was dating, but of the one she wasn't. And along images of Pip Thomson came the words she kept hearing about Trystan and his callousness, his casualness where it came to other people's feelings. Especially the girls he dated. Now his own sister repeated what Penny had said, what Eli had hinted at, and Nyx couldn't help being worried she'd made a mistake. She couldn't help being worried Trystan would soon find that she was too much trouble, and things around her were far too messy and complicated, what with a brother who wasn't keen on their relationship and an uncle who was having an affair with Trystan's own father.

"Shut up," he said, voice hoarse and threatening. Bryn sniggered. "You're appalling, you know? Whenever you're in a bad mood, you always lash out at others; you go and punish everyone around you for your lack of self-esteem, your bitterness, your disillusions. You can only feel somewhat better about your crappy life when you're making someone else's day hell. You're only happy when someone else is in pain, pain inflicted by your callous words, that you dish out as if absolute truths, but guess what, Bryn? It's just your opinion, and it doesn't matter to anyone but you. Or it shouldn't."

"Then why do you get so offended?"

"Look, it's enough, you two." Pip stood up. His eyes were watery and pained; there was a wince on his face, as if his body ached, something inside him hurt.

Bryn lowered her eyes, took back her seat next to Jamal, his arm folding around her shoulders and pulling her to him, as if to shield her from outside attacks.

"Sorry," she said.

Nyx's heart stampeded, her lungs tightened by an unknown grip. She could hardly breathe, and found herself wishing she hadn't invited them over, if it was for everyone to end up at odds with each other. Hand reaching for Trystan's, she held it, lowered her head onto his shoulder. What if his sister was right, everyone was right, and he simply played her affections to his will, for as long as he was having fun, but then ditched her to pick up the pieces of her broken heart? What if she'd willingly placed herself in his hands, for him to do as he wanted? What if Eli was right, and they weren't meant to be?

The soft touch of Trystan's lips upon hers brought Nyx out of the dark cloud she'd fallen into, and they kissed. No, they were wrong. No one kissed someone else like this if there weren't feelings involved. They were wrong; he cared for her, and would never hurt her. *This* wasn't wrong, this was perfect, this was where she should be, in Trystan's arms, with him.

The music shifted from the loud, blaring guitars and speeding drums to something mellower, softer. Lights dimmed, shading the room in a cocoon of obscurity, and Nyx searched for the culprit. Pip grinned back at her, raised his tumbler and downed his drink.

"You need to teach me how to do this," she said.

"Whenever you want me to."

"Is Eli of the blood?" Bryn inquired, bending forward to stare at Nyx. "Does he know anything about this, the town, the Craft?"

The girl shrugged. "We haven't talked about it. I never saw him use magic, but I can feel something weird from him. Maybe he's dormant, from so many years..." She pressed a hand over her lips, it wasn't her place to talk about Eli's past. Not that there was anything wrong with it.

"Yes?" Bryn urged, and now everyone's eyes were on Nyx, as if longing to learn more about the elusive, mysterious brother. "You were saying?"

Shaking her head; she came to a decision, it wasn't anything shameful, after all, was it? It wasn't even a secret. "He was in a coma for seven years. Couldn't be using magic, could he?"

Eyes widened and gasps erupted from half-open lips.

"Seven years in a coma? Blimey," Jamal shook his head. "Mum doesn't know this, does she? She'd be fussing all over him if she did. Even if he's not really her nephew. Or my cousin."

"He's my brother, though, so of course he's your cousin. I don't understand why you don't like him," Nyx spat. "Or you," she finished, turning to Pip, who blushed.

"I never said I don't like him, he's the one who's got a problem with me."

"He's got a problem with everyone who comes near his sister." Trystan and Pip exchanged a grin.

"He's not that bad, come on," Bryn insisted, pouring more gin into her glass. "That explains a lot, him spending seven years in a coma. On top of being adopted, of course he'd latch on to Spencer and Nyx as if they're a lifebuoy."

"I do like him," Jamal insisted. "He's ok, he's just not... well, our age, is he? He acts weird sometimes, but I can understand why, now that I know about his coma. Bloody hell, that must have messed him up real bad."

"How do you know my brother?" Nyx stared straight at Bryn, watched her attentively.

The other girl's cheeks covered in a light blush, and her eyes sparkled with an odd glint. She lowered them, and cleared her throat, alerting Nyx to her being rather uncomfortable with the course of the conversation.

"Met him on the night of my bash. Wanker went and ran into my bike, didn't he?"

A bevy of loud cackles erupted at Bryn's words, and she smiled openly, relief washing across her face. Nyx cocked an eyebrow, studied her further, there was something here. Why was Bryn so interested in her brother, why all these questions, the sudden awkwardness?

"That's how he got into my sister's black list, anyone hurt that bike of hers, and they're screwed. Massively." Trystan laughed, joined by Jamal.

Pip eyed Bryn, his eyes narrowed in deep concentration, a lopsided smirk on his lips. Nyx's attention veered to him. Whatever she'd sensed, Pip had, too.

"I'd have killed him," Bryn said, "if he'd ruined the bike. Turns out it was fine, no harm done. We had a little chat, and he seemed ok, I invited him in for the party, but he declined. Looked rather lonesome, though, and I felt sorry for him. Does he not have a girlfriend, Nyx?"

There. The inflexion in Bryn's voice, the slight tremor as she asked about Eli's love life. Could she have a crush on him? Nyx stole a quick glance at Pip, saw the same doubt in his eyes, knew she was on the right track. And didn't feel so weird, or so wrong, anymore. It was normal, after all, to feel attracted to two different people, even if you were in a long-term relationship like Bryn and Jamal. It happened, and what mattered was how you handled the attraction. Knowing Bryn was somewhat interested in Eli assuaged her, and Nyx felt less lonely for it. It wasn't a sin, that she had feelings for Trystan but also for Pip. As long as she channelled them correctly, and kept her emotions guarded and in their respective places - Trystan her boyfriend and Pip her friend - there was nothing wrong with the way she felt. There was nothing wrong with Bryn's apparent infatuation for Eli, either, except for the fact he was far older than her.

"I'm not sure. He didn't have one, told me so himself, a couple of days before your bash, actually. But he's been going out a lot, lately, even though he hasn't said anything. Think he may have met someone, he's always hanging out at the auto-repair shop." Her eyes latched on to Bryn again, expecting a reaction.

It didn't take long to register, Trystan's sister blushing deeply and once again diverting her focus to her own hands and the half empty glass she held.

"How old was he, when...?"

"He was fifteen when he went into a coma," Nyx clarified. "If you're wondering, nope, he didn't have a girlfriend before that, not a proper, real girlfriend, I mean."

Trystan held up one hand and counted off fingers. "That means he was twenty-two when he woke up. Crikey, bloke spent his entire adolescence asleep. He didn't get laid all those years?"

Another burst of laughter erupted, this time only from the boys. Both Nyx and Bryn glared at them, as if offended by their mirth.

"What?" Trystan asked. "Look, it's only natural; most people start their sex lives somewhere around their teens, don't they? Come on, which one here hasn't yet? Only if it's Nyx; all the others I know for sure have gotten laid already. Plenty of times, the two of you." He nodded towards Bryn and Jamal, smirking. "Eli's got what, ten years on us? It's just mental that he's never done it, know what I mean? I'm not poking fun or anything; it's just unusual, all right? Bloke's an adult."

"And a fit one, at that," Pip added.

"That he is," Bryn joined in.

"Oh, good, now everyone's got the hots for my brother."

"Oi, I don't have the hots for him." Pip chuckled. "Only saying he won't be inexperienced for long, I think."

The ringing of the bell put an end to their exchange, all sitting up to attention at the sound. They eyed each other, faces paling somewhat, taking in the tumblers and glasses with drink still in them, and the bottle of vodka on the floor.

"It must be my mum, look at the time," Jamal said, and stood up, wiping nervous hands on his jeans.

"Well, let's clear up." Bryn downed the rest of her drink, took Jamal's tumbler, and reached for Pip's. "Hide that bottle; I can't carry it to the kitchen along with these." She grabbed Trystan's and Nyx's tumblers and vaulted for the kitchen. "Go open the door, Nyx!"

Stumbling on her feet, bottle falling on its side and rolling under the armchair she'd been sitting in, Nyx fixed her hair, her clothes and walked off to the door, where the bell rang again. Plastering a smile on her face, she waited for Bryn to cross the hallway back to the living room before opening the front door to let her aunt Sarah in.

VI

"Seven years?" Jacintha asked again, sipping the G&T.

Eli grinned, nodded, reached for her hand. He still couldn't believe he'd kissed her and she hadn't pulled away. Entwining their fingers together, thumb caressing the softness of her palm, he sighed in a mix of relief and utter joy. When had he ever felt this happy? When had his heart halted its beat at the sight of a woman, when had he ever experienced anything as exquisitely painful as the range of emotions taking over him whenever he thought of Jacintha? When had he last wanted anyone this much?

The overhead lights flickered, the loud music from the speakers cut by static. A mere disturbance, but one Eli couldn't help attributing to his intense emotional state. He must take better care, lest people regard him with even more curiosity and distrust than they seemed to, at the moment. Erin Vaughn's long-lost son; Erin, the runaway, girl of many secrets, who no one talked about. As if afraid of raining down a curse they'd barely avoided. His mother had been like him, like Nyx; they had magic, powers coursing their blood, but the rest of the town seemed unaffected by such afflictions. Why did no one talk of it? His adoptive parents had spoken of Erin's talents freely, but here, the place his mother had been born and raised, no one seemed to know who and what she really was. Had this been the real reason behind her escape from town? Was that why Spencer had left, too, why they never brought Nyx to see her grandmother? Because of their magic and the bigotry the locals might hold against them?

No wonder Nyx and Spence kept silent.

"Seven years..." Jacintha insisted, bringing Eli back to the present. He kissed the back of her hand. "I can't even get my head around it. Must have been so strange, waking up and no longer being the same as you remembered."

"It was a shock, but I'm doing much better now. Used to have panic attacks at the slightest, stupidest things. Being around women was one of them." He laughed.

"So, you haven't been in a relationship?"

What was he supposed to say? He'd lived a life elsewhere. As dim as the seven years he'd spent at his father's world were becoming, Eli had lived his life there. And that included having been in love, deeply, madly.

"I had a girlfriend, before," he said. It wasn't really a lie. "Things never got to progress, though, and I'd met her when I was a teen. It was very different being face to face with women my own age, experienced, confident, self-sufficient, when I wasn't anywhere near that stage in life. I still feel very awkward around anyone I find attractive, anyone I like."

Jacintha pressed his hand. "You don't have to feel that way around me, Eli. You can be yourself; it's who I fell for."

"*Fell* for?"

The blush covering her cheeks rendered her face even more charming. It lit a spark of mischief, which forced a rush of heat through his body, as images of the two of them together pried a pathway in his mind.

"Look, I'm not going to deny it, I like you. I'm attracted to you, I want to be with you, get to know you better. Yes, I believe I may be falling in love with you. Does this shock you?"

His grin lit the whole of his face. "Like I said, I feel very awkward around confident, self-sufficient women who know what they want and aren't ashamed of saying it. I feel very awkward, but very into them, too. Into you. Maybe I've fallen in love with you. I shouldn't be afraid of admitting it, right? But I don't want to get hurt, don't want to be betrayed and left to pick up the pieces..." Averting Jacintha's eyes, Eli finished his beer, he was going too far. She had no need to know of his past, nor would she ever understand, let alone believe him.

"No one wants to get hurt. But do you want us to be together?"

"Of course I do. It's just that there's a lot of new stuff for me to take in and I don't always know how to deal. I'm constantly scared I mess everything up."

"Listen, we have a lot in common, you and me. You spent seven years in a coma, only woke from it three years ago, right?" Eli nodded. "Well, I had an accident three years ago, woke up from it with the world's biggest case of amnesia. I can't remember anything about my previous life. Sometimes I have these... flashes, but they're so quick I can hardly make sense of them."

The lights flickered again, this time for longer, bringing Jacintha's attention to it. She eyed the lamps, a frown on her brow to match his own. This time, it hadn't been Eli's emotions setting it off, maybe it was the approaching storm? Glancing at his watch, he pushed the beer away, a look of dismay settling over his face.

"It's almost Nyx's curfew, I should be heading home. I'm sorry I have to cut this short."

Jacintha shook her head, a tumble of brown hair falling over her shoulders. "It's fine, you have responsibilities, I totally understand. Come on, let's get out of here."

Outside, the rain pelted down, forcing Jacintha to pull up the hood of her parka. None of them had thought to bring an umbrella, and Eli only had his biker jacket, the collar of which he straightened to somewhat protect the back of his neck from the cold raindrops. Spencer's car was only a few steps away, parked in front of the building where Jacintha had her flat. Holding her hand, he ran towards the door, under whose awning they found some respite from the storm.

"Call me when you get home, all right? Just so I know you got there safely?" Jacintha threw her arms around Eli's neck, placed a loud kiss over his lips.

"Will do. Am actually worried about Nyx, I hope they're not riding that stupid bike."

"Trystan's a very responsible boy, Eli. He wouldn't do that. His sister, on the other hand..."

"She's a wild one, I bet," he added, thinking back to when he'd met Bryn Everley the night of her birthday bash. "I'll give Nyx a call, see where she is, pick her up if she needs a ride. I'll talk to you later, yes?"

Eli bent down to claim one last kiss, his lips lingering over hers as if unable to part. Finally, he found a remnant of will deep inside him, worry for his sister's wellbeing forcing him away from Jacintha's enticing company and the lush warmth of her arms.

"Call me," she said, sliding through the half-open door, eyes still firmly locked with Eli's.

"Will do."

He waited for her to shut the door, then ran to the car, black jeans drenched, water running down the back of his jacket, wetting the seat. Taking it off, Eli threw it into the backseat, belted himself and drove away, wanting to change into dry clothes before he picked up Nyx from wherever she might be. As the car turned the bend around the Everley estate, Eli's attention was once more drawn to the dark patch of woods. This was where it all started; this was where his mother had somehow found herself elsewhere and met his father. This was the way back for him, to where Eli believed he belonged. This was where he must bring Nyx so she could Weave a pathway for him to enter. He should have braved the dark woods already, why hadn't he? What stopped him? It was three weeks since he'd arrived at Weaversmoor, and the closest he'd come to that patch of forest had been the day he'd almost ran over Jacintha, who'd been fleeing those woods. Eli hadn't even dared cross the meadow that separated the backyard at Vaughn's cottage from the forested areas. What was stopping him?

Jacintha was. The thought of entering the woods and going back to Ephemera, this time for good, held little allure for Eli. It held especially less interest now they were together. But it wasn't just that. Coming clean to Nyx, telling his sixteen-year-old sister the truth about his seven years in a coma - the truth about what he was, that she must be too - kept holding him back. How was a person to talk of such things? He'd be regarded as crazy, unless Nyx was well aware of what she was. If only they'd take the initiative of starting that awkward conversation, Nyx and Spencer, thus easing the burden for him. Eli kept hoping, waiting for them to say something, but so far, no talk of magic had been made amongst the Vaughns of Weaversmoor.

He drove the car up the wide lane, noticing the open gate. Training the spotlights on the parking space in front of the old garage, he spotted his bike still under the awning, and a car parked in front of it. The colour and plate soon assured him it was Sarah Wilson's, and his heart sped at the thought something might have happened to Nyx, to Spencer. He parked the car in the vacant slot to the right, and jumped out of his seat, running towards the house under heavy rain, bolting inside. Hands shaking, Eli still thought to take off his drenched jacket, noticing the number of unfamiliar coats hanging from the rack. He marched towards the living room, from where the sound of loud voices in laughter and cheery conversation drifted out.

The room was full to capacity, or so it seemed to him. Sarah Wilson stood by the door, blond hair tied in a messy bun, arms crossed over her chest, while she reminisced on her own youth, the kids perched on chairs and the sofa, laughing out loud.

Nyx was seated over Trystan's knees, who'd taken hold of what they called Spencer's armchair, the one his uncle favoured. They had their arms around each other and traded soft kisses in between laughs. The couch had been commandeered by Jamal Wilson and his girlfriend, the rebellious Bryn Everley, whose dark-smudged eyes were set on Eli. Lounging on the other armchair, the one he'd claimed for his personal use, Pip Thomson kept an attentive watch over Trystan and Nyx's every move.

Something about the boy's expression brought Eli to attention, and he studied it. Exactly what was he seeing here? Who was Pip watching so intently, with such fire in his eyes? Was there some sort of triangle going on? Was it Nyx the boy seemed so interested in, or Trystan? Was it both? Before Eli could come to any sort of conclusion, the boy turned his head and faced him, as if he'd sensed the older man watching him. A mocking smile caught his lips, one Eli made sure he delivered back, and then Sarah Wilson was turning round and grinning at him, arms already spread wide to embrace Eli.

"We didn't hear you come in," she said, hugging him, planting a kiss on each of his cheeks. "Did you have a good time? I was just about to take these kids back home."

Eli smiled, cheeks blushing. He waved a hand at the teens gathered inside his living room, nodded at Trystan and Nyx. "I did, thank you, Sarah. Do you want me to drive anyone home? The Everleys are just down the road, I can take them."

"No, dear, it's no bother; I have to go past their place to get home. Pip, are you crashing with Trystan?"

The boy exchanged a look first with Trystan, shrugging. "I was going back to the Academy, but it's way too late. Can I stay over, Trys?"

"Of course you can, you know you're always welcome," Trystan replied.

Pip smiled, looking somewhat relieved, and for a split second Eli experienced a connection with him. Both felt like outsiders, never sure where they belonged or where they were welcome. At least Eli had a whole other world to call home; Pip had nothing but his own self.

"Right, that's everything sorted, then. Come on, children, let's go, it's raining cats and dogs and I don't want to be caught in this downpour longer than I need to. Eli, it was great seeing you," Sarah said, turning to hug him again.

He returned the brief hug, stepped inside the room so the door was clear, and nodded at each one of the teens walking out. As she came closer, Bryn Everley reached a hand to his arm, pressed it gently, tips of her fingers lingering over the skin of his wrist, his hand. He eyed her in confusion, which only increased at her enigmatic smile.

"Good to see you again, Eli. Heard you've been spending time at the auto-repair shop?"

"He's thinking of applying for the job there," Nyx said, marching hand in hand with Trystan. "I'm just gonna walk them to the car, is that all right?"

Eli nodded, fled further into the room, away from Bryn's stare. When he heard them leave the house, he fished his phone and called Jacintha. She answered on the second ring, her voice sending shivers through his spine.

"Hey, I'm home."

"Everything all right, then?"

"Yep. You?"

"Fine, I was about to turn in. Will I see you tomorrow? Want to do lunch?"

Eli closed his eyes, took a breath, unsure of what to say. It was his birthday next day, and he'd kept it from both his uncle and his sister, now from Jacintha.

"Spencer's away for the weekend," he said. "I already told Nyx we could go out for lunch. The two of us, like brother and sister." He still had to fill Nyx in on those plans, though.

"Sure, we can catch up later. Give me a call and we can work something out, all right?"

He winced, fiddling with a loose thread on his jersey. Jacintha's voice sounded different, not so joyous. Was she upset he wouldn't meet her for lunch? Maybe he should forget about his plans, spend time with her instead. The intricacies of romantic relationships were still a bit foggy for him; Eli had no idea how to handle them. He wanted to be with her, but also wanted to spend time with Nyx getting to know her, if not winning her trust. And he wanted the Sylvains to meet her.

"I can have lunch with my sister any other day," he said.

"Absolutely not, you've only just found each other. It's important you bond, Eli. For you and for Nyx. Go on, call me later and we can meet for a drink, all right?"

"If you're sure."

"I am. Talk to you tomorrow?"

"Yep."

"Ok. Have a good night, then. Sleep tight."

"You too." Hanging up, he dropped the phone on the side table.

One hand running through damp hair, Eli sighed loudly, frustrated at his lack of understanding of social rules. Talking on the phone was a torment, never knowing what to do or say, when to hang up, how to end the call. Nyx and Spencer poked fun at him, but didn't help; well, not where women were concerned. They simply accepted him for who he was and how he was, not bothering to put him through the ropes or dishing some light on issues he found himself struggling with.

As he was about to take a seat, his eyes happened upon a bottle lurking under the opposite armchair, which looked a lot like the one he'd stashed in the freezer. Not that Eli was much of a drinker, but he enjoyed sharing a drink with Spencer in the evenings, once in a while, and seeing both seemed to favour vodka over the drinks Corinna Vaughn had kept in her bar cart, he'd gone out and bought a bottle he could share with his uncle.

A bottle his underage sister seemed to have brought out, so she could drink with her friends, and which she must have tossed under the armchair as soon as Sarah rang the bell. Before he had time to get up and retrieve it, though, he found Nyx standing by the door, eyeing him in a strange way.

"Who was that on the phone? Your Mum?" she asked.

Eli blushed. He should talk to her about it, shouldn't he? After all, Jacintha was her tutor, Nyx should know of his involvement with the woman, she should know what kind of relationship they had. But what was it, really? Did he know? Were they dating, were they together, was this a casual fling? What should he tell Nyx, when he himself hadn't the slightest idea what to expect of Jacintha?

"Why is there a bottle of vodka under that chair?" he asked instead, trying to steer the subject from himself.

Nyx had the grace to blush, lowering her head in silent shame. "Bryn wanted a drink. Then they all did. Are you very mad at me?"

"Nyx, come sit." He waited for her to plunge herself on the sofa. "Did you drink?"

"A shot. It's not like I never had a drink before, Eli, come on. I'm sixteen. When I lived at Havenleah, I went to parties, drank a few beers, some vodka too, once or twice. Never got plastered, though. But I should have asked you before you took off."

"You're all under age. What if something happened? I'm not mad at you, just worried. I never know what to say or do, would Spence have let you offer alcohol to your teenage friends?"

She shook her head. "Don't tell him, please. And I didn't offer, it was Bryn who asked for a drink. And it was just the one drink, I promise. Better that we do it here, in the safety of our home, than outside in fishy bars or parking lots, Eli. We weren't getting hammered. And Bryn's eighteen, so she's technically of age."

"That girl's a mess." He shook his head, but smiled. "I won't tell Spence, but next time, please, clear it with him before. Because I don't know what's appropriate in situations like these, and he *is* your guardian, he's like a father to you, isn't he? So talk to him, please."

"Bryn's into you."

Eli's eyes widened in shock. "She told you this?" He'd sensed her interest; more than that, he'd noticed her play at seduction, but had chosen to ignore it. The girl was far too young and he wasn't into her. Even though Bryn's green eyes had made sudden, unexpected appearances in his mind's eye.

"No, you think? But she kept asking about you, including if you had a girlfriend."

He blushed again, turned his face away, to the sound of Nyx's caw of victory.

"I knew it; it wasn't your Mum on the phone."

"Never said it was."

She got up from her seat and threw herself on her knees in front of her brother, one hand reaching for his, a grin devouring the lower half of her face. He couldn't help but smile at her excitement, felling rather thrilled himself.

"Dish," Nyx begged. "Come on, tell me everything, who is she, how did you meet, how long has this been going on? Oh, I want to meet her, is it serious or just a fling?"

Eli lowered his head, shaking it, a snigger leaving his lips. "I'm not sure you're gonna like this. It's your tutor, Jacintha Tate."

He'd expected her to be shocked, annoyed, discomforted. Had prepared for her displeasure, her disapproval. But he hadn't expected nor been prepared for her shriek of joy, and the arms Nyx threw around him as she hugged her brother tightly, all the while howling in his ears words he couldn't even make out.

"Nyx, I can't tell if you're mad at me or glad."

She pulled back, looking straight at him. "Oh, this is perfect; she's the one I wanted to match you with."

"You wanted to match me with someone?"

"I told you I'd find you a girlfriend, didn't I? So you could make up for all the lost time. And it was Miss Tate I had in mind, today, when I asked you to pick me up from school. I was going to introduce you to her."

"That's why you were being so difficult about me not wanting to go. You should have told me."

"What, and risk the wrath of Eli?"

They both laughed.

"I wouldn't have been mad at you."

"No, but you'd have been so awkward you'd scare her away. Oh, tell me everything, how did you two meet? When did it happen, how long have you been seeing her? When was your first kiss? Have you already...?"

"Nyx, please!" Colour rose from his cheeks to cover his entire face, even his forehead. "Easy on those intimate questions. We met the day I got to Weaversmoor. I nearly ran her over."

Nyx giggled. "What's with you and running over people? You also ran into Bryn and her bike, right?"

Eli smiled and shook his head. "Only her bike. Jacintha came running from the woods, straight onto the road. If I'd been driving a car, I would've hit her, it was all so fast."

"Why did she come running to the road, though?"

"Said she scared herself jogging in the woods. But that's how we met. Then I didn't see her again for, oh, I don't know, what felt like ages. Though I couldn't get her out of my mind. Thought about asking you and Spence if you knew anyone named Jacintha, but..."

"But what? You should have, Eli."

"I felt awkward. We'd only just met, I'd only just been legally made a part of your family, didn't want to push my luck. Just wanted to get to know you and Spencer. But I ran into her on Halloween, and we had dinner together. Since then, we've seen each other regularly."

"Ah, so you had your first kiss on Halloween, it's kind of... well, romantic, if you're a goth, I guess." She laughed, but hugged her brother again. "I'm really happy for you."

"We had our first kiss tonight."

"What? But you've been seeing her for the past two weeks."

"This was only our sixth date, I didn't know if it was appropriate to..."

Nyx burst out in giggles. "Oh, Eli! Couldn't you tell she was into you? Because if she kept saying yes whenever you asked her out, then she was game, you should have kissed her on your second date."

Eli grinned again. "I didn't know. But I kissed her today. She said something about us being just friends and I lost it. Thought she was going to wallop me for having the gall, but no, she... she kissed me back."

"So now you're together?"

"I guess? She said she wants to be with me, wants to get to know me. Think I'm in love with her. I don't think I'm ready for this, you know? How am I going to do this?"

"Oi, you're all right, you'll do fine. You need to give this a chance, Eli. Promise me you will. If you need to talk, I'm always here for you, you know that? And Spence too."

"He's with Max, isn't he?" Eli asked, wanting to change the subject.

Nyx's expression sobered. "How do you know?"

"Call it a hunch. He told you?"

She shook her head. "Bryn did. I wonder why Spencer's kept this from me, from us."

"Maybe he's ashamed? After all, Max Everley is still a married man. And the father of your own boyfriend."

"So you're saying you don't support this? He's already left his wife and filed for divorce, you know?"

Eli shrugged. "It's not my place. As long as they're happy, that's all it matters. I'll stand by his decision, of course, but it won't be easy for them. It's all very sudden."

"No, it isn't. Max was the love of his life. It's… complicated, Eli. And it's not my place to tell the story, I'm sure Spencer will talk to you about this, when you tell him about Miss Tate."

"You think he'll frown on it?"

Nyx smiled. "She *is* my tutor, and you my brother, it's kind of awkward, if we're to look at it dispassionately. But Spence will get it, don't worry. Just make sure you're as open with him as he's been with you, right? I'm off to bed, feeling knackered. Are you staying up?"

Eli studied her for a quick moment, wondering if he should tell her, or anyone. It was almost midnight, which would officially make it the seventeenth of November, his birthday. He'd shied from mentioning the date to Spencer, in fear he cancelled his plans of going away for the weekend. In the end, Eli had given up on his own intention of spending the date with his parents, just so he could keep an eye on Nyx and allow his uncle some respite. But he'd arranged to meet them for lunch at Sunderleigh next day, and he was hoping Nyx would join him.

"Not for long, no, I'm also tired. I'll just clear up in here after you and your messy friends," he said.

"Hey, we didn't make a mess. Leave it, I'll sort it in the morning. Just put that vodka away, and let's keep that our secret, ok?"

Eli stood up and retrieved the bottle from under the armchair. "Just this once. I don't like the idea of keeping this kind of thing from Spence. Promise me you'll talk to him about this, next time you want to have your friends over. Which I'm guessing will be tomorrow night?"

"No, tomorrow Trystan and I are going out. You can have the house for yourself, maybe ask Miss Tate over for dinner. I promise I'll text before I come home, so the two of you can have some privacy. Or I can kip over at Trystan's."

Eli laughed, petting his sister's curly head. "As if. I'm not letting you sleep over at your boyfriend's without Spencer's permission. Listen, are you doing anything for lunch tomorrow?"

"Not really," Nyx said, eyeing him. "Why?"

"I'm meeting my parents at Sunderleigh, thought you might join us? I wanted them to meet you, do you mind?"

Her entire face lit up. "Of course not, I'd love to!"

Eli grinned back at her, relieved. "Good, then it's a date. Go on, young lady, off to bed. Sleep tight."

"Don't stay up too late daydreaming of Jacintha," Nyx whispered, and ran off to the stairs, leaving Eli grinning and blushing on his way to the kitchen, vodka bottle unstoppered and reaching to his lips so he could take a swig.

"Bryn's just gone into the woods." Pip walked to the window, vacating the leather armchair next to the bookcase.

"There's something off with her," Trystan said, arms behind his head as he lay on the bed watching shadows play across the ceiling. "She's been worried, must want to centre herself. Wish I knew what's up with her."

Pip sniggered. "You don't know? She fancies your girlfriend's brother, and it's doing her head in."

Trystan sat up, eyes veering towards his best friend. "She did ask an awful lot of questions about him, didn't she? What of Jamal? Thought he was, like, the love of her life, know what I mean?"

Shrugging, Pip eased the window open and lit a cigarette. "This troubles her, I mean, can't be easy for someone like Bryn. To fall for two different blokes."

"Someone like Bryn?"

"Your sister plays the rebel, but she's not all that bad, is she? Jamal's been a big deal for her, but I can see how this Eli may have such an appeal."

"You really don't like him, do you?"

"It's not like that."

"What's it like, then? Do you also fancy him?"

Pip's gaze rested over Trystan. His brow furrowed, tongue wetting his lips. "Why, are you jealous?"

Trystan smirked, rolled over, avoiding Pip, who came to sit on the floor by the bed. One gentle finger alighted over Trystan's forehead, shuffled lose strands of hair away, travelling down to trace his jaw.

"Are you?" he insisted.

"Are you in love with Nyx?"

Throwing his hands up, Pip sighed. "What is this, an interrogation?"

"She's my girlfriend."

"I know she is, you won't let me forget it. Why do you find you need to remind me of this, every single minute of the day, Trys? She chose *you*, it's not like it matters how I feel about her. It's not like it matters how I feel about anyone."

Trystan grabbed hold of his wrist, locked it in a tight hold. "So you *do* fancy her brother."

There were shards of ice in his eyes, and Pip couldn't help shiver. Not in fear or apprehension, but in realisation of their meaning. No matter how much Trystan denied it and ran from his feelings, those were real, they existed. The one time they'd kissed hadn't been a drunken accident, or rather, it had been brought about not only by Trystan being utterly plastered, but also because he *did* feel something for Pip. Something he was just too scared to face, or too angry to admit to, because of his father's past.

"You know damn well that's not true. I fancy *you*." He grinned mischievously at Trystan. "And Nyx, of course."

"Can't you ever get real?"

On the verge of losing his patience, Pip stood up, paced around the room, the pyjama bottoms he'd borrowed from Trystan sliding down his slimmer frame.

"You want me to get real? I can get real, only you don't want to hear, don't want to know. It's you and it's always been you, but yes, all right, I'm in love with Nyx. There, are you satisfied? I love you and am in love with your girlfriend, how sick is that? How sad? How much of a twat does that make me, Trystan?"

"Not much, or I'd already have jumped you."

Both boys laughed, a soft, low cackle. Pip came back to sit by Trystan, one hand grabbing his. "I know you feel it too, that's why it didn't work between you and Penny, why those other girls didn't last longer than a couple of months. What are you scared of, Trys? I'd leave *everything* for you. For you and Nyx."

"Sod off. You're being dramatic, you hardly know her, to feel anything like this."

"I know *you*."

Their eyes locked, stood gazing into each other's pupils for a long time. Trystan was the first to look away. "Pip, I'm not like that."

"Like what?"

"Like my father, gay."

"This isn't about being gay! Nor is it about being straight, or bi. It's about how you feel for people, certain people. You think I fell for you because you're a bloke? Or Nyx, because she's a girl? Why do you have to make everything so black and white? Because of your parents? You're headed the same way as your dad, living a lie because you're too scared to admit to your deepest feelings. We don't fall for people because they're boys or girls; we fall for them regardless of gender, Trystan. Look, life's messy, it is, and we don't always get to make sense of things. How long have we known each other?"

"Three years, give or take." Trystan risked a glance at Pip, whose expression had softened.

"I've been in love with you for that long. And I've seen your feelings for me grow, and change, and become..."

"What, Thomson? Become what? You're deluding yourself."

Pip reached a hand to the back of Trystan's neck, cupped the base of his head and pulled him closer. Foreheads touching, they closed their eyes and stood like that for a long, heavy moment. The room was draped in silence and lit by the glitter of stars upon the night sky, a pale, round moon spreading its barren, weakened light. Fingers entwined, they traced each other's skin, eyes closed, hearts speeding, breaths raspy and throaty as emotions overtook them. Time stood still, for a brief span, where they were outside space and matter, where they were the only living creatures in the whole of the universe, standing in a place where there was no judgement and no expectations, for only they existed and were safe, free of constraining boundaries.

Lips parting slightly, Pip reached his mouth to Trystan's, heart hammering, sweat running down his back. As much as he was in love with Nyx and couldn't get the girl out of his head, it was Trystan he loved; it was Trystan he longed for; it was Trystan who made him complete. It was his touch he wanted, his lips, the twirl of his tongue on Pip's, the entwining of their limbs, the slow, slow, sweet motion of their bodies together. It was Trystan, yes, but it was also Nyx.

Realising what Bryn must be going through, Pip almost smiled at his own predicament. How was it possible for someone to feel like this? How could he be in love with two people so different from one another? How could he claim this was more than hormonal teenage angst, spurred by the physical attraction he felt for both, in all of their differences? He fancied Trystan; he fancied Nyx, and any notion this might be him falling in love with them was an elaborate lie he told himself, just so he felt less base, less vulgar.

No, this was what the world tried to force on him, these notions of what was right or wrong, this cataclysmic black and white, with no shades of grey in between. Nothing was this simple, this pristine. He wasn't depraved or wanton just because he nurtured strong feelings for both a boy and a girl. He wasn't sick and soiled just because he fancied both genres; he was outside those binary equations a dated, conservative society tried to impose on him.

The same values Trystan fell prey to, and that prevented him from freeing himself, no matter how much he wanted, or how strongly he felt for Pip, no matter how intense his desires were. Trystan was bound to dated notions of love and propriety, as was

Bryn, but not Pip. And from what he was coming to realise about her, neither was Nyx. Maybe she'd be the one swaying Trystan, opening his eyes and mind, his strait-laced integrity; maybe she crumbled his walls down and they could be happy, the three of them, together. He saw no harm in it, and believed neither did she. Screw the rest of the world and their shallow-minded views.

He reached closer, mouth alighting over Trystan's, tongue at the ready to claim his, was stopped midway to the kiss by Trystan lowering his head even further, now completely out of Pip's reach.

"I'm not gonna do this to Nyx," he said, and Pip sighed. "Not gonna do the same mistake I did with Penny. She doesn't deserve it."

"It's that serious, huh?"

Pulling away, Pip walked over to the folding bed, needing the distance between them to shower some cool into his blazing core.

"She's... like no one I ever met." Trystan's eyes narrowed, glinting with emotion. "She's like you. It's almost like being with you."

Pip shook his head, a sad smile washing over his lips. "Nyx and I are nothing alike, you're just fooling yourself."

Trystan shrugged. "You know I love you, Pip. I really *do* love you, but I can't do this. You'll always be my favourite person; I just can't be who you need me to be."

"No, Trys, you're just too cowardly to be who *you* need to be." He slid into bed and turned over, eyes on the window, hands shaking in sudden fury at the unfairness of life and of having fallen in love with someone so uptight he couldn't admit to who he was. "I'm not gonna beg that you love me, Everley, I'm never gonna beg."

"Because you already know I do."

"You said it, not I."

"Wonder if she's back yet."

Pip smiled, turned back round. "Who, Bryn? She'll sort herself out. Fact is, he looks at her differently. I mean, she clearly has some sort of effect on him."

"Nyx's brother? You think he's not indifferent to Bryn?"

"I was watching him tonight. The moment she came up to say goodnight, he blushed, and became jittery. Kept stealing glances at her, but I don't think he was aware of it. She unravels him. I wouldn't be surprised to learn they hit it off."

"Nyx seems to believe he's met someone, maybe it's Bryn. Maybe they're out in the woods as we speak, a secret rendezvous."

"Trystan Everley, the romantic."

"I'm not being romantic, just saying they might be doing it even as we speak. Maybe Bryn's his first."

Both boys giggled. "Your sister would like that; she's a bit of a control freak."

"Why don't you like him, Thomson?"

Pip shrugged. "It's not that I don't. You know how things are with me, being an Empath and a Haruspex. You know the number of sigils I've had to ink just so I can have a semblance of peace inside my own brain. Even with all these seals, I can tune into other people's emotions, their thoughts, if I want to. I walk into a room or meet someone and I'm immediately aware of their overall composure, most times I can even read their thoughts. Well, not with him."

"What do you mean?"

"Eli Vaughn's like a wall, a very strong one. He's unreadable, unbreachable, unknowable. I don't know if it's a natural thing, if he was born that way, or if he's honed it over the years, this intense shielding of his. Maybe the coma changed something in his brain and he can't be read by people like me."

"Do you think he has magic? Think he knows about it, about this place? Do you think he knows of the Craft?"

"He's got to be of the blood, Trys. I mean, he's a Vaughn."

Trystan lay on his back, eyeing the play of shadows on the ceiling. "Mum used to say the weirdest things. About their mother."

"Erin Vaughn? I think I remember her mentioning it."

"Mind, she would have to be hammered to start dishing about it, but... she always said Nyx's Mum could open the secret of the trees? That those woods were haunted and dangerous to people like her. That Erin had lost her mind and her heart out there, to the shadows, and that those shadows had come for her. I wonder if she meant Eli's dad. I wonder what happened to Erin Vaughn in those woods. Swear to you, sometimes I get freaked out in there, don't you?"

Pip nodded. He'd felt uneasy once or twice, as if something lurked there, behind a veil, trying to break free.

"But then my powers are stronger for dwelling inside it, and I'm charged, my energy levels just rise. Bryn too, although I wish she wouldn't go alone. I've often wondered if Nyx's mum didn't..." He stopped, a sudden jolt of fear taking over his throat, closing it.

"Didn't what?"

"Get assaulted out there. Eli's father." Trystan rolled over again, locking eyes with Pip. "I mean, the way my mother spoke has always made me think something really bad happened and she barely escaped. Erin wasn't as lucky, though. Can you imagine if Eli Vaughn's the son of a rapist? Do you think these things are genetic? What if he's hurting my sister as we speak? What if he's a psychopath who *is* of the blood and knows his Craft and is using it against Bryn?" Sitting up in bed, Trystan reached for his jeans.

Pip mimicked him, suddenly scared he might have a point. The entire town knew what had happened to Erin Vaughn when she was fifteen, how she'd fallen pregnant to a stranger no one seemed to talk about; how she'd run away from home with the newborn only to return five years later, tail between her legs, forced to give up the child against what seemed to be her will. No one spoke of that, and yet, everyone knew how Corinna Vaughn had pushed her own children away, both leaving Weaversmoor in the wake of whatever had happened to Erin in the woods, twenty-six years ago. What if it happened again, now Eli Vaughn was in town? What if whatever his father had done to his mother he came to do to Bryn, or any other girl for that matter?

What if he was dangerous to Nyx?

"Come on," he urged, "let's find Bryn."

Both boys ran out of the room, across the long, darkened hallway to stop at the landing, relief washing over them.

Bryn Everley was climbing up the stairs, wrapped in her ceremonial cloak; backpack hanging from one arm, hair dishevelled, cheeks blushed from the cold, eyes sparkling in what looked like joy. Reaching careful tendrils of cognisance, Pip tried to further read her mood, let out a sigh of utter relief. Bryn was excited, charged, happy. Maybe she'd found some peace out in the woods. The sound of her humming between her lips attested to it, Bryn wasn't scared, nothing bad had happened to her. Stealing a glance at Trystan, they both smirked and shrugged, she was fine and they had spooked themselves with making Eli Vaughn a monster, something both very much doubted the young man would turn out to be.

"Everything all right?" Bryn asked, noticing their presence.

"Yeah, we were feeling peckish, so went down to grab a bite," Trystan lied. "'Bout you? What were you doing out in the woods at this hour?"

Bryn shrugged, dished them a secretive half smile. "Oh, you know, harnessing my powers, centring myself. I'm knackered, boys, see you tomorrow."

Hips swaying in slow motion, she walked across the corridor, clearly inebriated. A loud sigh reached them in her wake, a sigh that spoke of pleasures unknown, of secret emotions and sensations she kept to herself but was hard-pressed to hide.

Pip nodded Trystan back to his room, a mocking grin over his lips. "I think it's safe to say your sister just got laid. Only mystery is who the lucky partner was...

WITCH CRAFT

VII

The rain had stopped, as had the wind. Clouds no longer covered the sky, now turned to a velvety blanket sprinkled with stars. The air was still cold, though, a bite of frost covering the vegetation and the soggy grounds. Bryn eased her way through the woods, inhaling deeply of the petrichor, focused on reaching the clearing she favoured for working on her magic. She needed it, tonight, needed the grounding of earth below and sky above, the settling of familiar elements - just so she stayed her restless mind and made sense of the chaotic emotions she'd been experiencing since the night of her eighteenth birthday.

Since coming across Eli Vaughn.

If Bryn were to be honest, he was the reason for her restlessness, her unease, not the fact she'd turned eighteen. If she were to be honest, there wasn't one single minute of her day when her mind didn't veer in his direction and she didn't play out in her head the few times they'd crossed each other's paths. From the moment he'd run the car into her bike to their running into each other all through town, casually saying hello, even stopping to chat for brief seconds. She replayed it all in her head to exhaustion, and would rather be left alone daydreaming of his every expression and his every smile than spending time with her own boyfriend.

This couldn't be happening. This couldn't be real.

Just a stupid schoolgirl infatuation, surely. He was the mysterious stranger, the newcomer, the risqué older man, attractive and slightly dangerous, with his leathers and his bike, but not staying material. Not for her, at least. How old was he? Twenty-five, twenty-six? The age gap between them was far too wide, surely a man like him would go for someone his age, not a little girl, as he'd called her. And Bryn had been in love with Jamal for so long. When he'd first asked her out hadn't she thought herself the luckiest girl on earth? Hadn't she been the happiest person to walk down the crowded hallways of Weaversmoor Academy, knowing she was Jamal Wilson's girl, the one he'd fallen for, when at least half the female population at their school carried a torch for him? Hadn't Bryn invested her time and focus on making him fall for her, hadn't he been the one person she wanted by her side? And were they not good together?

Jamal centred her, he grounded and calmed her. Persistent and focused, Jamal was driven for success and accomplishments, and so was Bryn, they'd worked so well together, as students, as friends, as lovers. He accepted her odd, rebellious ways, she was secretly delighted at his polite, educated manners, and they'd allowed each other enough freedom to not suffocate their personal liberties. Not tied by the hip, as Trystan had been with Penny Lattimer, always together, immersed into each other to the point of obsession. No wonder her brother had tired of the girl so quickly. But that was not her way, and it wasn't Jamal's either. They'd never smother each other.

So why this, now? Why this fixation on Eli Vaughn and his eyes, his dimpled smile? Why this rushing of her heart, this cartwheeling of her stomach whenever he showed up, be it in her life or her thoughts? Why this rising heat across her chest, her face, when she pictured the two of them together? And why was she

WITCH CRAFT

picturing the two of them together when she had a boyfriend who she loved? Or did she? No longer sure of her own truths, Bryn had found herself losing sleep over the confused state of her emotions. If only she could get Eli out of her system, if she could at least have him once, maybe kiss him, just to know, see what it was like, maybe then she could put him behind her and move on with Jamal.

Move on. Where to? They were kids, Jamal sixteen, she barely eighteen, where were they moving on? How many high-school sweethearts made it, in the long run? Well, there was her father, and Spencer Vaughn. Those two had been in love since their school years, and it hadn't changed, despite all the time apart and the heartache imposed upon each other. Maybe she and Jamal were just like that.

But if so, she wouldn't spend half her time daydreaming of a man eight years her senior, fantasising of his kiss, and how his hands upon her body would feel like, how she'd feel if he smiled that wicked, crooked, dimpled smirk at her. What she needed was to be one with the earth, the night; what she needed was the wisdom of the surrounding elements, infusing her; what she needed was a good meditation session out in the woods, by the clearing. Where magical forces ran stronger and became enhanced by whatever power flooded the forest in that particular spot.

Coming to its opening, Bryn sighed, her mind already more focused, her emotions more grounded. She stepped into the clearing and started setting up her circle, placing candles on their allotted cardinal spots, crystals forming the ring inside which she'd sit and meditate, for as long as it took to shed some clarity into her messed-up head. Ditching the dark cloak she'd wore, Bryn stepped naked into the circle and sat on the still sodden ground. A shiver ran the course of her spine - it was cold, but soon the heat from inside the earth's core flooded through her skin, and she could no longer feel the temperature. Only the elements around her, as they shed a blanket of peace and safety over her.

Nothing could touch her, nothing could harm her, here. She was in the arms of the world and protected by the power of her own connection to her magic, her particular kinship to the element of her craft. The earth would guide and safeguard her, and no one could enter the safe space she'd built, no one could cross the threshold of the sortilege she'd threaded on this clearing. No one would find her, or see her, she was alone, and invisible to the world. Opening herself to the elements, Bryn closed her eyes and allowed the craft to speak to her. To down peace and clarity over her.

Eli Vaughn's face was what came to her mind. Not the empty, blank space that led her into a trance, not the void chasm that lured her deeper into a state of oblivion, not the familiar drowsiness of letting go and becoming one with the earth's core, no. *Eli*. It was all she could think of, all she could see, all that reached out for her.

It wouldn't do. This was an obsession.

Or had she fallen in love with the dark, mysterious stranger? She giggled, he wasn't even dark, not with his blue eyes and the golden five o'clock shadow of a beard, the rosy skin and honey-hued hair. He wasn't dark but in his heart - according to Pip, who kept insisting there was something not quite right with Nyx's elder brother, something shifty and cagey, lurking. Maybe Pip was afflicted by the same disease Bryn had fallen prey to: an intense, immense attraction to Eli Vaughn. Maybe Pip wanted him as much as she, as much as he'd wanted Trystan all these years, as much as he'd confessed he wanted Nyx. Another giggle left her lips, this wouldn't do, she must focus, centre herself.

An unfamiliar energy print breached her wards, seeped into the conjured protections she'd placed around the clearing. Someone was here, close by, moving towards her private, personal space. Someone she didn't know, and with magic as strong as hers, as wild as the one she commandeered, but as tamed, as well. Someone whose will was as much ruled by rational thought as hers. A strong, powerful talent she'd yet to come across. Eyes snapping open, Bryn shivered in fear, searching through the trees for a clue to who'd dared break into her lair.

The silence of the night exploded in a cackle of birds cawing and screeching. They flew from the large, wide tree to her right, that old sentinel she'd known since childhood and which looked so unlike any other tree in the woods. Heart thrumming wildly against her ribs, Bryn jumped on her feet, twirling around as her eyes followed the colourful, bashful birds on their flight. She'd never seen that kind of bird around, had she? They looked like kestrels or some other bird of prey, but their plumage was unlike anything she knew. From deep greens to royal blues, crimson reds to bright fuchsia, oranges and golden yellows, they were like jewels against the blackened night. A smile graced her lips as she watched them hide amid the canopy of leaves on the various trees, a smile that died as soon as her eyes came down to rest upon the shadowy figure hiding, lurking by the edge of the woods. A figure that was far too familiar, one she'd fantasised about, dreamt of holding against her.

With a silent step, Eli Vaughn crossed the threshold of her protective spell and came to stand at the rim of Bryn's circle, bathed by the dim candlelight that cast shadows upon his already darkened brow. She shivered, not so much in cold as in anticipation, and remembered she stood naked before him, cloak discarded outside her reach. Eli's gaze wandered through her body, lingering over the dark core of her womanhood, her small breasts, until it met her eyes, and there was lust in his - oh, yes, there was, he couldn't deny it. There was lust and curiosity, and also fear, as if he had no idea how to handle this sudden trouble he'd found himself in. As if he had no idea how to deal with the emotions he experienced by standing in front of a naked girl, who'd been playfully teasing him since they first met.

Goosebumps erupted on Bryn's arms as she recalled what Nyx had confided, that he'd spent seven years in a coma, losing his teenage years and missing all the hallmarks of adolescence. Knowing he'd never even been with a woman, Bryn took a step forward, an impish mood taking over her, the after-effects of her drinking clouding her judgement, impairing her rational thought. He was here, and she'd longed for his presence all along. He was here, and they were alone. There was no one to say what was right or wrong. There was only will and want, and the freedom to do as they wished.

Ambling towards him, Bryn came to stand in front of Eli, mere inches from him, the heat of his body reaching for her naked skin in waves of fire, telltale signs of his own lust, his own want. She wasn't wrong, had not misread the looks they'd exchanged; there was something between them. His constant visits to the auto-repair shop, a place she frequented often and where some of her friends worked part-time, those hadn't been a coincidence. He'd gone there in the hopes of running into her.

Needing no further assurance, Bryn threw her arms around Eli's shoulders and glued her body to his. Mouth diving for his lips, she kissed him, tongue parting an entrance, shuffling in so it met with his, twined and danced in urgency. Eli's hands came to rest over her hipbone, cold skin against her feverish one, a gentle, soft caress from his thumb coursing the length of her waistline. It lasted less than a second. Before she could deliver herself into the barely initiated kiss, Eli pushed her away, taking a step back, an awkward, confused look on his face. A terrified, self-disgusted look.

"Put your clothes on," he said, voice harsh. His expression spoke of a sudden, ill-hidden rage he struggled to keep under restraint.

WITCH CRAFT

Bryn shuddered, searched around for the backpack and the cloak, at a loss for what to do. He'd been compliant, returned her kiss, so why this coldness, now; what was this? The age gap, and the fact she was dating his sister's cousin? Reaching a tentative hand, Bryn placed it over Eli's chest. His eyes came down to stare at it, front teeth biting his lip, and her innards melted at the sight, a low, soft moan threatening to rise up her throat. She swallowed it down.

"What's wrong?" she asked, voice hushed as if to ease him. "We're both consenting adults."

Eli cackled, bent down to grab the discarded cloak, threw it her way. "Do you know how old I am, Bryn Everley?"

Pulling on the cloak, she shook her head. Good lord, the way he always spoke her name drove her mad.

"You're in your mid-twenties, I suppose."

He looked around, as if searching the trees, blue eyes darker for the lack of light. "It's past midnight, right? So that makes it my twenty-sixth birthday today. And you're what? Sixteen?"

"First of all, happy birthday." Bryn reached down and grabbed her backpack, from where she fished a small bottle of vodka. "Think a drink's in order. Second, I'm eighteen. So I'm of age, allowed to drive, drink, and consent to kissing older men. As long as I fancy them."

Eli smirked, shook his head, eyes on the toes of his boots. Bryn watched the soft blush rise up his cheeks and smiled. Opening the bottle, she took a swig, handed it to Eli, who glared, as if he couldn't decide what to do. After what felt like a long time, he took it, fingers brushing hers and sending jolts of electricity up her arm. He drank a long gulp, a search for reassurance, or maybe to make up for the fact it was his birthday and he was out in the woods, alone. Well, not alone, she was here and would be glad to keep him company.

"Haven't you done enough drinking at my grandmother's?" he asked, returning the bottle.

"Your grandmother's? According to my dad, the house is as much yours as Spencer's and Nyx's. Corinna Vaughn has been dead a while, now. Here, have another drink, live a little. It's your birthday, after all, and you've spent enough of those sleeping."

His face shadowed, Eli still took the bottle and downed another unhealthy swig. "Who told you? Nyx?" Bryn shrugged. "She said you'd been asking questions about me. What's it to you, little girl?"

She slid closer again, placing cool fingers over the hand still holding the bottle, guiding it to her lips for a quick sip. "Can't you tell? Not even after that kiss?"

Eli sniggered once more, pushing her away, but Bryn clung to him. He downed another shot, clearly uncomfortable. But there was a light in his eyes, that of curiosity - more than that, it was the light of eager lust, of want. He wasn't drunk, but nor was he sober.

"You're dating someone," he whispered, leaning down to touch his lips to her ear. Bryn shivered, but wrapped her arms around him. "I don't go after other blokes' women."

"I'm no one's woman but my own, you chauvinist pig." Pulling away, Bryn walked back into the circle, candles swaying at her passage. "And I do what I want with myself."

"Even if you're betraying someone else's trust? Do you know what that makes you?"

Bryn spread out her arms to her sides, palms up towards the sky. "I don't care. I don't care what you think of me. I don't care what you say, or how many times you deny your feelings for me, Eli, I know you want me. It was so obvious in that kiss. Not to mention your constant hanging at the auto-repair shop, looking for me."

Eli cackled, tears of mirth brimming his eyes. "Are you serious? I went there to service my bike and apply for the job opening. Good lord, you *are* conceited, aren't you? Little princess who thinks she's centre of the universe. You're nothing but a spoiled brat, entitled and selfish, uncaring of others."

Her face dropped, heart skipping a beat. Bryn bit back the words looming at the edge of her throat; she wouldn't give him the pleasure of seeing how much he'd unravelled her. Taking another swig of vodka, she handed him the bottle. "Here, finish it."

Eli took it and downed the rest of the drink in one long gulp, his face caught in a wince.

"I care about others. Do you think this hasn't messed me up? I was fine, satisfied with my lot, until you came and threw my world upside down." Marching towards him again, Bryn took hold of his jacket's lapels, pulled him to her, noticing the blurriness in his eyes, of someone who'd drank a bit more than his fill. "You shook my world apart, Eli Vaughn, and I don't know where I stand anymore, or who I am. I don't know what to do, where to go, how to even begin understanding this spell you seem to have placed on me."

Eli grabbed the back of her head, palm cradling the curve of her skull. His face came closer to hers, his breath warm against her skin. "What the hell do you want from me, Bryn Everley?" he asked, voice husky enough to raise the soft hairs on her arms and send jolts and shivers down her body.

"Don't you know? Can't you tell? All this time, taking me for coffee, chatting with me at the shop and you don't know how I feel? You don't know how much you've made me want you, Eli?"

Their eyes met and locked, a long, charged look passing between them.

"I'm so gonna regret this," Eli whispered, but reached down to glue his mouth to hers.

Bryn let go of all restraint. Her hands came up to cup his chin, lips and tongue eager for his, as if trying to smother a hunger she'd never get rid of. Taking a step back, she re-entered the protective circle of her former magic, bringing Eli with her. They stood at the centre, his hand on her body - hard, pressing, urgent in its journey through her skin. Bryn fought with the biker jacket he wore, pushing it down his back, his arms, dropping it on the now dry, musty forest floor. Then she assaulted the grey jersey, pulling it free from the waist of his jeans, hands eagerly searching for his skin. Eli helped himself out of the garment, stood shivering before her, watching Bryn discard the cloak and lay it on the ground so they could lie on it. Good heavens, he was so awkward, hands shaking in whatever emotion had grabbed hold of him, eyes wide with lust and fear, cheeks and neck reddened in whatever embarrassment he might feel.

Then Nyx's words made reappearance, and Bryn couldn't help but smile. A sweet, gentle smile, as she recalled her brother comment on how Eli had surely never got laid. Trystan must have been right, hence the discomfort, the odd fear. The fact he'd been awake for the past three years didn't necessarily mean he'd already made up for his former inexperience. From the look on his sister's face as the issue was discussed, Bryn gathered he hadn't. Eli was as much a virgin as she had been two years ago. Going back to throw her arms around him, she sought his lips, the kiss urgent and inflamed. Her hand came down to rest on the buckle of his belt, which she loosened. Eli stiffened in her arms, tried to pull away, she locked him in place.

"Shh, it's all right," Bryn whispered.

"No, I can't do this." Again, Eli tried to flee her grip, but it couldn't have been hard enough, for she managed to hold on to him, fingers already unbuttoning his jeans. "Bryn, stop. Please."

Her lips traced a line across his cheek to his ear, tongue coming out to play along the whorl, teeth biting the soft flesh of his earlobe. Eli moaned, back stiffening and chest pressing against her naked breasts.

"I can tell you want me, it's not like you've been hiding it. It's right there, in your eyes," she said. "And I've wanted you from the moment we met. There's nothing wrong with this, just let yourself go. It'll be all right, I'll guide you through it."

"None of us is free."

"Forget about that, consider this your birthday present."

Guiding him by the hand, Bryn helped him kneel over the cloak, facing each other. Her eyes studied the feather tattoo on his arm, from which a flock of black birds flew up his shoulder, across his upper chest, towards his neck. One tentative hand reached for it, touched one of the birds, the larger one, felt it thrum against her fingers, as if alive, wanting to break free. She steered her fingers up his neck, his chin, to his lips, which she caressed, thumb swiping across the lower one, parting them, until Eli took her finger between his teeth and softly bit into it. Bryn sat astride him, he reached for her mouth to claim one more kiss, and as their tongues met, so did they ease themselves down on the cloak.

"I don't know how to do this," Eli whispered into her ear, his face hiding against the mass of her hair.

"I'll show you. Let me make love to you, Eli. Let me show how to make love to me."

"This isn't love, Bryn. It'll never be."

With a smirk, she met his eyes. Oh, how wrong he was. Maybe it wasn't yet love, but one day it would be, she could feel it in every nerve and inch of his skin, deep in her own core. It may be nothing but lust now, she thought, as she helped him out of his jeans, but time would change it, and Eli would love her and she him.

For that was what the very earth whispered in her ear, that was what the wind sang through the leaves, it was what the unfamiliar birds chirped in their hideout on that odd, strange tree.

Eli lay by Bryn's side, panting. His entire body tingled, and his legs and buttocks spasmed in cramps. But he couldn't deny the intense, immense jolt of pleasure he was still wrapped under. He couldn't deny how good this had been, despite the impropriety of it all, the wrongness, the lurid, rotten treachery of his actions. Memories - fickle and fleeting - of his time in Ephemera came to the front of his mind. His heartache at realising he'd been lied to, tricked, betrayed by the girl he'd given his heart to; the pain he'd experienced at her callous treachery, the heartbreak such loss of trust had inflicted upon him, it all washed over Eli in the space of a heartbeat. He'd been devastated by Stella's treason, but had gone and done the exact same thing to Jacintha. His stomach coiled at the thought.

Pulling his jeans up, he sat and pressed his head against his knees, a wave of dizziness washing over him, alongside nausea. Bryn's smooth hand met his naked back, shedding a few caresses. Her voice reached him from afar, as if they were worlds apart. Which they were - she was a teenager, a girl on the cusp of womanhood, but a girl, nonetheless. He was a grown man, in love with a grown woman, how had he let himself fall prey to such base needs?

"Are you all right?" she asked, still lying on her back, naked body exposed to the elements, safely guarded by the wards she'd placed around them.

Eli nodded, then shook his head.

"Was it that bad?" Bryn insisted, her voice belying the words.

It hadn't, it had been the best thing Eli remembered doing, aside kissing Jacintha. Which made it all the worse for that. If having sex with Bryn Everley was this good, how much better would it feel to make love to Jacintha Tate? Which was what he should have done; she should have been his first, not this crazy, rebellious girl out for thrills and mindless fun. Anger rose, clouding his mind even more. Another wave of nausea washed over him, and Eli heaved.

Jumping to his feet, he ran out of the circle, stumbling over one of the candles, its light extinguished under his foot. Grabbing the knobbly trunk of the nearest tree, he gasped, coughed, head lowered, back bent. Retching loudly, Eli spewed the contents of his stomach - not that there was much to spit. His dinner, fully digested by now, left only the vodka he'd been drinking here and at home, as if somewhere deep down he'd known this was to happen, coming here and meeting Bryn, doing this, with her, not with the woman he'd lately dreamt of doing it with.

He flinched, straightening at her touch. Bryn's perfume assaulted his nostrils when she glued herself to him, still naked, still shameless, still giving. And what she seemed to deliver was an unusual, unexpected amount of peace. Finding he wanted her again, Eli forced what had already taken place between them away from his mind. How was he ever going to face Jacintha, after this? How would he be able to look her in the eye, if he repeated the offence? No, he must wash the stain off him, despite knowing he'd never feel clean.

"What's wrong? Had a bit too much to drink?"

Wiping a wrist across his lips, he turned, faced Bryn. The sight of her naked body roused him, and the smile she dished let him know she wasn't fooled by his coldness - Bryn knew he wanted her as she wanted him. Why? Why was he so attracted to this girl? Obviously he had a type: brown-haired, light-eyed, rosy-skinned. Hadn't Stella been blond? He could hardly remember her. His grip on Ephemera was dwindling, and would be lost forever if he didn't hurry, if he didn't find a way in. But did he really want to go back there, the place he'd been cast out of?

"I shouldn't be here," he said, and pushed past Bryn to grab his jersey, the leather jacket.

"Don't be like this. Eli, there's nothing to it, as long as you don't want it to be. It was just a shag."

He searched her eyes, confused at the dispassionate way she regarded what had just taken place between them.

"You have a boyfriend," he said, "And I also happen to be in a relationship."

"Then why did you do it? Don't be a hypocrite, you wanted to, as much as I did. So much time hanging around the places I go to, you now want me to believe you never thought of us doing this? Wasn't it good? Then what's wrong? It's no biggie."

"So you cheat on your boyfriend and it's no big deal? Well, it is to me. It sure wasn't you I wanted to do this with, not on my…" Shutting his mouth, Eli pulled the jersey on, tucked it into the waist of his jeans.

"Not on your first time, right? Well, think about it this way, when you finally make love to this lady you're seeing, you won't be this awkward, this… stumbling. At least you'll have an idea of what you're doing, and who knows, might even be nice for her, unlike what we had here."

His face reddened, heat mixing with anger and not a little shame. Of course his first time had been awkward, lacking. Of course she hadn't had much out of it, despite Bryn's constant telling him to slow down, guiding him through the entire thing. It had still been too hasty, too messy. Satisfying for him, but lacking in everything. And it didn't look as if it had been any good for Bryn. Pride made him want to take off his clothes and have her again, this time working on showing her he was a quick, avid student, capable of doing for her what she so gladly had done for him. But then Jacintha's eyes flocked his mind, and his resolve strengthened - this wasn't where he should be nor was Bryn the woman he wanted to be with.

And how did she know? How could she know it was his first time? Had he been so blatantly transparent, his performance so bad even a teen saw through it?

"What has my sister been dishing about me?"

"She mentioned your seven-year coma. And the subsequent... inexperience."

"Why would she do that? Nyx isn't like this."

"I asked if you had a girlfriend, it just took on from there. Why are you making such a big deal of it?"

"This was a huge mistake. I said I was gonna regret it, and I do. I'm sorry."

Bryn pulled up the cloak round her shoulders and shrugged. "It's no biggie. I had to get you out of my system, and the only way was if I had you. Like a nagging itch I had to scratch, you know, now it's taken care of and I can go back to my life. We can pretend this never happened."

"What were you doing out here?" he asked, suddenly uncomfortable with the circle of crystals and candles.

"Meditating," she replied.

"In the nude?"

"I feel more connected, like this."

"It's dangerous, Bryn."

Her smile widened, the spark of mischief in her eyes growing. "Not for me. Are we good?"

Eli shrugged into his jacket, training his eyes back on her. "I should never have done this."

"Then forget it ever happened, for heavens' sake," she cried, voice loud in the silent night. Birds took flight, suddenly disturbed in their peaceful nests. "It's not like it was mind-blowing or earth-shattering enough to have me pining over it. Just pretend we never did it and let it go, Eli." Bryn closed the narrow gap between them, hand gripping his chin in a claw-like vise. "But don't try to convince me you didn't feel it, don't try to convince me you never wanted this, or that I lured you into it. Your lust was as strong as mine, Eli Vaughn, and that, you must never forget. Don't go around making me the villain."

He escaped her hold, regarding the girl with a newfound respect. "This never happened," Eli insisted, and Bryn nodded.

"If that's how you want it, I'm cool with it. This never happened. Until it happens again."

Eli stomped off towards the meadow, not bothering with saying goodbye. Bryn's parting words worried him, what if she was right? What if he came upon her again and found it as hard to resist the call of his want as he had this time? Fastening his pace, he found himself running home, eager to put as much distance as he could between him and Bryn. Silently, he climbed up squeaking stairs and hid in his room, certain he wouldn't get any sleep, guilty as he felt over the betrayal he'd brought on Jacintha, the very same day they'd gotten together.

Morning found him wrapped in the duvet, as if he'd struggled with it all night, wearing nothing but a pair of briefs and sweaty socks. He hopped off bed and jumped straight into the shower, skin clammy and stinking of Bryn's perfume. He must wash it off; he had to wash every trace of her off. Scrubbing until he was raw and red, Eli stood under the scalding flow of water, Jacintha's face taking over Bryn's when he relived the details of the past evening: the look in her eyes, their first kiss, the feel of her skin. It was her he wanted, her he longed to be with. Wrapping a towel around him, Eli ran back to the bedroom in search of his mobile.

Jacintha's voice greeted him after a couple of rings, warm and husky, as if she'd still been asleep.

"Good morning."

"Good morning. Did you sleep well?"

"I did. You?"

He closed his eyes, Bryn's naked body flashing in his brain. "I slept. Jace, I want to see you. I need to be with you."

She chuckled on the other end. "I miss you, too, Eli. Let's meet up when you get back from lunch with your sister, all right?"

"It's my birthday," he spat, too fast to stop himself. "I'm taking Nyx to meet my adoptive parents. But I want to spend the rest of the day with you."

"Why didn't you say? Happy birthday. What do you want to do?"

He shrugged, grinned. "Have no idea."

"How about we have dinner and then go dancing? Unless you have to stay in because of Nyx, that is."

"No, she's going out with Trystan. I'll have to be home by eleven-thirty, though, that's her curfew."

"So no dancing. I can come over, if you prefer. Unless it's too soon? For me to be officially there? As your... what? What are we, Eli?"

A fist knotted around his gut, such was the longing he felt for her. Such was the guilt of what he'd done. "In love. We're in love. Yes, I think I'd like that, have you here. Will you come?"

"I'd love to. We can go to dinner and then back to yours. That's a date, then. A birthday date."

"I'll call you when I get back from Sunderleigh, is that all right?"

"Of course it is. Talk to you later, then. Bye."

"Bye."

Eli got dressed and stomped down the stairs towards the kitchen. His head throbbed, tongue fuzzy and mouth tasting weird. All after effects of too much to drink, certainly. Maybe coffee would help. He stopped, staring at the kitchen table, jaw slackened and mouth open in an odd mix of awe and confusion. The place was empty, and silent, although coffee had just been freshly brewed and its scent infused the entire room. The table was spread with a lavish breakfast, consisting of what seemed to be croissants, orange juice, butter, jam, ham and cheese, scrambled eggs and fresh fruit. A small, beautifully wrapped parcel was placed in front of Eli's chair, its bow threading curls over the plate it sat on. Tears brimmed his eyes, a knot shut off his throat.

"Oh, you're up already!" Nyx's voice broke the trance, his eyes rising to meet hers as his sister walked in from the garden, carrying a glass jar with a single rose in it. "Just went out to get this." Placing it at the centre of the table, she joined him at the door, throwing her arms around his torso and hugging him. "Happy birthday," she chirped, delivering one loud kiss on his cheek.

"How did you know?"

She pulled away and dished Eli a slightly offended look. "Not through you, it wasn't. When the will was read, the lawyer said all our birthdates. I took note of yours. Why didn't you tell us? Spencer would have stayed back; he'd want to spend the date with you."

Eli pulled his sister into his arms. "I didn't want him to cancel his plans. He needed this break, Nyx, I could tell he was getting more and more frustrated with our bickering."

"Well, we're not bickering now, are we? So, what do you want to do today? We're having lunch with your parents, but after that, do you want to do something? I can cancel with Trystan, you know."

"I made plans with Jacintha, if you don't mind? I don't want you to change your life for me, nor have it revolving around mine. But I do want you here by half eleven tonight, though."

"Let's eat, before it gets cold. Open your present, go on."

Eli sat at the table and carefully unwrapped the parcel, to come upon a medium-sized bottle of cologne. He eyed it doubtfully, then grinned at Nyx. "Thank you, you didn't have to get me something."

"Don't you like it? We can return it. I couldn't find the one you wear, but this smells similar. I noticed it's nearly empty, your bottle."

"I'm sure I'll love it, Nyx. Thank you. I mean it."

His eyes brimmed with tears again, and a flaming ache climbed the walls of his stomach. He didn't deserve this, not after his behaviour the previous evening. What he deserved was to be ignored, shunned for his betrayal. What he deserved was to have Jacintha breaking it all off, Nyx turning her back on him.

"Are you all right? Why are you crying?" She stood up from her seat, came to squat beside him, hands frantically grabbing his.

"I'm fine, just emotional. Never mind me. Here, give us a hug." Wrapping his arms around her, Eli kissed the soft, large curls of her hair, one hand stroking her back. "I wasn't expecting this."

"Well, then, eat. You kind of need the food to soak up the booze."

Eli blushed, what did she know? How much did she know? Had Bryn lied and as soon as his back was turned, spilled out everything?

"The vodka bottle's nearly finished, Eli, and I'm pretty sure it wasn't my doing. You had a bit too much to drink last night, didn't you?"

Relieved, he shrugged, gave her a lopsided grin. "I can assure you I've learnt my lesson, won't be doing it again."

"That bad, huh?"

Nodding, Eli tucked in on the eggs, stomach rumbling with hunger, his mood suddenly changed from the previous sombreness into something akin to excitement, exhilaration. He'd do what Bryn had said, put it all behind him, forget the whole thing, pretend it never happened. And in time, who knew, maybe it would be as if it hadn't. Maybe he could really ignore the entire thing. Just like he was forgetting Ephemera and the details of what he'd lived throughout the seven years he'd been lost to this world. Maybe with time, he could lose every trace of the one night he'd spent with Bryn.

VIII

Nyx blushed again at the intent look Trystan's mother set on her. She melted deeper into the chair; food forgotten on the plate pushed away from her.

"You *do* look a lot like your mother," Cressida Everley repeated, for the fourth or fifth time since Nyx had walked into her house.

"Mum, you're embarrassing her," Trystan said, reaching a hand under the table to hold hers.

"I'm sorry, darling, didn't mean to. So, how are you coping? With the Academy and being back at Weaversmoor?"

"Mum, she never lived here before. Nyx was born when her mother was already at Havenleah."

"Oh, right. I forgot you never met Corinna. Can't say you lost much, there. She was not an easy woman, that grandmother of yours." Cressida poured more wine into her glass and downed it in one go. "How's Spencer doing?"

There was a hint of bitterness and mockery in her voice, which ruffled Nyx's feathers. She sat up straighter and faced the woman across the table, frowning. "He's fine. Settled down well, I should think."

"Well, now he doesn't have Corinna to hound him, I suppose he'll be fine here." She gulped another glass of wine, pushing food around her plate, which she wasn't obviously going to eat. "What of your brother?"

Nyx paled. She'd expected questions about Eli, but was unsure how to respond. Cressida Everley had been around during her mother's pregnancy, probably knew everything about Eli's father. It was one of the reasons Nyx had promptly agreed to come over for dinner at the Everleys, in hopes Cressida might dish some details about Eli's parentage. She hadn't expected to be left alone with only Trystan and his mother, though, assuming Bryn would be present, and Jamal with her.

"What of him?" Smiling politely, she drank some water only to steady the intense beat of her heart.

"Well, I thought you'd be spending the day with him, seeing it's his birthday. Twenty-six already, how time flies. I remember him being this tiny, reddish little thing, all fury and fists in his father's arms. Bet he's done a bit of growing, hasn't he? Must be tall. Not as tall as his father, though. No one could be *that* big."

"You saw Eli when he was born?" Nyx asked, sitting closer to the table. "You knew his father?"

Cressida laughed. "I wouldn't say I *knew* him, Fionn wasn't someone one got to know, unless he wanted you to. I met him, though. It was I who called upon him that night, so he knew his son was coming. Corinna would have kept it all from him and done away with the baby as soon as it was born, but Erin wouldn't have that. Good God, she really loved that... creature."

"Mum!" Trystan sounded shocked, face darkening as he glanced at his mother and the near empty bottle of white wine in her hands.

"What, Trystan, it's true. Fionn Sylvannar was more creature than man. He was huge, and terrifying, even Corinna feared him. Stunningly gorgeous, too, more akin to a god than to mere mortals. Of course he was none of that."

Nyx frowned, wondering what she meant. "What was he like? Was he a nice person? I'm sure Eli would love to know."

Cressida giggled, finished the wine and pushed the bottle away from her, searching around for another. "No, he wasn't nice at all. Stuck up and aloof, fancied himself better than the rest. But he was good to your mother, and loved that child of his. Even when he was forced to give them up, he loved Erin and their son above all else. That's why he had to let them go, see. They'd never make it there, she told me herself. They wouldn't have been safe, same as here. Although she cut all her threads, but there are other ways, as I found out when I called Fionn here. Erin taught me how to."

"You didn't know how to call him?" Nyx wondered at the true meaning behind the woman's words. Why would she need to learn how to make a phone call? Unless she didn't mean that kind of call. Unless she meant she'd summoned Eli's father to Weaversmoor. But summoned him from where? "What do you mean?"

Cressida's eyes widened, she looked away from Nyx, aware she'd already said far more than she should. "So, anyone wants coffee? No, you're too young for it, aren't you? Think I'll go up and drink mine in the bedroom, if the two of you don't mind? It's been really great meeting you, Nyx, you remind me of your mother. I'd like to meet your brother, too. Oh well, maybe one day. Have a good night, children, behave. Hear me, Trystan? I expect you to act like a proper gentleman."

Leaving behind two uncomfortable, stunned teenagers and a wave of heady perfume, Cressida Everley exited the dining-room on unsteady legs, humming some hit from the early nineties under her breath.

"Wow, that was awkward," Trystan said, getting up from his seat. "I'm sorry about Mum; you shouldn't have to deal with this."

Nyx joined him at the door, threw an arm around his waist, hugging him. "It's fine. I want to be here for you, no matter what."

They kissed, Trystan ushering her up the stairs to his room.

"Thought your sister would be here, with Jamal, Pip too."

Trystan sniggered. "Why would Thomson be here? If you want to hang around him, maybe you should be dating *him*, not me."

"Jealous, much?" she asked, face closing and eyes darkening in sudden anger.

"Well, yeah, you two went on a date when we were already together, now you're asking after him. Of course I'm gonna feel uncomfortable about it."

"You said it was fine. I could've cancelled, but you said it didn't matter. Why is this an issue, now?"

Trystan blinked, ground his teeth. "I'm sorry. I just... look, I don't want to lose you, Nyx."

"You won't, don't be silly. What do you want to do now? Only have to be home by half past-eleven."

"We can watch a film; Bryn's got a few I fancy you might like. Wanna go raid her shelves?"

They giggled and Nyx followed Trystan to his sister's room, a haven of teal walls and dark blue ceiling with golden stars hand-painted across it. The entire chamber, large as it was, felt dark, but not oppressively so. It was Bryn from top to bottom, with several leather jackets discarded over chairs and settees, crystals gracing every surface, throws and pillows in bright peacock colours thrown around the floor, bed and sofa. They searched through her film collection, settled on one, and ran off to Trystan's room to watch. A room that was as different from his sister's as he was from her. His was a boy's room, in all its glory, with blue walls and plaid throws, leather armchairs, a sturdy desk, a comfy bed. They settled on it, attention soon swerving from the film to focus on each other and the tentative discovery of their bodies through fondling and kissing, which soon became quite intense. When Trystan tried to pull down Nyx's tights, she stopped his hand. It was too soon in their relationship to jump into this, no matter how much her body claimed to want it.

They faced each other.

"Not yet, Trystan."

He nodded, placed a soft kiss on top of her forehead. "We'll take it as slow as you want. Is it your first time?"

Nyx blushed, wondering how he'd react to her response. "Is it yours?"

"No."

"Neither is mine. But it's too soon for us to take it next stage, don't you think?"

"I hadn't realised there was an established timeline for this to happen. Can you tell me where it falls into? After the ten-thousandth kiss, before the weekend away together, when we're eighteen?"

Nyx jumped off the bed, rearranging her clothes. "Now you're just being a git, Trystan." She took a peek at the bedside table clock, realised she had less than twenty minutes to make it back home. "It's late; I'll give Eli a call so he can pick me up."

"Don't be silly, I'll walk you. I'm sorry if I upset you." Trystan dished her his best puppy-eyed stare, bringing a string of giggles out of Nyx. "Come on, say you forgive me, give us a kiss."

She went willingly to his arms, surrendering to the heated kiss, finding herself having to push him away as soon as Trystan tried to free her off her clothes.

"Look, I said no. You better understand I really mean it."

Trystan held out his hands in shamed surrender. "Fine, I get it. Let's grab your coat and walk you home. Do you mind cutting through the woods?"

She nodded and followed him down the stairs, where both shrugged into warm jackets, scarves, gloves and beanies. The night was clear but briskly cold. A gust of icy wind greeted them as they stepped out through the kitchen back door, and ran off to the property's edge, where a rusty old gate awaited to let them into the woods. They walked in silent companionship across the now much clearer path threading between the trees, towards the meadow that separated the forest proper from Vaughn cottage, stopping at intervals to kiss. Soon, the soft glow of the backyard's light signalled the cottage lay just ahead, and both sighed.

"Don't want to say goodnight," Trystan whispered, hugging Nyx to him.

"Neither do I. But Spence will kill me, and so will Eli. He wasn't very happy we drank his vodka. Come on in, just for a little, will you?"

"Won't he kill me for having pinched his booze?"

She giggled. "He's not that bad, you know? He's actually a very sweet, if awkward, bloke."

"You've sure come round to him."

Nyx cocked her head to the side, in thought. She had. After the first friction and her resistance to accepting Eli in her life, she'd come round and welcomed him in. She couldn't think of a life where he was no longer here, where he didn't belong to her, wasn't her brother.

"Had lunch with his parents today, the adoptive ones. They're sweet, too. They raised him well, and you can tell they love him like a proper, real son. And are damn proud of him. He's overcome so much, is still trying to overcome all that happened to him."

"Do you love him? Like Spencer?"

Nyx shook her head, slid the key to the door and opened it. "Not like Spence, no. But I do love him, that's true. He's my brother and I really don't want to lose him, you know? I'm actually glad he exists and came into my life."

They filed quietly through the kitchen, ditching Nyx's umbrella on their way, to come stand at the living-room door, cheeks flushed and hands over their mouths as they tried to contain their mirth and embarrassment at the sight in before them.

WITCH CRAFT

Sprawled on the sofa, his jersey untucked and rumpled up his chest, Eli Vaughn was busy sliding one hand through the back of a woman's top; a woman who sat astride him, mouth glued to his, from where soft moans erupted at regular intervals; a woman both teens were quick to recognise as Weaversmoor Academy's most sought-after tutor, Jacintha Tate.

Eli's skin broke out in goosebumps the moment Jacintha's lips alighted on his neck. A smile of pure delight lit up the whole of his face, and he hugged her tighter, hands sneaking inside the flimsy blouse she wore. A sudden jolt of cold flared through his spine, the unmistakeable sense of being watched sneaking in and waking his every sense. He'd learnt long ago to listen to his instincts. It was something that had returned with him from his time in Ephemera, where living alone in the woods forced him to use every single sense, lest he fall to his own demise. Opening his eyes, he prepared to search for the source of his unease.

Not that he had to.

Standing at the door of the darkened living-room, two slack-mouthed teens contemplated the couple with discomfort and amusement. Nyx was home, and she'd brought Trystan along.

Eli sat up, nearly dislodging Jacintha from where she balanced precariously astride his hips. She locked eyes with him, registered the embarrassment on his face, turned round to happen upon the young couple, who pressed hands to their mouths and seemed about to break out in a fit of giggles. Vexed, Jacintha took to the sofa, as far from Eli as she could, face as red as the blouse on her back.

"Oh, hi, good night," she managed to whisper, blushing even more.

"Good evening, Miss Tate," Trystan said, ever the gentleman.

"Hi, Miss Tate. Sorry to barge in, thought you'd heard us." Nyx faced her brother, apparently too ashamed to look her tutor in the eye.

"We didn't. Sorry."

"No, I'm the one who should apologise, didn't mean to... anyway, I'm home now. We're just... I'm just gonna walk Trystan to the door, you two..." she gestured one hand in the air, voice low and cracking. "You two carry on."

"Happy birthday, Eli," Trystan offered with a smile, before following Nyx back to the kitchen.

"Well, that was awkward." Jacintha stood up, hands grabbing the mass of dishevelled hair falling down her back. She twisted it into a bun, wrapped an elastic band around it, under Eli's attentive eye.

His heart jolted at the sight of what rested at the base of her neck, inked along the width of it, underneath her hair.

Barely visible, but there.

Eli joined her, tip of his fingers pressed to the black design. A sense of affinity gripped him, as if their meeting had been pre-destined, meant by whatever magical forces ruled the world.

For upon Jacintha's skin lay a feather much like the one he had, a match for his own tattoo. He covered it with the palm of his hand, shuddering at the possibilities it hinted at, pulled her to his chest and rested his chin on the crown of her head.

"I can't begin to tell you how much you mean to me, Jace," he whispered, laying a kiss on her hair. "But this was awkward, all right, I'm sorry."

She looked up. "Can't remember ever being caught at it by my boyfriend's little sister. Bet they're laughing their heads off. It's not as if they don't do the same, when they're alone. But you don't need to hear this," Jacintha added, reading the look of displeasure in Eli's eyes.

"Can I ask you something?"

Before she had time to reply, Nyx was back at the door.

"Eli, a word, please?"

He sighed, let go of Jacintha. "Won't be a minute."

Following his sister into the kitchen, Eli composed an apology, an explanation for what she'd walked in on. "Listen, I'm sorry you had to witness that..."

She discarded his words with a flick of her hand. "Please, it's not like I don't get to see Bryn and Jamal at it all the time. It's not as if I don't do the same, myself. Stop looking at me that way, Eli, I'm sixteen, and have dated before."

"Fair point. What was it you wanted to tell me?"

"Right, about Trystan's mum. Actually, it's about our mum. And your dad."

Shards of ice ran through Eli's veins, his entire body seeped in a sudden surge of cold frost he couldn't shake. As if an impending doom had descended over them, a sharp sword dangling over their heads. He shuddered, but nodded his sister on.

"She was fairly drunk, but kept saying such odd stuff about your father. That he was more creature than man, that Mum wasn't safe with him, and neither were you, so that's why she had to return? Kept talking about Mum cutting threads with him, and how she was there when you were born and she was the one who called your father to let him know before grandmother did away with you. Only she didn't say it as if she gave him a call, know what I mean? It was... so weird, Eli; she spoke as if she'd *summoned* him, like he was a demon or a spirit or something. Totally freaked me out. Anyway, thought you'd like to know, seeing Spencer can't tell you much about him. I have a feeling Cressida Everley knows a lot about your dad, though, and she mentioned she'd like to meet you. Maybe I can arrange it for you one of these days, if you want to find out more?"

Eli grabbed hold of a chair's back. Knuckles white from the strain, he fought against the wave of dizziness that claimed him, stomach cartwheeling, his previous meal sitting awkwardly in the sudden rolling motion of his innards. Forcing a grin to his lips, he was painfully aware Nyx could read him like an open book and knew he was in a world of pain. Her hand folded over one of his, gentle and soothing.

"Are you all right?"

Why did everyone keep asking him that? As if he was some sickly child who couldn't provide for himself, a thing of weak limbs and weak mind, in need of others' protection.

"I'm fine, it's just..."

"Too much to take in. I know. But I'm here for you, and Spence, too. You don't have to meet her now; you can take your time. I'm sorry I mentioned it."

Folding his fingers through hers, his smile became more at ease, genuine. Eli shook his head. "No, I'm glad you did. It was just the shock, I'm fine now. How was your evening?"

Nyx shrugged. "Fine. Sorry I crashed yours. I'm going to bed, do you mind? You and Miss Tate can have downstairs all for yourselves; just shut the living-room door, will you? I don't want to inadvertently watch the two of you at it, if I happen to have to come down to the kitchen, all right?" Her smile carried a mischievous layer that put a smirk up his face.

Eli ruffled her curls and followed his sister back to the living-room.

"I'm off to bed," Nyx announced, grinning at Jacintha. "Have a good evening, Miss Tate."

"Good night, Nyx," she replied.

Eli joined her back at the sofa, after shutting the door behind him, one arm immediately snaking round her shoulders.

"Is she all right? What was it you wanted to ask me?"

"Huh?" His mind was distracted by what his sister had told him, curiosity ploughing a road to his heart, preventing him from focusing on anything other but the meaning of Cressida Everley's words.

"You wanted to ask me something? Just before you left to talk to Nyx?"

"Oh, right." The image of the tattooed feather on her neck brought Eli back to the cottage, to Jacintha, thoughts of his father and his world momentarily pushed aside. "When did you get that tattoo on your neck?"

Jacintha's eyes widened as if in surprise. "What tattoo?"

"Jace, the one at the base of your neck? The feather?"

"What feather? I don't remember having a tattoo."

Eli reached for his mobile, turned its camera on and trained it on Jacintha's skin, snapping a photo. "Here."

She studied the image. "Blimey. Must have had it done before my fall. Can't remember getting it but I must have known it was there, somewhere deep in my mind."

"Why's that?"

Something shifted in her eyes, Jacintha looking avoiding Eli's stare. She was hiding something, keeping some crucial, vital information. His gut coiled with the sense of betrayal, sweat erupting down his back and under his arms, a blast of cold folding over his body. It wasn't just him keeping secrets, after all; Jacintha had hers too. It worried him these pertained to the one thing they had in common - a feather tattooed on their skin. Disregarding appearances and consequences, Eli took off the grey jersey he wore, exposing a naked torso to Jacintha's eyes. She blushed, looked away, only to focus back on his skin. One shaky hand reached out to touch his tattoo. He shivered under her fingers, goosebumps forming all over his arm.

"What the hell?"

"I know," Eli said, and saw the same shift come over her eyes. Yes, she was definitely hiding something, but he couldn't just come and force it out of her, could he? If only he could read her mind, but Jacintha's brain was like a fortress, a wall of grey static thrown right at him. "It's just like mine, only smaller and minus the birds."

"What does yours mean?"

There it was, again - the shiftiness, the elusiveness. Why would she keep secrets from him? Eli knew well enough what his tattoo stood for, at least the feather; it was his claim to the Weaving Craft, marking him as a Weaver, as Ora had patiently explained. But if Jacintha had the very same feather inked onto her skin, albeit in a different place and with a different size, then it must mean she had magic, too. It must mean she kept her powers from him, but why? Because she wondered if he could even understand or accept them?

Eli had kept his magic from everyone - his uncle, his sister, and now Jace; was it really any wonder she did the same? How many people at Weaversmoor knew of the existence of people like them? How many were ready to believe and accept? How many would hunt them? No wonder all those who carried the powers in their blood instinctively kept quiet about it. The world would never be ready for the existence of magic. Witches were still being burnt at the stake, if not literally, at least morally. People were still being persecuted and killed for their differences. No one in their right mind would expose themselves to harm, willingly. Not even at Weaversmoor.

Weaver's.

Weavers like him, like his mother before him, his grandmother, his sister.

Like Jacintha too, the feather on her back claimed her as one. What if she didn't even know? That would be impossible, her powers would have manifested, those random, fleeting shards of talent that came out of nowhere, unexpected and unplanned. She knew, and that's why she hid it. Because, just like him, Jace was unsure of who to trust. Eli pulled her closer, lips alighting over her fragrant hair. She hid her face against his torso, inhaling deeply of his skin, shedding a soft kiss on his sternum, then another and another, all the time moving towards the tattooed birds, her tongue trailing a line across his chest. Eli shivered, held her tighter, body demanding they didn't stop just at kissing, his every instinct requiring he carried her upstairs, to his room, his bed.

He claimed her mouth, parted her lips, entered them. Jacintha returned the kiss, as frenzied as Eli, hands as curious, exploring every inch she could gather of him, as he did with her. Moving back to the sofa, he helped her down, resting gently on top of her, one hand sliding beneath the hem of her skirt, the flesh of her leg locked inside thick tights he longed to rip off her. Only the thought of his sixteen-year-old sister upstairs stopped him from going further. Panting, he sat up; face red, lips swollen from the bites and kisses.

"I'm sorry," he said. "Nyx's upstairs, I don't feel comfortable with it."

"No, neither do I, not after they walked in on us already. I better go."

"I don't want you to."

She pressed herself to him, laying a caress over the feather, his arm, across the chest. "Neither do I. But we can see each other tomorrow, can't we? When's Spencer coming back?"

"Tomorrow night."

Her eyes mirrored a slight disappointment, a chagrin that he'd still have to babysit Nyx and wasn't completely free for her. Eli smiled, kissed her cheek.

"We can have next weekend just for ourselves," he promised. "If you want to."

"Think I'd like that."

He pulled on the jersey, stood up, one hand extended to help her. "Call me when you get home, so I know you're ok. And drive carefully, please."

They walked to the door wrapped in each other's arms, lingering outside on the porch, kissing. Finally, Jacintha broke free and ran to her car, waving Eli goodbye. He stood outside until he could no longer see her round the bend, then shut the gates and walked back home, his emotions conflicted. How was he to address the fact he, too, had magic, how was he to pry the truth from Jacintha? How was he to find if she knew about her Weave? The fact she was one meant she could help open the portal for him, a passage he was no longer sure he wanted to take.

Why couldn't he simply let go of the whole thing, let the past rest, forget about Stella's betrayal and whatever had happened after, whatever had taken place that meant he'd been cast out by his own brother and could no longer return by his own hand? Why couldn't he simply forget?

Because it was unfair.

Eli was Fionn Sylvannar's son as much as his brother Rhysondel, and like him, he was entitled to walk that land, roam that world. He was entitled his honour back, for that was what Stella had stolen from him. How, he didn't yet know, but he had faith of one day remembering everything. Perhaps the day someone weaved a path to Ephemera again and he could enter freely. Perhaps it wasn't his sister who was supposed to help him, but Jacintha. Maybe she was better equipped and better prepared to assist, to believe, to want to aid him on his quest. What if she was tutoring Nyx on her own powers, on her Weave? His sister was still so young; she'd be struggling with her Craft. Jacintha, being a Weaver, must have been assigned to help the girl control her talents and learn how to use them safely.

Which meant someone at Weaversmoor Academy knew about the Craft, the magic in certain individuals' genetic print. What if the entire school was in on it? What if every single student attending it carried the taint of powers in their blood? What if the entire town was composed of witches, every resident being *of the blood*?

His heart thrummed, banged loud and vigorous against his chest.

Images from the previous night streamed like a catalogue of sins into his head.

Bryn had been playing with the witches' Craft out in the woods, when he ran into her. Bryn must be of the blood. She'd said she was only meditating, but Eli knew the Craft well enough to understand Earthens worked better in complete communion with nature, the soil, the surrounding elements. Ora had joked about it often, how Earthen witches liked to go out at night and dance naked under the moon, making a spectacle of themselves. Ora herself was a Healer, with water magic coursing her veins, one who'd attached her life and heart to an Earthen who, once a month, did get himself naked in the privacy of their little home garden, and communed with earth and sky and nature at will. What Eli had caught Bryn doing was exactly that: replenishing her powers and links to her element like his adoptive father used to do. She knew about magic, and knew how to use it. And she attended the same school his sister did. Jamal, too, Bryn's brother, and that tattooed boy, Pip.

Tattooed.

Those weren't mere tattoos gracing Pip's adolescent skin. Those were sigils, wards, spells to keep him safeguarded, reined in. Much like Eli's birds. He'd worked those in Ephemera, except for a couple he'd had tattooed at Daylesford, Crafted to keep his mind from being entered, pried upon, his thoughts his alone. Weavers had a knack for getting glimpses of others' minds, and Eli hadn't wanted Nyx stumbling around his brain. Nor anyone else, for that matter. So he'd had sigils inked onto his skin, and that was exactly what Pip Thomson did. They were all witches, they all knew of the Craft. And none trusted Eli enough to bring up the subject in front of him. They all hid behind innocent eyes, dishing out betrayal and lies at every step. All but Cressida Everley.

He must see her. He must speak to her and learn from the woman's lips how she'd called upon his father, how she'd summoned him. Because if there was a way for Eli to contact the man responsible for his existence, he wouldn't hesitate. If only to let his father know how his son had been treated while dwelling in his barony, how his son had been cast out by his own brother, victim to the treachery of a lying, conniving girl intent on... what? He simply couldn't remember what had taken place between Stella and him to have her turn against Eli. What had she done, really? He knew she was the person behind his eviction from Ephemera, but had no memory of the hows and whys. Maybe his father did. Maybe his father could shed some light on the subject and bring a measure of peace to Eli's fevered brain; maybe if he was told the reasons for his banishment he could put those lands and those people behind him, and fully commit to a life in this world, with his family, with Jacintha. He must see Cressida Everley.

The buzzing of his phone inside the pocket of his jeans brought him back to the present reality. He slid the screen, pressing the phone to his ear, Jacintha's voice metallic and distant.

"Hey, I'm just in. What are you up to?"

"I was about to turn in," he lied, and felt no qualms about it. Wasn't she hiding so much from him? Why should he feel guilty?

"Sleep tight, then. Will I see you tomorrow?"

"Sure, give me a call mid morning. Bye."

"Ok, bye," Jacintha replied, her voice tentative and slightly suspicious.

He knew he was being purposefully, stupidly, immaturely cold, but couldn't help feeling betrayed by her secrecy. Cutting the call, Eli climbed the stairs to his room, stopping by Nyx's, trying to discern through the darkness across a half-open door. She lay in bed, back down, mouth slack, a soft snore coming out of it. Her hands clung tightly to the pleat of the linen sheet and duvet, as if afraid the clothes were ripped off her and she woke up uncovered and cold. She was deeply asleep, though, and Eli's eyes swerved to the phone resting on her bedside table.

A phone he was sure would have Bryn Everley's number. And only through Bryn could he come to reach Cressida on her own, privately. Bracing himself, Eli sucked in a deep breath and slithered through the door, silent as he could. Tip-toeing across the wooden floors, his hand reached towards the phone, fingers alighting over it, still too far for him to reach. He slid one foot forward, the other.

Nyx turned on her side, facing directly to where he stood. Eli's heart hammered against his chest, how weird would it be for her to open her eyes and find him here? What could he say, that he'd heard her whimper in her sleep and had come to check if she was all right? Might work, but he'd rather not risk it. Her breast rose and fell with the balance of deep, restful sleep; she was far from waking up and Eli already knew how deep his sister could sleep. Not like him, or Spencer, who'd be awake at the slightest, most trifling noise. He stood very still, though; wanting to make sure Nyx was deep in her slumbers. When he was certain she wouldn't suddenly open her eyes, he grabbed the phone and exited the room as silently as he walked in.

Unlocking the screen, Eli searched through his sister's contacts, and sure enough, there was Bryn's.

He marched to his room, closing the door behind him, and walked off to the window. Staring out, Eli searched beyond the meadow and amidst the trees for a sign of Bryn out in the woods, crafting whatever spells she'd been playing with. The unwanted, uncomfortable thought she might have put a seduction hex on him crossed his mind, forcing a deliberate grin to his lips. It could justify his willingness in giving in to her. A willingness that could as easily be explained by the fire in his loins at the sight of the girl's naked body and her blatant, open offer. Hormones, it was, not Bryn's witchcraft; he couldn't put the blame on her alone. Like Ora used to say, it took two to do that dance. Steadying his pulse, Eli pressed call, holding the phone in a tight grip. Three rings was all it took for Bryn to pick up.

"Look, Nyx," she snapped on the other end, voice hushed but slightly angered, "if Trystan doesn't pick up his phone it's because he's either asleep or doesn't want to talk. So there's no point you calling me."

"Hi, Bryn," Eli whispered, doubting this was a good idea. "It's Eli." The silence stretched like an elastic band, to the point he could feel it break and snap. "Bryn?"

"I'm here. Why are you calling me on your sister's phone?"

"I don't have your number."

"You could have copied it, she's gonna know a call was placed from her phone, to me. Not hard for her to figure out it must have been you, and then all your efforts to keep this secret go down the drain."

He shuddered, she had a point. But he could deal with Nyx later, make something up. Right now, he had more important issues at hand. "My sister said your mother knew my father. Mentioned a couple weird things she said about him. Look, I know this is unwarranted, but I need to speak to Cressida. Tonight."

"Eli, it's past midnight, she's probably asleep."

"Please."

She sighed, and he could almost picture her, jaw squared, eyes squinted, a frown of annoyance all over her face, as she pondered her options. "Fine, meet me at the clearing, where you found me yesterday. I'll be there in five."

Before Eli could reply, she cut the call, leaving him hands sweating, heart thrashing, legs wavering in the sudden realisation he might be closer to Ephemera than he thought.

IX

"Are you sure you want to do this?" Bryn asked, eyeing Eli askance. He ran shaky hands through his hair, shook his head. "I have to. It's like a pull, one I need to follow. I need to know who I am, where I come from. I don't expect you to understand."

Bryn stopped walking; they were mere steps from the rusty gate opening onto the Everley estate. "I'm not half as dim as you take me for. And I *do* understand, they're your genetic heritage, your birth parents, of course you need to know more. Of course you must wonder why they left you. She used to say the weirdest things about your father, you know? My mother." Picking up pace, she guided Eli to the locked gate, and ushered him in.

They roamed through thick clusters of trees, Bryn seeming to know her way in the dark like the palm of her hand, but Eli wasn't fooled anymore. This was *her* magic, her natural power, her link to the earth that guided and permitted her to never get lost and always find the right way. The very soil must lead her correctly, something travelling from the core of the ground to Bryn's insides, so innate as to her not even noticing it happened every time. Finally, they alighted on a manicured grass expanse leading to a large, stately house. An eyesore of a house, Eli mused, with its round turrets, the dark grey stone of the walls, the slate roofs. It looked like something out of a fairytale, one of those massive castles in Germany or Austria he'd seen in books, something fit for an evil queen. Eyes shifting towards Bryn, who walked ahead, he imagined her as that evil queen, lady of the manor, dishing pain and death on her subjects and everyone around. A grin graced his lips.

"Come on, through the side door," Bryn whispered, and Eli followed.

The house was dark and silent. They came into what looked like a pantry and a mudroom combined. The girl pressed a finger to her lips, other hand pushing softly on a wall panel, the hinges creaking far too loud in the still of the night. The panel slid, Bryn pushed it open to reveal a hidden staircase leading up.

"Servants' stairs," she clarified. "The house was built somewhere in the 1700s, and there are all these passages for servants, areas that were specific to them. Trystan and I used to run around using them as secret passages, but they're still pretty much in use by the house help. This one leads straight to the first floor."

He followed her up the narrow staircase emerging on a wide landing that opened to a corridor. The Everleys lived lavishly, and ostentatiously, judging by the luxurious décor of the landing alone. Which belied everything about Bryn. She wasn't ostentatious nor arrogant where it came to material goods or money, wasn't entitled; but she did have a mean streak about her that came from knowing she held a position in the social order that outranked most of the people she knew. One that came not only from the money her family had, but the weight their name carried in a place like Weaversmoor.

"Mother's at the end of the hall," Bryn said, pulling on the sleeve of his jacket and rushing him along. "Look, Eli, she's probably plastered, you need to take everything she says with a huge pinch of salt."

"Why would she be plastered? I'm sorry; I don't get what you mean."

Bryn's eyes sparkled with amusement. "Means she's drunk. Like you were last night, only more."

Eli blushed, turned his eyes away. "Why is she drunk?"

Bryn's expression went unnoticed, but the sourness in her voice let him know all he needed of how damaging the entire situation had been for her.

"Because she can't accept dad doesn't love her and never did. Because she wants to own him and force him into something that'll eventually destroy them both and us with them. Dad fights back, and it drives her into drinking, just so she can cope with the truth."

"Which is?"

Her eyes rested on his, harsh, cold, but with the liquid glint of impending tears. "He's gay. Was forced to marry her. Huge mistake. She's refused him the divorce for ages, and…"

"You don't have to tell me this, Bryn," Eli said, one hand taking hold of her arm. "It's none of my business."

She shrugged, embittered smirk on her lips. "It's more your business than you think. Come on, be quiet, Trystan's room's next door and I don't want him to wake up."

They crossed the hall in silence, stopping at a large, double door. Bryn knocked softly, turned the knob, her head pushed into the narrow gap.

"Mum, are you up?"

"Bryn? I was just about to turn in," a swaying, slurred voice replied from the confines of the room.

"Eli Vaughn's here. Remember I told you he was coming to visit?"

Eli stepped closer to Bryn, watching her back. The way she spoke to her mother, as if *she* was the parent reassuring her own child, pulled at his heart. This girl was far from what he'd made of her, there were depths to Bryn Everley he couldn't even begin to fathom. He was suddenly sorry for her, who'd obviously had to grow up far quicker than other girls her age, simply because neither of her parents was available to do their job within a family. Bryn had had to be mother and father to her and Trystan, to both her parents, as well, and of course this was bound to leave scars, wounds that would never heal. As much as the wounds he and Nyx had to nurse from their mother's abandonment.

"Oh, of course, let him in."

Bryn widened the gap in the door, glueing herself to its panels, inviting Eli in. He slid through, brushing against her breasts with his upper arm, a shiver running down his spine, hairs standing on end at the back of his head, his arms, his legs.

"I'll be right outside," she said, and closed the door as she left.

The room was dim, but not fully dark. The curtains were pushed aside on the three tall, wide windows across the front wall, letting in a sliver of moonlight that bathed the insides with a blue-ish, silvery shimmer. Sitting on a chaise longue, a glass of something in her hand, Cressida Everley watched him with eager eyes, studying his gait as if in search of similarities that assured her he was who he claimed. Eli studied her back, saw Bryn in every trace.

The woman was as beautiful as her daughter, if not more. Hair slightly lighter than Bryn's, with a sheen that hinted at gold streaks running through it, eyes a little wider than her daughter's, more like Trystan's, but her colours were the same as Bryn's: the rosy cheek, the green eyes, the alabaster skin. Everything about her was wider and larger than Bryn, as if her daughter was a toned-down version of Cressida. Eli realised Trystan had inherited his mother's traces in the shape of his mouth, the curve of his chin, the round of his eyes, while Bryn had been endowed with her colours and beauty.

"Hi," Eli managed to croak, suddenly ill at ease. He should have asked Bryn to stay.

"Come closer," the woman said, gesturing with her glass, the drink sloshing inside.

He took a couple of steps forward, came to stand above her, facing the woman down. It felt disrespectful to look at her thus, so Eli squatted by the chaise longue, at hand's reach. Cressida rested cold fingers over his brow, traced the line of his forehead, the jaw, the chin.

"You don't look much like him. It's Spencer and Corinna I see in you, not Fionn, not Erin."

"But I *am* their son."

"Noctifer Sylvannar, because you were born in the dead of night. Known as Nox, for you'd be like the night, enchanting and luring, a king in two worlds."

Eli shuddered at her words. This woman knew it all. And she wasn't keeping secrets from him. "Is that what he said, my father?"

"Yes, he made sure to seal your fate the moment you were born. Such a heavy burden to place upon a child, don't you think?"

"What kind of man was he? How were you able to call him? You're also a Weaver, aren't you?"

Instead of looking shocked, Cressida was amused. She giggled like a little girl, hand shedding a soft caress on Eli's cheek.

"No, no. The Vaughns were the Weavers, always. So was my father-in-law, a fluke in his genetic lineage. It was Erin who Weaved a path for Fionn to come here, she placed her threads, I only helped strengthen them. And then I summoned your father like she told me to, the night you were born. He came blazing like a sun, the light of a million stars on his wake. The monster inside him burning through his eyes, anger and pain at war within him. Only Erin could appease his beast, the curse every single one of them was born with. The curse they had to endure for living such long life spans."

Eli nodded, unsure what Cressida meant. He knew it was Weaver magic that provided the Everlasting with their powers and their near immortal status, and the mention of monsters and beasts seemed to wake up a faint memory from his time in Ephemera, but he couldn't quite recall what it meant.

"He was a handsome man. Well, he was more than that, for he was more than a man. A creature, and one that was pleasing to the eye, if scary to the mind. You're as handsome as him; no wonder my daughter's caught so tight in your spell."

Eli blushed, surely she had it wrong. He was no more than a whim for Bryn, a game she played, a dare she'd placed upon herself. Soon she'd tire of trying to seduce him; soon she'd sicken of Eli and go in search of the next big thrill.

"Can you tell me how to call him? Like my mother taught you?"

"Nox, where's your mother?"

A shiver clawed at his back, it was a long time since someone other than Serge and Ora called him that. Eli shook his head.

"I don't know. According to my adoptive parents, she came to the hospital when I was still there, but then disappeared."

Bringing the rim of the glass to her lips, Cressida finished her drink, placed the empty beaker on the small side table to her right.

"Your grandmother severed every single thread Erin weaved to your father's world. At some point, she had six Weavers posted in town to lock down the portal. But they sent their Hounds, and took them one by one, fuel for their dark magic, their tainted spells. When Erin was forced back here, she knew she must make sure there were no more of her threads, so they couldn't cross and come after her, for they'd want her for being a Weaver."

"You mean my father sent people to hunt my mother?"

Cressida shook her head. "He *did* send them to take the Weavers your grandmother brought in. Those lives rest on Corinna's head, Fionn was brutal and heartless, she should have known that. He cared for nothing but Erin and you, of course he'd never stand to having Corinna step in and keep him away. She knew this, and still went ahead."

It didn't make sense, and yet, there was a familiarity to all she said; as if deep inside him, Eli knew what she meant. He just couldn't remember.

"But when Fionn was forced to let go of you and Erin, he did so to keep the two of you safe. Because both were Weavers, and if anyone in his world knew, *they*'d come after you."

"You know what I am, then. So show me how you called my father to our world."

Again, she shook her head. "Erin severed her every single thread. You can no longer use her Weave to reach Fionn. If you were to place a Weave of your own, you'd be endangering us all. Your sister and yourself, especially. *They*'ll come for you, if *they* find out."

"No, that doesn't make sense. I can keep us safe, Nyx and me."

The woman sniggered; Eli's patience bristled.

"I've been there," he finally said, voice hoarse as if it cost him to speak. "For seven years, I've lived there. And no one, not one single person that came across me in that world, realised what I was."

Cressida reached across her lap to hold his hands. "When you went into a coma and the Sylvain called Erin, she knew. She knew your mind had Weaved you there, and this was why you couldn't wake up. She said your body was so dim at times it was almost as if you were no longer here, in our world. It was her and Corinna that arranged for you to be nursed at home, it was your grandmother who made sure your condition was kept hidden and not looked upon by social services or any such thing. Corinna and her battalion of lawyers saw to it you were safe in our world, while Erin tried to find a way back there so she could rescue you. I gather she must have made it, because here you are."

Eli shook his head. "It wasn't her. I was cast out, though I can't remember why."

Cressida sighed in relief. "That means you can't weave a path back. Of all the small miracles."

"What if I *want* to return?"

They locked eyes, cold glints of steel in both of them, a battle of wills and forces. Suddenly, Cressida didn't look half as drunk as he'd taken her to be. Suddenly, she didn't look half as mad, or as vulnerable.

"Your mother came here before she left to find a way in. Made me promise if ever you or Nyx happened to turn up at Weaversmoor, I'd look out for you. I was to do my best keeping you safe. And I'm going to do that for her, for Fionn."

"I got the feeling you didn't much care for my father."

A cackle fled her lips. "Oh, I liked Fionn, all right. I liked him because he made your mother happy and stood up to Corinna, who bullied this entire town and had us all under thumb. I liked him, for he warned me, but I refused to listen to him. When he came to deliver you and Erin back to our world, he told me I was headed for disaster, and I shouldn't listen to Corinna, but did I care? I let her lure me to her web, and it made my life hell. But your grandmother, as much as Erin, wanted to make sure you and Nyx were safe."

"Then why did she force us back here? Aren't we vulnerable in this place? My parents told me there's a rip in those woods, a place where the fabric that separates both worlds is weaker. Where Weavers can cast threads and open the breach so they cross over at will. Why would Corinna want us here? Seeing both Nyx and I are Weavers?"

"So that you can keep the rip sown. As much as you can widen the gap, being Weavers, so can you use your powers, your magic, to sow it back, keep it locked tight. Corinna and my father-in-law did that for a number of years, they even brought about another

Weaver to help, but Clarence Everley passed away before they could train her, and for some reason, your grandmother never really trusted the girl. When Corinna died, we lost our wards. She knew this would happen, so arranged for you and Nyx to return. Your sister attending the Academy will ensure she learns what's expected of her, and your grandmother must have believed the couple who raised you had filled you in on all this."

Eli nodded, but a shudder ran through his body. Corinna had brought in another Weaver, one she never came to trust. It must be Jacintha - Weavers weren't all that common. The feather inked on the back of her neck claimed her as one, and she'd already told him she'd been brought to town three years before. But Jace seemed unaware of what she was or what she could really do with her powers; she seemed unaware of the existence of another world right at their doorstep, one only those like them could breach.

Head swaying, he sat on the carpet, shuddering with the implications he could now see. It was all so clear. Jacintha's presence at Weaversmoor, her tattoo, the way they'd met. She'd said she'd freaked herself out in the woods, but that wasn't quite so simple, was it? What if she'd inadvertently opened a doorway to Ephemera, and that was the reason behind her fright, and had her running terrified into the road? What if she didn't know what she'd done? Shuddering, Eli tried to rein in the sudden blast of his heart; he must think, make sense of this, getting himself upset wouldn't help. Jacintha had come to town three years before; he'd risen from his coma at around the same time. She had no memory of her previous life, much as he struggled to remember his time on Ephemera. If not for his adoptive parents', Eli would be as much in the dark about his powers as Jacintha seemed to be.

What if she'd come from that other world? Cressida had mentioned Hounds sent to search other Weavers and collect them, so that the ruling class of Ephemera could siphon their power.

What if they weren't actual hounds, dogs trained for the hunt? What if they were Weavers, too? And Jacintha one of them? Was this what she was hiding from him? She'd come to take Eli and Nyx, she was hunting him? No, he couldn't believe it. His powers, although they came across a blank whenever trying to reach inside her head, were still accurate enough to understand she wasn't warding him off. No, Jacintha really had no memory of her past. Static was what he got from her, not a fortress built to keep others out, like the one he erected in his brain. What if she was like him, and had suffered some accident in *her* world, was now lying in a coma somewhere, her body getting dimmer and dimmer as she took on a new hold in this world? What if, like Eli, she'd Weaved a path across the worlds, only the other way around? He must look further into this.

"So, you can't help me reach my father?" he asked, heartrate back to normal, breathing eased by the decision he'd taken. "What about my mother? Do you think she made it there? Do you think they're together? She could be in danger, could even be dead."

Cressida's eyes pooled with tears. "Erin sacrificed herself for the wellbeing of her children, Eli. You owe it to her to make sure you treasure her gift, which is your life, your freedom. You must never try to reach your father and his world. You must let go of Nox Sylvannar and fully embrace Eli Vaughn. It's who you are, now."

He nodded, if only to appease her. "No one talks of it around me. Of the Craft."

"They're testing their waters. Spencer must be doubtful you have any powers, and he must have warned Nyx to keep hers secret. Perhaps you need to take the first step and come clean to them, show your uncle you're of the blood."

"Of the blood?" Eli wondered how she knew the expression, had Fionn taught her?

"Those who have magic in their veins. We say we're of the blood. Weaversmoor is a haven for those like us, so we tend to congregate here. Rare is the person who doesn't carry some ounce of power, residing in this area."

So they called them the same as in Mythos, here. *Of the blood.*

"Thank you for your time, Mrs Everley," Eli said, and stood up, legs stiff from having sat for so long. "I'm sorry for disrupting your evening."

Cressida stood up too, shaky on her feet, and Eli held out one hand to support her. "I've wanted to meet you ever since I heard you were back in town. It's been a pleasure seeing you again, dear boy. You're your mother's son, all right; your father's child. That's why I urge - no, I beg you - to be pondered, Eli. They were far too hot-headed, too rash, I urge you to think deep before you act. Here, I'll show you out."

The door opened just a crack and out slid Eli, head down, hands flung into the pockets of his jeans. Bryn emerged from where she hid in the shadows by the wall, took a step towards him. They faced each other, Eli looking like someone who'd sucked a bitter lemon, Bryn wincing at the sight of him. She reached a hand, which he ignored.

"You ok?" she asked, nodding towards the door behind her. "Come on in, take a seat, I swear you're positively turning green."

The smile on his lips widened, and she breathed out relief. Eli followed her, studying the room while she scooped up discarded clothes from the small sofa pressed against the wall.

"Sit." She carted the garments to the nearest chair, fiddled with her iPad, the soft, low sounds of Patti Smith's *Because the Night* swaying into the room.

Unexpectedly, he obeyed her, long legs stretched ahead of him, head leaning against the dark green wall, eyes closed, breathing in fast, small gulps of air. Bryn knew if she were to place a hand over his heart, it would hammer like a machine gun.

"Can I get you a glass of water? You really don't look well."

He shrugged, ran shaky hands through his hair, kept his eyes shut. Bryn stepped away, but before she could move out of his reach, Eli grabbed her by the wrist.

"Just sit here with me a few seconds, will you?"

Bryn eased herself by his side, her thigh in contact with his. Shivers shook her spine, like hands running nails softly down her back. Ghost hands, that pushed into her and tightened a grip around her lungs. Breathing had become a near impossibility, from sitting this close to him. Stealing a glance at Eli, whose eyes were still closed, she studied his features, noticing for the first time the creases on his forehead, the tiny wrinkles around his eyes. How she longed to soothe them with a caress, how she longed to soothe *him*, repeat last night's pleasures.

"Did she tell you anything useful?"

"I suppose. My mother came to my grandmother when I was in a coma and asked for her help. It was Corinna who provided I was so well taken care of, after all."

"What about your father?"

Eli shrugged, finally opening his eyes, rolling his head on his shoulders so he could look at her. Bryn's stomach erupted in flames, which melted to hot coals under the force of his stare. Unable to stop herself, she reached the tips of her fingers to his temple, ran them through his hair, until her skin met his, the caress moving to his neck, the shoulder where she knew black birds took flight from their restraint on a feather inked up his arm. She'd like to see that tattoo of his again; hell, she'd like to see so much more of him again. Her hand rested over his arm, curled around it, and still Eli didn't move, hardly blinked at all. Their eyes were still glued together, in the dimness of the room; his, dark and unreadable, while hers were an open book. Bryn rested her head against the sofa's back, lips so close to Eli's shoulder she could have kissed it. His head slid down an inch, their noses almost touching.

And still they said nothing, just sat there with eyes upon each other, music floating around them, its lyrics setting a mood that echoed through Bryn, eager for Eli to make the first move. But he was like a statue, only the intermittent blinking and the rise and fall of his chest betraying him alive. She could smell mint on his breath, and the subtle, musky cologne he wore, notice the pores on his skin, every single bristle of his beard, the ridges in the soft pink of his lips. She could see the grey subtly streaked across the blue of his eyes, and the lengthy, golden eyelashes, like velvet folds casting shadows on his cheek. She could see the lust inside his eyes, and scent the smell of want from his skin; she could sense his heat coming out in waves that threatened to engulf her, to inflame her even more. How could he have such an effect on her?

Letting go of his arm, Bryn slid her hand down the length of it, grasped his fingers and twined hers through them. Eli didn't shove her away, didn't pull back.

What had her mother told him that left him in such an altered state? He seemed a shell of himself, lost of will and strength, prey to her every whim, only a body for Bryn to use. Well, she certainly didn't want him *that* way. Would he react, if she tried to kiss him? Would he pull back? Anything was better than this look of utter confusion, this apathetic attitude, so unlike him. Her chin inched further, settled over his shoulder. Their lips were so close as to nearly touch, eyes still locked together, his brimming with tears she couldn't place.

Thinking back to the times her mother had mentioned Erin and the strange, older man she'd fallen in love with, Bryn tried to remember anything Cressida said that might have had this effect on Eli. Whenever the subject of Erin Vaughn's trespasses came up, Cressida would go on and on about how inappropriate their relationship was, what with the age gap. Erin had been what? Fourteen, fifteen, when she'd gotten herself physically involved with a man Bryn had assumed to be over forty, by what her mother said. That was abuse, plain and simple.

It *did* make sense that Eli reacted like this.

His parents' relationship had been anything but normal, or morally acceptable. In fact, the more she thought about it, the more it disgusted her. As if Erin had been seduced by a pervert, a paedophile stalking little girls through the woods, a monster hunting his prey in the dark. Shivers ran down her back again, this time in fear of the very same woods she felt so grounded at, the woods that fed her magic and made her stronger. Erin must have been caught in the man's snare while doing precisely that. No wonder Eli looked so shaken. Nothing about his origins was clear, or clean. It was all a swamp of morally shaky choices, from both father and mother. Emotions gripped her, a sigh that resembled a sob forcing its way from her lips. Bryn reached her free hand to Eli's cheek, caressed the soft, short bristles of beard, head inching even closer over his shoulder. She shut her eyes when he shut his and parted her lips, ready for the kiss.

Only to snap her head up as Eli pulled away, hands over his face, a groan of frustration leaving his mouth.

"No," he said. "I can't do this."

"But you want to."

Eli trained his eyes back on her, anger having taken the place of bewilderment. "I'm in love with someone and won't betray her. Not again."

Bryn stood up, smoothed the black jersey down her stomach, walked away to her desk where she turned off the iPad. "Miss Tate, huh?"

"How do you know?"

"Trystan mentioned he and Nyx walking in on the two of you nearly at it. Well, can't say it doesn't run in your family."

Eli pushed himself up, stretched his arms and back. "What does?"

"The tendency for inappropriate relationships. I mean, she's your sister's tutor, right? And your uncle just ran off to spend the weekend cooped up with a married man. Not to mention your parents..."

Two strides of his long legs carried Eli closer to Bryn, and he wrapped a strong hand over her wrist. "Then don't mention them."

Bryn lifted her chin, stared defiantly.

Eli let go of her arm, suddenly detached. "That's why I won't ever touch you again. I'm not going to repeat the same mistakes my father did. I, at least, won't take advantage of a little girl who craves attention because she has daddy issues."

Her face darkened, a blush covering her formerly pale cheeks. Fury rimmed her eyes, which had narrowed. "You're a total git, aren't you, Eli? I don't crave attention, nor do I have daddy issues. You know nothing about me. At least try to be a little grateful that I brought you here so you could meet my mum and get all the dirt on yours."

"You're right. I'm sorry."

"Is it that bad? What she told you? I mean, you're clearly upset."

"My mind's a mess, right now. But don't think I don't appreciate what you've done. I won't forget this, Bryn. Thank you."

She shrugged. "Don't mention it. Blimey, this room is dark."

The small lamp on her bedside table lit up without any of them touching it. Eli's face stood out from the shadows, eyes narrowed as he searched hers. Bryn's widened with surprise, a little shock.

"You *are* of the blood," she gasped. "I sensed such strong magical energy last night, before you came up on me. Restrained and secretive, yes, but so strong. Your print lets loose out there, but I can hardly sense it here. You keep hiding it."

"And you weren't meditating in the woods, last night."

She let out a cackle. "Busted. Why are you hiding your magic from your family? They have no idea if you know of the Craft."

"I'm not hiding; I just didn't know how to bring this up, seeing they're also keeping their powers from me. I never seem to know what to do."

"Be honest. Be you."

They faced each other once more, both smiling.

"I better take off now, left Nyx alone."

"Look, this doesn't have to be awkward, Eli," Bryn whispered, standing well away from him. "We could be friends, you know?"

His eyes rested over hers, warm, tempting, the look inside them assuring Bryn he'd like to be far more than friends, if only he was free.

"Think I'd like that. You're... well, you're like no one else I know, Bryn, and I think I could do with a friend like you. But now I really should get going."

"Want me to walk you down to the clearing?"

"I can find my own way. Would really appreciate if you showed me to the door, and the gate."

"Sure, come on, then."

Pulling on one of her many discarded jackets, Bryn ushered Eli out of the room, a sense of loss slowly seeping into her veins, as if she'd just been robbed of some essential part of herself. As if a preponderant piece of her had been shattered.

Swallowing down a gasping sob, she understood what it was she missed - her very own heart.

It had been ripped off her chest and shred to pieces outside her.

WITCH CRAFT

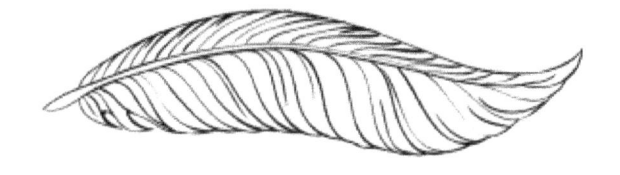

X

The lights flickered briefly, a minute event that would have gone unnoticed by anyone not of the blood. Spencer, though, *was* of the blood and his eyes took due notice of the momentary disturbance. He flashed what he hoped was a significant look at Nyx, who silently replied with a shrug of her shoulders, signifying she had nothing to do with the electrical disturbance. Maybe a natural event, then, not magically provoked. It wasn't unheard of, and the weather *did* call for it, what with the storm raging outside. As if mother nature herself raged against Spencer's return to Weaversmoor, after the weekend away, where he and Max had absolutely no worries but what to order for lunch and where to go to dinner, aside making up for all the years apart. It was as if the entire universe portended an omen of doom to rain upon them because they'd returned.

Pushing away dire thoughts, Spencer eyed the two siblings, aware of a shift in their relationship. Something had happened during his absence, something had changed between them, their bonds had strengthened. They seemed tighter; the bickering gone. He smiled - this was a change for the better, surely. When the lights flickered once more, he cast annoyed eyes on the chandelier, watching the lamps go on and off. Then the stereo came alive, blaring loud music into the room, Spencer jumping from his seat along with Nyx.

This wasn't a natural event. This had been magic-made.

Slowly, he faced Eli, who cast his eyes down, shied away from meeting his uncle's glare. So he was of the blood, too; he *did* have magic. This must be his awkward way of bringing the subject up, in the hopes either Spence or Nyx understood what was going on and spoke of it openly. It fell to him, being the eldest, the paternal figure, if not outright unit.

"You'll ruin the cables, if you keep this up, Eli," he said, as if it was the most natural thing in the world, to play around with lights and sound just by exercising your willpower. "And do turn that down, it's late."

Nyx inched forward on the sofa, her attention on her brother. "What does this mean?" she asked. "You're versed on the Craft?"

Eli nodded. "Aren't you?"

"Nyx is just learning, she was a bit behind on a few subjects. Hence the tutor."

"Who he's dating," Nyx added, her hand slapping her mouth as she realised she was out of line; it wasn't for her to tell, but Eli. "Sorry," she said.

Eli shrugged, but his eyes filled with worry as he trained them on Spencer, fearing his reaction.

"You're dating Jacintha Tate? Now, there's one I didn't see coming. How did this happen?"

The younger man shrugged again. "How do these things happen? Naturally, I'd think." The blush on his cheek was endearing, and Spencer found himself caught in a flood of love for his nephew. "We met when I first got here, and ended up falling in love. Do you think it's gonna cause her problems, me being Nyx's brother?"

Spencer shook his head. "As long as the two of you are discreet, I don't see a reason why. And Nyx will soon no longer need tutoring, so you're fine. Hey, I'm happy you met someone."

"Don't you have anything to tell us?" Nyx inquired, one eyebrow cocked playfully.

Her uncle met her stare. "By the looks of it, you know already."

"Wasn't sure, until Bryn Everley told me."

"Do you mind if we don't talk about it just yet?" Spencer looked ill-at-ease, not quite ready to admit to the depth of feelings he carried for Max. "It's still early days, and he's in for a nasty divorce. We need to take it slow. Besides, I'm more curious about Eli and his Craft, do you know what yours is? I'm an Earthen. How have you coped with it all? Who taught you to work it?"

Eli sat back, stretched his legs. "You have no idea what a relief it is to be able to speak of this freely. My adoptive parents taught me, Serge is an Earthen, Ora a Waterling. I'm like Erin."

Spencer and Nyx exchanged a look, eyes wide in sudden concern. So Max was right, Corinna had known Eli was a Weaver, and planned ahead to ensure both he and Nyx came to meet at Weaversmoor. But how were they supposed to close the chasm and keep the portal into that other world locked forever? She'd left no instructions, no clues on what and how to do it. How were these two supposed to pull off magic that momentous?

"Do you have any tattoos?" Eli asked, Spencer's head reeling with the change in subject.

He grinned, though, and unbuttoned the shirt he wore, taking it off and exposing his back to Eli's eyes. It was entirely covered with one large tattoo, that of a fern leaf. His nephew stood up, came to kneel on the rug before him, tips of his fingers alighting over the detailed design.

"It's... wow, it's really beautiful," he said. "So delicate, it almost looks like a feather instead of a fern leaf. Why this?"

"Do *you* have tattoos, Eli?" Spencer inquired.

Eli nodded, and proceeded to get rid of his jersey. As he exposed his body, turning the arm so Spencer could see his ink, a gasp from his sister brought attention back to her. Cheeks blushed, Nyx focused on Eli's shoulder and collarbone.

"What?" he asked, suddenly uncomfortable.

"Spence, look at his tattoo."

"I know. Show him."

Eli faced his sister as she pulled down the collar of her pyjamas, exposing the upper arm to view. On the exact same spot where Eli had his feather tattooed, Nyx sported an equal design, complete with a couple of birds taking off from it, just like his. Only Eli had far more birds inked onto his skin than Nyx.

"Do you know what this is?" she inquired, voice shaking.

"Weaver's mark," Eli replied.

Both Spencer and Nyx sighed in relief.

"The feather marks the Weavers," Spencer explained. "Erin had one, too, on her ankle. But those birds, I only saw them on Nyx. Now you. Erin had stars tattooed onto the lower half of her back; they were sigils and wards to help rein in her Weaver's powers and the consequences they carried."

"Like the mind-reading?" Eli cackled. "Yeah, that's this big bird here. All these birds are meant either to protect or enhance my Craft."

"But why birds?" Nyx asked.

"I could ask you the same."

"It's what came into my head, and I felt they were appropriate. Nothing else would do."

"Exactly."

"Well, I'm glad we got this out of the way," Spencer said, getting up from his seat. He walked off to the bar cart and poured a measure of water into a glass, fishing around his pocket for the small vial he carried. Measuring a couple of drops with a pipette, he poured the inky purple liquid into his water and downed it in one gulp, wincing.

"What's that?" Eli asked.

"A fortifier," Nyx clarified. "Spence's a Draught-Maker. It's like vitamins."

"Like a tincture, then?"

Spencer faced away from him, nodded his head. "Nyx, it's rather late, you should get some sleep. Tomorrow's a school day."

The girl shuffled out of her comfortable sitting arrangement, yawning and stretching her arms. "You're right. Have a good night, you two." She crossed the room and exited, leaving the door ajar behind her.

"Listen, I'm sorry I missed your birthday. We could do something to celebrate next weekend. A party, maybe?" Spencer studied Eli, who grinned and shook his head.

"Please, don't. And stop apologising for it, you needed time away, Nyx and I were driving you mad. I really don't mind."

Nodding, Spence eyed the bar cart. "Do you want a drink?"

"Nah, I'm off to bed, myself."

"Don't. I need to talk to you and didn't want to do it with Nyx here." Walking towards the door, he peered out, focused on the sound of his niece upstairs, brushing her teeth and getting ready to sleep. He closed the door gently behind him, walked off to the large French windows, signalling Eli to follow. "How much do you know of your father?"

"You're finally going to tell me about him?"

Spencer grinned. "I've been shying from it, it's rather awkward, you know? But we do need to address that subject."

Eli gazed outside, taking in the stormy night. Rain poured like there was no tomorrow, drenching the deck and grounds. "How much do you know about the couple who adopted me?"

So, he was aware of it all. It made things easier, at least. "I know my sister trusted them enough to hand you over. I know your father did, too."

"They were his subjects, and very loyal to him. Do you know how your sister met him?"

Spencer nodded again. "She's a Weaver. Threaded a portal into your father's world. A portal that's left a chasm there, one my mother and some of the town's elders have struggled to keep locked. I'd hoped this wouldn't come as a surprise to you, the existence of a parallel world where your father lived."

"Does Nyx know?"

"Not yet. Will have to tell her one day, but figured she could do with being carefree a couple more years. Until she knows how to work with her powers, at least. Until she's attuned to the Craft. But you're an adult, Eli, and I had to address this. That portal cannot be opened again, *ever*. It needs to stay locked, or you and Nyx will be in danger, as well as everyone of the blood."

"Why's that?"

Spencer ran his hands through his hair in a gesture that was reminiscent of his nephew when he was anxious. "Your father wasn't like the others in his world. Have your adoptive parents told you nothing?"

Eli faced his uncle. His blue eyes had acquired a steely glint, one that bore down on Spencer, trying to breach into his soul. As if he carried a secret that was so heavy it had become an impossible burden, and was unsure whether to share it or not. Was unsure whether Spencer was trustworthy enough for him to share.

"You can tell me anything. I know how much Erin loved Fionn. Despite the wrongness of it all, according to my mother. She loved him, and even after marrying Tom, went on loving him. There was only Fionn for her. Mother made it sound perverted, dirty, and Erin was already so vulnerable, after..."

"After having been forced out of Ephemera by my elder brother."

Their eyes met, measured forces, studied the depths of each other's thoughts. "Yes. Erin lived in Ephemera with Fionn and you for five years. You spent your early childhood there. But I don't suppose you remember much of it."

"Oh, I remember far more than you think, uncle. I may have come back to this world when I was five, but those weren't the only years I spent there."

~ "What do you mean?"

Eli took a deep breath, as if bracing himself. "Did you ever cross over, with my mother? Were you ever there?"

Spencer shook his head.

"It's beautiful. Nothing like this world, of course. Remember when I said I was in a coma for seven years? That wasn't quite true."

"Really?" Wondering where this was going, Spencer looked longingly at the bar cart, he could do with a drink just to pull himself through this.

Despite knowing for a fact an alternate, parallel world where creatures with strange powers existed was true, he still struggled around it. Still found it unbelievable, even after having seen Fionn Sylvannar first hand. Nothing like him had ever roamed the world Spencer lived in.

"I did suffer a freak accident, was unconscious for years, but it wasn't as much a coma as it was a Weave. Does this make sense? I lost consciousness here to regain it there. My body was a husk, empty, hollowed, and at times so dim you could see through it. Because I was alive in Ephemera, Spence. I was alive there. Mum says there were days she feared I'd simply disappear from this plane to become fully alive there. I was *that* dim."

"So what happened? How come you're here?"

Eli studied the outside again, and Spencer appraised his nephew. No wonder he struggled with everything about this world, from social conventions to technology. It was a wonder he'd managed to find himself in a relationship with a woman, seeing how awkward Eli was around them.

"My father had another son, besides me and Fioll. That's the one who cast out my adoptive parents and threatened to hand Erin over to the Everlastings if Fionn didn't put an end to their affair. You're familiar with these terms, I gather?"

"I am, yes."

"I lived in Ephemera for seven years. In the woods, as a Silvares. Do you know what that is?"

"I have a vague idea. Like a gamekeeper?"

"Something of the kind. I lived and grew into manhood there; my inkings came to my skin there. I don't remember everything, some details fail me completely. I know my brother cast me out, but can't remember why. I don't think he knew who I was, I only realised we were related when my parents mentioned him being the gentlest of Fionn's sons. The name rang a bell; I remembered he was the one casting me out of Ephemera; much like his brother had done to the Sylvains years before. The moment he cast me out, I woke up in my old bedroom, strapped to a hospital bed, seven years having passed me by. I fainted one day in the woods, when camping with my father at the age of fifteen, and woke up a twenty-two-year-old man. It was... difficult."

"I can imagine. So being cast out means you can't return?"

"Yes. I can never cross to Ephemera. I may be able to Weave a thread or two into that world, but it'll never be a gateway, and I'll never be able to cross myself back there."

Relief washed over Spencer. If Max Everley was right, they didn't want creatures from that world breaching into their peaceful lives, wrecking havoc just so they could get their hands on Weavers they could use for their terrifying ends, killing anyone who stood in their way. Not only Weavers, but anyone with magic, seeing the creatures used in the hunt for those of the Spirit element fed off magic, any kind. The stronger the better, and once they'd crossed over, their energy levels would need constant replenishing, only brought about by tapping into someone's magic and draining it, along with their lives.

"The thing is, I think Erin may be in danger. I think she might have Weaved herself back there."

Spencer paled. "You think she went after Fionn? He made her promise she wouldn't. A binding promise. She couldn't break it, to the risk of hers and his life. Their sanity, at best."

"No, she didn't go looking for my father. When Mum realised I wasn't in a coma but in a Weave, she called Erin, who came to see me at the hospital. She was very upset, and knew straight away I'd Weaved myself to Ephemera. So she took off, and was never seen again. But I spoke to Cressida Everley recently."

"You did what? Was that wise?"

Eli shook his head, rubbed his cheeks, his chin. "Going off with Max like that, is it wise? He's a married man with an unstable wife. And children, Spence, they have children. This will take a toll on them. It's Trystan and Bryn who are going to get hurt, in the end. And you, I mean, he's already hurt you once, hasn't he?"

Spencer took a cautious step back, where had this come from? Eli hadn't struck him as the sort of person who passed judgement on others. "Have you ever been in love?" he asked.

"Yes. I was once as stupidly in love as you are. What Max did to you when you were about my age, she did to me, back in Ephemera. I don't recall the details, but she was behind my casting out. Betrayed and used me, manipulated me, and when she had no use for me anymore, made sure she got rid of the nuisance. I'm just afraid Max does the same to you, and you end up shattered and broken. Nyx needs you. She's already lost far too much."

Spencer eyed the floor, dust gathering by the window. The entire house needed a good clean. What if Eli was right and Max ended up emulating what he'd done sixteen years before? Was that a risk he was willing to take? Was he ready to face the consequences of what his choices would do to Max's children? As far as he knew, Bryn supported her father's decision, but would Trystan?

"I get it. But my eyes are open, this time. Look, you were hurt by a woman, and still you've fallen in love again. You found it in your heart to give love a second chance. I'm giving Max a second chance, too, but I'm not going into it blind. What did Cressida tell you?"

Eli sighed. "She said Erin came to Corinna for help, after seeing me at the hospital. It was your mother who arranged for everything. That I was sent home and taken care of only by Serge and Ora, that I was provided for, that social services stayed away. It's what Cressida told me. That Erin knew I'd Weaved myself into Ephemera, that I was in danger there, and she went to look for me. She Weaved a thread to search for me and clearly didn't know if she'd ever make it back, for she had Cressida promise to look out for Nyx and me."

They locked eyes, Spencer's narrowing as his mind tried to put together all the pieces of a puzzle he'd long tried to solve. Erin hadn't left her daughter and husband because she was selfish. She'd left because her other child was in danger.

"Spencer, she could be dead, I understand. But she can also be held prisoner by the Regia in Chymera, so she feeds their eternal lives. She could be about to be turned into a Nigrum who'll come hunt her own children. I think it's clear we need to find her."

"What if she's not in Ephemera? Nor Chymera? What if she never managed to cross over? Her threads were all severed here, my mother made sure of that. Maybe she didn't leave to search for you, Eli, but to stay away from Nyx. If hunters made it into our world, they could have traced her through Fionn, maybe my sister only wanted to make sure her daughter was safe, seeing she'd failed to protect her own son. I think it's too risky. What if something enters, from their side? What if you go and can't make it back? No, Eli, we need to keep that portal locked."

"There isn't a portal anymore, don't you understand?"

"Eli, Erin's a grown woman, who made her choices, for whatever reason. My job is to make sure you and Nyx are safe. I know you're an adult, but you're still my nephew, and I'll do anything to guarantee you're not in danger. There's an evil there, in the Ephemera woods, Erin mentioned it often. There's an even bigger danger in Chymera, which she never really went into. All I know is what those creatures do there is something dreadful, terrible for the likes of those like us. I'm sure you can understand this."

Spencer watched him turn his face away, eyes narrowed to slits as Eli pondered his uncle's words. Seeming to have reached a decision, the young man faced him, a tentative smile rising up the corners of his lips.

"You're right. I won't try to find my mother. But Nyx needs to know this, Spence. She'll be in danger if she doesn't; ignorance is not an option, here."

"We'll tell her. Or you tell her, seeing you lived there, twice. I'm off to bed now, if you don't mind. I'm glad we cleared this, though. It was about time our family was done with all the secrets."

Dishing one final, warm glance at Eli, Spencer turned back and left the room to his nephew, who looked lost in thought.

Nyx wrapped her scarf tighter around her neck; the day had been cold and grey, a fog clinging constantly around town, obscuring the skies. Training her eyes up, she gazed at the white-ish quality of the light, the frosty dimness of it, her thoughts back to Eli and his magic. It had been so relieving to know her brother was of the blood, and a Weaver like her. It made her feel less alone, less of a freak. Not that she regarded herself as one, but Nyx was aware most other students did. Weavers were rare, and unreliable. Able to tap into all sorts of magic, they never excelled at anything, and always seemed to come up short, whatever they tried. Thinking about her brother's Craft led to Jacintha Tate - who also happened to be a Weaver - and her entanglement with Eli. Was Miss Tate aware Eli was of the blood? Had he brought up the subject with her, before doing so with his family?

Nyx seriously doubted. Eli was very wary of sharing his secrets, and although he seemed to be in love with Miss Tate, it was probably too soon for him to open up, given his secretive, suspicious nature. She found herself blushing at the memory of walking in on them, Jacintha striding Eli, both about to take off their upper garments, so urgent in their kissing and their groping, so inflamed with passion for one another. She and Trystan had already had a couple of laughs about it, but it was still awkward, and the first tutoring session after the event had been a quiet, tentative one, both her and Miss Tate leery of overstepping any boundaries. They'd now fallen back into rhythm, though, and as the weekend loomed just around the corner, Nyx had even suggested Eli brought Jacintha home for dinner on Saturday, so that Nyx and Spencer could socialise with her in a more intimate setting. Maybe she should bring Trystan along, too?

As if by magic, the boy materialised near the gates of Weaversmoor Academy, his step rushed as he marched across the gravelled path. They hadn't arranged to meet today; Nyx was counting on Eli to pick her, seeing Spencer had gone off to view real estate for his project. As much as Nyx was uncomfortable with the thought, she'd encouraged her uncle to find an activity that fulfilled and satisfied him. Eli was intent on doing the same, and he'd started training at the auto-repair shop every morning. Which didn't explain for him being late. Waving at Trystan, she fished for her phone, they could walk home and Eli didn't have to bother coming to the Academy. Or he could, but for Miss Tate.

The smile on her lips lost strength, dwindled and died, as Nyx studied Trystan's darkened face. Something must have happened, he looked troubled. Her gut twisted, cold filling her body. An impending sense of doom wrapped itself around her, and didn't let go. Her instincts told her Trystan must have found out, or been told - that his father and Spencer were together. Max Everley must have finally come clean to his son, seeing his daughter was privy to the affair even before it started. A memory intruded her mind - that of Bryn asking Nyx to tell Spencer to give Max a call. Trystan had been livid at that. As much as he seemed to be now. Bracing herself, Nyx composed a speech in her head that would serve to ease him into accepting the tryst. After all, love was love.

"Hi," she greeted when Trystan was close enough. "I didn't expect you today."

"No, I'm sure you didn't," he spat, and Nyx winced. "It didn't cross your mind to tell me? You've known for a while, and didn't find it important that I also did?"

"What are you talking about?"

"Your uncle! My father. You knew they went away for the weekend and kept this from me, Nyx?"

She paled, icy sweat running down her back. Trystan seemed to regain some sort of composure, one hand reaching for hers, which Nyx relented immediately.

"Look, I get it; this must be as hard for you as for me. It *is* your uncle, after all, and he did raise you like a father, you must be shocked at his behaviour."

"Shocked?" she managed to croak, heart speeding.

"Tearing a family apart like this, acting like a callous home wrecker, I understand you're ashamed. That's why we must do something about it; we need to keep them apart."

Nyx retrieved her hand, face reddening with the sudden dismay caused by Trystan's words and his assumptions of her opinion on the subject. "Spencer isn't a home wrecker; he didn't break your family apart. It was already broken, Bryn said so. You've hinted at it yourself."

His eyes widened, mouth slacking into an 'O' of bewilderment, as if he couldn't believe what he heard. "Are you for real? Your uncle seduces my father, makes him leave his home and his family..."

"My uncle did no such thing! Have you heard yourself? Your father asked for the divorce before they got back together. He moved out before they became involved. And it was *your* mother who came between them, years ago. Your dad and Spencer were a couple, for years, did you know that? It was your grandfather, my grandmother, that broke them apart. Your mum was as much a victim as they were, yes, but she's been unreasonable, not letting Max go."

"You support this? You mean to tell me you're taking their side? What kind of person are you? You make me sick, you're not who I thought you were. What a mistake I've made, I thought you were different, but you're disgusting."

Nyx's eyes brimmed with tears; this wasn't going as she hoped. Reaching a hand towards Trystan, she tried to grab his, but he pulled away. Her heart collapsed, air fled her lungs.

"Don't touch me," Trystan yelled, flickers of fire erupting from his nails, and Nyx looked around in fear they were overheard.

Shame claimed her, but he had no right to make her feel this way. She did nothing wrong, he who the one being unreasonable.

"Trystan, they love each other," Nyx insisted, tears streaming down her face.

"Who are you, even? How can you defend them? I never want to see you again."

Turning his back on her, Trystan ran down the road, stomped through the gates, disappearing from her sight. Nyx stood rooted to the ground, legs shaking. Silent sobs rattled her shoulders, lungs unable to draw breath, head swimming and heart racing. She jumped up, though, at the hand folding over her shoulder, strong, but gentle. Pip Thomson's worried eyes met hers, narrowing even more at the sight of her tears.

He gathered her into his arms, still watching the gravelled incline after Trystan's disappearing figure. He caressed Nyx's back through the thick overcoat.

"What happened? What's wrong?"

Nyx sobbed into his chest, unable to stop. "He's a git. A wanker. I hate him." Her voice came out muffled.

Pip tightened his hold, fondling the curls on her head while shushing her. It was soothing, warming. As warming as being here, in his arms, safe from the world outside, cocooned in a nest of tender care. Albeit his rebellious attitude and the bad boy looks, Pip was really the gentlest soul she'd ever met, the most caring, too. He was also the boy she'd found herself fantasising about more often than not, despite her involvement with Trystan. Which had been a blatant mistake, given he was such a chauvinistic, prejudiced person, after all.

Her sobs dwindled to mere sniffles. Pip pushed her away and searched her eyes.

"Are you all right? Wanna talk about it?"

Nyx shook her head, only to nod a couple of seconds later. "We broke up," she said, voice faltering again. "Well, *he* did, I just stood there taking his abuse."

Pip's hand wiped the tears from her cheeks, cupped her face. "Trystan's not an easy person, but he's well worth it, Nyx. I'm sure this was just a tiff."

"Oh, no, it wasn't. I wouldn't go back to him if he crawled on his fours, begging."

Pip laughed, and Nyx found herself smirking. "You're overreacting."

"Not I, *he*. Made all this fuss because of his father and my uncle. Well, I guess the cat's out of the bag, now," she added, seeing his eyes widen either in shock or surprise. "You're not gonna act like a total git, too, are you?"

Pip stepped away from her, shoving his hands in the pockets of his dark wash jeans, looking sheepish. "I don't know."

"Oh, come on, why's everyone so homophobic around here?"

He reached for her hand, took hold of it. "I'm the last person to be homophobic, Nyx, believe me. Trystan's father is involved with your uncle?"

She sighed. "Looks like it's been a well-kept secret, after all. Spence and Max Everley were together all through university. As in a couple. They broke up soon after returning to Weaversmoor. And now he left his wife. But Spencer had nothing to do with it; they only got back together afterwards. Apparently, Trystan doesn't believe this, so he's being a total wanker accusing my uncle of ruining his parents' marriage."

"It's been ruined for years," Pip said. "Look, Trystan has a very hard time dealing with his father's sexuality. Hell, he has a hard time dealing with his own sexuality, so it's no wonder. He'll always blame someone else for his parents' constant arguing, and will never accept his father might even be right, where it comes to his mother. For Trystan, she can do no wrong and is just a victim."

Nyx eyed him pensively. "What about you? Do you think it's wrong? That Max Everley wants the freedom to be whom and what he's always been?"

"Of course not, don't be silly." Once again, Pip eyed the ground, a sheepish grin over his lips. "I'd be a hypocrite, otherwise."

"What does that mean?"

"Come on, Nyx, you must know. Other students talk about it, like, *a lot*. I'm sure Penny Lattimer must have said something."

He wasn't making sense. Whatever Pip meant, Nyx had never heard a comment about it, nor had Penny ever spoken of him other than to say he was troubled and the Everleys overprotected him.

"I don't know what you're talking about."

"I'm bisexual, Nyx. I'm bisexual and polyamorous inclined. The last thing I'd do is judge someone else on their sexual and affective choices, you know? Now you're the one looking shocked."

She averted her eyes, aware he was right. "I just didn't expect it. Never seen you with anyone, except for that date with me."

Pip cackled. "Which date? Bryn's bash, the tattoo parlour, the study date, the coffee shop? Before you decided to go monogamous with Trys? I swear I'd put you down to being a little like me, what with Spencer being outside the norm. I presumed you were more... open-minded, I think."

Blushing, she tried to disguise how uncomfortable the entire conversation was. Eli's admonishments made perfect sense, now, he'd insisted plenty of times Pip might interpret their dates as something outside the friend zone, more romantically inclined, and it looked as if her brother had been right. And how could she keep a straight face and swear she'd regarded the whole thing as friendship, how could she claim to have seen Pip merely as a friend? That was a blatant lie, Nyx had been as much attracted to him as to Trystan, and the only reason she'd stepped into a monogamous relationship with the later was because it was the norm. Anything outside it scared her. Even though her entire life had been lived outside whatever norm composed the world.

"Look, I don't want to upset you," he insisted, reaching for her hand again. "Trystan's complicated and reacts like a wanker where his dad's concerned. But he'll soon come round, and you'll make up."

Tears brimmed her eyes again. "I don't want to. He was so mean, and cruel. I don't want him back in my life, if this is how he acts."

"Come here, don't cry," Pip whispered, pulling Nyx back to his arms.

"What's going on?" A cold, detached voice interrupted them, both teens shuffling away from each other to face the newcomer.

Eli scowled at them, a doubtful look in his eyes. Nyx pressed her lips, cheeks still wet with the streaming tears, shook her head.

"Trystan found out his father and Spencer are together, apparently," Pip clarified. "He wasn't very happy with Nyx taking their side and overreacted, but he'll soon come round."

Eli's hands curled into fists, knuckles paling under the strenght he exerted. Nyx folded her fingers around his, tried to ease them open.

"Did he hurt you?"

She shrugged. "Only my feelings. Pip's been comforting me."

"I can see that." Eli's voice oozed sarcasm. He dragged his sister into his arms, and kissed the crown of her head. "Thanks for looking after her," he still said, acknowledging Pip's efforts.

The boy blushed, nodded in reply. "Your brother's here, now, I'm gonna take off. I'll have a word with Trystan and call you later, all right?"

Nyx stared at him, blankly. "Gimme a call, but I don't want to hear of him," she replied, bursting into tears again.

Eli held her tighter. Pip walked off, leaving the two siblings alone, Nyx sobbing into her brother's leather jacket.

"I've brought the bike, but you're in no fit state to ride," he said, fondling her back as if Nyx was a child.

"I'm fine," she insisted, pulling out of his hold. "I'll be fine."

"I know what it's like to feel like this, you know? Being in love with someone who ends up hurting us. All I can say is it'll pass, Nyx. I swear it does, it gets better with time."

"We weren't together all that long, I'm not gonna kill myself for losing him. You should have heard him, Eli, the way he spoke of Spence. I wanted to slap him for it, you know? He's not who I thought, I should never have started seeing him."

Eli directed her to the bike, handed Nyx a helmet which she busied herself with. "Put yourself in his shoes, for once. It's got to be hard, his parents divorcing, his family breaking apart. He's only sixteen, don't expect him to act cool and composed like an adult, not even *we* manage to do it. Cut the boy some slack. I'm sure the two of you can work this out. If you want to, that is."

Nyx hopped on the bike, arms snaking round her brother's waist. "Problem is I'm not sure I want to."

"You're hurting, give it some time. Here, let me take you somewhere and tell you a bit of a secret. Are you up for it?"

She nodded against his back, and Eli took off towards the river, taking the road that passed in front of the Everley estate towards Vaughn cottage, instead of going the other way around. They sped by it, Eli only braking when the house was no longer visible, hidden by the thick cluster of vegetation spreading between it and their home. He pulled up not far into the trees, stopped the engine, jumped out of the bike, gesturing Nyx along. She took off the helmet, shaking her head to free the curls, and followed her brother into the forest. The fog was thicker here, wet, dampening her hair, her tights and shoes. She'd end up with a cold, if she wasn't careful.

"Where are we going? What do you want to tell me?"

Pressing a finger to his lips, Eli took her hand and carted Nyx along, until they came to the same small, round clearing where she'd once found Trystan with flames dancing across his body. The memory tightened her gut, and she had to force down an impending sob. It was also the same clearing near the strange, odd tree, where the flock of jewel-coloured birds that looked like kestrels, but weren't, perched amongst the thick, long boughs, hiding within the canopy of leaves. She peered at her brother, questioning glare across her eyes meeting the sparkle of anticipation and eager fear in his.

"What is this?" Nyx asked.

"Those birds you have tattooed across your shoulder? Who drew them for you? And the feather?"

She blushed, took a peek at the tree, it was empty. It was empty of birds, but not of leaves. The boughs were still covered in russet, brown and yellow leaves, a mass of them, contrary to most of the other trees, who'd shed the largest part of their canopies with the approach of winter. What was it Eli really wished to know?

"Why?"

"I've seen birds like those before."

Of course he had, they were also tattooed across his shoulder and collarbone. "I don't see your point, Eli."

"Let's go closer to the tree," he invited.

The moment they stepped out of the clearing to stand under the large boughs, something in their surroundings changed. The air wasn't as cold, or as brisk, although there roamed a gentle breeze. It carried a scent of running waters, the wilderness too. Closing her eyes, Nyx inhaled deeply, spreading arms to her side as if she wanted to embrace the tree, the entire place. Eli grinned. A soft, hushed chirp sounded from the highest part of the tree, where a red-feathered bird perched, beady black eyes set on her. A blue one hid to their right, its claw-like beak so close to Eli she feared the bird might go for his ear.

"I drew the birds," Nyx finally said. "Inspired by these. Where have you come across them before? Why do you also have them tattooed on you? The feather I get, but the birds…"

"Because I'm not just a Weaver, and nor are you, Nyx. We're bird-charmers too, and this is our flock. Ours alone. Only we can connect with these."

Her eyes widened, she'd never heard of such. "Bird-charmers? Since when is that a thing?"

"Listen to me. You've heard us speak of my father, do you remember his name?"

"Fionn something."

"Fionn Sylvannar. Have you ever heard anything alike?"

"No."

"Of course not, for it's not of this world. My father is not from our world.

They sat against the massive tree trunk, side by side, the carpet of fallen leaves serving as cushion. Nyx still looked stunned, her silence only driving the point. Eli feared he might have made a mistake and his sister wasn't yet ready to be told of the hidden world existing just on the brink of theirs, at hand's reach for those who - like her - could summon up a breach that opened to it.

"I can see you don't believe me," he said, a grin gracing his lips.

"On the contrary. It explains these blasted birds that Trystan couldn't even see. It also accounts for this weird tree, and Mrs Everley's words about your father. That he was more creature than man. Of course he was, if he came from another world. This is mind-blowing, Eli, despite making some sort of warped sense. So you say mum was able to summon him here, is that it?"

He shook his head, took her hand. "No. Our mother opened a portal to this other world. Its inhabitants call it Mythos, and it's huge, Nyx. I've only seen a small part of it, and have knowledge only of some of its regions. The capital is Chymera, where the Everlastings live. My father was one of these creatures. He ruled Ephemera and the East Baronies, and held his court at a place called Thorne Ridge. That's where our mother opened a portal to. This tree's the gateway to it. Marks the border between our world and theirs, but can't be breached unless a Weaver threads a weave through it."

"As mum did. Was it a spell? How did she do it?"

Eli shrugged, leaning farther back. "I have no idea. No one seems to know how it's done. I guess there are many ways, depending on the Weaver."

"So this means we can both do it? We can travel between here and there? Eli, you could meet your father!" Her enthusiastic voice died at the sight of her brother's sour face. "What?"

"I wasn't fully honest with you, when I told you of my coma. I wasn't really in a coma, you see. I was in a Weave."

"You went there? In your head? While your body stayed in a hospital bed, you lived there in your mind? This is insane!" Her excitement belied Nyx's words.

"It's not as simple as that. I Weaved myself to that world during the coma, but I had a body there. It's like all I left behind was an image, a print? Immaterial, almost. A husk, a shell. A simile? And that's still not the right word."

"A clone?"

"Yes, I think it fits better. A *clone*. There was a clone in my bedroom, at my parents' home, but I was in Ephemera, living another life. The life of a boy named Noctifer Sylvannar, who happens to be the youngest son of Fionn Sylvannar. I didn't go by my father's name, then, I didn't even know I was his son. It was only after my return that I started remembering everything, and my parents filled in the blanks. Some of them, at least."

"So your coma weaved a thread that placed you in this other world, but then you got better and that thread what, was cut?"

Eli squinted, as if in thought. "No. I got better because I was cast out of Ephemera. If it hadn't happened, I might never have returned, and that clone lying in my bed, that husk, would have dimmed itself to extinction."

"How do you know these things? Who taught you all this? Was it our mother? You said you came to Havenleah often to meet her, did she tell you this?"

"My adoptive parents came from Ephemera. They were my father's subjects, and were cast out when Fionn's relationship with our mother was uncovered by his eldest son. He forced my father to renounce her in exchange for her freedom, but he cast out the Sylvains along with Erin because they were loyal to Fionn. He thought I was their son, so he allowed me to come along. I was five."

"Bloody hell, Eli." Nyx trained her eyes on the expanse of trees, noticing for the first time the air shimmer and twist as if in a heatwave. This must be the spot where the breach opened, were she talented enough to weave her thread into that other world. "And you want to go back there?"

He met her eyes. Once, he'd wanted to. He longed to leave this world and get back to what was familiar, what he knew. He'd come to Weaversmoor with that very intent, finding a way back in. So he could clear his name, avenge the harms Stella had done him and reclaim his just place in that world. But now, he wasn't so sure anymore. He had Nyx, and Spencer, and was at a good place in life. He'd met Jacintha, couldn't bear the thought of being parted from her before allowing their romance to even develop. Closing his eyes at the thought of Bryn Everley, her open smile popping into his mind, Eli realised he really didn't want to return, if it weren't for that deeply ingrained longing for his parents. He must admit he'd like to meet them, and the thought Erin had gone after him into a place she'd been evicted from, placing herself in danger, did cast weight on his decisions. He found himself of two minds, divided between desire and obligation, want and must, honour and need.

"I honestly don't know, Nyx." They stared at each other. "There's this void in me, a hole that quietly demands to be filled. A need to face them, know them. My real parents, I long to hold them. But at the same time, I find I can live with their absence, it's just not all that demanding. Because Ora and Serge, those were my mum and dad, those were the ones who sat by me when I was sick, who drove me to and from school, who helped me with homework, who nursed me while my body lay unresponsive in a bed. The Sylvains are my real parents, even though I wasn't born of them."

Nyx held his hand. "I get it. I don't miss mum, either, hardly remember her at all. Dad and Spencer were my parents; she's just the woman who gave birth to me. But there's a part of myself that longs to know her, ask why she left..."

"Because of me. She left because of me." Eli's eyes took on a pained look, but he still kept them on his sister, braving the storm of emotions she was bound to find herself under. "She left when she realised I'd Weaved myself back to Ephemera, I think she went after me."

Nyx shook her head, lost. "Why? She gave you to others, cut off all contact with you, why would she go back somewhere she'd been sent away from? Somewhere that could possibly be dangerous?"

"Precisely because of that. She must have thought I'd be in danger. I don't know, Nyx, but what if she *did* go after me? To make sure nothing happened to her son? Shouldn't I follow? What if something bad happened to her, is it not my responsibility to try everything I can to make sure our mother's all right?"

Shaking her head, Nyx tightened the grip on Eli's hand. "She left us. Both her children. It was her choice, and she told no one why she was doing it. How can you simply assume she took off to save you? Did you come across her, back there?" Her finger pointed towards the space among the trees where the air kept shimmering. "Why would you go and place yourself in harm's way for something you don't even know it's true? Your place is here, with Spencer and me. *That's* your responsibility, Eli, to stay here with me. I've already lost too much. Please, don't talk like this, not today. I don't want you to even consider leaving."

Eli wrapped an arm around her shoulders and hugged her. "I don't really want to leave, either. Not after having found you and Spence, not when... well, when there's also Jacintha, you know." He blushed and his sister giggled, the trace of impeding tears gone from her eyes. "And it's not as if we can open a portal; as a cast-off, I can't Weave threads back there. I can enter, but through someone else's Weave. You'd have to do it for me."

Nyx cocked her head to the side, studied the air ahead of her, eyes squinting against a sudden erupting glare. "You mean like this?" Her voice came out strained.

Eli jumped, heart racing, took a step closer to where the scenery had changed almost drastically. Ahead of them no longer stood a clearing surrounded by dainty woodland, it was now a dense, lush, deeply forested area, of which they could hardly see beyond thick trunks of tall trees. This was the place he'd lived and grown from boy to man, the place he remembered so well, as if he'd left only yesterday. This was where Eli had made a home for himself, one he missed nearly every second of every day, the memory of which becoming dimmer and dimmer in his mind's eye. This was Ephemera, the East Baronies; this was the forest near Thorne Ridge where his father ruled supreme, these were the woods leading to Viridans, where Stella had lived. This was where he himself had built a life as a Silvares, the only life he remembered.

He faced his sister, smiling. Pushing one finger over suddenly dry lips, Eli begged her for silence, gestured her forward so Nyx joined him by the rim of this alien world she'd opened for them. Both trained their eyes on the forest, as far as they could see. A loud caw broke through the silence, the siblings raising eyes to the sky, following the flight of a large bird of prey. A white-faced owl swooped down on its prey, small mice running through the carpet of leaves covering the forest floor. It was followed by a raven the size of which Nyx had never seen, and Eli sniggered at how her eyes popped open in surprise and excitement. The last bird to fly down from its perch on a tree was a gyrfalcon, feathers red like blood, beak a razor so sharp it gleamed in the mid-afternoon autumn sun. The quality of light was different in this other world.

The bird came to stand by the edge of the portal, head cocked as its eyes locked first with Nyx, then Eli. He shivered, uncomfortable with the open passage and what it had attracted, found himself getting lost in the bird's hypnotising glare. It was only when Nyx jerked his arm to force his attention on the sight her finger pointed at, that he seemed to wake up from whatever trance the bird had set on him. He focused on what Nyx showed him, grinned openly. A white doe peered through the trees, ears flickering, body poised ready to flee. The snap of twigs had it turn its head to the left, then bolt with a jump that hid it from sight, running for safety. More birds flocked the skies now, swooping down to join the owl and the raven, the red gyrfalcon at their feet.

"Shut it, Nyx," Eli shouted in alarm.

The girl reacted by instinct, taking one step back, hands curling into fists. The air shimmered and Ephemera was gone. Where they'd had a glimpse into another world, now stood only the same old trees, and the autumn skies weren't golden with the warm light of the setting sun - they were whitish grey, clouded, barren in a mid-November that already announced the coming of snow. The white doe was gone, so was the owl, the raven as big as a medium-sized dog, the red falcon whose sentient eyes had seemed to study Eli attentively. Nyx took a look around, satisfying herself everything was back to normal, then turned to her brother, face shaded with worry.

"What happened? Why did you want me to collapse my Weave?"

Eli shrugged, the gesture lost within the shudder his body released. "Remember I told you we were also bird-charmers? Well, that's a pretty common thing in Mythos. And some charmers can see the world through the eyes of their flock. The gyrfalcon belonged to someone, Nyx. We were being watched, studied, not by the bird but the person who's Craft's linked to it. Spencer was right; it's dangerous to leave this breach here."

"What? Why? What does Spence know of this?"

"That other world isn't safe. Some of its creatures feed on people like you and me. They use our powers, our magic, to lengthen their lifespan. If one of them found out there were Weavers opening a portal to Mythos, they'd come after us."

"Well, you were there, nothing happened to you. Why would we be in danger now?"

Eli shook his head and led her back to the bike, mind momentarily lost in an attempt at securing a lock over the severed threads of Nyx's Weave. He could only breathe once assured he'd broken it into a myriad tiny pieces no one could put back together. There'd be no Nigrum crossing through that breach, because there would no longer be a breach at Weaversmoor.

"Being a bird-charmer cloaked my powers as a Weaver. No one knew what I was. Beyond a Silvares and a bird-charmer, that is.

Your Craft was also hidden by it, but the longer you maintained that Weave, the more visible it would become, like a beacon to the Everlasting. They'd know a Weaver was at work out here, and they'd come for us. With an army of Nigrum so they could thread a path to our world. And make no mistakes, Nyx, they would hunt us down and take us to Chymera so we could feed their immortality, and they'd let those Nigrum kill any magical beings they came across. If we'd lingered for a second longer, Weaversmoor would be lost. You and I would be lost, all your friends and family dead. Promise me you'll never open that breach. Promise you won't Weave yourself back there again."

A terrified stare in her eyes, Nyx nodded. "I won't. I'll never put us in danger, Eli."

He hugged her tightly, knowing they'd come very close to being found, the thought of losing his sister like a blade pushed into his heart. The border was being watched, then. This hadn't been the place Rhysondel Sylvannar had taken him to, when the current Lord of Thorne Ridge cast Eli out of Ephemera for good. This was the place Erin Vaughn had once built a Weave so strong any Ephemeral could have crossed it. Someone must have known there were Weavers here, and placed a watch on the border, to keep an eye on the portal. They mustn't summon one, ever again, for someone would be there, on the other side, waiting for them. Someone who was desperate enough to betray friends and family in their wish of ascending, intent on securing a place in the cortège of Sponsas who were to grace the Grand Ball at Thorne Ridge. Someone who always had a flock of mismatched birds following around, from red gyrfalcons to white-faced owls to corvus colossus and other such winged beings.

Stella.

Part Three

I

Jacintha sipped the wine sedately, her eyes darting to Eli every once in a while. Saying she was anxious was probably the understatement of the year, what with being thrown into the dinner table with her boyfriend, his younger sister - who happened to be one of her students - and an uncle she didn't know how to behave in front of. Spencer was Nyx's legal guardian, Jace was Nyx's tutor, and her involvement with Eli came close to breaching every moral code she could think of. So saying Jacintha was anxious was indeed an understatement.

She allowed Eli to grab her hand under the table, his dimpled smile showering her taut nerves with a wash of hunger unlike the one her stomach insisted on not experiencing. He leaned in to steal a kiss, Jacintha dipping her head lower to try and avoid it, self-conscious for the presence of others as she was.

"Awww, they're so cute," Nyx swooned, her voice tender. "Aren't they just perfect together, Spencer?"

Blushing, Jace ventured a look across the table, meeting Spencer Vaughn's eyes. Instead of unease, she was given a smile, and the tension her entire body had been under seemed to vanish like a trick of magic. *Magic.* Another subject she'd eventually have to broach around Eli. Sighing with yet a new worry, her shaky hand led the glass to her lips, and this time, Jacintha did take a large gulp of the full-bodied red wine.

"You're not eating?" Spencer asked, sounding preoccupied. "Are you vegan? Eli didn't say anything, I assumed you..."

"No, no, I'm all right," she hurried reassuring him. "I'm just... well, nervous. It's weird, isn't it? Dating the brother of one of your students and sitting at their family table to eat. I mean, I'm not even sure in what capacity I'm here."

"Eli's girlfriend," Nyx and Spencer said.

"My girlfriend," Eli added, with a touch of pride.

Jacintha smiled, and allowed him to fully kiss her on the lips. This was getting serious, she couldn't stop thinking of him when they were apart, and spent her days counting the hours until they saw each other again. Did he feel the same? Or was she just getting ahead of herself, rushing things, headed for a disappointment?

"So, how long have you been dating?"

"Three weeks," Eli replied.

"One week," said Jacintha, and frowned at him, but a smile was still on her lips. "It was a week ago that you first kissed me."

"A week and a day, if you need to be precise," he joked. "But we've been dating for longer."

"Well, it doesn't count if there was no kiss." Staring at Nyx, Jacintha raised her eyebrows. "Right? There has to be a kiss."

"There definitely has to be a kiss," Spencer agreed, and laughed.

"She's right, Eli, if you didn't kiss, it doesn't count, you were just friends hanging out."

"You're all going to gang up on me, aren't you? Fine, I give up. We've been together, officially together, for a week. But we've been dating for three. And I've wanted to kiss you since day one," Eli said, lowering his voice and stealing one more kiss, while Jacintha blushed deep red.

The buzz of a mobile phone led eyes away from her. Jacintha watched Nyx hurriedly read a text, grateful for the distraction. She'd never liked being the centre of attention. Unless it was Eli's attention, of course. More at ease now she'd downed two glasses of wine, Jace leaned her head against his shoulder, inhaled deeply of the dark, leathery, richly wooded fragrance of his cologne, a scent that roused and calmed her senses at the same time. He placed a soft kiss on her forehead, but Eli's focus was set on his sister.

"Everything all right?" he inquired.

"Yeah, Pip wanted to catch a film."

"Are you going?"

Jacintha noticed Spencer turn slightly annoyed eyes towards Eli, realised there was some sort of tension there, with him controlling his sister and their uncle clearly opposing it. Nyx merely shrugged, going back to her Beef Wellington.

"You should go," Spencer cut in.

"Should she?"

Nyx and Spencer exchanged one curt, knowing look, assuring Jacintha this was a subject they didn't usually see eye to eye on.

"I'm not in the mood," the girl replied, and Jace studied her more attentively.

Nyx had been somewhat sombre, the past few days, inattentive and shying into herself. She hadn't been hanging around Trystan Everley as usual, the young couple using recess to lock lips in what looked like everlasting kisses, the teachers who came across them or watched the teens from the window in the staff room wondering how on earth they could breathe. Jacintha had spied them at it a few times, but didn't question their capacity to breathe; she knew well what it was like to be so immersed in a person you forgot the world around you, forgot to eat, drink; you forgot to breathe. She knew what it was to be that much in love, and the look in the girl's eyes clarified it all for her: the young couple must have broken up and Nyx was in the process of nursing a broken heart.

"Your uncle's right," she added, knowing to be bang out of order, but not caring, what with yet another glass of wine coursing her veins, turning her into the daredevil she'd never been. "The worst thing you can do now is stay home pining over him. Go out, enjoy yourself, show him it's his loss, not yours. Don't ignore your heartache, of course, but don't feed it more than it needs. Obviously, I sound like a complete git."

Nyx smiled, eyes sparkling with unshed tears. "No, you don't. So you think I should go? Pip's his friend, won't it be too awkward? What will he think?"

"Who cares what Trystan Everley thinks, Nyx? After the way he treated you and spoke of Spencer, frankly, you can do without him. But you and him only just broke up, how do you think it's gonna look like if you're suddenly seen going round with Pip?"

The girl's eyes darkened, storms on the brink of unleashing hidden behind the curtain of lashes.

"You're so narrow-minded it hurts," she whispered. "And who cares what *you* think, Eli? You're not my father, only just got here; think you can order me around because you happen to be older than me? Let me tell you one thing, you are as much a kid as I am. You're as immature as I am. What do you know of the world, of life, of being love?"

Jacintha watched him take a deep breath, hands curled tightly over the cutlery he held, knuckles white from the strain.

"I know what it's like to be heartbroken. I know what it's like to lose that person you think is the centre of your world, what it's like wanting to put that someone out of your head and going to whatever extremes to achieve it. I also know what it's like to be lied to, used by someone who actually cares nothing for you. And I don't want you to do that to Pip. If you're only trying to find a way of putting Trystan out of your head, you can't go round using Pip."

"I'm not." Nyx's voice came out sedated, as if she were hiding something deeper, of further import.

Eli sighed, shook his head, a smile slowly drawn across his lips. "Go on, text him. Jacintha and I will drive you. You don't mind, do you?" Eli asked, after all, it was her car.

"It'll be a pleasure."

Nyx turned her attention to Spencer. "How'm I gonna get home after? Think it's gonna rain, don't fancy walking back here, and forcing Pip to have to return to the Academy under a rainstorm. Unless Eli comes get me?" She eyed her brother.

Jacintha blushed again; already sorry she'd suggest the girl should go out. All week long she'd been longing for Friday, so she could have Eli all to herself, alone. The family dinner invitation he'd sneaked up on her had taken her by surprise, but Jace had soon adjusted to it. They'd sit down with his family for a meal, then leave for a drink at the pub, then back to her place, where they'd have all the privacy required for what she had in mind.

"I'll come get you, just give me a call when you're ready to come home. And I'll drop Pip at the Academy," Spencer offered, getting up from the table. "Nyx made dessert; I hope you're all still hungry."

"I could do with something sweet," Jacintha said.

"I'm not sweet enough for you?" Eli teased, nose brushing against her cheek.

"Eww." Nyx broke out in laughter. "My brother's so cheesy it hurts."

"You're just an ungrateful girl, you are." His smile belied his words, the light in his eye evidence of the love he nurtured for his sister. "Text Pip, tell him we'll pick him at the Academy. It's starting to rain; no point the boy walking all the way to the theatre under the deluge."

Jacintha stole a glance of him, heart swelling with an immensity of feelings she could just barely recognise. The memory of having experienced something akin tugged at the edge of her mind, but she couldn't quite place the when or who. Not that it mattered;

Eli was the only one she wished to remember, at least for the time being. There was something inherently good about him, shown through his loyalty and the way he bonded with family he'd never even heard of. The love he'd allowed to grow in his heart for Nyx and Spencer was something to be admired, as was the way he tried to handle all this. Being adopted, learning about his real parents, having his life turned upside down and a new family forced down his throat in the wake of his coma, it was nothing short of surprising he handled this so well.

But there was something of the mysterious about him too, and it pulled on Jacintha's wild imagination. There was something dangerous in Eli - it came out through his eyes, his smile, the daredevil way he rode his bike, as if he thought himself immortal, untouchable. It pulled on her imagination and nearly brought about images of another life, another time, another place. Where certain people didn't have to worry about such petty things as death or disease, where those people ruled supreme, and monsters haunted the night; no, *hunted* the night. Shaking her head minutely, cold sweat sliding down her back, Jacintha forced a smile on her lips as Spencer returned to the room carrying a cheesecake between his hands, Eli close behind him with clean plates and cutlery. Whatever her often feverish brain tried to feed her, it didn't matter. This was all she wanted, what she had right here. A nice, cosy family gathering, a sense of safety, of belonging, a quiet, steady life.

And Eli.

"There isn't a single film that sounds interesting," Nyx whined.

Pip smirked, studying the posters; he could think of a couple he wouldn't have minded watching. "What do you wanna do, then? You're the boss; I go where you tell me."

She turned a wary eye on him, soon morphing into something slightly wicked, challenging.

"I want to get plastered."

"No, you don't."

"Why's that? I just want to act wildly, you know? No restraints, nothing binding me to be this perfect girl everyone demands I am. I want to be free, act out, numb body and brain so I can stop thinking, so I can forget. Drinking will do that, won't it?"

Shaking his head, Pip tried to grab Nyx's hand, but she fled him. "Don't let anyone rule you like this."

She sniggered. "*Rule* me? That's the opposite of what I want to do. I want to be my own person for once, and do what I want, not what others think is right."

"No, you want to give Trystan this much power over your life and mind that you need to drink yourself stupid just so you can cope with his imbecility."

"I'm in pain, here," she shouted. "I'm the one who's suffering."

Pip grabbed her by one arm, dragging Nyx out into the rain, to stand in the middle of the empty road, the storm washing over them. "Then give it a good cry. Go on, no shame in it. And even if there was, no one will see you crying in the rain. Scream, howl, shout, cry, but let it out, Nyx. Don't numb it, just let it out. Life's about joy and pain, you have to live through one to experience the other. Embrace your hurt, let it take hold of you, rage against the world, against him; hell, rage against me for being here, witnessing this. Break apart, melt down, have the biggest crying fit of your life, just don't bottle it up. Let it wash off you, so you can heal. Drinking yourself to oblivion is not going to change the fact Trystan acted like a git, it's not going to erase the fact the two of you broke up, and it sure isn't going to make you feel better tomorrow morning when you wake up with a hangover and your uncle and brother mad at me that I let you drink. Which, of course, I'm not gonna do."

Nyx palmed strands of wet hair from her eyes, face sodden with tears and rain, a grimace of rage on her face. She took a step towards Pip, hands curled into fists with which she delivered punches to his chest, as if he was to blame for all she was feeling - the hurt, the pain, the confusion from what Eli had told her earlier, what they both had seen. He hadn't asked Nyx to keep it to herself, and yet, she'd known instinctively not to breathe word of it to anyone. Her brother's fear had infused into her core, Eli's eyes at the sight of those birds had carried more panic than Nyx had ever seen, and she couldn't remember a moment when she'd seen Eli that terrified, not even when he'd waited at the door of Vaughn cottage to let her and Spencer know he was Erin's long-lost kid.

On top of all the changes in her life, the fact she was able to open a door into a world where she and her brother were prey to whatever entity he seemed to fear so much, had been the final straw breaking the camel's back. No wonder she collapsed into tears in the middle of an empty street, rain washing over her, with only Pip to witness her misery. He'd put it down to Trystan and the breakup, and wouldn't be far from the truth - Nyx had bawled her eyes out coming out of the forest with Eli. After closing the portal into that other world, her brother wrapped his arms around her, reassuring her it'd all be fine, Trystan was a wanker who didn't deserve the likes of Nyx. But she'd also cried herself hoarse once back home, when Spencer asked what was wrong, noticing her puffy face and swollen eyes. Hadn't she done enough crying for a boy who couldn't have cared that much, if the fact she supported her uncle's pursuit of happiness had been enough for him to break up with her?

Only she wasn't crying for Trystan, or the end of their short-lived relationship.

She was crying for herself, the girl whose mother had left when she was barely five, the girl whose father died at sea and left her alone, the girl whose uncle now inched away from a life solely dedicated to her care in search of his own bliss. She was crying for having been lied to all these years, for the secrets kept from her, the family members she'd been kept from. She was crying for having been forced out of her familiar surroundings at Havenleah, dropped into a school where she was behind every other student, moved out of the house that lodged the memories of her entire life, and compelled to make new friends at the risk of ending up an outcast and a loner. She was crying for being so confused about so many things, namely the fact Eli believed their mother might have gone to that other world searching for him - she'd never come search for Nyx, would she? - placing herself in danger; or the fact she'd jumped into a relationship with Trystan when she went on nursing feelings for Pip.

She was crying because everything was so bloody hard and she had no idea how to deal with the hardship.

Mouth open, Nyx unleashed a loud wail of anger and pain into the night, bending at the waist, jeans sodden with rain, parka dripping water to her feet, clad in knee-high wellies that let moisture in through the top. She screamed for a long while, Pip standing before her, unfazed, not at all shocked or disgusted by her behaviour. As if it was his normal fare, to go out with girls who broke down sobbing in front of him every Friday night. It only served to anger her more - that he simply stood there, after she'd punched him, now that she was acting like a lunatic. It angered her that he'd ignore her like this.

Pulling herself back together, Nyx straightened, wiped water from her face. Their eyes met, Pip's electric blue sending sparks of energy into her core, shaking her every belief, drowning all her wants and needs with a stronger, much louder, new emotion. He stared with such intensity it was as if he was about to ravish her soul, unearth every single one of her secrets, unleash a beast she carried and that was akin to his. She stared into his, and what Nyx thought she saw must mirror the very look in hers: a wild fire threatening to raze everything that dared stand in its way, and which would leave only devastation in its wake.

How many days since Trystan had broken up with her? Three, four? It felt like weeks had gone by, and she'd already gotten over it. As if she'd never really cared that much about him, and all she'd ever wanted was right here, standing with her in the rain, unwilling to leave. This was all she needed, someone who'd be there no matter what, who understood what it was like, someone she'd tried to push out of her thoughts and away from her skin, but failed every time. Someone like Pip.

"I am so madly in love with you, Nyx Vaughn," Pip said, his voice a mere whisper.

But she heard him, and it was all she needed.

Closing the gap between them, Nyx threw her arms around him. Their mouths sought each other; lips glued together, tongues darting for the kiss. And the rain kept pouring, careless of the moment they experienced, unrelenting in its wish to drench the entire world. They didn't care for the rain, either, what if they caught a cold? All they cared, all Nyx cared was for this never-ending kiss, and everything it made her feel. It had never been like this with Trystan, had it? She'd never felt like this. She'd never felt their kisses must go on forever, for none would be able to breathe if they parted lips.

But part they must, and Pip finally broke contact to touch forehead to hers, thumbs caressing Nyx's wet cheeks. "I'm so madly in love with you," he repeated.

Nyx's mouth broke into a grin. "This is just wrong, in so many ways."

"Come on; let's get out of the rain."

"Do you still want to catch a film?" she asked, as they took cover under the theatre's large awning. "At least it's warm in there."

"But then we wouldn't be able to speak. No, let's go somewhere else."

Dragging her by the hand, Pip led them down a side street towards the vicinity of the tattoo parlour. Nyx had never paid much attention to the door on its right, having registered it was a black door, lacquered and forbidding. But now, as they stood in front of it, she realised this must be some sort of club. Music blared from within, the door slightly ajar, and a muscular man with a bald pate stood at the entrance, chatting with a girl who wore too much make-up. He nodded at Pip as if he knew him well, stepped aside so the newcomers could enter.

"What's this place?" Nyx asked, following Pip to a darkly lit room, away from the narrow staircase leading to the lower floor, from where music reached upstairs. It must be a nightclub, and they were about to break every single rule, being under age, far too young to be allowed in a place like this.

"Somewhere kids can come and listen to music, or dance. It's cool; they won't serve us any alcohol. Well, unless you're Bryn." Pip led them to a table secluded in what looked like a booth. It gave them all the privacy she needed, with even a gauzy curtain they could draw. "I'll get us drinks, is soda all right?"

"Yeah, thanks."

It didn't take Pip long to return with a couple of sodas and a stash of paper towels. He handed Nyx half, and proceeded to wipe his hair and face dry with the rest. She'd taken off her coat, the jeans on her legs starting to dry. Patting dripping wet hair, Nyx tried to dry it as best she could and pulled it into a tight bun. Pip sat by her, one arm snaking round her shoulders and dragging her to him. Their lips met again, this time the kiss not so wild or fiery, a tentative, soft peck.

"Why is this wrong?" he asked, boring into her eyes.

Nyx shrugged. "Look, just days ago I was dating Trystan Everley. We just broke up and I'm already smooching another bloke, how do you think it's gonna look like, Pip? If I were a boy, hurray for me, applause would ensue and I'd become some sort of hero. But I'm a girl. I'm well aware of the array of *pretty* names soon to be attached to me at the Academy. Just because I'm already seeing someone else."

"You care too much what others think." Wrapping cold fingers through hers, he squeezed, smiling. "Do you love Trys? Do you hope the two of you get back together? Why did you kiss me, Nyx?"

Blushing, she looked away, brought the glass to her lips and drank deep. Why had she kissed Pip? Because he'd said he was in love with her? Or because she'd been falling for him and Trystan both, ever since meeting them? How could she be in love with two people at the same time? How could she make peace with this, with herself, if it was contrary to everything she'd ever been led to believe?

"I care about him, I like him. Thought I was in love with him, dunno, maybe I am. But the truth is, I've also been thinking of you. Like, constantly. Not when I'm with him, no. But when I'm home, or at school, I think about the two of you. I long to be with both of you. I simply don't want to choose."

"You did. *Chose* him."

"Well, I couldn't go and start seeing the two of you, could I?"

"Why not?"

Nyx laughed, hiding behind cold hands. "Spencer and Eli would have freaked. Well, Eli would. He was rather shocked at me going with you to Bryn's bash when I'd already started seeing Trystan. If I'd have told him I was dating both, he would have a fit."

Pip averted her eyes, giving Nyx the distinct impression he was hiding something.

"What is it?" she urged. "You also think I was dragging the two of you about? Playing you both? Because that's what Eli insinuated."

He shook his head, sipped his drink. "I doubt your brother's that squeaky clean. He may have spent seven years in a coma, but I don't think he's still as inexperienced as he used to be."

"He and Miss Tate must have done it already; they're so all over each other. One night Trys and I walked in on them, they were close to doing it on the sofa."

Pip laughed. "I doubt that, Miss Tate wouldn't have. Nor would your brother, he's too uptight to expose himself like that." Locking eyes with hers, he caressed Nyx's cheek. "I'm in love with you. Have been for a while, Trystan knows this. He also knows I'm here with you."

Nyx blushed, her pupils glinting with sudden anger. He knew and said nothing? Well, that did it; Trystan didn't really care for her.

"He knows?"

"The other day, after you left the Academy, I went over to the Everleys to have a chat with him. Told him if he wasn't going to apologise for being bang out of order, you'd never forgive him. He shrugged. So I told him I was going to ask you out. He shrugged again. I felt free to do as I see fit. Look, Nyx, he's throwing a tantrum. Trys has always had a very hard time dealing with his emotions, and I know he's gonna regret this. But I don't want to back down; no matter how bad a friend that makes me. I'm in love with you and want a chance at this. I think you care enough about me to also want to see where it leads. But if you're uncomfortable, no one has to know. We can go about as if we're just friends hanging out together, and see if we fit. If later on we decide that we do wish to be together, well, there's nothing weird about a couple of friends falling in love, is there? Look at Jamal and Bryn."

"You wouldn't mind?"

Pip shook his head. "Nah. Just as long as you give us a chance. Will you? We can take it as slow or as fast as you wish."

She lowered her head, unsure of what to do. "You said you're bisexual. Does that mean you've been in love with boys as well as girls?"

"Yes."

"And you've dated both?"

"Again, yes. Does this vex you?"

"No, please, I've grown up with a gay uncle; he's made it a point of turning me into a broad-minded, accepting human being. I'm just trying to figure out where I belong, in this."

"Right now, you belong in my arms," he whispered, pulling Nyx to him. "Yes, I've been with both boys and girls in intimate relationships, it's no big deal. I don't fall in love with someone because they're a boy or a girl; I fall because they're…"

"Them."

"Exactly."

"Was Trystan one of those boys you were involved with?"

Pip cackled. "No. But only because he didn't want to. I was in love with Trystan for a long time. I think part of me will always love him. But right now it's you I want to be with. Is that all right?"

Sensing he longed to change the subject, Nyx nodded, finished her drink. "Can I ask you something?"

"Sure."

"How do you feel in those woods? The ones separating my house from Trystan's, I mean."

Pip seemed to ponder, eyes lost in the distance. "How do I feel?"

"Yes, have you ever experienced anything... weird? I mean, you're an empath, and a Haruspex, have you ever come across something out of the ordinary out there?"

"You mean the birds? The ones resembling your tattoos?" He faced Nyx, studying her reactions attentively.

"So you've seen them? No one else seems to."

"Once or twice, yes. Like kestrels, but with colourful, bright feathers. Trystan and Jamal never see them, neither does Bryn, I think. But she has a strong link to that place, that clearing where the weird tree sometimes seems to shimmer and disappear. Have you experienced anything different, in there?"

"What do you know about being a Weaver?"

Pip shrugged. "What I've told you already."

"Don't you find it weird that Weavers aren't very good at anything? We're like... weak, or something, because we can't specialise in any one element, or any one Craft."

He shook his head, clasping Nyx's hand. "No, you're of the Spirit, that's your element. And you can temper with every single Craft. Weavers aren't weak, you're... multi-faceted."

"But being able to work a little of each Craft doesn't really make us any good at one specific thing. And it doesn't explain the name. Why Weavers? I can get Draught-Makers, the name explains it all, right? Spellcasters too, and Sigilists. Even Hexers, Empaths, it makes sense. But Weavers? Why that particular name?"

"Well, maybe because you can weave..." Pip tentatively explained.

"What? What is it we weave?"

"Magic?"

"What if our ability is to weave *threads*? Pathways? Magical paths others can follow or use?"

"What are you talking about, Nyx?" He inched closer, ear to Nyx's lips, eyes narrowed, trying to focus and make sense. "What do you mean?"

"Eli's a Weaver too. And you know the strangest thing? He has a tattoo just like mine. Pip, it's just like mine. The same feather, the same birds, only he has lots more. It's even in the same spot, only the other arm. Like mirror images, but mine's incomplete."

He sought her eyes, held them. "So he *does* have magic." Pip sounded surprised, as if he'd expected it but couldn't quite believe. "You're siblings, and your mother was also a Weaver. As was your grandmother. Maybe the bond between you is stronger than anyone ever conceived. Or maybe he saw your tattoo and had one done to match it, like I did."

"You say that like it's a bad thing. Why don't you like him? He doesn't like you either, and I don't get why. You're very alike."

"No, we're not. And it's not that I don't like your brother, it's that he puzzles me. Most people are easy to read, and I have to shut them off willingly. Eli's like a brick wall. Worse than that, he's like a sheet of steel. Can't get through, can't reach in. He disconcerts me and makes me fear he's hiding something."

Nyx lowered her chin to her chest, breath taken away. Should she tell him? Besides Spencer and Eli, there wasn't a person she trusted more than she did Pip Thomson. Not even Trystan had been so deserving of her trust, or Penny, who she counted as her best friend, currently. If she were to be honest, it was Pip who was her best friend; it was him she believed she could trust with anything.

"He *is* hiding something. Only it's nothing like what you may think."

"So you know what it is?" Nyx nodded and relief seemed to wash over Pip, his shoulders relaxing, a sigh leaving his lips. "That makes it enough for me. As long as he doesn't keep secrets from his own family, I mean."

"Pip, you'd never believe it if I told you what being a Weaver really means."

"Try me."

She searched his eyes, looking for a sign, a trace of that which would make her spill everything, tell a secret that wasn't hers to share, betray her brother and the trust he'd placed upon her. It wasn't as if Eli had sworn her to secrecy; he hadn't even mentioned she was to keep quiet about this. But no one else seemed to know the truth about being a Weaver, not even Miss Tate. She wondered if her brother had shared his secret with Jacintha, if he'd shown her the other world that was half his. He'd said they were in danger from that other world, though, and that should make it enough for Nyx to keep quiet. Still, Pip did see the birds no one noticed, Pip did witness the tree shimmer and grow out of focus, as if it wasn't there; Pip did catch a glimpse of this other world her brother had dwelt in for seven years. Shouldn't he be allowed to know? Shouldn't he be warned?

"What did you mean with having a tattoo done to match my own?"

Pip laughed at her sudden change in subject. "You're impossible, you are. Fine, keep your secrets. Here," taking off the chequered shirt he wore, Pip turned the right elbow round so Nyx could see.

Inked onto the large spider web tattoo covering his elbow was a recently acquired design, a feather just like hers, only smaller. It looked woven into the web, trapped there, stuck to it. For a split second Nyx felt the proverbial fly caught in the spider's web, such was the intensity of emotions she experienced in that instant. Like a sigil, it was; a probable one too, but this didn't have Bryn's touch, her magic. Pip had got this one on his own, and no magic had been weaved to it, except for the one pertaining to Nyx's Craft, or Nyx herself. She realised it wasn't *her* trapped in Pip's web, but the other way around. He'd made himself hers, etched himself to her.

Unable to restrain herself any longer, Nyx claimed his mouth again, demanding one more urgent, inflamed kiss, with lips and tongues and hands all working together in the discovery. They curled into each other, hidden behind the sheer curtains of the booth, lost in their own world, their newfound passion. Breath laboured, both brought the kiss to an end, lingering with hands entwined and lips touching, briefly, softly.

"Why did you do that?" Nyx finally asked, tip of one finger tracing the well-known lines of the feather design on his elbow.

Pip shrugged, stole another kiss. "I felt compelled to. It's like an anchor, it grounds me, and also lets me know if you're... well, troubled. I have one for Trystan too, this flame. He has it on his chest. Having a replica of your Craft tattoos means I can lock you off whenever I need to, but I can also tap into you and know if you're all right. It gives me a choice." He smiled, watching her troubled face. "You still struggle with this, don't you? I'm sure your father had tattoos, Spencer must have them too."

"Yeah, but I thought they were just that, tattoos. Not some sort of branding. It'll sink in, eventually."

Pulling her deeper into his arms, Pip rested his chin over Nyx's head. "I don't want to talk about magic anymore, nor of your brother or Trystan. I want to talk about you, about me, the two of us together like this. What do you say?"

"I can go with that."

"Then I'll get us another drink. Don't go anywhere."

Nyx nodded, and watched him stroll away. She had no intention of going elsewhere, despite knowing how wrong it was of her to be here, with Pip, so soon in the wake of Trystan breaking up with her. But knowing didn't mean she cared, nor that guilt assaulted her about it. Watching Pip saunter back, her chest caught, lungs swollen and unable to function, heart plummeting. No, she'd never manage to feel guilty about this.

Because everything about it felt right, like a spell she'd woven into perfection, a magic so strong it was unbreakable. Together, Nyx thought, she and Pip could be unbreakable.

The thought scared her to death.

II

He woke up with a start, and the sound of shouts breaking through the darkened silence of the room, only to realise they were his. Fear gripped his gut, or maybe it was the cheesecake that hadn't sat right with him. But a dessert wouldn't explain for the accelerated rate of his heart, the shallowness of his breath, or the fact he had no idea where he was. Until a pair of warm, reassuring hands grabbed his shoulders and turned him towards her.

Jace.

Heart rate slowly returning to normal, Eli pulled his arms around her, hugging her with what was nothing short of utter dread.

"You're all right," she crooned, "I'm here. Was it a nightmare?" Backing away, Jacintha trained her eyes on his.

Eli shook his head. No, it hadn't been a nightmare, for that would imply the images assaulting his brain had belonged to the realm of imagination. And he knew this was far from the truth. He hadn't dreamt at all; what his mind had re-lived while he was asleep were memories, from a not-so-distant past but a now distant life.

"I don't know," he lied, "can't remember."

"Your heart's beating so fast, let me brew us some tea. Camomile, I think, to help soothe you and settle us back to sleep." As she eased from his grasp, Eli tightened the hold, keeping her in place.

"I can think of other ways to soothe me, much better ways, in fact." His voice held a promise he hoped she wouldn't resist.

Sure enough, Jace raised her eyes to him, smiled mischievously. "I think I'd prefer that to a cup of tea, yes."

Kissing her, Eli dragged Jacintha down, covering her body with his own, eager for a re-enactment of the previous night's lovemaking. The thought of Bryn nagged at the back of his head, despite the desperate attempts at keeping her green eyes from his mind, as well as the memory of what had taken place between them. But the truth was he'd come to Jace better prepared, not so in the dark about what to do and how to act, and the sex between them had been very different from what he'd experienced with the Everley girl. Contrary to Bryn, Jacintha had enjoyed it as much as Eli, and he'd make sure the same happened again.

After both were spent, but still wrapped in each other's arms, it didn't take long for Jacintha to drowse back to sleep. Her soft, smooth breathing was like a lullaby, one that failed to send Eli off to the realm of dreams, one he'd avoid at all costs. It did give him time and space to ponder, though, on what he'd remembered of his previous life, while lying safely in this woman's arms. A woman he couldn't envision giving up, not for the time being. And yet, if all his memories were true - and why wouldn't they be? - did he really have a choice? He might lose Jacintha at any given moment, without warning, due to none other but the fact she was entirely like him - a soul of two worlds, one life in this one, another elsewhere.

Eyeing the ceiling, Eli breathed deep, trying to bring forth the dream, his memories from a lifetime at Ephemera. Stella, always Stella, pale blond hair and icy eyes, flocks of odd birds constantly following her through the woods, the white-faced owl that perched by her windowsill, like a sentinel keeping watch over her. He'd remembered her parents too, the Dellacquas, Domina Primrose and Domine Fluvio, one of the most respected families in the village of Viridans, the nearest to the seat of the Governator, Thorne Ridge - an estate so immense he'd hardly covered its entirety in the seven years spent there. He'd remembered the baker and her fragrant loaves of caraway seed on a Saturday afternoon, the Saturnalia buns he'd come into the village to buy, after selling his game and pelts over at the vectum; he'd remembered the girls who clustered together like locusts at the market square on Sundays, and the way they'd look at him; he'd remembered the elders, the youngsters, the children. Each market stall, each forest road, each smell, sound, sight, he'd remembered.

And Stella's sister.

Eli had remembered Stella's sister.

Casting a look at the woman sleeping next to him, her head resting over the shoulder where his birds flew free from the constraints of a feather inked on his arm, Eli shuddered. For he'd suspected it before - that Jacintha might be like him. That she was the Weaver Corinna had brought into town but never managed to trust enough to let her in on the secrets of Weaversmoor. His grandmother hadn't trusted Jacintha for a very specific reason, although Corinna never really knew it. Jacintha didn't belong here. Jacintha hadn't even been born here. Hence the lack of memories from a prior life, the absence of family. Hence her waking up in a hospital bed, victim of an accident practising a sport she didn't recall; hence her not even knowing who she was, what her name was. Because it had never been *Jacintha*.

Her real name was Hyiacinth Dellacqua, and she was Stella's younger sister. Her life had been spent in Ephemera until something catapulted her into this world at about the same time as Eli had been cast out of that realm. And while he'd returned to his proper life, she was surely sleeping away somewhere in Ephemera, perhaps even dying, with no one knowing what was happening to her. What if she was lost in the woods? What if wild beasts came to find her shell, disrupted her slumbers, accidentally killed her? What if she died out there, from exposure to the elements, her body - already weakened by the fact she now lived another life elsewhere - unable to resist? What would happen to Jacintha if Hyiacinth were to perish?

She'd be forever locked here.

Come to think of it, this wasn't such a bad thing.

Although his memories were still foggy, unclear on certain issues, the image of Hyiacinth's face was very distinct. Jacintha and she were one and the same; of this he had no doubt. But as much as she hadn't been Jace out there in Ephemera, so hadn't he been Eli, and as far as he remembered, Nox and Hyia weren't lovers, they were friends. Stella was the woman he'd been in love with, the one who'd shattered his heart and destroyed his life in that world. And Hyia, as everyone called her, had nursed no other feelings for him but those born of friendship. For she, too, had kept a secret. There was a man she loved, a man she longed to be joined with. What of him? Why wasn't he trying to wake up Hyiacinth back in their world, why did he let her roam elsewhere as if she were free?

A fiery surge of jealousy ran through his veins, he'd not let her go. Jace and Hyia may be the same woman outwardly, but they were very different. Jace was outgoing and fun-loving, Hyia had been shy. Always in the shadow of her sister's magnificence - Stella of the birds, the charmer of anything with a feathery pair of wings - Hyia had been introspective, quiet. She never stood up for herself, nor demand attention was given her. She went about life as a shadow, a ghost, as unseen as she failed to see, for Hyia had been blind. And everyone failed to acknowledge her existence, except for this man she'd loved so much as to betray her family for him. What had she done, really? What had Eli helped her do that ended with him being cast out of that world for good? Something to do with Stella, who'd finally revealed her true nature to him.

No, he mustn't let Jace return, he couldn't let the breach be opened again.

Taking Nyx to the woods wasn't a mistake, but letting her play with her powers to the point she'd conjured Ephemera had been an error. One he wouldn't let her repeat. Spencer was right, as had Corinna been. While the birds came swooping down to stare at Eli and Nyx, he'd sensed the call of danger lurking behind them. He'd known those birds had been about to send out a message to whomever their charmer was, and apart from him, he'd known only one in Ephemera - Stella. What if there were Everlasting and Nigrum searching for him? What if Erin had made it back to Mythos, and was captured by the Regia at Chymera, strapped to their twisted contraptions so they could slowly milk her essence, her magic, her life? What if she'd been tortured and they now knew Fionn Sylvannar had a Weaver son, who'd taken after his Weaver mother, the same woman who'd given birth to Eli's Weaver sister?

What if they came after them?

He, Nyx, and surely Jacintha, would be in danger, had the thread his sister Weaved been enough to alert the packs of venators stationed at the spots where breaches had once appeared. Surely Rhysondel Sylvannar had posted a couple of sentinels by the spot where a Weaver had opened a door to this world, at his order, so Eli was cast out of Ephemera through it. Surely there'd be a lookout to assure nothing passed, the breach was locked. Or maybe he'd posted his minions there so he'd learn of Hyia's return, for he must know all of her secrets, and must have been looking for her. It must have crossed his mind Stella's sister might have been inadvertently pushed out by the same shunning used to get rid of Eli. It must have crossed Rhys's mind Hyia could be locked away, but looking for a way in, she who was a Weaver, with the capacity to thread her path back to him. For Rhys, the current Governator and Eli's brother, was the man Hyiacinth Dellacqua had secretly loved, and with whom she'd been secretly involved, their encounters often aided by Eli when he had been Nox.

The portal could not be opened again; there could be no further communication from this world to that, it was too dangerous. And it would mean losing Jacintha, which was something Eli simply wasn't ready to risk. But didn't he owe her that much? To let her have a choice? Shouldn't the decision be hers? What if, one day, her memory returned, as Eli's had? What if one morning Jace woke up knowing all about her other life, her other love? She'd never forgive him for not telling her, and she'd hardly believe him to be in the dark about it. Or would she?

Maybe he should run this through his parents when he went to Daylesford for a visit on Sunday. Maybe Ora and Serge could shed some light on what he must do. What if they longed to return to the world that had seen them born and grown to young adults? They'd been about his age when forced out of their home. Eli himself had pined for Ephemera, and he hadn't spent as many years there as they did. But now, he no longer wanted to return. His long-lived desire to go back to where he should have ruled as a king suddenly lost strength. He no longer cared for Stella's treason, for his out-casting, for his family heritage and his place in the Mythos hierarchy. All he cared about was his life at Weaversmoor, his sister and uncle's safety.

And what he had with Jacintha.

Eli patted the seat of his bike and strolled off towards the cottage, the shrill ring of his mobile breaking through the constant pattern of confusion his brain had fallen into. A welcome distraction from the thoughts going round his head, worrying at his stomach like claws, ever since he'd remembered Jacintha wasn't her but Stella's younger sister - Hyia of the blind eyes, betrothed to someone other than him. He couldn't bear the thought of losing her in this world, but neither could he keep out of his head the danger he feared she must be under, with an unconscious body lost somewhere in Ephemera. If only that husk would break and Jace was trapped here forever, with him. If only none of them had to ever go back.

Fishing the phone from his jacket, Eli frowned at the sight of his father's number on the screen. Both he and Ora called daily, but in the evening. It was lunchtime; he'd just left the auto-repair shop. Unless something had happened. Heart in hand, Eli answered the phone.

"Hey dad," he greeted, "what's up?"

The breathing on the other end was harsh, wet. Was Serge crying? Eli's stomach coiled around itself, a noose of fire tying it.

"Son," Serge whispered. Yes, he was crying. "Son, you have to listen, I don't have much time."

What was this? Doom folded around Eli, like a mantle, black and cold as the darkest Winter night.

"Dad, what's wrong?"

"They got her, son. Your mum, my Ora, they took her away. I was just coming home when I saw them round the corner, dragging her to a car. They didn't see me, though she did, and gave me that look."

"You're not making sense." The dread that only seconds before had been a mere whisper now turned to a loud clamour, a shriek that went on and on in Eli's head.

"She gave me that look, you know which one. That I was to stay away and do as we'd agreed all those years ago. Make sure you're safe and they can't find you."

"Dad, what are you talking about?" he shouted, unable to contain himself any longer. The doubts and suspicions creeping up made perfect sense, and yet didn't. He refused to let them in, this couldn't be. He mustn't let these thoughts into his head, or he would surely go mad.

"Eli, you're in danger, and so is your uncle, your sister. You need to grab them and leave that place. They must have taken her back, so it gives you some time, but..." Serge's voice dwindled to silence.

Ice froze Eli's body, the sky above clearing of the dark curtain of clouds it had worn all morning, a promise of rain which wasn't to materialise. He forced a breath down his lungs.

"I'm coming over."

"You're doing no such thing," Serge barked, and Eli stormed back to his childhood days, a little kid again, being grounded for some mischief or other.

"Then talk to me in a manner that makes sense, dad, because so far you sound like a maniac."

A long silence, broken only by the sound of someone breathing harshly, ensued. Finally, Serge cleared his throat. "Somehow, they found us, Eli. And took Ora with them, back to Mythos. *Hounds*, son. A trio of them. They had a Nigrum, too. *Your mother.*"

The last two words stopped his heart. All he'd feared, all he'd dreaded, the wild thoughts that had run through his head days and days on end, came to fruition in the split second it took his father to inform him of what Eli had already foreseen. Erin had Weaved her threads back to Mythos and been caught on arrival, used for the Everlastings' foul purposes in Chymera, transformed into a Nigrum ready to turn against her own kind. And now she came for her children. Now, she came to hunt her own children, those she'd tried to protect in her own clumsy way.

"Eli, Ora's a gentle woman, you know this. They've taken her to Chymera for interrogation; it won't take much to break her."

"Mum's much stronger than what you give her credit for," he whispered, tears already pooling his eyes. A headache started forming behind them.

"Listen to me, son. She'll try to hold back, and will manage, for a while. That should give you time. But be assured, they'll return, and head to Weaversmoor. Erin will know to go there. You need to leave and take that sister of yours. Your uncle too, they'll use him to find you and Nyx."

No, he couldn't run. He couldn't place an entire village in danger. He couldn't simply pack up and leave, condemning the lives of all those people just for the sake of his. He couldn't go and leave Jacintha vulnerable to the Hounds, the Nigrum. Maybe he could bring her along. But then he'd be forced to tell her everything, and risk losing her. What if, as she remembered the truth about herself and her other life, Hyia woke up from her slumbers in Ephemera and Jace simply ceased to exist? What about Ora? He couldn't leave her there, in Chymera, prey to the machinations and torture of a corrupt, rotten society. He couldn't let her suffer for his sake. Not his mother. Erin may have given him birth, but Ora was his mother. It was she he loved as one, and he couldn't let her die like this.

"Are you listening to me?"

"Dad, come here. Together we can..."

"I'm the first person they'll come after, son. We must stay apart. I'll find a way to contact you, but for now I need to leave Daylesford and you need to leave that town as of now. Do you understand? Ora's about to make the ultimate sacrifice, and you can't let it be in vain. You can't let her death be in vain. *Promise me.*"

The sound of his father sobbing was what undid him. Serge already counted Ora as good as dead. Was there really no hope? Halfway to accepting it, Eli nodded. "I promise."

"I love you, son. Please, be safe. We'll see each other again."

The call ended before Eli could reply. He was left paralysed, standing under a sudden ray of sunshine that turned his hair into spun gold and his eyes as bright as a summer sky, while his entire world shattered at his feet. What would they do to Ora, in Chymera? He couldn't let her give her life for him. It was Eli they wanted, wasn't it? Surely he must still have time to convince his uncle and sister to help; they wouldn't let an innocent woman die in vain. Nyx would Weave a thread through which Eli could cross to Ephemera, he'd go to Chymera and trade his life for Ora's, or try to save her. Spencer would grab Nyx and run - leave Weaversmoor, the UK, Europe even, if it was mandatory. They could torture him as much as they liked, if Eli had no idea where his uncle and sister were, they'd be safe.

But what of the rest of this town? What of Nyx's aunt Sarah, her children? What of the Everleys? Max would join Spencer, surely; Cressida would know to run. She'd met Fionn Sylvannar, knew how dangerous Everlastings were, she'd make sure her children were safe. He'd warn them before leaving, or Nyx and Spencer would. The town would be deserted, and they could send as many packs of Hounds as they wished - there'd be no one for them to capture.

Yes, that's what he must do, Eli had to go back to Mythos and make sure Ora wasn't harmed. Gathering himself, he ran to the house, eyes wide with fear but face set in a rictus of purpose. He found Spencer busy with cooking lunch for the two of them, his uncle's entire demeanour changing from his usual carefree frame to a mask of worry at the sight of his nephew. Pulling up a chair, he forced Eli to sit.

"What happened, are you all right? Is it your parents?"

Turning a blurry, confused gaze on Spencer, Eli shuddered at his uncle's capacity to read him. The man had known straight away what ailed him. He nodded, a tear fleeing the safety of his eye, rolling down his cheek, trapped between the bristles of his short beard. Spencer busied himself with one of his endless tinctures, choosing a pale yellow one he then mixed with tap water. Shoving it into Eli's hands, Spence nodded him to drink. Eli gulped it down mindlessly, as if he was outside himself, no longer present, no longer here. He felt dislocated, dislodged, unable to focus but on the thought he was wasting time and needed to hurry back to Mythos. What time did Nyx leave school?

"Tell me what happened, Eli," Spencer prodded him.

He turned wide, vacant eyes back on his uncle, another tear falling down his cheek. "I must get back there."

Spencer paled, understanding immediately. "No."

"They took Ora. They'll torture her, *kill* her. After she tells them where they can find us. They'll come for me, for Nyx. Everyone in this town will be taken, killed, you included. Max too, his children. Can you really allow for this?"

Spencer shook his head. "This town's protected. As long as no one Weaves a thread to that world, they can't enter. Not through a portal and not through our physical borders. Eli, as much as my mother failed, she excelled in her Craft. Corinna made sure the wards held and Weaversmoor was safe. As long as the entire town maintains those shields up, no one from that world can come in here."

Eli cackled, knowing Spencer to be wrong. The wards Corinna Vaughn had placed around town couldn't be very strong, if an Ephemeral had found her way here. Jacintha Tate was not from this world, she was in fact everything Corinna had fought to keep out. But then it hit him, Jace hadn't entered Weaversmoor of her own volition, Corinna had *brought* her in. Because she'd needed Weavers to keep up the spells. Much like the Everlasting did in Chymera, trapping the lifeforce and magic of Weavers so they could persist. So their own wards and spells could persist. How ironic his grandmother had chosen to safeguard her town and family by use of the exact same instruments that had made Mythos abhorrent to her.

"Vacate the town, make sure everyone leaves. Grab Nyx and go, see that everyone does the same, but I won't be stopped, Spencer. It's my mother."

"So you'd risk the lives of many, including your friends, your family, your girlfriend, for the life of a woman who isn't even your *real* mother?"

Eli stood up, the chair underneath him clattering to the flagstone floor. Heart hammering, hands clenched in a claw-like gesture, anger coursed through him. He narrowed his eyes on his uncle, and there was a menace in them, a death-wish, directed at Spencer, not at himself. There was hatred and disbelief, that a man who'd witnessed his own sister give up her children would now come throw at his face Ora wasn't his mother, Erin was.

Erin, who'd never been there for him. Erin, who, for whatever reasons, had let go of him. That she'd done it all to assure her children were safe only gave strength to his plea. As much as his birth mother had sacrificed herself, so did Eli find he must sacrifice his life and wellbeing for Ora.

"She *is* my real mother. Erin gave up the right to call me son the moment she let the Sylvains take me. And now she's working against us, Spencer, and she'll know you're here, she *will* come, no matter what. Whether I open a breach or not, Erin can come and go between worlds at will. Corinna's wards pale in comparison to the powerful magic Nigrum can create. You all need to leave, this place is doomed."

"You have no idea what you're saying. My mother saw to it, Eli. Max's father too. Or do you think Fionn Sylvannar was the first creature ever to come into contact with the people here? Do you think you're the first child born of such a liaison? Every single one of us who are of the blood is somehow descendant of this other world. We all carry their blood, be it Chymeran, Ephemeral or Everlasting. Every one of us, Eli. We know how to counter their magic; how to use their very Craft. And we've *far* surpassed them. So put this idea out of your head, you're not going back there."

"I am. And you won't stop me."

"Eli, don't be a fool. You're safe here, Nyx too, do not ruin this."

"How can you stand there as if everything's all right, Spencer? They took my mother; they'll come back for my father, and won't stop until they have me and Nyx!"

"They won't know of you and Nyx."

"They already do! Erin's with them, she's been turned into a Nigrum."

Spencer's face darkened, eyes widening in shock.

"I see you're familiar with the term. Your own sister will lead them here, unless I put an end to this. So you see, I have no choice but to go back there."

"No!"

Eli shuddered, took a step back in sudden alarm. He'd never seen his uncle quite like this. Spencer was a mild-mannered man, placid and moderate. He didn't raise his voice, nor did he lose his cool. He didn't rage, didn't order around. But what Eli had in front of him was a version of Spencer he'd never met, and he wondered if this was the man who'd turned his back on his own mother, and left her house for good, because she couldn't accept who he was. Still, Eli would not be intimidated, he'd fight Spencer as his uncle had fought his mother, and just like him, he would prevail. Ora would not be left to die a horrible death because of him.

"Don't try to stand in my way, uncle," he whispered, voice cold, devoid of all feeling. "For I will destroy you if I have to."

Spencer's expression lost all the anger, there was deep regret in it, now, heartache and pain for Eli's predicament. There was understanding too, for his hurt, his rage, but also a strong resolve; he would not be moved. Eli shook his head, anger overpowering every other emotion. Curling one hand into a fist, he banged it on the table, Spencer grabbing at his chest. The older man paled, shuffled on his feet, lost his balance. Clutching the shirt he wore, trying to rip it open, he clawed at his heart, face turning purple, lips losing colour, eyes bulging. Spencer dropped to his knees, still scratching at the fabric and skin over his heart.

"Help... me..." he begged, voice failing him.

Eli's eyes widened in fear, but he found himself unable to move. Standing there, in the kitchen, watching his uncle struggle with a pain that seemed to deliver consecutive attempts against his life, Eli couldn't think. Unprepared for this, he was, powerless to change what reason told him was about to take place, all he could do was watch, and let tears stream down his face while Spencer struggled against the force that threatened to take him; while his uncle fought for his life. There was nothing Eli could do - he was impotent, inadequate, incapable of helping.

Or was it he was unwilling?

WITCH CRAFT

III

Pip approached the house from the back, having cut through the woods just outside the Everley estate. This saved him precious minutes, he was due at school in less than half an hour, Nyx needed her book.

The silence was what first warned him.

It was eerie, unnatural.

Spencer and Eli should be chatting in the kitchen; this wasn't the first time Pip Thomson made his way to Vaughn cottage during lunch break in the past three weeks - since he and Nyx had started dating. He'd either be walking her home or picking her up, but he'd been coming here regularly since that Friday night in November. And Spencer and Eli were *always* chattering away, Nyx's brother excitedly talking about cars and bikes and motors, Spencer smiling while he cooked, replying when solicited, or putting his nephew up to date on the bookshop he intended to open next year. More often than not, music would be playing in the background.

This silence was uncanny, unexpected.

With careful footsteps, he approached the window, eyes scanning the interior, wide in their sockets as Pip took in what he was seeing. Spencer, kneeling on the floor, hands clutching his chest. Face caught in a grimace of pain, lips purplish. He looked as if he couldn't breathe. Before Pip had time to do anything, Nyx's uncle collapsed, body spasming. Shocked into action by the thought Spencer was alone, Pip started for the door, but caught sight of a figure standing to the left. Eli was there.

Eli was in the house, with Spencer. So why wasn't he doing anything, why didn't he help? Just stood there, eyes narrowed, from where a steady stream of tears trickled down. What was wrong with him, that he was about to let his own uncle die?

Running for the door, Pip threw it open, convinced he knew what was going on.

"Call an ambulance," he screamed.

Eli didn't move, he was rooted to the floor, paralysed. Kneeling by Spencer, Pip tried to remember the first aid classes they'd been forced to attend at the Academy, but nothing came to mind. He should have paid more attention. Maybe that was why Eli wasn't moving, he was terrified, had no idea what to do.

"Call an ambulance, Eli," Pip shouted again, and this time Eli *did* move, he shuddered and blinked, as if waking from a trance.

"Spence," he whispered, the flood of tears intensifying.

Good lord, he was hopeless. Seven years in a coma had really turned Eli into an immature, unprepared little boy inside a man's body.

"What's wrong with you?" Pip fished his phone, dialled 999, Eli finally approaching the spot where Spencer lay dying on the floor.

When the operator answered, Pip shoved the phone into Eli's hand, placed two fingers on Spencer's neck, searching for a pulse. There, but barely.

"It's my uncle," Eli was saying, his face so white it looked like chalk. "I don't know, he won't speak. Collapsed on the floor, clutching his chest. I don't think so, no."

Pip closed his eyes, forcing his mind back to the classes. They'd covered this; he'd been taught what to do in a case like this, why couldn't he remember? What was it he was supposed to do when witnessing a heart attack? Give the patient his medicine? Water? Put his legs up? Oh, he just couldn't think. And Nyx. Waiting for him at the Academy, unaware of what was going on in her own house. Shuddering, he heard Eli give the operator the address before hanging up.

"They'll send help straight away."

Kneeling next to Spencer's head, Eli grabbed his uncle's face between his fingers, shoulders shaking. "Look at me," he whispered. "I didn't mean it, Spence, please look at me."

Pip frowned, wondering what had happened. At first, it seemed Eli was purposefully doing nothing to help his uncle. As if he'd wanted him to suffer? But walking in, Pip had been confronted with a world of panic in Eli's eyes, and looking at him now, he couldn't help but think he must be in shock. Still, a suspicion that refused to vanish kept biting at him, an intuition he'd long ago learnt to give heed to. For some reason, Eli Vaughn had refused helping Spencer, leaving him in pain. The belief was made stronger by his hushed apologies.

The sound of an ambulance wailing its way to the front gates cut Pip's thoughts short. He stood up, unsure if it was wise to leave Eli alone with Spencer. But someone needed to let the paramedics in.

"Is it them?" Eli asked, eyes so wide they looked about to pop off his head. "Will you stay with him? I'm gonna let them in."

Not waiting for a reply, Eli darted off, leaving Pip alone with Spencer. What about Nyx? Someone had to warn her. She should be here. He thumbed the phone, this wasn't the kind of thing that should be told over a call, he must come get her at the Academy.

As soon as the ambulance left for the hospital, he'd pick her up and they'd take a cab, if necessary.

The paramedics stormed into the kitchen, pushing aside chairs and table to get to Spencer's unconscious body. Pip stood up and walked back to the door, where he placed himself out of the way. His eyes made contact with Eli's, still stunned, still shocked. Terrified, in fact.

"My sister," he whispered.

"We have to take him to hospital. Do you wish to follow?"

"What? The hospital? What hospital?"

"Mr. Vaughn will be taken to Queen Anne's, sir," one of the paramedics replied, both still working on getting Spencer's body onto the stretcher.

Pip crossed to where Eli stood, placed a hand on his arm. "I know where it is, we can go get Nyx and follow. Are you all right to drive?"

Eli shook his head, watching the paramedics run out the kitchen with an unresponsive Spencer between them.

"How'm I gonna tell Nyx this?" He covered his face with trembling hands, a sob hushed between his fingers. "Max needs to know, too."

As if finding new purpose, Eli reached for Spencer's mobile, searched through the contact list. Pip made as if to leave, but he held him in place, the same terrified look still in his eyes.

"Hi, this is Eli, not Spencer," he said, Max Everley's voice clearly audible to Pip. "He's been taken to hospital, Queen Anne's. I'm sorry to bother you, but I didn't know who else to call. I have no idea what to do. Nyx is at school, I still have to go and tell her. I have no idea. Would you? I'll meet you there, then. Thank you." Facing Pip, shoulders slumped, Eli let out a moan. "Max's picking us up at the Academy. Can you please tag along, Pip? Nyx is gonna need you, I think."

"Maybe I shouldn't, she'll need her family."

Eli trained blazing eyes on him, Pip's skin crawling, his back shuddering in sudden fear.

"You're her boyfriend, aren't you? Then step up to it. I was so against her carrying on with you, please don't prove me right. My sister's gonna need you. *I'm* gonna need you."

Pip nodded, shoving hands into his pockets. "Then we should go, lunch break is almost over."

Eli rushed him to the door, grabbed his jacket and the keys. "What were you doing here, if Nyx's still at school?"

"She forgot one of her books; I came to ask Spencer for it."

"Well, I'm glad you were here." Eli sounded calmer, more composed. "I never seem to know what to do with myself, most of the time. As if I'm... a helpless incompetent. How'm I gonna tell her this? He's all she's got."

Pip shook his head, directed Eli across the woods, towards the part of the forest that led to the Academy. They walked in silence, hurriedly, the brisk air of early December failing to freeze their bodies, warm with the exertion. In a few minutes they came upon the Academy's tall, surrounding walls and its large gates. Nyx was standing at the bottom of the stairs, eyes travelling between her wristwatch and the entrance, clearly looking for Pip. When she saw him, a smile danced across her lips, to die the second she spotted Eli. Face crumbling, Nyx ran down the stairs, and Pip realised she needn't be told, she knew.

Somehow, she just knew.

Maybe it came with being a Weaver, maybe her brother had lowered his walls and she was able to read him, maybe it was Pip that had allowed her a glimpse into his head. Whatever it was, Nyx knew and tears already coursed down her cheeks as she ran to them, passing Pip and throwing her arms around Eli, sobbing convulsively in time with him.

"What are you saying?" Jamal asked, for the third or fourth time, managing to grab hold of Bryn's hands.

She eyed him with a mix of pity and impatience, unable to hide her discomfort. Why was he making this so hard? It shouldn't be difficult to understand.

"I need space, Jamal, some time for myself. That's why I think we should take a break."

"Take a break?" he inquired, voice rising. "Or do you mean we should break up, altogether? Frankly, Bryn, I don't have time for this. You're acting like a spoilt brat."

"Takes one to know the other," she mumbled, searching around her satchel for the mobile that wouldn't stop buzzing. Fishing it out, she narrowed her eyes at the name on the screen. Why was her father calling her at this hour? "Yeah, dad, I'm kind of in the middle of something, mind if I call you back?" She found herself hushed, eyes careening towards Jamal, as what her father disclosed slowly sank in. "Were you with him? Who was, then? *Eli*? Is he all right? Is he gonna be ok? Yes, all right, dad. I will. See you in a bit."

Killing the call, Bryn pushed the phone back into her bag, head swinging from side to side as if looking for someone.

"What's wrong?" Jamal asked.

She locked eyes with him, tears already brimming in hers, which she pushed back. "Call your mum. Spencer Vaughn's been taken to Queen Anne's."

"*What*? What happened?"

Shaking her head, she started walking away. Jamal closed a hand round her fist, forcing Bryn to stay put. "I don't know, ok? Eli was with him, had to call an ambulance, then he phoned my father. I have to go find Nyx, they'll be here to pick us up soon."

"Eli? So it's *him*, huh? That's why you want to take a break."

"Oh, screw you, Jamal; I really don't have time for this. A man's in the hospital, all right? He might even be dead, I dunno, but he's your cousin's uncle, he's my father's..."

"Your father's what? Bryn, please talk to me."

"Call your mum, grab Trystan, meet us there." She pulled out of his grip, running towards the central staircase, knowing Nyx to be on the second floor for her afternoon class.

Dashing through the swing doors, Bryn came to a halt at the front hall, barely avoiding crashing into Jacintha Tate.

"Bryn Everley," the teacher scolded. "You know you're not to run in the hallways. What's with you?"

"Have you seen Nyx Vaughn, Miss Tate?"

"No, I don't have Nyx today. Why?"

"Her uncle's been taken to hospital. I'm to go get her, my father's picking us up at the front gates."

"Where's Eli? I mean, where's her brother? He should be warned. I'll give him a call."

"Oh, don't bother," Bryn huffed. "He's meeting us here; it was him who found Spencer. I really have to go, now."

"Yes, of course."

Bryn took a step away from the teacher, who remained by the swing doors, lost in thought. As she passed the front entrance, her eyes caught sight of a head full of curls bobbing up and down a girl's back, running down the gravel to the gates.

Nyx.

She halted, swerved right, dashed through the door and down the steps, mouth opening to call for the other girl. But then she saw Pip, and Eli behind him, looking dishevelled and haunted, paler than she'd ever seen him. Their eyes met the second before Nyx crashed into her brother's arms, who hugged her tight. Even at a distance, Bryn could see tears coursing down Eli's face. Taking the steps two at a time, she searched the road behind, looking for her father's car.

Pip curled one arm through hers, his countenance pasty and yellowish, as if he was about to be sick. Their eyes met, Bryn registered how terrified he was, how shocked, and wondered how he came to be here, with Eli.

"My dad called," she explained. "He's out of his head with worry. Why are you here?"

"I was with Eli when... Bryn, I think it's bad." He'd lowered his voice to a mere whisper, trying to keep it from Nyx. "I think it was him. *He* hurt Spencer."

Bryn's eyes narrowed, trying to make sense of Pip's words. Was he accusing Eli of having done something to his own uncle?

"There's dad," she replied, longing to change the subject, already anticipating the world of pain and chaos about to shatter around her. "Eli, my father's here."

The young man disentangled himself from his sister's hold, took one look at the car now entering the Academy. Then met Bryn's stare, a message passing through them, one she couldn't quite interpret. He looked so desperate, so scared.

A shiver ran down her back. How she longed to assure him all would be well. How she longed to take Eli in her arms and soothe him, make it all better for him. But the female figure at the front door reminded her he wasn't free, and it wasn't her he wanted by his side for comfort. It was her, Jacintha Tate, who now hurried down the steps, ready to meet them before they left. Eli broke eye contact with Bryn; turned towards her - his lover, his girlfriend, the woman he really cared for and of which Bryn must remind herself daily.

"Meet me at Queen Anne's," he said to Jacintha. "Please?" The woman nodded and ran towards the back, where teachers parked their cars.

WITCH CRAFT

Max's vehicle halted by Bryn's left, her father jumping off with a cloudy look on his face. This really wasn't fair, he'd just found his happiness, managed to break free from the claws holding him prisoner to a life that wasn't his, a man he never wanted to be; to have him now stand on the brink of losing it?

"Come on," he called, "we're wasting time here."

Eli seemed to wake up from whatever dream state he'd been in, and ushered Nyx to the back seat, Pip taking the other side of her. Bryn joined her father up front, hands grasping the doorhandle as Max sped all the way to the hospital. No one spoke; no one said a word, the inside of the car like a silent hearse broken only by the sound of Nyx crying. Bryn couldn't remember a longer ride anywhere. Her eyes met Eli's through the mirror, and what she seemed to glimpse made her wonder if something more wasn't on the verge of taking place. Like a doom settling around the entire town, it was - a foreboding that chilled her to the bone. Something was coming; for him, for them, and only Bryn and Eli seemed able to see or feel it. Suddenly lost for breath, she opened the passenger side window, took a large gulp of the frosty December air.

Finally, the long drive up the hospital came into view. Nyx had stopped crying, head resting against Eli's shoulder, one hand firmly held in his, the other clasping Pip's. Max drove towards the visitor's car park, near empty at this hour. Soon it would be full, with three o'clock visitors. They glided out like an entity, scared of crossing through the doors and entering this place of doom, where bad news would be served left and right. Bracing herself, Bryn squared her shoulders, reached for her father's hand, a soft, loving look in her eyes.

"Come on," she whispered, "the sooner we get there, the sooner we'll know."

And maybe it wasn't bad news; people fell ill and recovered every day, everywhere. Why would Spencer be any different?

Stealing a glance at Eli and Nyx, she shuddered. Because it was *them*, her mind wailed, because it was them and they were ill-fated, doomed. Just look at their history, both abandoned by mother. Eli had never even known his father, who, according to Cressida, was some sort of monster, a very dangerous man. Nyx had lost hers recently; she had no one left but her uncle, her newcomer of a brother. It was like a curse hanging over the girl, and Bryn suddenly feared for Eli's wellbeing. What if he was the next victim of this doom that seemed to follow Nyx around? How was Bryn going to deal with it? The sight of Jacintha Tate entering the hospital's reception area sobered her up, and Bryn turned to her father, who stood by the front desk talking to one of the girls behind it in hushed tones.

Following Jacintha, Sarah Wilson and her husband Tyronne dove through the rotating doors, closely followed by Trystan and Jamal. Bryn found herself wincing at the sight; this wasn't good, at all. Feelings were already running high because of the stressful situation, the not knowing how Spencer was faring; tempers were sure to rise due to the stress. Especially where it came to Trystan and Pip, because of Nyx. Or Jamal, she deduced, by the way he looked at her. Like shards of ice directed at Bryn, and the cold got hold of her. Her brother had run to Nyx, and hugged her, the girl seeming to melt in his arms, locked tight inside what looked like a safe cocoon. Why must Trystan be so difficult? It was clear how much he cared for Nyx, why would he let his prejudices against their father stand in the way of his own happiness? Bryn forced her gaze away, trained attention back to her father, who'd joined them with the information he'd gathered at the front desk.

A nurse gestured them. Max, taking the lead, was the first to reach her. She directed the group to a waiting room, where uncomfortable looking seats awaited them.

"The doctor will be in presently, with news of Mr Vaughn's condition," she said. "May I ask who are his next of kin?"

"I'm Mr Vaughn's lawyer," Max clarified. "His nephew and niece will be his next of kin."

Eli joined Max, having delivered care of Nyx to Pip. "Mr Everley is my uncle's life partner, he's also his next of kin."

Max's face lightened at the acceptance, his eyes brimming with tears, and Bryn had to hold herself back from running to Eli and hugging him. Or even kissing him for it. Whatever she did and wherever she looked, it was him who always came back to her mind, it was every little thing Eli did or said that made a dent in her certainties, widened the hole already there, to the point she knew she'd already fallen in love with the man. A man who didn't want her, nor would he ever, despite what the earth and the trees had whispered in her ear the night they'd met in the woods and made love.

Hanging her head down, Bryn took a deep, uneven breath. She watched as people filed in, Sarah Wilson pushing Pip out of the way so she could hold Nyx, who glared at her aunt in a terrified and offended way. Sarah seemed not to notice, simply pulling Nyx's head to her narrow bosom and caressing her curls in a failed attempt at soothing her. Nyx looked uncomfortable, as if she wished to be anywhere but here, at the hospital, yes, but especially in her aunt's grasp. Free hand searching round, she darted it at Pip, who held it tight. The cat was out of the bag now; no one would doubt Pip and Nyx were together. Bryn had known for a while, and kept it to herself, respecting their wish for secrecy because of Trystan. Who knew about it, of course, and looked none too happy for it.

Well, it was his fault, wasn't it? He'd acted like a git, and still refused accepting Max and Spencer's relationship. The thought brought Bryn's attention back to her father, but her eyes were diverted by Eli's figure as he joined his sister, taking the chair next to her. Nyx disentangled herself from Sarah's arms and hugged Eli, her aunt's face darkened by the girl's preference. Tyrone Powell had sat himself next to his wife, and Jacintha Tate slid towards the seat on Eli's left. Trystan and Jamal stood in the middle of the room, like a sore, an open wound, and she wished they'd just take a seat, stopped making themselves conspicuous. Max paced by the door, clearly uneasy, and Bryn decided her place was by him, he'd need her on his side when the news came.

For they would, and every single nerve on her body, every one of her instincts told her they wouldn't be good. As she reached her dad, a tired-looking doctor opened the door and stepped inside, searching around until his eyes locked with Max's, acknowledging him as the one responsible adult present. He shook his head minutely, Max paled, Bryn held her father's hand.

Their world was about to collapse.

IV

"Mr. Vaughn's next of kin, please?" the doctor called, his attention still on Max Everley.

Nyx's stomach somersaulted, cold sweat drenching her. Eli stood up, pulling her with him, but Nyx's legs seemed made of rubber, or maybe it was steel - she couldn't move them, no matter what.

"I'm Eli Vaughn," her brother said, voice shaking. "Spencer's nephew. This is my sister Nyx. Mr Everley is my uncle's life partner." He sounded like a broken record, repeating the same thing.

"I'm afraid we don't have good news."

Nyx's heart stopped. The entire world stopped. There was no action, no movement, no sound. There was nothing but the sudden void she was thrown into. As if hiding from reality, she found herself wrapped in a cocoon that kept her away from what she already knew was about to be said. But if she didn't hear it, she'd never know, and it wouldn't be real. She'd be safe, here, inside her head, away from whatever was about to rain on them: the shattering of her life yet again, the pain, the loss, the despair. Nyx never wanted to go through that again, and as long as she hid here, in this warm, hollow void, she didn't have to.

It was the wail that brought her out of her shell. The loud, long, piercing wail, echoing from the walls and windows of the tiny waiting room. A howl so filled with pain she assumed it must be

Max, it had to be him, she'd witnessed the love he had for Spencer during the several times the Everley patriarch had joined them for dinner – with Bryn tagging along more often than not - or even to stay the night, something both Nyx and Eli had insisted upon. He'd made himself part of the family in the three weeks that had elapsed since she and his own son had broken up. Max had slithered his way in, and both Eli and Nyx had been glad to welcome him, for there was no doubt how much he loved Spencer, there was no mistaking how much he cared for him.

But the voice wasn't male, so it couldn't be Max bawling his grief before the doctor even had a chance to say what Nyx refused to hear. It couldn't be Max, so who was it that had forced her out of the safety she'd hidden herself in, who'd brought her back to deal with something she couldn't face, shouldn't *have* to face?

Then it hit her - it was her.

It was Nyx screaming her pain even before it had been awakened. Eli's arms held her tighter, but her brother felt weak, as if he couldn't hold himself up. Legs buckling under him, Bryn Everley reached out to grab Eli by one arm, her voice soothing and calm, dishing out words Nyx couldn't make sense of. Such hollow, empty words that didn't make sense and didn't make it better for her, nor did it look like it was working for Eli.

Sobbing, Nyx searched her brother's eyes, registered his tears, and found them bonding through the pain, for only they could understand what this meant, what this felt like. Only they had experienced the same amount of loss. No one else inside this room belonged to Spencer as much as they did.

"I'm so sorry," Eli cried, legs buckling again, this time the tired doctor coming forth to help him up.

"No," Nyx blubbered, "no, this isn't happening, this isn't real. Eli, tell me it's not real. Where's Spencer?" She pulled away from her brother, whose face had gone pale, lips lost of colour, eyes rolling to the back of his head.

Was Eli about to faint? Was she to lose him as well? The doctor held him as his body flopped down like a rag doll, Bryn trying to pull him up by the waist. Rage flew through Nyx, rode her like a mad wind, a wild fire, and forced her to her brother's side, one hand pulled back to lash out with a loud slap against his cold, clammy cheek.

"Don't you dare," she whispered, "don't you dare, Eli. You're all I have."

His eyes fluttered, her brother regaining consciousness, weakly fighting the grasp the doctor and Bryn had on him. He pushed forward to take Nyx in his arms, both upholding each other as they sobbed together, Max Everley coming to join them and wrapping strong, long arms around their shoulders. The three people who most loved Spencer. The three people he had in the world. His family.

"No, we don't know yet," Nyx said, voice muffled against her brother's chest. She broke free and searched for the doctor, read the truth in his eyes. "He's going to be fine. I know he's going to be fine."

"I'm sorry, Miss Vaughn. Mr Vaughn was dead on arrival, we couldn't revive him. It was a massive stroke, and there was nothing we could do."

Nyx pushed away, hair flying wild about her head. She was like Medusa, head full of coiling snakes, fury gleaming in her eyes, a figure of doom, to be feared. She was a weakling who'd lost everyone she'd ever loved, all those who'd been her safe harbour. She was nothing but a lost little girl, alone in a rotten, cold world.

"A stroke? Spencer was too young for a stroke, he was thirty-nine, no one has a stroke at thirty-nine."

"Nyx, your uncle had a heart condition." Max's voice cut through the loud rumble of thunder in her brain.

She turned towards him, head askance, doubt in her mind as a string of memories rushed her. The tincture he constantly consumed drops of. The ashen colour of his lips when the news Tom had been lost at sea reached them, back in Havenleah. The hand over his heart when the phone call came to tell him his mother had died. The purple hue of his face when he'd ran into Max for the first time. The constant, repeated rubbing of hand over chest, over his heart. The signs had been there all along, and yet, she'd failed to see them. She'd ignored them. Because she'd been too busy with her shallow little life, and her silly little problems, wrapped up in her tiny, little, privileged world, being a nuisance, selfish as only a sixteen-year-old could be. Swerving to Eli, she locked eyes with him.

"Did you know this?"

He shook his head, tears still streaming down his cheeks, then bent down, hands over his knees, retching, gasping.

"Spence had me promise not to tell you. And he only told me because I insisted. Because I could tell there was something wrong with him, that first weekend we went away," Max informed. "He refused to see a specialist, said he had it under control. Obviously, he didn't." His voice was thick, wet, filled with the unshed tears he'd been holding back.

Like slow motion, Nyx watched Bryn let go of Eli and walk to her father, hugging him.

"We'll have to perform an autopsy," the doctor said, "and there are a few legal procedures that will need to be taken care of."

Legal procedures? How was she going to handle this? Eli looked far from capable of coping, and she was too young to deal with all this. Max Everley stepped in; assuring the doctor he'd see to it, Nyx sighing in relief. How horrid of her, that she felt relieved for not having to deal, for having someone else willing to do it for her, thus saving her the hassle, the bother of facing up to the truth and keep living. She wasn't quite certain she could go on living. As her eyes came upon her brother, she knew she'd have to. Eli needed her as much as Nyx needed him. A wide step took her back to him, and it was Nyx who pulled her brother into her arms, directing him to the chairs, where they sat together, wrapped in each other, sobbing softly.

Nyx had no idea how long it was until the sobs dwindled to hiccups and the tears dried out on their cheeks. It was a long time; that much she knew; and the room had gone silent aside the shuffle of feet, the opening and closing of the door, as people streamed in and out to use the toilet, grab coffee, tea. Finally, she held up her head, taking notice of those still in the room with them - for these were all that mattered, the people who stuck by them in their direst hour, their moment of need.

Sarah sat across the room from Nyx, holding hands with her husband, Jamal to their right. Trystan had taken the seat next to him, and he trained bruised, mournful eyes on her, but one of his arms was wrapped around his father's shoulder – at least something good seemed to have come out of this. Bryn took to her father's other side, her attention focused on Eli, kindling Nyx's suspicions. She pushed those thoughts away, now wasn't the time. Looking at her brother, she noticed he'd calmed down, there was colour back on his cheeks. Jacintha Tate sat beside him, their hands entwined, a loud admittance to how things stood between them. The soft, warm touch of a hand upon her knee brought Nyx's attention to where Pip squatted by her. He smiled tentatively, reached his free hand to her face, wiped tears from her eyes. When she nodded, he sat by her side, pulled Nyx into his arms, kissing her forehead first, then searching for her lips. No point hiding the truth anymore, she needed the comfort of someone who cared, someone who'd be there. She needed Pip as much as her brother needed Jacintha.

A shadowed figure broke into her line of vision, Nyx raising her eyes to see who it might be. Cressida Everley stood before her, holding two plastic, steaming mugs. She pushed them at Eli, at Nyx.

"Here, both of you, drink this."

"What is it?" Nyx inquired, while Eli took his mug and sniffed the rising steam.

"Chamomile," he said, "and a hint of valerian?"

Cressida nodded, smiling a sad, bitter grin. "It'll help calm you. I know this must be very hard on you."

Nyx sniggered, she had no idea. How could she? Her family was around, alive and kicking. Cressida's parents still resided at Weaversmoor, her children were healthy and happy, right here, in the same room as she. The most hardship the woman had ever been through was her disrupted, failed marriage, and the loss of the man she'd loved, but he was still alive, he was still here. What did she know of being alone in the world, with no one to count on, having lost ground and anchor and her safety? She knew nothing; none of these people did; only Eli came close to understanding what Nyx was going through. Lights flickered above her, the window panes rattled disturbingly. Realising she was about to lose control, Nyx gulped down half the steaming mug of tea, coughing and spurting with the burning of her tongue and lips.

"We need to talk practical things." Sarah Wilson's voice cut through the hushed conversations, all eyes converging on her. Apparently unfazed, she softened the skirt over her knees, looking around innocently. "Tyronne and I can take care of the funeral for you; take that load off your back. Then there are the legal issues, what with Spencer's estate and everything, but I'm sure Max will get someone to look into this. As for Nyx, she needs to pack a few things and come stay with us, until the guardianship is legally passed on to Tyronne and me."

"The *legal* guardianship?" Eli inquired, his voice cold and menacing.

Nyx's heart did another cartwheel. How could this be happening on top of everything? She had no wish to go to Sarah, leave Vaughn cottage; all Nyx wanted was to stay with Eli. He was an adult, and her closest kin. Surely her guardianship would fall onto him.

"Well, you're in no condition of looking after your sister, are you? I mean, you're still a kid; this has come as a shock for you. Until a couple of months ago, you didn't even know there was a sister, did you? No one expects you to uproot yourself just so you can take care of Nyx, and no one will blame you for being unable to do it."

"Unable? Uproot myself? This is my home, as much as hers, or yours. This is where I live now, and Nyx is my sister. She's all I have."

"I don't want to live with you, Aunt Sarah," Nyx said, voice threatening a new burst of tears. "I love you, but I don't want to move in, I want to stay at Vaughn cottage with my brother."

"Honey," Sarah insisted, speaking as if Nyx were a five-year-old being unreasonable, which only served to make her bristle. "You're in no condition of making this kind of decision. I mean, Eli can't take care of you, he has no idea what to do, doesn't even have a job."

Eli tightened his grip on Nyx's hand, she winced but withstood. They needed to put up a convincing, united front. Sarah would not part them.

"Not that this is any of your business, and not that I *need* one, but I do have a job. I work part time at the auto-repair shop down at Remington Street. And I'm twenty-six-years old, an adult; I can take care of my sister. In fact, it's what I'm going to do from now on, she's all I have and I won't let anyone take Nyx away from me."

"She won't be taken away from you; you can visit whenever you wish. But she needs a steady, familiar environment around her."

"And I can't give her that?" He stood up, risen to full height, tall and menacing. "Nyx stays with me. Unless she wishes differently, of course. But you don't care what we wish for, do you?"

Sarah blushed, eyes narrowing to angry slits. Jacintha jumped from her seat, curled her hands around Eli's arm, trying to soothe him.

"She's a child, has no idea what's best for her. And you're clearly unfit to look after her, just look at the two of you! That's just wrong, morally, isn't it? I mean, she's your sister's teacher and you're all over her? Is that the kind of environment you want Nyx to be raised in? No wonder she's dating the most troubled boy at school, something both you and Spencer should have already put an end to."

Nyx shuffled back in the chair, Pip holding her tighter. "You're a horrible person," she said, staring straight at her aunt. "I never knew you were like this. My father never knew…"

"Oh, he did, all right," Cressida Everley whispered, Sarah's eyes darting angry looks at her.

"Jace is my girlfriend," Eli said. "There's nothing wrong with that."

"And I'm not Nyx's teacher, only her tutor. Besides, the school board is aware of this, right, Mr Powell?"

Sarah turned a stunned face at her husband, and Nyx pitied him. He was in for a world of pain, later on. But how could her aunt act like this so soon after the loss Nyx and Eli had suffered? Had she no respect, no feelings at all?

"And none of you see anything wrong with this? What with his father's track record, you're all willing to let someone born of that man take care of a child?"

"I am not my father!" Eli's face took on a deep red hue, eyes darting swiftly towards Bryn, who turned to look at him.

It was a brief moment, something so quick no one noticed, except for Nyx. The suspicions she'd harboured earlier took deeper hold, aided by Bryn's blushing cheeks. Trystan's sister had nursed a crush on Eli, of that Nyx had no doubt, and she must have advanced herself to him on numerous occasions. Sarah's words had been like a sharp knife to her brother, Nyx being aware how the age gap between his parents troubled him. They'd both heard his father being referred to as a pervert who'd seduced an underage girl. Bryn's advances must have made him feel pretty much a pervert himself. How could Sarah be so cold, so mean?

Despair washed over her, sobs gripping her chest, rising through her throat. She stood up and ran to Eli, crying desperately. "Don't let them take me away from you," she begged. "Please, don't let them part us, Eli."

He ran a hand up and down her back, whispering words of reassurance to her ear.

"Actually, Sarah," Max Everley interrupted, "Spencer left a will. Nyx's guardianship is to be passed on to her brother, as her next of kin, and the estate to be shared equally by both. Of course you can contest this, but I assure you I will give you a very hard time. I'm going to make sure Spencer's last wishes are respected."

Sarah stood up, signalling her husband and son to do the same. "Well, you're all wrong. Can't you see he'll soon get tired of it? Eli's just going to play house for a bit, and when he gets sick of it, he'll pack up and leave, like his father did, his mother too. That's what runs in his veins, and he'll ditch Nyx as his parents ditched him, as Erin abandoned her children. Then you'll all come looking for me, begging that I take care of things and fix it all up."

With a furious twirl of her head, she left the room, followed by her husband, who kept dishing apologies to everyone, as he shook hands with the people present. Jamal followed his father's lead, but when he came up to Eli, who extended a hand towards him, instead of taking it in his, the youth swerved a blow at Eli's cheek. The punch was spot on, hitting him across the chin, head careening back on his neck, lip splitting and blood oozing from the cut. Tyronne Powell grabbed hold of his son, while madness ensued, everyone shouting at the same time. Nyx's head wheeled from one side to the other, she wanted to cover her ears with her fingers to keep out the din. Had everyone gone mad? What was going on? Spencer had just died, why didn't they respect this, why didn't they just let her and Eli grieve?

A pair of arms shrugged around her, Pip pulling Nyx to him. "It'll be all right," he whispered, "it'll all be fine in the end."

But Nyx very much doubted it.

***

"She's not going to take Nyx, Eli; I'll see to it. Spencer wanted the two of you to stay together, and his wishes will be met." Max Everley paced the floor of the sitting room, hands gesturing wildly about him, clearly irritated.

Eli lowered his head, nodded. He trusted Max, knew the man would do all he could to make sure Spencer's last wishes were carried. What he didn't trust was Sarah Wilson and her righteousness, her desire to see to it Nyx was properly taken care of. Her heart was in the right place, Eli shouldn't let himself hate her for it; the woman was worried about her niece's wellbeing. But time was running out on them, he'd have to tell Nyx everything soon, and couldn't well do it with Sarah Wilson butting in every second. He couldn't well do it now, either.

Watching his sister, his heart tightened. The girl was distraught, which was no wonder. Spencer had been the last remnants of family Nyx had. Eli was the newcomer, and they hadn't known each other for long – despite the instant connection and the love Eli couldn't deny feeling for her. Spencer had seen her grow; he'd been there from the start, as much a father as Nyx's real dad. His head reeled with the weight of what he'd caused her.

If anyone was to blame for Nyx's loss, it was Eli, and he'd need to come clean; he'd need to tell her so she could make a choice. If all else failed, he'd have to grovel to Jacintha, have her open a portal to Ephemera for him. And risk losing her. Not that he wasn't bound to, Eli realised. Any time now, she might wake up in her other body, her real life, that of Hyiacinth Dellacqua, the girl who'd tried to help him win the heart of her sister.

He turned his eyes to Jace, gut coiling with the prospect. But what was he to do, what choice did he have? He'd already caused Spencer's death, couldn't allow Ora or Serge to lose their lives for him. Couldn't allow Erin to come and drag Nyx to a destiny as bleak as hers. There was really nothing else to do, Eli must find a way to cross back to Mythos, and maybe if he could find his real father, there'd be hope to put a stop to all this. Maybe he could keep Nyx and Jace safe, if he gave himself up. It would atone for Ora's predicament, Spencer's death. It would ensure Hyia had at least a chance of coming back. For the moment Eli entered Ephemera, he knew he'd lose Jacintha for good; he knew he'd never return. Sarah Wilson could have Nyx, then. He'd see the girl understood it was their only chance. He'd see to it the people of Weaversmoor were safe and Erin took her Hounds elsewhere, in her search of him. Surely they'd know, in Chymera, that a portal had been breached, surely they'd know someone had crossed over, entered their world from another.

Of course.

The breach.

Nyx had played around and weaved a thread, she'd opened a breach.

Chymera had sensed it, and sent their Nigrum, their Hounds, to hunt down the trespassers. That's why Erin had come after Ora and Serge; they'd known it was her print. Erin must have assumed it was Eli, the son she bore Fionn Sylvannar, the one most likely to have the power to return to Mythos, the one she'd crossed over to find. Maybe Erin thought he'd weaved his way back to this world, leaving Ephemera for good. That was why she'd gone to Daylesford straight away, she'd thought him there.

And now she had Ora to torture into giving her his whereabouts, so Erin could come after Eli. He doubted Fionn would allow her this. The man held such high standing in Chymeran government, how could he condone this? Unless he had no idea. The only solution was to go back, really. Eli must cross over, the sooner the better. And the only way to make sure the Hounds were none the wiser as to who opened the breach, was to assure it was Nyx who did it. She'd carry her mother's print as much as he, and Erin already knew Eli could weave pathways to Mythos. No one would think of Nyx, or Jacintha; the two would be safe.

But he must make sure. Someone must be told, warned Weaversmoor might be in danger. Someone who'd listen to him. Someone he could trust.

Eli's eyes fell upon Bryn Everley, who, sensing the weight of his stare, turned to face him. It was as if she already knew. The bright green of her pupils dimmed. Distress and a deep ache danced inside her eyes. But Bryn would do as he asked; she'd believe. Her mother would, at least, and he'd beg the girl to tell Cressida.

Mind made up, his attention returned to Max, who was saying his goodbyes. He'd also look after Nyx. When everything was said and done, Eli wouldn't be abandoning his sister to a dire faith, he wouldn't betray her like he had Spencer. Grabbing the hand the man reached out to him, Eli shook it, pulled him in for a brief hug. Max looked shocked, but grateful at the same time. Both men smiled awkwardly at each other, let go, the lawyer turning to shake hands with Jacintha. Bryn approached him next, bringing a blush to Eli's cheeks. He couldn't help being awkwardly aware of what had happened between them, that night. It felt like a thousand years ago, and yet, it was so vivid in his memory it could've taken place just the previous evening. He could still scent her perfume in the air, feel the touch of Bryn's naked skin under his fingertips, and was painfully aware of what a disappointment he must have been. He was also very much aware this girl, eight years his junior, had provided him with his first clumsy attempts at sex.

Arms wrapped around his torso, she pulled Eli into a hug. He tensed up, knowing he must speak to her urgently. But he must wait for night to fall and everyone was asleep, before even venturing out to meet her. If she agreed to it, that was.

"I need to talk to you alone," he whispered. "Do you mind meeting in the woods later tonight? I'll text you."

Bryn eyed him suspiciously, but nodded. "Is it about your uncle? Did you do something to him?"

Eli blushed, turned his face away. Could she read him this easily, was he no more than an open book to her? Not even Jacintha was as well attuned to his moods, why should this girl be? Why should she make him feel as if he was safe with her, no matter what he did or said; no matter how afraid he was? Why must she appease him so? Curling his fists, he shut his eyes for a second, collected his thoughts, took a deep breath.

"Will you come?" he insisted.

"Yes." She then moved on to say her goodbyes to Jacintha and Nyx.

"Pip, want us to drop you off at the Academy?" Max asked.

Eli's eyes converged on the boy, who also looked at him. If everyone left, he'd be alone with Nyx and could tell her everything. But the girl needed a respite, she needed a break, a rest from all this. He couldn't add to the stress she was under, not yet. He couldn't put himself through it, either; the thought alone made him want to throw up, curl up and sleep. They both needed time, which Eli knew they didn't have. Surely one night wouldn't hurt. He couldn't yet bring himself to do all that was needed of him, not before he made sure Bryn would be up to the task Eli was about to set on her. Preparations had to be made, of course, but his brain wasn't functioning properly, his entire body refused to work conveniently. Listless, weak, tearful, he was; haunted by the look in Spencer's eyes as he fell down on his knees to die. And Eli had put him on his knees. Eli had been responsible for him dying. He must find a way to deal with this, before setting out to tell Nyx the danger they were under.

"Do you mind staying? I'll drive you back later, if you want to," he said, eyes still on Pip.

The boy nodded, returned to the sofa, and sat next to Nyx. Max and Bryn exited the room, Eli following to let them out. Nodding again at Bryn to make sure she didn't forget his request, he shut the door and returned to the living room, where he was met by the sight of Jacintha grabbing her handbag, as if about to leave. A flare of panic rose through Eli's chest.

"Must you also go?"

She nodded, a brief smile gracing her lips. "I just don't want to give Sarah Wilson any more ammo against you, Eli."

"Screw her," he barked, did a double take as he looked at Nyx. Sarah was her aunt after all, her father's sister, she was also her family. "I'm sorry."

"No, you're absolutely right. I can't believe she threw this on you, on us, so soon after Spencer… it's as if she doesn't even care how we feel."

Eli hung his head down. "It's all my fault," he whispered. "I killed Spencer. He died because of me."

The silence was terrifying.

Eli's hands shook, he curled them into fists. Jacintha's fingers alighted over the nape of his neck, rubbed it gently. A sob fled his lips, a tremor shook his shoulders, the memory of Spencer clawing at his chest, face contorted in pain, like a hammer pounding into him.

"Shut up," Nyx begged, anger seeping through her voice.

He faced her, tears ready to fall again. Would he ever do anything other than cry? "It's true, Nyx. I as good as killed him, just ask Pip."

The boy blushed, shook his head.

"I simply stood there, doing nothing; if I'd acted he might have lived. If I'd called 999 sooner, Spencer might still be alive, but I froze. See, Sarah isn't wrong when she says I'm not fit to care for you, I'm useless."

"Eli, you need to stop this." Nyx's voice had become very cold; suddenly she didn't sound like a teenager anymore, she was an adult. She was an adult and in control of everything. "I seriously can't deal with you breaking down on top of everything. You froze, fine, anyone would. Anyone in your situation and with your past would. I'm just glad Pip was here to help you. But I need you to stop blaming yourself and saying these things. Or Sarah will use them to tear us apart, and I simply can't have it. I won't lose you, you hear? I will *never* lose you; you're all that's left me."

"Don't you get it? It's my fault he died!"

"No it isn't, it's *his*." Tears ran down Nyx's face. "Spencer shouldn't have kept his condition from us; he should have consulted a specialist, taken better care of himself. It was his irresponsibility and stubbornness that killed him, Eli, not you. So stop blaming yourself."

"I'm sorry," Eli wept, pushing away Jacintha, who tried to take him in her arms. "I need some air." Running out of the room, he dashed to the kitchen, threw the door wide.

Once outside, he breathed of the cold air of late autumn, eyes searching the back garden, the sight sending jolt after jolt of pain through his heart. Evidence of Spencer was everywhere, his mark upon everything, his memory vivid and clinging to the place like a vengeful spirit.

"I'm sorry," Eli whispered to the darkening skies. "I'm so sorry. I didn't mean for you to die, I don't know what I did, it wasn't really me. I'm so sorry, Spence, I'd do anything to have you back." Tears ran down his cheeks, a sob shook his shoulders. "I'd do anything to have you back, Spencer."

Collecting himself, Eli wiped his eyes, glanced around once more, attention falling on the array of potted herbs his uncle had kept. His homemade remedies, that had failed to save his life. But would he have died, if Eli hadn't pushed him too far? Would Max eventually have managed to convince him he must see a specialist? Would he have lived, if Eli had controlled himself? Those were questions he'd never have answered, and the doubt would always haunt him. He must make Spencer's death count for something, and he must make amends.

But for now, he had to pretend. He had to go back inside and go on as if he didn't plan to leave, as if he didn't mean to sacrifice himself for the sake of his sister, his girlfriend, the people in that village who he didn't even know and meant nothing to him. Or shouldn't. Truth was, they did, and he refused to put anyone else in danger because he was wanted for crimes that weren't his. Maybe he hadn't done what he was accused of in Ephemera, but he was responsible for Spencer's death in this world.

And for that, he must pay.

V

Jacintha stood up, tired of the countless hours sitting on that armchair. She wasn't one to simply stand around doing nothing; it drove her mad being this useless, this purposeless. But Sarah Wilson had taken the funeral into her hands, Eli clearly not up to the task, and it was too soon for him to clear his uncle's room. It would only bring him more despair. His guilt worried her. How were they to know if the outcome would have been any different had Eli been better prepared for his uncle's weak heart? It wasn't as if he'd done it on purpose, Eli was like a child in most things, having been locked in his own head for so long, outside the world. There was so much he still needed to catch up to. Unlucky, it was; that he and Spencer had been alone, although Pip Thomson's arrival had been a godsend. But not even the paramedics had been able to save Spencer Vaughn; from where she stood, the man had been condemned all along.

"Do you mind if I go into the kitchen prepare something for us to eat?" Jacintha asked, her eyes on the mantle clock striking eight. How long had they sat like this, in the dark?

"I'm not hungry," Nyx replied.

"You need to eat something, can't go round on an empty stomach. Your aunt will have a field day if I let you get sick," Eli barked from where he sat.

Jacintha could barely make out his eyes, but the thickness in his voice told her he was far from being well, and far from being on the mend. Despite Eli not having known Spencer for long, it had been clear the two shared a strong bond, and he missed his uncle as much as Nyx did.

"I'll eat if you eat," the girl said, and Jacintha couldn't help grinning. She was a smart one, all right.

Reaching for the light switch, she turned on the chandelier, the room brightening instantly. Eli squinted, Pip and Nyx looked relieved. A dark shadow seemed to have been banished, just by lighting the room. Before anyone could stop her, Jacintha pulled the thick curtains shut, keeping the world outside, intent on building them a cocoon. She then piled a few logs on the fireplace, lit them, the scent of wood burning giving the room an immediate sense of comfort.

"How about I make us some cheese toasts and a tisane, huh?"

"I'll help you." Eli pulled his frame from the chair and walked off to the kitchen, dragging his feet.

Moving seemed to pain him, he couldn't even breathe. This amount of grief worried her, and Jacintha found herself resenting Sarah Wilson for having disrupted Eli and Nyx's already fragile frame of mind with her talk of taking over the girl's guardianship. Eli was clearly troubled by it, as was Nyx, but Jacintha sensed there was more. He was worried; he was scared, but putting on a brave face - a martyr on his way to sacrifice. Maybe he'd come to the conclusion Sarah was right, and Nyx would be better off with her. Maybe he was bracing himself to let go of his sister, move on with his life elsewhere. Away from Weaversmoor, and consequently Jacintha.

For Nyx's sake? Well, he was wrong, and she'd let him know. Eli was as capable of providing a stable environment as Sarah and her family. And he clearly needed his sister; he needed the grounding she gave him, the responsibility, the reason to stay here. Had he not been happy, so far? Was he not in a good place, was he not part of a family?

Despite Spencer's death, he couldn't just quit; Eli owed it to his uncle, Nyx, himself. He mustn't quit. If only he'd talk to her. He was so private, where it came to his emotions, always bottling things up. How long had it taken him to finally kiss her and be honest about his feelings? She must make sure he shared his pain with her. Maybe then he'd not see things as bleakly as he now did.

Following him into the kitchen, Jacintha took the loaf of bread from Eli's hands, set it on the counter and wrapped her arms around him.

"Do you have any idea how I feel for you?" she said, and his body tensed up under her hands.

As if it vexed him, distressed him. As if he found himself unworthy of it.

"Eli, look at me."

He didn't try to hide, staring straight into Jacintha's eyes. There were clouds and storms gathering on his, threatening to break into clapping thunder. He looked ready to burst, and if Eli broke, no one would be able to pull him back together. She could see it in his eyes and feel it in the tense, taut lay of every muscle, every nerve. He didn't need her to push him into speaking of his hurt; what he needed was some peace and quiet, some silence - a respite from everything. He needed the comfort of a soft bed, a dark room, a soothing hand.

"I swear it'll be all right. It'll pass, you'll be happy again," Jacintha whispered.

Eli nodded, kissed the top of her head. "I know. I'm just exhausted." With clipped gestures, he disentangled himself from her grasp, set about cutting the bread into slices.

Jacintha filled the kettle, plugged it in, searched around the fridge for cheese and some non-existing ham. There was bacon, though, so she pulled it out, and got working on the sandwiches. Soon, the kitchen filled with the mouth-watering scent of oozing cheese and crisp bacon, hiding the odour of the burnt food on the stove, where Spencer had been cooking lunch for him and Eli when he suffered the heart attack. She should get rid of it, scrape the contents of the pan to the trash; wash it so there was no evidence of that food left.

Clearing away the reminder of the moment he'd collapsed, never to return again.

Eli beat her to it, leaving Jacintha to prepare the tea and pile the sandwiches on a plate. She was nearly done, when the sound of sobs brought her to a halt. Putting down the tray, she turned to where Eli stood, shoulders shaking, both hands clasping the sides of the stove, the pan in front of him. It reeked, and filled the kitchen with its sour, acrid stench.

It reeked of death, standing as a reminder of what was once familiar and taken for granted, the keepsake Eli must get rid of before Nyx happened upon it. The memento he dreaded most, surely, and she shouldn't have let him touch it; she shouldn't have let him deal with this. No one could expect him to be made of stone. Rushing over, Jacintha took Eli back in her arms, shushed him, hands running along his back in a gentle, comforting dance.

"I can't deal with this," he sobbed into her shoulder. "I want to step up, be a man, Nyx needs someone to be strong, so she can grieve, but I can't. I look around and expect to see him grinning, calling me over to watch something stupid thing on the telly, or to listen to those silly songs he liked. I look around and all I see is him. His presence lingers everywhere, but then he's nowhere. Spencer's not here and I miss him, and I shouldn't have gotten mad at him; he died thinking I didn't care. But it's not true, I did; I loved him and

I miss him like hell. He was strong and selfless, and he was always here. Now there's a void, and nothing, no one will ever fill it. There's a void and I can't come close to taking his place, because I *can't* take his place, can I? I'm not half the man Spencer was."

Jacintha kissed his wet cheeks, in search of his lips. Eli surrendered, they lingered on with mouths locked together, the kiss as soothing to her as it was to him. Finally, his tears subsided. They stared at each other for what felt like a long time, Jacintha taking note of the dark blue specks in Eli's eyes, the slivers of silver-grey, the secretive, terrified look at the back. She wished she could heal him, assuage his pain, but this was something only Eli could do for himself. This was something he must go through, no matter how much it broke him. And he should be going through it with Nyx, not her. Maybe Jace should pick Pip and drive the boy back to the Academy, get herself home, leave the siblings together to nurse their wounds.

"Listen, maybe Pip and I should go. You and Nyx could do with..."

Eli hugged her back. "No. Please, stay. I can't deal, not tonight. She needs Pip, too; he'll do her good. Come, let's join them and eat."

He sounded less unsettled, which served to lift her mood just a tad. Running ahead of Eli, Jace opened the living room door for him, tray balanced in his hands, a tentative smile rising up his lips. Nyx and Pip were still wrapped around each other on the sofa, but both lifted eager-eyed faces as the older couple entered, attention set on the food, the scent of which oozed into the room, forcing stomachs to rumble. They'd all missed lunch, no wonder they were starved.

When Eli placed the tray down on the coffee table, the teenagers attacked the hot sandwiches, relief washing over Jacintha. They'd be all right, Eli and Nyx. It might take them a while to pull themselves back together and heal the wound left by Spencer's death, but they'd grieve and come back the stronger for it, more united, too. And that was just what they needed, to be even closer, tighter, bonded. They needed to become a family on their own, so that no one could step in.

The door to Spencer's room stood ajar, beckoning from the left of the hallway, closer to Eli's room than Nyx's. She wouldn't even need to walk past it, if she didn't want to. But it would still be there, glaring at her, beckoning, reminding her it now stood empty, and always would. That room, where Spence had found happiness again, acceptance from his dead mother, a purpose, a will, would now stand like a gaping wound, bleeding into her, into the entire house, screaming his absence. Bleeding Nyx of joy, of peace.

If Eli didn't pull himself together soon, she was going to lose it. Because, want it or not, he was the adult, here, and needed to step up. She was just a kid, how did he expect her to deal with all this and his moping around, blaming himself for everything? How could he demand she put on a brave face when he was breaking apart? After everything he'd told her? After everything they now knew about themselves? After what he'd hinted at and the horror stories her mind had made up, of those things across the breach, the creatures in that world, the birds staring them down, as if they were watching, waiting, abiding?

Eli needed to pull it together. And so did she. But how was Nyx to live without the last remnants of normality she'd had? How was she to go on without the last parental figure she'd known? What if Sarah was right and Eli just wasn't up to it? Shaking her head, she pushed the thoughts of impending doom back, drove them out of her mind. Turning slightly, her eyes met Pip's. Although he smiled, there was worry on his face, showcased in the way he bit his lower lip. Of course he was uncomfortable with this. Of course he must feel awkward.

But Eli had practically begged him to spend the night, Miss Tate driving further the request. Oh, Eli had *not* been well; at all. And Nyx owed him this much - that he got his melt down today, tonight; that he shut himself in his room and hid from the world. As long as he stepped up next morning and did his part. For she was not going to lose him, and she was not letting him out of her sight, she was not letting Eli leave her behind. No more losses, she could deal with no more pain. Her entire body felt bruised and raw, as if she'd been repeatedly hit with a stick, or fallen down a long flight of stairs. If her brother needed the palliative of Jacintha Tate's company in his bed, so did Nyx have need of Pip. Eli had clearly understood as much. Spencer would never have allowed the boy to stay overnight, both alone and unattended. But Spencer was gone, and it was his absence that sprouted their need.

"Come on in," Nyx invited, opening the door to her bedroom.

Pip slithered in, the girl following, casting one final look at her uncle's room. Eli's door was closed, and no sound came from within. He and Miss Tate must surely be asleep, Nyx had seen to it she gave them plenty of time to have the upper floor for themselves, she and Pip had ended up falling asleep on the sofa. But now she needed her bed, the solace of her bedroom, the comfort of her boyfriend lying next to her. So she locked the door behind them, turned on the small bedside lamp, pulled the curtains shut, attention lingering on the treetops at a distance, achingly aware of what hid in those woods. For a split second, she wished she could go to that other world, lose herself there. At least until the pain was gone and she could face living in this house again, without constantly being assaulted by memories of her uncle, able to accept Spencer was never coming back. But running away was not an option.

She sat on the bed, tapped her hand over the duvet, a request for Pip to join her. He smiled awkwardly, head cocked to the side, a blush covering his cheeks. That smile was like water cooling her fevered skin, a breeze on a blazing hot day, food for the starving, the kindle that set her guts on fire and made her want him more and more. Some days, she found herself missing Trystan: the way he held her hand, the look in his eyes when they were together, the sound of his voice in her ear. Some days, she wished he hadn't left; and this was one of those days. But at the same time, Nyx was unwilling to let go of Pip, and if she were to be honest, although her attraction for Trystan was still as immense as it had been since they'd first met, her feelings for him were a fraction of what she experienced with Pip. If the world were any different, she'd love them both freely. If the world were any different, she'd share her heart with both, and knew Pip would do the same. If the world were any kinder, less judgemental, no one would care that they went around the three of them; no one would bat an eyelid they loved each other, all three of them; no one would even notice they weren't a pair but a trio. Only, the world wasn't any kinder or any different, and she wasn't prepared to face its prejudice.

Suffice it she had Pip, for now, and that she was enough for him. The future was unimportant, she couldn't look into it, didn't care what it might bring. Any given moment, she could lose it all - people being taken away from her, the rug pulled from under her feet. There was no safety net anymore, and there never had been, but Nyx had refused to see it. Life insisted on teaching her one single lesson, that she kept failing to learn. Nothing was granted, nor did it last forever. There were no certainties but death, and when she least expected, those she loved most would be taken away, until she either learnt never to open her heart again or throw herself into love as if life was about to end. Because it was. Every single moment, life was about to end, and she might as well live it like that. Extending one hand, she gestured Pip to join her; the boy reaching out to curl his fingers through hers.

Sitting beside her, he pushed the coiling locks of hair from her neck, claimed her mouth, the kiss long, soft yet fiery, a study in seduction and arousal. Oh, he knew how to do it; he knew well how to set Nyx on fire, and although he'd never pushed her further than this - the kisses and soft caresses they exchanged - he didn't shy from losing himself in her, and making sure Nyx nearly lost her head to him. Well, tonight he wouldn't be pulling away, dropping her off home or stopping their antics before it was too late. Why, he could be walking down the street next day and be hit by a car. She could fall down the stairs and break her neck. Her brother could crash his bike, her aunt could drown in the pool, her entire family could be wiped off the face of the earth, she could lose everything.

Tomorrow she could lose everything, including her life, but this was now, this was what they had and they must make it count. They had this moment together, which would never repeat, and they owed it to themselves, the universe, to make the most of it.

Nyx reached for the tie Pip still wore, his uniform as dishevelled as hers, the blazer discarded on a chair downstairs, along with his parka, which hung from the hallway coat-hanger, next to hers. Loosening the knot, she tried to pull it out, Pip lent a hand. It landed on the floor, instead of the trunk at the feet of her bed. An unexpected laugh peeled from her lips, hushed and warm in the silence, which served to embolden her. Unbuttoning the uniform shirt, Nyx pulled it off, dropped it on the floor, arms breaking out in goosebumps now she had only a thin cotton camisole over her bra. Pip's eyes widened, blushing again, the telltale sign attesting to how uncomfortable he was. Which was belied by the sudden spark in his eyes, the rush of want Nyx captured there. She reached for his shirt, fighting with the buttons to set them loose. His hand coiled over hers, forcing Nyx to stop.

"We shouldn't," he said. "Your brother's just there."

Nyx smiled, despite the tears pooling in her eyes. "Eli's asleep. And he's not stupid, Pip, he knows what's bound to happen. He knew it would, the moment he asked you stay over, and that means he's fine with it. *I'm* fine with it."

"You're not yourself tonight, Nyx. You just lost your uncle, you're in pain."

"Then help me soothe this ache."

Another shake of his head, this time Pip lowering his eyes to avoid facing her. "It doesn't work like that."

Nyx cupped his chin, forced his head up so he must look at her. "You don't want me?"

Pulling her back into his embrace, Pip drowned his face in her hair. "I want you more than anything; I just don't think it's the right time for this. You're so vulnerable, Nyx, I don't want to..."

She pushed him away. "You can be taken from me tomorrow, like Spence was. I can die any minute, like he did. When's it going to be the right time, Pip? It's now, the right time is now, *this* is all we have. This moment, the present, and we get to live in it. There's no point aiming for the future, leaving things undone, unsaid, because there'll be time. There won't. The only time is now."

They stared into each other's eyes for long, Pip's hard and intent, stubbornly sticking to his guns, Nyx inflamed and urging, leaving no doubt as to what she demanded of him. What she would have from Pip. He blinked once, twice, lips twitching in the longing for a kiss, she knew he was about to cave in. She knew him well, all his tiny, little tells, the expression on his face, the look in his eye, she knew how to read and interpret his every whim.

Saw him battle himself, a raging war between his wants, his passion, and the will to live up to what he believed her brother expected of him. Saw the fight ensue for a long moment, and saw the losing side retreat, the blue in his pupils darkening with desire, the longing to be together as one with Nyx. She smiled - a slow, small curl of her lips - and dove in for a kiss. Her fingers fumbled with the buttons on his shirt. Pip broke apart from her only to take it off, his own hands searching for the zipper on her skirt, the waistband of her tights, the clasp of her bra.

They fell back on the bed, limbs entwined and bodies glued together with the sort of hunger that wouldn't take long to appease. Soon, they were left panting, holding each other's naked bodies under the duvet, eyes locked, lips gifting soft pecks upon silky skin - and Nyx felt all the better for it. She felt sated and complete, comforted of her pain, she felt something akin to relief. It may be wrong, it may be immature of her, trying to cover up the hole in her heart with this, but at least for a while the pain was gone, and the world didn't look half as bleak, and she didn't feel half as alone. For a brief moment she dared hope it would all be fine, one day, and she'd heal, and the world was not a terrible, terrible place that kept taking from her, that kept punching and fisting and stomping all over her. For the time of a heartbeat, Nyx felt whole again, and that was a relief.

Laying her head over Pip's chest, she kissed the tattoo he'd gotten the first time they'd met. The cross, the one he'd tattooed for her, the first to have tied them to each other. One of her hands darted to his arm, caressed the length of it until it came to his elbow, where the feather that stood for her Craft was imprisoned in the spider's web that stood for his. Had he locked her to him, or he to her, she wondered? Did this feather allow him to tap into her powers, could he unlock the access to that other world where Eli had lived, could he open up a breach just as she? It'd be dangerous, Pip knew nothing of it, he had no idea what it meant to be a Weaver. She should have told him, already. Had tried to, the night they'd first kissed, but courage had fled her and Nyx ended up changing the subject before she came clean. Well, now was as good a time as any.

"Remember when I asked you what you knew about being a Weaver?"

He nodded. "I got the clear impression you were keeping something from me."

"I was. Because part of it wasn't my story to tell. It wasn't entirely my secret."

"Eli."

Nyx pushed herself on both elbows, searching his eyes. "Yes. You know we're both Weavers. And I told you our Craft isn't really that of tapping into other Crafts and being able to perform all sorts of magic half-heartedly. We *do* weave threads, like I said. Threads that form pathways, roads, portals."

"That lead where? Are you telling me you can weave yourself from here to, let's say, China?"

She cocked her head, pondered on it. "Perhaps. But I'm sure it's been seen to, there must be wards or locks that keep Weavers out of doing that kind of thing."

"Then where do those paths lead? You're hardly making sense, Nyx."

"Another world."

Pip let out a woof of amusement, but stopped before it turned into laughter, the seriousness in her eyes telling him she meant every word. "Get out."

"It's true, I've seen it myself. I went into those woods with Eli, when he told me of it, and I opened a doorway into his father's world."

"His father's...? What are you saying?"

"You've been around Mrs Everley often, haven't you? Did she ever sound funny? Like she was talking nonsense? She was the first to hint at this other world, the night Trystan took me there for dinner. It was just the three of us, and she kept on about my mother, Eli, his father. That my mother had brought a creature from another world into ours, and that creature was Eli's father."

Pip nodded. "She sometimes spoke a lot of nonsense, but I thought it was the wine. You mean this is real?"

"He spent seven years living there, Pip."

"Who did?"

"Eli! When he was in a coma, he weaved himself there, and lived an entirely different life. But that's unimportant, now. You had that feather tattooed into you, what if it allows you to access my powers, or the powers of any Weaver near you? What if it permits you to tap into my Craft? You could unwittingly open a breach and place everyone in danger, yourself included. That's why I'm telling you all this."

He shook his head, clearly doubtful of the veracity of her words. "This is mental, Nyx, it's... unreal."

"It's the truth. Eli told me they can sense when we Weave a thread that opens a portal there. And they can hone in on us, so they can find us and take us to their world."

"Why would they want to? Who are *they*?"

"The creatures from that world. Because we feed their immortality."

"This is insane."

"Pip, you must believe me. You can never let yourself Weave a thread in those woods, you promise me?"

He nodded, but Nyx saw the same look in his eyes that assured her he wasn't quite sold on what she said, wasn't yet convinced this was real. She couldn't prove it, not now, not like this. But they could go to the woods during daytime, and she could show him the birds and try to charm them, as Eli had said. Maybe then Pip would believe.

"I'll be careful. But you have to convene this is surreal, Nyx. Still, Mrs Everley did say some weird stuff, when she drank more than her fill. I thought they were drunken ramblings, but given what you just told me, well, some of her outlandish stories seem to tie in. And your brother lived there for seven years? No wonder he has such a hard time with technology and adjusting to this world. Was it all very different? What was it like? What did he do there?"

Nyx lay back on his chest. "I don't know, he hasn't told me much. He was going to, said he'd sit me and Spencer down and tell us the whole thing, but…"

Tears choked her voice, Nyx blinked. She found she couldn't speak, the blade that had momentarily been pulled out of her chest back there again, this time with a vengeance. The pain seemed to have doubled, the despair of knowing her uncle was forever lost to her having trebled. Pip caressed her hair, and Nyx gave herself to the comfort of his touch, willing it to be enough to at least lull her into sleep. Come morning, Pip would have to leave, he'd have to go back to the Academy and attend classes, go on as if nothing had happened. She'd stay back, withheld from school for the time being, mourning her loss as society deemed she must, when all she wanted was a distraction, something that numbed away all this pain.

Closing her eyes, she wondered how Eli was coping. He was the adult, so that meant he'd have to put on a brave face the moment a new day was born. He'd have to bite the bullet and push down his own ache, pretend he wasn't in pain. It suddenly hit her they were in fact alone, for no one else understood what it was they'd lost. They were alone in this, but together, aware they had only each other to hold on to, to help them push through, move on. If anything, Spencer's death had served to bring them closer together.

WITCH CRAFT

VI

Eli watched the rise and fall of Jacintha's back as she lay sprawled, stomach down on the bed. Her hair fell over one shoulder and the grey pillowcase, her face looked serene, rested, and his heart turned cartwheels at the sight. His heart, which was soon caught inside a fist of iron, aching and throbbing with the pain of letting go. She may be at risk elsewhere, and he the only one who could help. She may be perfectly safe, here, away from the dangers of the world that had seen them grow. What would not make her safe was his presence. Just like Nyx, Jacintha would be better off without him. Reassuring himself she was fast asleep, Eli slid off the bed and grabbed his clothes, mobile shoved into the pocket of his leather jacket.

Out in the darkened hallway, his eyes were pulled towards his sister's room, whose door was closed shut. Only silence reached from within, he figured both she and Pip would be sleeping. Trying to keep it out of his mind, he moved to Spencer's room to get dressed. There was no point letting himself become upset at Nyx having a boy sleep over, it was Eli who'd asked Pip to stay. Sarah would have a blast, were she to find out, but soon she'd get her wish - Nyx would come to live with her, and Eli would have left his sister's life for good.

At least, she'd have a life.

Breaching the doorway, he stepped into Spencer's room, wondering how many times had he been inside, in the few weeks they'd shared house. How many times had he sat in that armchair, talking to his uncle, listening to him, Nyx hovering at the door? How many times had they lingered here, going through mementos of Spencer's youth, him showing his nephew tokens of the family he'd never known? It hadn't been enough; he wished he'd had more, the fact he didn't being no one's fault but his. Shaking his head to clear his thoughts, Eli pulled on his trousers, his socks, the boots. Sliding into the warm grey jersey, his fingers typed a hurried text for Bryn to meet him in the woods. Jacket hanging from one arm, he silently left the room, taking the stairs with doubled attention to avoid the creaking step halfway through. Then he left the house via the kitchen and ran to where the forest met the Everley estate, straight for the clearing he'd come across one night, where he'd found a girl doing her Earthen rituals by the light of flickering candles, a girl who'd given herself to him so freely he still reeled from the memory.

Bryn was there, huffing and puffing, walking around in a tight, small circle. A grimace took over her face at the sight of Eli. There was so much raw emotion in her eyes, such longing spread all over her countenance, he found himself shaken by it. Resolve failed him, as did his certainties that Jacintha was the one, *his* one. If that were true, why was he always so moved by this girl? Was it her youth, her brazenness, her open admittance of how much she wanted him? Eli had never come across someone like Bryn Everley, who he could make no sense of except for the fact he wanted her too, maybe as much as she wanted him. But there was nothing emotional about such want, this was all physical, lust and desire. Not what he experienced for Jacintha, not what he'd felt for Stella.

WITCH CRAFT

This was raw and bleeding and new, and Eli had no idea how to deal with it. He tried to pull himself together.

"Took you long enough," Bryn said. "Don't want to leave dad alone, although Trystan's staying with him. But my brother's difficult, and I should be there. What is it you want from me?"

They locked eyes, Eli's skin breaking out in goosebumps. How was he going to tell her? "I'm sorry your father's going through this," he said, voice shaking. Bryn peered into his eyes, a wave of fear crossing hers. "I need a favour, Bryn. You must promise you'll see to this."

"It couldn't wait? Spencer just passed away and you want to ask me a favour? I don't understand you at all."

Shoulders slumping, he turned away, the prick of tears stabbing the inner corners of his eyes and forcing him to heave. "I miss him," he whispered. "It's my fault your father's grieving, my sister's heartbroken, it's my entire fault." Facing her again, Eli searched her eyes; saw the doubt inside them, the suspicion. "I killed him, and now must make amends. You understand this, don't you?"

She took a step forward, placed a hand on the arms he'd crossed over his chest. "Eli, you're scaring me. What on earth are you talking about?"

"I can put a stop to what's coming, but not on my own, Bryn, I need your help," he whispered. "Spencer's death cannot have been in vain. See, I didn't mean to hurt him, only wanted him to realise I couldn't do what he wanted, but it was like I couldn't control what took over me. It was as if I wasn't even there any longer, inside my own mind. I wasn't myself anymore, only a red hot fury that took his life. *I* took his life."

Bryn's eyes widened, her mouth slightly ajar in confusion. "No, dad said he had a heart condition, Eli. It was bound to have happened, sooner or later. It's not your fault, stop blaming yourself. You've done nothing wrong."

He shook his head, attention suddenly lost on the bow of her upper lip, quivering in fear. His tongue wet his own lips, parched as they were. He wanted to wipe away that quiver, shake off her fear. Jacintha was sleeping back in the cottage, alone in his bed, and here he was, hours after having caused his uncle's death, staring at a girl's mouth and considering covering it with his, in a kiss he'd do better to stay away from. But this was the last he'd ever see of her, and Eli realised he longed to take with him the memory of a girl who hadn't shied from going after what she wanted, a girl who hadn't been afraid of wanting him. Of taking him whole, the good and the bad.

"I must go away soon. I need you to make sure Nyx and Jacintha are safe. Your father will know what to do, your mother too, I think. Yes, Cressida will understand, she knows far more than the rest of you. But I must go after my father, my mother, they're in danger." Her eyes moved away from his, the girl hiding her face as if she couldn't bear to meet his stare. "Bryn, look at me."

She shook her head, tears sparkling over long lashes. "You sound like a lunatic."

"Bryn, please, I'm begging you. Make sure your parents know the portal has been breached. Tell Cressida Erin's alive but she's no longer the same, she's dangerous now, and can't be let near Nyx, or Jacintha. Tell your father he must make sure the town's borders are protected and can't be entered. Promise me." He grabbed Bryn by the shoulders, shaking her. "You don't need to believe me, just promise you'll do this."

Bryn's head shot up, their eyes meeting. Hers blazed with a fire Eli tried to ignore, it moulded into wonder and doubt, then sudden belief, followed by what looked like relief.

"It's true, then?" she asked, voice like a thin wail of wind. "There's another world out there, where your father came from?" As he nodded, she covered her mouth with weak fingers. "Oh my god. She wasn't going crazy; it wasn't the ravings of a drunkard, was it? Mum was right, she was *always* right. And we're in danger?"

"Only Nyx and Jacintha, because they're Weavers. Bryn, promise me!"

"Eli, don't leave. They need you, you can't leave." She hugged herself to him and Eli was shaken. His arms, sprouting a life of their own, curled around her shoulders, returning the hug, and he closed his eyes, breathing in the particular scent of her hair. "*I* need you," Bryn whispered.

And it unravelled him, undid his mind.

Holding her tighter - this girl who was far too young for him, who made him look as depraved as his own father had been, seducing a fifteen-year-old girl all those years ago; this girl he found himself wanting with too wild a hunger - Eli realised nothing was simple, where his feelings were concerned. Hands tangling with her messy hair, he pulled her away from his chest, Bryn's face covered in tears, her mouth twisted in an ugly wince of pain as she wept.

"Don't go," she begged again, and his heart broke a little more.

Down came his mouth, as hers reached up, and their lips met halfway, salty tears mixed with the taste of her lip balm, the mint drops Bryn liked to munch on. He kissed her as if their lives depended on it, aware of how wrong, how twisted this was, he a twenty-six-year-old man, she just eighteen, a girl nearly as young as his sister. But nothing felt right anymore, not since he'd remembered his former life in a world that shouldn't exist, his safety threatened by a mother who'd been lost for coming to his rescue, his uncle dead at his own hands. Nothing felt right but the fact he must make amends, and if he was to lose himself in Ephemera, he would take this with him. He would take this memory with him, Bryn Everley and her green eyes, her warm kiss. As hungered as his, as urgent too, leaving both with raw lips in the aftermath, as they came loose from the embrace.

"This is all sorts of wrong," Eli whispered, bent down to kiss her once more.

"You want me, I want you, how can it be wrong? We can make it, Eli, just trust that we can."

pushing her away, he curled his fists, suddenly angered. "There's no '*we*', Bryn. You have a boyfriend who's already got it in for me, as his actions at the hospital showed. And I've left my girlfriend asleep in my bed, what am I doing here, kissing a girl my sister's age? It's twisted and ugly and wrong, and I don't want to be this man."

"What man?" she shouted. "The coward who's too scared to admit to what he really feels? Jamal's not my boyfriend anymore, we broke up. There's nothing wrong with what I'm doing, Eli, because I *care* for you," Bryn whispered, one hand reaching out for his, which he surrendered. "I care so much for you. And I know you want me just the same. We can work this out, whichever way you want, just please, don't leave."

"I have to, I'm the one Erin wants, I need to see she comes after me. Bryn, I'm begging you. Will you give your parents my message; tell them Erin crossed to search for me while I was there? They caught her, and changed her, now she's dangerous and may come after me, if I don't give myself up first. Will you tell them this? If you care for me..."

"Yes, yes, I'll do it," she cut in, face twisted into a grimace of ache, tears back in her eyes. "I'll make sure mum and dad hear of this, and that both Nyx and Miss Tate are safe. I'll do whatever you want."

"Thank you," he whispered, relieved. "I'll never forget this. But now you need to go, and I have to get back home."

"I'll never forget *you*. And I'll never stop wanting you, Eli Vaughn. I'll never give up, even though you say this is goodbye."

His heart lurched at the feel of Bryn's body glued to his, the hidden meaning in her words. All thought fled him; there was only gratitude and the touch of her, her deliverance, her rendition. Reaching for her lips, Eli covered them with his mouth again, one hand cupping her cheek, thumb caressing the soft, soft skin. Despite the wrongness of it all, this was the one thing that actually felt right, having her in his arms, locked in this kiss. Bryn responded with the same eager urgency, tongue dancing around his, hands fisting the short-cropped curls on his head. It was over before they even had time to think, Bryn stepping away from Eli, fingers still locked with his as she walked away, knowing she must leave.

"I love you," she whispered, then turned around and fled.

Eli stood rooted to the ground, eyes following her departure, heart stomping wildly as his whole body shook.

I love you, she'd said, and the words echoed in his head, round his mind, through his brain. No one had ever whispered such words to him. No one had ever cared this much for him. But what did she know? Bryn was a child, an eighteen-year-old girl caught by hormones and the emotions riding her body. She was lured by the mystery of him, the fact Eli was older and out of her reach, the forbidding nature of their impossible relationship.

It wasn't love; it was a teenager's wet dream.

Shrugging, he wiped one final stubborn tear, headed back home, knowing he'd soon have to let go of everything that now seemed to warm his heart and his very life.

For he had a debt to pay, and amends to make.

Eli woke up with the onset of a headache pounding against his skull. He turned over in bed, shielding his eyes from the glare of the early morning sun drifting through the gap in the curtains. They'd been hastily closed, him being far more pressed with getting

Jacintha out of her clothes and into his bed. Only to find himself snogging Bryn Everley hours later.

One hand alighting over the soft skin of her back, he caressed it gently, fingertips poised to feel the smooth rise and fall of her breathing. The gaping wound in his chest was still there, it hadn't changed, hadn't moved, hadn't even lessened. Thoughts ran around his fevered brain in confusion, enhancing the headache. From Spencer dying thinking his nephew hated him to Sarah Wilson's threats of taking Nyx away from him, from Ora being held prisoner and tortured in Chymera and Serge hiding away in danger of suffering the same fate, it all muddled his head, and placed him under constant stress. Sleep had been a shoddy affair, done in batches from which he woke up with a start, sure that something had entered the house and was just poised there, biding its time, until it came for him. Or Nyx.

He must do something. He couldn't just stand still.

Sitting up, Eli reached for his phone, tried his father's number yet again, only to be awarded the same mechanical reply - that the number he'd tried to reach had been disconnected. Tears gathered at the corner of his eyes, a heavy weight set on his chest. He fisted his closed lids, rubbed them until it hurt. A smooth hand alighted on his back. Jacintha was awake, she mustn't see him like this.

"Hey, are you all right?"

Turning, he met her eyes. "No. No, I'm not all right, and I don't know if I'll ever be."

"Why don't you call your parents? Think you could do with them being here."

What was he supposed to say? That his parents, like him, like Nyx, like Jacintha herself, were in danger? He sniggered.

"They're away on vacation. It's hard getting a hold of them at the moment, the signal's bad where they're staying. I've left them a message."

"Come back to bed, then. I can call in sick, the principal will understand if I don't show up today."

"No, you should go. And take Pip, he can't miss his classes. Nyx and I can do with a little time alone, just the two of us, know what I mean?"

Jacintha nodded. "Of course. Give me a call later, then, I can come over at lunchtime, cook you a meal."

"Jace, I can get lunch sorted for me and my sister. Sarah Wilson would have a field day if she thought I couldn't even feed Nyx. But I'll give you a call."

"Right. Then I should get dressed. Maybe you could go and wake Pip?"

Eli blushed, wondering what he'd find if he were to open the door to his sister's room. He had no illusions the young couple would be inside, had no illusions about what would probably have taken place between them. Wincing, he tried not to see his sister as a child; she was a young girl on the brink of womanhood, and like it or not, sexually active. The fact Pip Thomson was in her room, in her bed, was his responsibility; after all, he'd practically begged the boy to stay.

Had he done it for Nyx, though, knowing Pip would provide her ample comfort, a soothing company, solace from the pain? Or had he wanted to irritate Sarah, knowing she was against Nyx's relationship with Pip? What would she think, were she to know of this? That he'd allowed two teenagers to sleep together under his guardianship? Did he really care? In the end, what Eli had wanted was to provide Nyx with something her aunt would hardly have given her: freedom. From the moment Sarah took Nyx in, her life would change, and Eli had wanted to at least give her this much liberty to do as she saw fit. He wanted her last memory of him to be this - the brother who'd respected and trusted her enough to treat her as an adult, not the man responsible for her uncle's death.

A knock on the door brought him out of his musings. Casting his eyes about, Eli realised Jacintha had locked herself in the bathroom, the sound of running water like white noise he'd failed to notice. Pulling on a pair of pyjama bottoms, he marched to the door, opened it wide. Nyx stood there, clearly uncomfortable. Her hair was a wild tangle of curls brushing her shoulders, face pale, dark circles under her eyes, and Eli wondered if he looked anything like that. Behind his sister, Pip lurked in the hallway, closer to Nyx's room than to his. They were both fully clothed, and he found himself sighing in relief.

"Hey," he said, "I overslept, sorry. Let me get dressed and I'll cook you breakfast."

"Don't bother; Pip's got to get back to the Academy before breakfast is over. I was wondering if Miss Tate could drive him."

Eli looked behind his shoulder, Jacintha now out of the bathroom and combing her hair. She nodded hastily, threw the brush into her capacious handbag, pushed earrings through the pierced earlobes.

"I'll be right down," she said, fishing around for her boots.

Nyx nodded, turned back to leave, Pip taking her place at the door. He reached out a hand to Eli, who shook it.

"Thanks for letting me stay over," Pip said. "I... I'm really sorry about your loss. I'm sorry I couldn't do more."

Eli's eyes widened in shock, heart slamming against his chest. Did the boy find himself responsible for Spencer's death? Did he think he'd failed to keep him alive?

"Pip, it wasn't your fault," Eli whispered, voice failing him.

Through the corner of his eye he spied Nyx halt at the end of the hallway; slowly turn round on her heels to face them. Behind him, Jacintha inched closer to the door, her hands alighting over his shoulders as if Eli needed steadying. He shook his head, everything kept going downhill, everything turned harder and harder at each second. And he was running out of time.

"It wasn't your fault. I'm really glad you showed up when you did, I was at a loss. If anyone's to blame, it's me. But let's drop this, please. Thank you for being here for us, for Nyx. I hope you keep looking after her. I hope you're here, when she needs."

Their eyes locked, and Eli saw the realisation in Pip's. The boy knew something was about, he'd sensed it in Eli's words, his entire gait. What was it Nyx had said his Craft was? An Aerial, right? Haruspex and Empath, no wonder he'd got a sniff of Eli's intentions. He only hoped the boy kept it to himself, at least for the time being. Letting go of Pip's hand, he nodded again, and stepped aside to let Jacintha out.

"Right, have you got everything?" she asked of Pip.

"My coat's downstairs."

"Go on, grab it, I'll be down in a second. It's early hours, we have time."

Pip sauntered off to join Nyx, their footsteps dimmer and dimmer as they climbed down to the ground floor. Jacintha turned back to Eli, one hand caressing the flock of birds taking flight over his upper chest. He pulled her into his arms, kissed the crown of her head.

"I'll call you during my lunch break, is that ok?"

"Sure. Drive carefully. Take care of yourself."

She peered into his eyes, studying them. Eli forced a composed, carefree look upon his face, not wanting to worry her or awaken any sort of suspicion. He'd have a hard time with Nyx, soon; adding Jacintha to the equation was sure to further drive him mad. And he doubted he could keep up his resolve if she begged him not to leave. They kissed, long and deep.

"Rest," she said. "Allow yourself to grieve."

"I will. Lemme just get dressed so I can walk you out."

"No, stay. I don't mind walking myself to the car. I'll see you soon, yes?"

Eli claimed another kiss, and another, wondering if they would see each other soon, if he would taste those lips ever again; make love to this woman once more.

"Of course," he lied, and forced a smile on his lips, but his heart bled bitter poison to his veins.

Jacintha walked away, turning to wave a hasty goodbye before she left the hallway for the stairs. He took refuge inside the bedroom, curtains still pulled shut, the sombre interior a perfect match for his mood. He couldn't linger. Bryn would have spoken to Cressida, he hoped, to her father. He must hurry doing what he'd purposed before, but had been set aside by Spencer's death. Taking a look around, Eli realised he had so much to lose. For the first time in his life, he had far too much to lose.

When he'd fallen into a coma at age fifteen, catapulted out of this world into that of his father, he hadn't left much behind, except for his adoptive parents. But he'd gone through his life in Ephemera as Nox Sylvain, with no memory of the world he'd left, and the thought of Ora and Serge had been a pale memory, convinced as he'd been that they were gone. When Stella betrayed him and he was cast away, Eli had believed himself cursed, thinking he'd lose it all, his whole life, but in fact he hadn't. What did he have back there in Ephemera that surpassed what he'd now achieved? He was alone in those woods, no family, hardly any friends, the girl he loved turning out to be far from what he'd thought her.

He hadn't had that much to lose, when Rhysondel Sylvannar brought a Nigrum to cast Nox Sylvain out of Mythos for good. This time was different. This time, he'd be making an immense sacrifice. He had a home, a father who was out there, hiding, lost in this huge, huge world. He had friends, people who cared for him. A job he loved. A sister he couldn't bear the thought of being without. A woman who made him happy, who put a smile on his lips, the mere thought of her enough to race his heart. A girl who loved him, and who he...

What? What did he feel for Bryn? Why couldn't he keep her out of his mind, why did he have to relive every single time they'd met privately, every chance encounter they'd had? Why had he kissed her? Why had he slept with her out in the woods, what was this power the girl had over him? And why did butterflies flutter his stomach, and wild flocks of birds took flight in his heart every time he closed his eyes and heard her voice whisper those three words, *I love you*, as she'd said just yesterday? Why would it matter this much to him? Why was he hesitating, when he knew there was no other way? If he cared for his friends, for Jacintha, for Nyx, even for Bryn, he had to leave.

Blinking away tears, Eli dove into the bathroom, straight to the shower, where he allowed the comfort of warm water to wash over his troubled senses and knotted muscles. Then he carefully dried himself, pulled on a pair of clean briefs and left the steam-filled bathroom to get dressed.

The sight greeting him forced Eli to halt, one hand to a heart that jumped against his ribs, alarmed by the unexpected presence of his sister sat atop an unmade bed, where just hours ago he'd made love to the woman he was now letting go of.

"Blimey, Nyx, you scared the hell out of me."

"I'm sorry. I just don't want to be left alone."

Their eyes met, Eli studying hers intently. What did she really mean? Had she somehow gotten an inkling of his intentions? Maybe Pip had hinted at something?

"Let me get dressed and I'll make us something to eat."

"I've made fresh coffee and toast. We should call Max and Sarah about the funeral. Maybe it's not such a great idea to let her handle things. She can say you're not fit to take care of me."

Eli grabbed a clean jersey from the dresser, pulled it on, settling on the black jeans he'd been wearing the day before.

"What if she's right? What if you're better off with her than me?"

Standing up, Nyx walked towards him in jerky steps, as if unable to move properly. Her hands clenched and unclenched, and she kept blinking away tears. He didn't want to hurt her, but how was he going to make her understand his need to leave? How was he going to make her see he'd only mean danger to her, were Eli to stay? How was he to make her realise he'd killed Spencer because his uncle had refused to let him leave, and he feared he'd end up doing the same were Nyx to stand in his way?

"Have you eaten?"

She nodded, stood her ground, eyes set on his.

"Then come into the woods with me. We need to speak."

"I'm not letting you get out of this. Eli, I don't want to lose you. You're all I have. You can't let aunt Sarah take me."

He pulled on his boots, wrapped a scarf round his neck, all the time avoiding his sister's eyes. Taking one final glance at the room, he willed the image to mind, something he could return to when in need. A memory that upheld him in the darkest of times he already envisioned ahead for him, of a place where he was once safe, and wanted, and loved. When Eli was satisfied he'd burnt every detail to mind, he exited the room, Nyx hot on his heels. They went downstairs, where thick winter coats were hastily pulled on, as well as warm leather gloves.

Nyx mimicked her brother's every move, fear printed on her face. Eli hated himself for it, and for what else was to come, how he must hurt her to ensure she wanted him out of her life, just so the girl was safe. How he must hurt and disappoint her with the truth of what he'd done, what he still had to do. How, like his mother before him, Eli must also abandon her, for there were those who meant more to him.

Only that part wasn't quite true. No one meant more to him than Nyx, not even Ora. He cared for her, loved her like the only mother he'd ever known, but she'd made a choice long ago, she'd known well what she'd gotten herself into. Ora had made sure Eli was aware of that, she and Serge alike. They'd hammered into his head how they'd chosen this, and when and if Chymera sent anyone for him, they were ready to stand up for Eli and face the consequences of their choices, for these had been made freely. Not Nyx. She hadn't chosen anything. She didn't deserve any of what had happened to her so far. So he must make sure she was safe, because Nyx mattered that much to him. He must make sure he stayed away from her, diverted attentions to him and only him; so that not even Erin remembered her daughter existed. As long as Weaversmoor was protected by its wards, and Eli was away from it, everyone inside would be safe, and that included Nyx.

Leading her to the kitchen, he grabbed a slice of dry toast from the rack and munched on it, reached for a bottle of water placed on the counter, not bothering himself with sitting down for a proper meal. Time was of the essence, and he had much to tell his sister. He opened the kitchen door, let in a gust of frosty morning air; the sun was just rising on the horizon. How glorious sunrise was, back in Ephemera, much more than here. Part of him missed the landscapes of that world with an ache he daren't explain, and that part was ready to go back, eager for it. But it was such a small piece of him, in the grand scheme of things.

"Come, let's take a walk," he suggested, and sped off towards the woods, Nyx running after him.

They made their way in silence for a few minutes, breathing heavy of the frosty air, lungs hurting with the effort of the speedy walk. Finally, they came upon the clearing where the strange tree ruled queen; its boughs now empty of leaves, winter truly come even to this borderland. Eli looked up and down the trunk; there was no sign of the birds, today, no sign of life at all. The entire forest seemed to have fallen asleep in her winter hues, coated in a grey, sleepy sheen.

"Why are we here?" Nyx asked, hands on her hips.

Eli's stomach plummeted with the jolt of love invading him - seeing her here, like this, his feisty little sister who refused to take any crap from anyone, the girl who didn't shy from throwing her opinion at him when he didn't want it, the girl who was as much a lioness standing up to him as she was standing up *for* him. The girl he knew would always have his back. She'd always have his back. How could he break her heart like this, then, how could he run and leave her behind like this?

"Can you climb a tree?"

She nodded, the beginnings of a smirk already curled at her lips. "Of course."

"Then let's get on top of that one. Race you."

He sped ahead, and started climbing up the massive tree. Nyx wasn't far behind, and soon they found themselves sat atop the sturdiest bough, the world at their feet. Light brightened around them, and the air shimmered, the breach clearly calling out for them. Soon; they'd open it soon, for the briefest of moments only, and he'd cross over and never return. These were his final minutes in this world, with his sister. He must make the best of them.

Glancing towards the deeper part of the woods, towards the Everley estate, Eli found himself caught by a sudden longing for a sight of Bryn, the last glimpse he'd have of her. But that was not to be, he'd said his goodbyes to the girl who believed she loved him, the only woman he knew to have ever felt that way. Regret filled him - that things weren't different, that he couldn't have come to feel for Bryn what she seemed to feel for him. All he could hope for was that the love she thought she had for him was enough to make sure she did as Eli had asked her.

"So," Nyx said, breaking through the cloudy whirlwind of his thoughts. "What was it you wanted to tell me?"

He hung down his head, eyes to the distant ground. How did he tell her this? Where did he start? How did one begin to break one's own sister's heart?

"I have to leave, Nyx."

Eli raised his head and met her eyes, saw their flat glare, understood she'd known all along this was what he'd come here to tell her.

"I won't let you."

"There's nothing you can do..."

"You're far from being a coward, Eli Vaughn, or an irresponsible oaf, so stop trying to act like one. You're not gonna leave me; I won't be carted off to Aunt Sarah like this. You're terrified, I understand; think this is too much for you. But I'm not a child anymore, we can do this. Together, we can do this."

He slid along the bough to come closer to her, dragged her into his arms. "There's nothing I'd like more than staying here with you, being a family, watching you grow into the outstanding woman I know you'll be. But I can't."

"Why the hell not? What possible reason can you have to abandon me like this? Because I won't let you go, you hear me? I'll do whatever to stop you from leaving."

"No, you won't." He held his sister tighter. "Spencer also tried to stop me and see what happened to him."

"Enough with that, already, you're not responsible for his death." Nyx loosened herself from his grip, glued her eyes to his.

"What if I am? He tried to prevent me from going and I... I just lost it, Nyx. I lost it, I wanted him gone, wanted him to stop and so he did. I provoked his heart attack, and he died because of me. What if I hurt you, too?"

Tears streamed down her cheeks. "Well, you're already hurting me. Why could you possibly want to leave? I thought you loved me, you seemed happy here. With your new job, Miss Tate, you seemed really happy with your life here."

"I was. *I am*. But if I stay, I'll be putting you all in danger."

"Eli, you're not making sense. Instead of speaking nonsense and playing the victim, why don't you try telling me what the hell is going on?"

Looking away, he clenched his teeth. Up ahead on the horizon the sun was fully up, bathing the land with a pale, creamy, white light. People would be leaving the comfort of their homes, now, to go to work, attend school, whatever it was they did. People who knew nothing of the danger they might be in, if he insisted on staying, luring to such a safe, sleepy town horrors they had no idea could even exist. Jacintha must be on her way to the Academy, freshly bathed and with her makeup on, wearing her dark maroon overcoat with the fake fur collar that hid half her face. Bryn must be now revving up her bike, skirts flying up her thighs, a provocative grin on her lips. And Nyx should be doing the same, leading a normal, secure life, like any other kid her age. But she also deserved to know; after all, this concerned her family.

"Remember me telling you I thought our mother had Weaved herself back to Mythos to look for me?" Nyx nodded. "Well, she was captured. An outcast of Ephemera, her entrance was forbidden everywhere in Mythos, under penalty of death if she dared trespass again. But they didn't kill her."

"No?"

Eli shook his head. "No. They turned her into one of their Nigrum. And then sent her back here, with a pack of Hounds. They've gotten to my mum, took her away to Chymera. Dad managed to escape, but Ora's being tortured into giving away my whereabouts even as we speak. I can't let my mum be hurt because of me. I can't let her suffer. And I can't let Spencer's death be in vain."

Nyx eyed him pensively. "You want to go back. But you were cast out; wouldn't that also put you in danger of a death sentence, Eli?"

"I've been thinking about this," he said. "When I was cast out, the ban was placed on Nox Sylvain. This was the name I went under during the seven years I spent there. But you see, Nyx, that wasn't me. I mean, it was never my real name, was it?"

"You lost me there."

"My father named me Noctifer Sylvannar because I was born in the dead of night. They called me Nox for short. When I was forced back here, Corinna changed my name to Eli. Eli Sylvain, after my adoptive parents. But that's not my real name, either."

"Then what is? Noctifer Sylvannar or Eli Vaughn?"

"Both, actually. And none was banned from Mythos."

VII

"There's something wrong, Bryn." Pip hastened his step, following her along the empty outdoor space around Weaversmoor Academy. "He spoke as if he was... saying goodbye."

Bryn faltered, feet dragging over gravel. Darting her eyes around, she searched for signs of other students, this wasn't the kind of conversation to be overheard. But what should she tell Pip? It was Eli's secret, Eli's origins; it respected no one but him. It was private, personal, and Bryn had no right going around telling others of this. He'd trusted her to keep quiet. Besides, talking about it would only reawaken the pain she already felt crushed by.

"Why did you break up with Jamal?" Pip suddenly changed the subject, arms crossed over his chest, head cocked to the side, a squint that told her he needed no answer to what he already knew.

Bryn shrugged. "I needed some time."

"Is that so? Is that why Jamal punched him at the hospital? Just after the man heard of his uncle's death? Because *that* made no sense, Bryn, unless..."

"Unless what?" She wheeled round, hair flying like cords around her head, eyes like green pebbles, hard on Pip. "What are you saying, here?"

"You're in love with him. With Eli."

Her shoulders slumped, defeated. "What if I am?"

"Then you need to help me. He's going to leave, I'm sure of it. Is that what you want? Do you want to lose him?"

Sniggering, Bryn pulled her hair into a hasty ponytail. "Lose him? Eli Vaughn's way out of my league. He has a girlfriend, remember? Who he's madly in love with."

"But he goes into the woods at night to have sex with you."

Her cheeks burned, entire body assaulted by heat so intense she couldn't breathe. It wasn't the blaze of lust she often experienced at that particular recollection - it was the fire of shame. That someone else knew how she'd offered herself to a man eight years her senior, who'd used and discarded her soon after. A man who'd still come to her when he needed help. It must stand for something, surely. She couldn't betray his trust. No matter what Pip said, she couldn't betray Eli's trust.

"This is none of your business. It happened, it's over, it had no meaning."

"Except for you. Bryn, please, I can see you're hurting. I can see you know more than you admit. You need to help me keep him here."

"Why? If he wants to leave, it's his life, Pip. He's an adult." Hiding the pain Eli's absence would bring her, Bryn put up a brave face, acting as if she couldn't care. "Look, he's made up his mind, I can't change it. Can't talk about this anymore; it's already breaking my heart. Please."

"What about Nyx? She just lost her uncle, and now her brother decides to leave? You saw how desperate she was at the thought of moving in with the Wilsons."

Bryn shook her head. "I can't be dragged into this."

"So you're going to let Eli Vaughn screw up everyone's lives?"

"Screw up? Why do you always have to assume the worst from him? Eli's trying to keep us safe, you know?"

"By being a martyr? By breaking his sister's heart? This isn't how he gets to atone for his actions! He needs to step up and face the consequences of what he did."

"And what did he do, Pip?" Bryn faced him, arms hanging limply to the side.

She was tired, hadn't slept at all the previous night, head going round in circles. More than once she'd considered going to her mother and telling Cressida everything, but fear kept Bryn locked in place, seated on the sofa against the wall, where Eli had once sat by her side, not that long ago. Pip was right, she didn't want him to leave, despite being aware she had no place in his life. Not in the capacity she wished. But hadn't he kissed her? Hadn't he come to her when in need? Hadn't she been the one person Eli trusted with his request? It had to stand for something. He'd known she'd do as he asked, but Bryn had failed him, kept it all to herself so far, still shying from going to her father, her mother. What if they didn't listen?

"He killed Spencer."

Eyes closed, Bryn held a hand to the side of her head, pounding with sudden pain. "You're unbelievable."

"I'm not saying he meant to do it, but he caused his uncle's death. I was there, Bryn. He was angry; you should have seen his face. Spencer was on his knees, clearly in pain, and Eli just stood there, frowning at him, his face a mask of hatred. Then it changed, and he wasn't a monster any longer, just a normal man."

A monster. Hadn't that been how her mother referred to Eli's estranged father? A monster, more creature than man, from another world. What was it Eli had said? That his father and mother were lost and he must go after them? What if he meant that *other* world, what if he'd been talking about his birth parents? How was he going to enter that place? What was he going to do?

Suddenly worried for his wellbeing, Bryn clapped a hand over Pip's arm.

"What is it you know?" He shook his head. "If you want my help, you must tell me everything."

"You're just gonna think I'm crazy."

A cackle echoed through her lips. "Have you heard my mother? You think you can top her amount of crazy, Philip Thomson?"

"What do you think *you* know, Bryn?" His face lit up with unexpected comprehension. "He asked you to meet him, didn't he? Later that night I thought I heard someone leave the house, it was him coming to see you. What was it he told you?"

She shrugged again, still awkward about sharing secrets that weren't hers.

"Bloody hell, Bryn. Fine! I know what being a Weaver really means. *There*. That's what I know. What Nyx told me."

Her eyes shifted, confusion settling over them. What did being a Weaver had to do with anything? Except for the fact Nyx was one, as was Miss Tate, and Eli was connected to the both. Suddenly, the truth hit her. Like a punch to the stomach, it was, robbing her of air. She knew Eli to be of the blood, but had no idea what his Craft was. He must be a Weaver. Like his mother and grandmother before him, like his sister, his girlfriend. He *had* to be a Weaver. And Bryn had been lied to all her life, as had every other child at Weaversmoor, every single student at the Academy. Being a Weaver was not just having a knack for using every type of Craft they came into contact with, it must mean more than this. Being a Weaver had to be something rare, powerful; why else would the town have the name of Weaversmoor?

Why would this particular town be a gateway to another world? Why would creatures from this other realm cross over and sow half breeds into the womb of the women of Weaversmoor? But not every woman, no. According to Bryn's own mother, she'd dodged a bullet when Erin and she came across the man who'd fathered Eli. Because he'd only wanted Erin, not Cressida. Only Erin had been a Weaver.

"What did she say? Is Eli like her?"

"They're both Weavers. And you know what they do? They *weave*." He laughed, but it was a terrifying sound. That sound of madness and utter fear, drenched with despair, hopelessness. It was the sound of sheer panic. "And I'm going to lose her if we don't stop him from weaving his sorry arse out of here."

"He's going to cross over. He's not just leaving Weaversmoor, Eli's leaving our world."

Their eyes met, and now Bryn's were as desperate, as terrified as Pip's. She had not signed up for this. She had not agreed to this.

"Nyx said as Weavers they can make threads that open portals to other places. Like, she could probably Weave herself here, if she wanted to, but she's never tried it. She *did* open a doorway to..."

"Another world."

"So you know of this."

Pacing around, Bryn forced long breaths into her lungs, trying to recall everything Eli had said. "Yes, though for years I thought it my mother's drunken ravings. There's some sort of parallel universe that can be reached through Weaversmoor. It's where Eli's father came from. And I think their mother is there too. He plans to go after them, said something about telling my mum Erin's alive but changed, that she's dangerous and will come for Nyx? Said dad would know what to do. Something about wards placed all over town to keep strangers away. I don't know, it all sounded so outlandish. Wait, I remember, he said he had to go, to keep Nyx and Miss Tate safe because they're Weavers. And if he wasn't here, no one would come for them, because it was Eli Erin wanted? It doesn't make any sense."

Pip clutched her upper arms, shook her slightly. "He means to cross over and give himself up, to keep them away from this place. To keep Nyx and Miss Tate safe. He wants to atone for Spencer's death. But Nyx can cross over, Bryn, and what Eli wants to avoid *will* happen, if she does. Which she *will*, the moment he leaves. The moment she realises what her brother has done, Nyx is going after him. Eli won't know, and her life will be at risk. I can't let it happen. I can't let her do this."

Bryn shook her head. "No. Eli can't leave. We better talk to Miss Tate, he'll listen to her."

Pip sniggered. "She doesn't know a thing. The woman's a Weaver, has been tutoring Nyx for weeks now, and has no idea of her own powers, no clue as to what her Craft really means. Jacintha Tate won't be of any use to us, Bryn, and her presence will only further Eli's resolve. We go to Vaughn cottage and talk to him. You and I and Nyx. Together, we can sway him, I know we can. Together, we can come up with a plan, we can try and put sense into that thick head of his."

"All right. We go now, before it's too late. And if we can't make him see sense, I'll cart him off to my mother, she'll put him to rights."

Pulling her satchel cross-body, Bryn walked off to the student's parking lot, where she had her bike. There was only the one helmet, now she'd broken up with Jamal, but they weren't riding far, Pip could go bare-headed. It would be faster than walking all the way from the Academy to Vaughn cottage, and she had a disastrous feeling they were running out of time.

Epilogue

"So, this means you're free to weave yourself back there?" Nyx inquired, studying her brother's face.

She'd been reading this all wrong. Eli had no need for her; he could weave his own threads to Ephemera and open a portal. But he'd chosen to tell her the truth. Although furious he intended to leave, she still appreciated the fact he treated her as an adult, respected her enough not to lie or hide things from her.

"Yes. I'll be doing that presently, but Nyx, I needed you to know, so you can be on your guard. So you can take care. Nothing good comes from lying or hiding things from people just to keep them safe. It's a wrong notion, ignorance only endangers us."

"I'm grateful you did, but I still don't see why you need to go, Eli. What can you do, there? You're safer here. I know she's your mum, but look, I'm your sister, I need you, and you need me too. We only just found each other, how can you think of leaving?"

"Because my presence here will only harm you."

Nyx huffed, crossed stiff arms over her chest, staring away from him.

"There's more. The moment you Weaved that thread and opened the breach, they felt it in Chymera. Erin's print, for you're her daughter. Soon they'll send her back, if Ora doesn't speak. And if our mother doesn't find me at Daylesford or you at Havenleah, she'll come *here*. She'll come here with lord knows how many Hounds, and endanger the lives of everyone around. See why I must leave?"

Nyx shook her head, grabbed her brother's hand. "No. Why must you leave?"

"So I can give myself up to them and make sure they set Ora free."

She cackled. "And they're going to do that from the goodness of their hearts? Eli, I may have no idea who the hell *they* are, but from all you've told me, what you're suggesting is contrary to nature, *their* nature."

"I can't leave her there, don't you see?"

"I *do* see. I understand your predicament, and that you feel you need to leave. But not like this."

"What do you mean?"

"Alone, unprepared. What do you expect to achieve like this? We need a proper plan."

"*We*?" He laughed, but there was no humour in his mirth. "There's no time for that."

"Fine, then we go, we open the rip and cross over, reach Ephemera and then what? Head to Chymera? Do you know where it is? How to get there? Do we walk, or are there cars in that world? We can try to catch a ride."

"You're not going anywhere, Nyx. This is something I must do alone."

"Because you killed Spencer. So now you must die, to pay for it." She watched him lower his head, one single tear dropping from his eye. "Stop being a martyr. If you go, I'll only follow, you know? I can weave a thread there as well, and you'll be aware that I'm in that world, which I know nothing of, probably placing myself in danger, just because you refused to take me along with you. But I won't be left behind, you hear me?"

Eli looked into the distance, while Nyx squeezed his hand. She could see him falter, mind working fast the implications of her threats.

"We can work together, Eli, two's better than one. I can help you, watch your back. And you'll do the same for me. Think about it, as long as we're together, you know I'm safe, right? Because I'm right beside you. If you leave me here, won't you be constantly worried something happens to me? And frankly, if our mother's been turned into this thing you said, and is coming for me, *for us*, we're much safer there. No one will think us in Mythos, they won't know we crossed."

"If I agree," he said, Nyx interrupting him by throwing her arms around his shoulders and hugging her brother, "I said *if*, it's not set in stone yet. If I agree, you must promise you'll listen to me. I know that place, and how to survive it, would take at least a couple of months to have you even slightly prepared for it."

"But we don't have a couple of months."

"We hardly have a couple of hours. That's why you must promise to always heed my words, once we're there." She nodded vigorously. "This tree, this is a borderland, I told you already. You know what that means?"

"No. But I feel safe here. Secluded. As if I can't be harmed."

"And you can't. No one can see us here, and time halts for us. This is a haven for Weavers. Once we're in Mythos, and if we get separated, you must find a tree like this and climb it. And then you wait for me there."

"How long, Eli? How long must I wait before I know you're not coming back?"

He shook his head, pulled his sister into the safety of his arms. "I don't know."

"I'm not going to lose you. And I won't be parted from you, you hear me? If they capture you, they capture me as well. Or I try and set you free. But for us to be at least moderately safe, we need to come up with some sort of plan."

"Before we start thinking in those terms, you need to learn everything you can about that world. You need to hear all I have to say."

"And that is?"

"What happened to me in the seven years I lived there, in Ephemera, at my father's estate. You need to know what it was like, my life as Nox Sylvain, a Silvares in the woods near the village of Viridans."

"Why's that?"

"Because I'm not the only Weaver from Ephemera to have come to Weaversmoor, Nyx. And there was a price on my head back there, because of it."

WITCH CRAFT

If you've enjoyed this novel, please consider leaving a review on Goodreads and any other platform you use for that effect, for us Indie Authors reviews are the best way to get our work out there, and it would be much appreciated. If you'd like to keep up with news of my work, don't forget to sign up for my newsletter:

[Newsletter Subscription (mailchi.mp)](https://mailchi.mp/46ad4cfd5de9/ruthmiranda)[1]

---

1. https://mailchi.mp/46ad4cfd5de9/ruthmiranda

Don't miss out!

Visit the website below and you can sign up to receive emails whenever Ruth Miranda publishes a new book. There's no charge and no obligation.

https://books2read.com/r/B-A-IONH-XRPDD

BOOKS 2 READ

Connecting independent readers to independent writers.

Milton Keynes UK
Ingram Content Group UK Ltd.
UKHW021920281024
450365UK00017B/865